PRAISE FOR ANGEL FALLS

"This heart-pounding novel doesn't stint on its characters . . . masterful."
—*RT Book Reviews*, four stars

"If you're looking for nonstop action and heart-pounding excitement, then *Angel Falls* is just the read you've been looking to find. Connie Mann deftly weaves danger and suspense into a story that left me sitting on the edge of my seat, flipping the pages."
—Debbie Macomber, #1 *New York Times* bestselling author

"A perfect blend of fast-paced thriller, inspiration and romance."
—Fresh Fiction

"In *Angel Falls*, Connie Mann has penned an edgy, gritty book that pushes the boundaries of Christian romance fiction while giving readers a hero and heroine to root for."
—Irene Hannon, bestselling author of the Guardians of Justice series

"A riveting read starting with the first page all the way through the book."
—The Suspense Zone

"Dark, intense, and breathlessly paced, Connie Mann's edgy novel, *Angel Falls*, is exciting, romantic suspense that kept me guessing. With tight writing and fast-paced action, Connie does a fantastic job of grabbing the reader from the first page and never turning loose until the last. *Angel Falls* is not your usual Christian suspense. Filled with intrigue, murder, and sensuality, and set in Brazil's steamy underbelly, Connie's debut is riveting."
—Linda Goodnight, author of *A Snowglobe Christmas* and *Rancher's Refuge* and contributing author of the Prairie Romance Collection

"*Angel Falls* is a powerful read from the beginning with a hero and heroine who emotionally grip you and won't let go. The chemistry between Regina and Brooks along with the suspense keeps you riveted to the story."

—Margaret Daley, author of the Men of the Texas Rangers series

"Connie Mann takes her readers on the heart-stopping journey of a woman who puts her life on the line for an orphaned baby boy and her heart in the hands of the man who came to save them. It was a remarkable story I won't soon forget."

—Sharon Sala, author of the Rebel Ridge trilogy

WHAT READERS ARE SAYING ABOUT *TRAPPED!*

"Romance, intrigue and suspense with a Florida twist. Great read!"

—Captain Shelia Kerney, United States Coast Guard–licensed captain

"In *Trapped!* the author lets the reader feel the heat and sweat and smell the fear from unknown dangers along the river. Her fast pace and stunning conclusion will give the reader a fascinating ride."

—Martha Powers, award-winning author of *Death Angel*, *Bleeding Heart*, and *Sunflower*

TANGLED LIES

ALSO BY CONNIE MANN

Angel Falls

Trapped!

TANGLED LIES

CONNIE MANN

This is a work of fiction. Names, characters, organizations, places, events, and incidents are either products of the author's imagination or are used fictitiously.

Published by Waterfall Press, Grand Haven, MI

www.brilliancepublishing.com

ISBN-13: 9781503934764
ISBN-10: 1503934764

Cover design by Michael Rehder

Printed in the United States of America

For everyone who has ever longed for "home," and with love and gratitude to those who opened their hearts and gathered them in.

Prologue

Boat captain Sasha Petrov called any day spent on the water a good one. If she got to test her mettle against one of Mother Nature's temper tantrums while out there, well, so much the better.

Sasha eyed the darkening early-June sky and grinned. Today might just have been perfect. The three-man crew had just stowed the day's catch and she had turned *The Mermaid* for home when the wind in northern Puget Sound kicked up and the sky turned an angry gray. She zipped up her windbreaker as she scanned the squall line building behind them and gauged its speed and distance, the weight of the pink salmon sloshing around the holding tanks.

She raised her face to the sky and laughed as the wind slapped her cheeks, spray making her hands slick on the old wooden wheel.

"We're going to get wet, Bella-girl."

Her yellow Lab scanned the sky as though she understood, then nudged Sasha's leg before disappearing belowdecks to join the rest of the crew. Since the day Sasha had found the shivering, half-drowned pup four years ago, Bella had never left her side—except to hide during storms.

The Mermaid handled the choppy surf like the old workhorse she was, oblivious to the churning waves. Sasha braced her feet against the swells, eyes on the horizon, ignoring the spray in her face and the rocking of the boat. Nothing beat the thrill of pitting her skills against the fury Mother Nature dished out.

Pete Trowbridge, *The Mermaid*'s handsome owner and the man she'd been sort of dating for the past few weeks, joined her on the bridge. When he saw her face, a smile split his own.

"You love this, don't you?"

Sasha sent him a saucy grin, then swept her eyes forward again. "Aye aye, sir. Always. Every day."

"My mother is going to love you. I'm taking you to meet her this weekend." He winked, and her heart stuttered.

Meet his mother? Dread stole her smile, and she tightened her grip on the wheel. Maybe he meant it in a casual, my-mom-is-awesome way. *Sure. Right.* And maybe King Neptune would appear from the deep and offer her a graceful way out. She wanted to bang her head on the wheel. She'd thought of their relationship as fun, a nice way to spend a few hours. How had she missed the signs? Again?

She chanced a quick glance in his direction and decided she'd better make this short and sweet. Kind of like the old saying about a bandage: rip it off fast and it won't hurt as much. She hoped.

"Look, Pete, it's been fun and all, and I love working for you, but I'm not really a meet-the-parents kind of girl."

"What are you saying, Sasha? That you were just passing the time with me?"

It wasn't the words so much as their underlying fury that raised goose bumps on her arms. She really had not been paying attention.

She tried for a casual shrug. "I just meant I'm not ready for anything serious, that's all."

He folded his arms, widened his stance. "Then I'll just wait until you're ready."

A second, sharper twinge of panic made Sasha's heart rate speed up. "I wish you wouldn't. Really. Can't we just say it's been fun and move on?" She threw a big smile his way.

His eyes narrowed, and she knew she'd overplayed it. *Too late.*

"I want to marry you, Sasha. This summer. We're good together."

Her eyes widened, and her mouth dropped open in pure shock. Marriage? Good gravy. She hadn't even been ready to commit to calling him her boyfriend.

"I'm just not the marrying kind, Pete." She had to raise her voice to be heard above the rising wind. "I don't ever see myself tying the knot. I love the freedom of the sea and all that." *And if I'm alone, I never have to worry about hurting someone—like I'm doing now.*

Pete grabbed her arm and jerked her around to face him. *The Mermaid*'s wheel slipped from her grasp, spinning wildly. The heavy boat turned to port, parallel to the ever-increasing waves as the storm caught up with them. If she didn't get back to the wheel, they would be running in the trough with waves hitting them broadside. Even a boat as sturdy as this one could get swamped if she didn't regain control.

"Let go! I need to hold her steady!" Sasha yelled, but Pete held fast.

Suddenly Bella burst up from below, sliding on the wet deck, barking frantically. She shoved against Pete's legs, but he wouldn't release his grip.

"No, Bella. Go below, girl!" Sasha shouted.

Pete ignored everything around them, eyes on Sasha.

"You're going to marry me."

A huge waved crashed over the side, almost washing Bella overboard. The big dog yelped and scrambled to get her paws back under her. Sasha lunged forward to help, but Pete wouldn't let go.

"Later, Pete. Please. The storm."

She saw him slowly look around and blink, finally realizing the squall had overtaken them. The wind whipped the waves into a frenzy, tossing *The Mermaid* like a cork. He shoved her away and she grabbed the wheel, fighting with everything she had to work against the heavy seas and keep them from capsizing. Muscling the heavy boat back on course took every ounce of her strength, especially with the wind blowing so hard she couldn't see past the rain hitting her face. Pete disappeared below and she blocked everything from her mind but the challenge of besting the storm.

It seemed like hours, though probably no more than forty minutes passed before the worst of the wind died down, the rain slowed to a sprinkle, and Sasha slumped against the wheel, exhausted. Her arms and shoulders ached from gripping the wheel, but her usual elation at winning another round against the sea had vanished. Pete had stolen that from her. She wanted to fight back, tell him what she thought of his crazy assumptions, but she didn't want to get him wound up again. It didn't matter anyway. She'd just take Bella home to their little studio apartment and get into dry clothes. Then she'd figure out their next move. She'd loved this job, had planned to spend all summer working *The Mermaid*, maybe longer. Pete had stolen that, as well.

Still, there was the proverbial silver lining. Now she had no reason to miss her foster mother's sixtieth birthday party in Florida. Last time she'd turned on her laptop and checked email, she'd found half a dozen messages from her sister Eve, nagging her to come home. After so many years away, the thought both tempted and terrified. Yet she owed Mama Rosa and Pop that much, and more.

As they approached the marina where Pete kept the boat, Sasha throttled back the engines. She looked over to where Bella had come back on deck to pace, eyes on the lessening waves.

"Almost there, girl."

Pete burst up from below. Bella growled, but before Sasha could respond, he scooped the big retriever into his arms and tossed her overboard.

For one frozen instant, Sasha could only stare. Then she sprang toward the railing, ramming both hands against Pete's hard chest to shove him aside.

"Are you insane?"

She spotted Bella paddling frantically in the boat's wake and climbed over the railing, slapping Pete's hands away when he tried to stop her.

Gasping when she hit the icy water, she reached Bella in a few quick strokes and grabbed her collar, offering encouragement. Bella paddled frantically, both of them fighting the pull of the cold water as they swam the final stretch to the dock. They climbed out at the farthest end of the marina, a safe distance from where Pete struggled to get *The Mermaid* into the slip. *Let him struggle, the snake.* Dripping wet and cold, they walked away without a backward glance.

Sasha didn't start shaking until they reached her apartment.

Time to go home to Florida. To face the past.

And maybe, just maybe, figure out the future.

Chapter 1

When a gorgeous 1946 mahogany racing boat like he was towing appeared in a town the size of Safe Harbor, Florida, people noticed. Jesse Claybourne eased his pickup to a stop at one of the only traffic lights in town and smiled at a little boy who skidded to a halt, open-mouthed on the sidewalk. The little boy's mother looked over her shoulder and her jaw dropped, as well. Jesse had toyed briefly with waiting until dark to make his appearance, but decided to wade in with both feet. He acknowledged mother and son with a nod as he drove through the intersection. He figured in the five minutes it took to reach the marina on the outskirts of town, everyone would be talking about *The Painted Lady*. And speculating about her owner.

That might, or might not, make things easier.

When he turned off the two-lane road onto the dirt track that led to the marina, he realized he should have waited until nightfall. Pickups of every vintage and description, along with a smattering of sensible sedans, lined both sides of the road. He'd stumbled into the middle of some big event.

In for a penny, in for a pound, his great-aunt Clarabelle had always said. He kept his pace slow and steady so he wouldn't bog down in the sand, and nodded to the people who turned to stare. At the marina, he pulled off to one side since all the trailer parking spots were filled. One look over his shoulder at the Martinelli house, where the marina's owner and family lived, and he knew the reason for the crowd. Through the haze of barbecue smoke, he glimpsed a hand-painted banner that read "Happy Birthday, Mama Rosa!"

He wandered over to the slips, looking for number sixteen, but none of them were marked. Most already held boats, so his shouldn't be tough to find.

"Can I help you, son?" a deep voice said.

Jesse turned to see Salvatore Martinelli and a couple of his captain buddies standing behind him. He held out his hand.

"Nice to see you again, Sal. It's been a long time."

Sal's eyes widened, and he glanced at *The Painted Lady*, then at the two captains frowning beside him.

"Is that you, Jesse Claybourne?"

Jesse sent him a half smile. "It is, sir."

Sal tugged him closer for a hug and a slap on the back. "Don't you *sir* me, now, son." He pulled back, met Jesse's gaze. "I was sorry to hear of your aunt's passing. Clarabelle was a fine lady."

"Who could also throw a mean left hook if you crossed her," Jesse added, and they both laughed. Then he sobered. "Thank you. She'll be missed."

Sal gestured to the men beside him, who were listening with unbridled interest.

"You remember Captains Demetri and Roy?" Demetri's dark hair and beard were going gray, but Jesse remembered his ever-present cigar from childhood summers in Safe Harbor. Short and squat, Captain Roy had gone almost bald, but he still had the look of a man who didn't suffer fools lightly.

Jesse held out a hand, but Demetri ignored it. Roy turned sideways and spit tobacco juice near his feet.

Jesse dropped his hand but kept his smile in place. "Good to see you both."

Two other men, obviously captains, appeared and scanned *The Painted Lady* with practiced eyes. The tall, skinny one gave Jesse an equally intense once-over, while his stocky friend merely scowled.

"Captains Bill and Jimmy," Sal said.

Jesse didn't offer his hand again, merely nodding to each in turn. He hitched a thumb over his shoulder. "Looks like quite a party. Didn't mean to pull you away."

"My Rosa is sixty today, praise be to God, and she is surrounded by people. She can spare me for a few minutes." Sal nodded to *The Painted Lady*. "She's a beaut. What brings you here?"

"Boat like that don't come cheap," Captain Demetri muttered.

Jesse ignored him and answered Sal. Aunt Clarabelle's unexpected legacy wasn't something he'd planned to explain. "I'm entering *The Lady* in the Tropicana in Clearwater in a couple weeks and need a place to work on her."

Sal started shaking his head before Jesse finished speaking. The other captains stepped closer, closing ranks, and Jesse had to admire the way they stood with their friend.

"Sorry you've come all this way, Jesse. But I don't have any transient slips for rent."

Jesse hid his disappointment at Sal's response, though he wasn't surprised. Safe Harbor had never been big on welcoming outsiders. He smiled.

"I don't need transient space. I'm going to keep her in Aunt Clarabelle's slip."

Captain Roy visibly started. He spit again. "But she's . . . gone."

Jesse nodded and noticed Sal looking off into the distance, clearly uncomfortable. He looked Captain Roy straight in the eye.

"Right, but my uncle purchased the slip from Sal years ago, and Aunt Clarabelle left it to me in her will. Along with her cottage." He met Sal's eyes. "And everything else she owned."

"You mean you're plannin' to stay in town?" Captain Roy looked him up and down. "Took you more for a city boy. Or a no-good ex—"

Jesse caught his eye, dared him to keep talking. Roy stopped, but his look said he knew all about Jesse's jail time. Jesse didn't blink.

Sal straightened as though he'd come to some decision. "Roy? You mind checking on the grill? I know Rosa loves your barbecued chicken."

Some kind of signal passed among the four men before they headed back to the party.

Sal took off his fisherman's cap, and Jesse was surprised to see a bald pate and nothing but fringe where his thick curly hair had been. Ten years had taken their toll.

"I can't deny you the slip, Jesse, but you know they won't make it easy." He sighed. "Clarabelle left you her share in the marina, too?"

When Jesse nodded, Sal shook his head. "Safe Harbor folks don't like strangers in their midst. Especially not rich ones. Or ones who, well . . ."

"Have been in jail?" Jesse finished.

Sal nodded. "Your arrest was big news here. I've always thought you were a good boy, Jesse. Least you were when you spent summers here. Clarabelle never did believe a word of what went on." He shrugged. "I figure everyone makes mistakes and is entitled to a second chance. But I wish you'd picked somewhere else for yours."

"I've always loved this town." Jesse decided to keep his plans to himself for now. Sal already looked rattled. He wasn't sure how he'd handle the news that Jesse planned to start his own vintage racing team right here at the marina.

"Sasha's coming home," Sal said.

The words hit Jesse like a fist to his heart. He kept his expression bland. "Really. When?"

Sal smiled ruefully. "She should have been here already. Don't rightly know how long she'll stay. Rosa is . . ." He scrubbed a hand over a face more lined than Jesse had ever seen it. "She's got the cancer."

"I'm sorry, Sal. Is there—" He stopped, unsure what to say next.

"They have her on some experimental treatment now." Sal shrugged. "We hope. And we pray it will work. My Rosa, she's a fighter."

Sasha now had a better understanding of how the prodigal son felt walking that last mile toward home. After a five-day cross-country trip in her un-air-conditioned Jeep Wrangler, it had taken two hours of roadside pacing and internal debate before she managed the last twenty miles.

Which made her two hours late to the party. Not that that would surprise her family. What caught her off guard, though, was the number of cars crammed into the marina parking lot and lining the gravel drive. She'd no sooner made the final turn leading to Pop and Mama Rosa's place—home—and parked the Jeep when she heard barking, a female shout of "She's here!" and then hurried feet on the porch stairs. After all these years, she hadn't known what to expect, but it certainly wasn't this, and it made her stomach clench and her hands shake.

Way before she felt ready, Pop yanked open her car door and pulled her into his strong arms before her feet even hit the ground.

"Ah, Sasha, it is so good to see my beautiful baby," he whispered, rubbing a callused hand up and down her back. He pulled back, cupped her face in his hands, and kissed one cheek. *"Tesora mia,"* he murmured. My treasure. He kissed the other cheek, then tucked her against his chest.

For a moment, Sasha couldn't respond past the wave of emotion that threatened to swamp her; she just absorbed the familiar, steady feel of Pop's work-hardened arms around her, the salty, Old Spice smell of his leathery skin. When she pulled back, tears shimmered in his dark eyes, and she had to look away for a moment, get her own emotions under control. They studied each other, and she saw the additional lines time had etched beside his eyes. He'd lost weight, too, something she'd have to tease Mama Rosa about. Mama's motto was simple: food was for family and family was about food.

Pop stroked her cheek with the back of his hand.

"We've missed you, Sasha. It's good you've come home."

"I don't know how long I'll be—"

He ignored her to pet Bella, who had hopped out behind Sasha and was prancing at his feet, fluffy tail wagging.

"Who is this beautiful girl? She looks like our Bella from years ago."

Sasha smiled and shrugged. "I thought so, too, so I named her Bella. I found her as a pup." No need for ugly details now.

"Sasha, is that you?" Before she could turn all the way around, she was swept up into Captain Demetri's arms, wrapped in the familiar smell of his Cuban cigars.

He set her at arm's length.

"Let me look at you." He kissed both of her cheeks. "Beautiful."

"Hey, Sasha," Captain Roy broke in, elbowing his friend aside to collect his own hug. And then Captains Bill and Jimmy arrived, and more hugs were exchanged.

She stood in the circle of these men who'd been such an important part of her life, and grinned like an idiot. Past and present collided and made her feel she'd finally come home.

"Sasha!" Her foster sister Eve appeared, nudged Pop out of the way, and pulled her into a bone-crushing hug. "It's about time you showed up, you crazy tomboy."

Out of the corner of her eye, Sasha saw Pop and the other captains ease away, giving the sisters some room.

She pushed back another unwelcome tide of emotion and hugged her sister close, acutely aware that her sweaty T-shirt and cargo shorts would muss and wrinkle her elegant sister's silk tank top and white linen pants. She should feel bad about that, but didn't. Funny how family could make you revert to your twelve-year-old self in two seconds flat. She eased back and took in the carefully tamed black curls framing Eve's perfect cheekbones and her beautiful, chocolate skin. Eve could have been a model. She was that gorgeous and always made Sasha feel like the ugly stepsister by comparison.

She held Eve's shoulders and grinned.

"How're things in DC with the environmental wackos?"

Eve rolled her eyes before she turned and grabbed one of Sasha's bags from the backseat.

"They're fine, thanks. You shouldn't judge, oh fearless captain, since without environmental wackos like me fighting the good fight against industrial fisheries, you'd be out of a job."

"Yeah, yeah, yeah," Sasha shot back, her earlier nerves easing at how quickly she and her sister fell into familiar banter. She grabbed her duffel in one hand and Bella's bed in the other and stopped short. "Where's Mama?"

Eve looked away, and alarm skittered up Sasha's spine.

"Eve? What's wrong? What don't I know?"

Eve huffed out a breath, seemed to come to a decision, then turned back to face her. "You've been gone a long time, Sash."

"Right. So have you. What does that have to do with anything?"

"I don't live here, but I stay in touch, visit." When Sasha opened her mouth to protest, Eve's hand shot up. "I know. You live in Washington State. Not exactly next door. But . . ." She stopped, chewed the inside of her lip, then nodded. "OK, here's the deal. Mama's sick. Cancer. Has been fighting it for a while. They thought they had it licked, but it's come back."

Sasha stumbled backward as though her boat had been slammed by a rogue wave. She struggled to stay upright. Mama couldn't be sick. She was invincible. A short round bundle of tough love and fresh cookies. She couldn't be sick.

"Why didn't anyone tell me?" Sasha turned on her sister, her fear seeking an outlet. "Why?"

Eve planted her hands on her hips. "If you bothered to turn your cell phone or computer on every once in a while, you would have known sooner."

Sasha opened her mouth to lash back, but the anger seeped out of her, replaced by a hard knot of guilt. Yeah, that was on her. She got tired of solicitors and spam and unwanted calls and regularly left the phone at home, turned off. She also forgot to check her messages and email for a month or six at a time. When she'd turned the phone back on last week, she'd found the voice mail from Pop to come home for Mama's party. And her laptop netted another two emails from Eve to go with the previous six.

"What kind is it?" she asked.

"Breast cancer. She's had a double mastectomy, so be prepared."

"Wait. What? How long has all this been going on?"

"Over six months."

Sasha swallowed hard, slapped again by how much time had passed and how much she'd missed. "No reconstruction surgery?"

"Not yet. They—"

"Hey, Sasha. Welcome home!"

Sasha found herself hugged again, and she searched for a name to go with the face. But when he grinned, the dimple did the trick.

"J. R. Renzo, is that you?" He'd been the high school heartthrob and never could understand why Sasha didn't want to go out with him. "Are you still working on the water?"

"Yep, Pop says he'll sell the fishing business to me when he's ready to retire."

"That's wonderful."

"Oh my," Eve murmured, and Sasha looked up to see the two very attractive men who'd arrived with J. R.

"Oh, hey, Eve. Good to see you, too," J. R. added. "This is Nick Stanton, with the Safe Harbor police, and Chad Everson, the high school football coach."

Eve and Sasha shook hands all around, and Sasha wanted to laugh. She'd thought they were brothers. Both were dark haired and dark eyed, but Nick came with lots of lean muscle, while Chad's linebacker build would have pegged him as a football player even without an introduction. The fact that J. R. practically ignored Eve also had Sasha biting back a grin. Men generally ignored Sasha, not Eve.

"Mama's waiting for you. She sent me to get you."

Sasha turned at the unfamiliar voice and found herself staring into a pair of angry green eyes, much like the ones that had looked back at her from the mirror for years. Tall and skinny, with bright-blue hair shorn on one side and piercings all over, the girl couldn't have been more than fifteen or sixteen. The way she stood with her arms folded and chin jutting out, she wasn't rolling out the welcome mat.

But scared-with-attitude was a breed Sasha knew well. She'd had to get past the same when she'd found Bella. She turned to the men.

"If you'll excuse us?"

She waited until they went back to the crowd before she stuck out her hand.

"Hi, I'm Sasha. Thanks for letting me know. Are you new around here?"

She knew instantly it was the wrong thing to say.

"No, you are. I live here." The girl turned and stomped off toward the house.

"Charming, isn't she?" Eve said, laughing. "That's Blaze, their newest foster child. Sort of reminds me of another stray I used to know."

Since Sasha had been thinking the same thing, she smiled, though her insides quivered at what she'd find inside the once-familiar old house.

"Guess we'd better get this over with."

Eve reared back. "What does that mean?"

Sasha sighed and shook her head. "Not what you think. I meant I have to steel myself to see Mama, not say the wrong thing—which I'm obviously still skilled at doing."

That drew a small smile from Eve. "I'll be right behind you."

The old cracker-style house looked exactly the same as it had the day Sasha left ten years ago. Hipped tin roof, white clapboard siding, porch that ran all the way around. Inside, a wide-planked hallway ran down the center of the house straight to the back door, with rooms opening up on either side. She stopped a moment to let her eyes adjust, cataloging familiar furniture, eyeing the narrow stairs leading to the big upstairs bedroom under the eaves she'd shared with Eve and Cathy.

"Where's Cathy?"

Again Eve looked away. "She goes by *Cat* now. And she's . . . she couldn't get away this weekend."

Which meant Cathy/Cat still hadn't forgiven her. Sasha wasn't really surprised, but a foolish part of her had hoped they could finally move on. Looking through the back doorway, she could see the crowd of people who had come to her mother's party, smell the burgers and chicken on the grill, hear the laughter and country music blasting from a boom box. Pop's choice, no doubt, since Mama would have preferred Italian opera.

Preparing herself, Sasha followed Eve down the long hallway to the back door.

At her first sight of Mama, Sasha froze, one hand on the screen door. She bit her lip to keep from crying out. No matter what Eve had said, she hadn't been prepared. This frail, sickly woman wearing a colorful scarf because she'd lost her hair to chemo couldn't be Mama Rosa. *Dear God, no.* Abject fear and a hefty dose of guilt slapped her, hard. She was tempted to turn around and run for her Jeep. But she wouldn't. Not today.

She forced the tears back, took a deep breath, and dug deep for a smile. For Mama, she could do this.

Jesse Claybourne had just taken a sip of his drink when the screen door opened and the star of all his teenage fantasies stepped out. He nearly choked as he realized, yes, it was in fact Sasha Petrov, the prodigal daughter come home. After all these years. And by all accounts, Mama Rosa and Sal had certainly killed the fatted calf.

Without conscious thought, he moved closer. She looked good, he decided, if a little tired and ragged around the edges. He supposed having a mother fighting cancer would do that to you. Beside her, Eve looked the same as ever: elegant and sophisticated, but with a heart as big as all outdoors. Sasha, of the amazing mane of hair and athletic body that begged to be touched, would as soon bite your hand as let you pet her.

She tried to laugh at something Eve said, and even through the strain in her voice, the rich sound slapped him hard. Yeah, he'd always been a sucker for Sal and Rosa's oldest.

The sisters moved down the porch to where Mama Rosa sat in a white wooden rocker in the shade. Sasha swallowed hard, twice, before she grabbed the gold mariner's cross she always wore to keep it from hitting Rosa as she carefully bent to kiss her mother on both cheeks.

He understood her shock. This was not the robust fireball who'd chased him off with a broom for stealing cookies.

Mama Rosa grabbed Sasha's hands when she would have pulled away and whispered something that made Sasha nod and take a careful breath. He waited a moment before he eased up onto the porch, pretending he didn't see Sasha turn her back toward her mother and close her eyes as she rubbed her heart.

"Happy birthday, Mama Rosa," he said. "Had I known it was your birthday, I'd have brought you flowers." He leaned in to place his own kiss on her cheek, smiling when she held his face in her hands.

"Jesse Claybourne, let me look at you." She scanned him from head to toe, then patted his hand. "You're a good boy. You can bring them next time." She hitched her chin toward Sasha. "At least you'll come to visit me."

Sasha blanched.

"That's because you're the best cook around." He glanced skyward. "No offense, Aunt Clarabelle."

"Thank you, Jesse." Rosa shrugged. "We all have our talents. Your Aunt Clarabelle was a good woman and a fine schoolteacher. She will be missed."

Jesse nodded and, out of the corner of his eye, watched Sasha casually check him out. When their eyes met, he winked, and a lovely flush spread over her cheeks. Clearly uncomfortable, she wrapped her arms around her middle as she stepped in his direction.

"Surprised to see you here, Money-boy."

He sent her his best smile. "And miss the chance to hassle you? Wouldn't dream of it."

She huffed out a breath. "Some things never change, I guess."

"You'd be surprised," he drawled, matching her stance.

Pop stepped up onto the porch, gave Mama's face a quick scan, and gently kissed her cheek.

"Jesse is moving into Clarabelle's cottage while he works on his vintage powerboat. Big race coming up in Clearwater."

Jesse saw the interest spark in Sasha's eyes before she carefully masked it.

"Want to go for a ride one day?"

She snorted. "Ride? With you? Please." She propped her hands on her hips, head cocked at a saucy angle. "Not unless I take the helm."

Now it was his turn to snort. "In your dreams, Petrov."

"Sasha is a licensed boat captain," Mama said. "She's been working—"

Whatever else she had been about to say was drowned out by Pop, who stuck his fingers in his mouth and let out an ear-piercing whistle Jesse hadn't heard in many a year. But now, as then, silence fell instantly. Pop gestured to Eve, who stepped out of the back door bearing a huge cake. Then he turned back to the crowd.

"Friends, thank you for coming and for celebrating with us today. God has granted my Rosa sixty years, and we are thankful. For her. And for all of you who have shared our lives."

His eyes filled with tears as he tugged Sasha's hand and walked over to the rocker with her. He took Mama's hand in his other one and kissed it tenderly. Eve stepped over and held out the enormous sheet cake with its two candles displaying *60*. Blaze stepped up beside her and held the other end. Sasha started "Happy Birthday" with her lush, off-key voice, and everyone joined in, all eyes on Mama Rosa, who smiled a huge smile and finally blew out the candles on the third try.

Jesse watched the scene play out, smiling, then stiffened when that familiar itchy feeling crept up his shoulder blades. He was being watched. Not surprising, really. It was only a matter of time before his recent incarceration became public knowledge. He glanced around, but he didn't see any obvious scowls aimed his way. Nor worse, someone fingering a weapon. But the feeling persisted, so he slipped away. No way would he bring the ghosts of his past here. The Martinellis had enough to worry about.

The standard summer thunderstorm blew in about three o'clock and broke up the party. Sasha watched from a corner of the porch as families rushed to their cars amid shouts and waves, holding towels over their heads, casserole dishes tucked under their arms. Within minutes, the driveway cleared. Fifteen minutes after that, the storm blew out to sea, leaving behind sunny skies and slightly cooler temperatures. At least for a little while.

She wished her own emotions could be swept away as easily. It had taken every bit of her inner strength to keep from rearing back in shock when she first spotted Mama. Her throat closed up again, and her hands clenched with the need to punch something in frustration. This couldn't be happening. How could she not have known?

Of course, Eve and Pop had tried to tell her. Would it have made a difference? Would she have come home sooner?

Sasha stepped off the porch and crossed the yard, her back to the house. She paced the edge of the weedy lawn where rocks bordered the water as it sloshed against the shore. She'd neglected her family for a long time and deserved every bit of this guilt. She owed them more than this. So fine, she'd stay awhile and help Pop with the marina, as Mama had asked. She'd try to put some meat on Mama's bones, too, though since she couldn't cook, that'd be a challenge. But she could try, *would* try, doggone it. It was the least she could do.

"Mama wants everyone in the house."

Blaze's voice came out more growl than words, but Sasha caught the drift. She turned and saw the teen, arms crossed over her skinny chest, looking like a strong breeze would blow her out to sea. But what she lacked in heft, she made up for in attitude. Sasha smiled and leaned down to pet Bella.

"Have you met my dog?"

"We have a dog."

"Right. And for now, we have two."

Blaze's eyes widened. "You're not staying."

Sasha stood and realized she towered over the girl.

"Actually, I am." She shrugged. "So maybe we could get along, huh? For Mama's sake?"

Blaze huffed out a breath. "Nobody wants you here. Especially not Mama." She spun around and stomped back to the main house.

Sasha sighed and followed her across the now-empty yard.

Sasha found Pop and Mama in the living room, with its sagging flowered sofa and the lumpy loveseat that she and Eve and Cathy—oops, Cat—used to fight over. Now, Mama sat in one of those fancy electric recliners, eyes closed, feet up, while Pop sat beside her in the old wooden rocker, gently holding her hand. Blaze huddled in a corner of the loveseat, arms still in the upright and tightly crossed position. Eve sat beside her and tried to put an arm around her, but Blaze shrugged her off and leaped to her feet. She crossed the room and plopped down on the floor at Pop's feet. An aging beagle lumbered in and flopped down beside her. Bella pranced in behind the dog and immediately collapsed on Blaze's other side. Bella sent Sasha a questioning look, as though asking, *OK to be here? She needs me.*

Sasha smiled as she sank down on the sofa and nodded. Bella put her muzzle on Blaze's knee and promptly dozed off. Her loud snoring coaxed a reluctant smile out of Blaze and woke Mama with a start. She opened her eyes and smiled groggily as she looked around the room.

"Where is my Cathy?" she finally asked.

Sasha had wondered the same thing. Eve, who had always known everything about everyone, said, "She couldn't come, Mama. She's very sorry. She'll call you soon."

Blaze huffed out a breath. "She didn't even bother to call."

Pop stopped rocking. "You will not talk about your sister with disrespect."

Blaze ducked her head, a flush spreading up her cheeks. "I just meant—"

"Enough," Pop said gently. "Let's enjoy those who are here."

Sasha hid a smile as Blaze managed—just barely—to bite back another deep sigh. It would have been funnier if Blaze didn't remind Sasha so very much of herself as a teen, all attitude and prickly desire for affection hidden behind walls of insecurity.

Just then the door opened and Cathy breezed in, movie-star shades hiding her eyes, straight black bob swinging around her face as she slowly walked to Mama in heels so high and a skirt so tight it was a wonder she could move at all.

Mama's eyes widened and filled with tears. "My Cathy. You came."

Cathy bent, careful not to tip over, and kissed Mama's cheek. "It's *Cat* now, Mama. Happy birthday."

"You missed the party," Blaze announced, earning a stern look from Pop. "I'm just sayin'."

Cat straightened and noticed Sasha for the first time. "What are you doing here?"

Sasha stood and forced a smile. "Same thing you are, sister." She took a step to hug Cat, but her sister retreated to a safe distance.

"I can't believe you had the gall to show up here after what you did."

"Cat, look, I'm sorry. Truly. I never meant to—"

Cat held up a hand. "You never meant any of the horrible things you did. You just didn't think. Ever. Not about anyone but yourself." She shook her head. "This was a mistake. I need to—"

"You will sit down."

Every head turned toward Pop. Cat automatically plopped down in the nearest chair. Nobody argued when Pop used that tone of voice.

Mama fumbled with the remote, and the chair slowly raised her head and lowered her feet. Once she squirmed and settled, she looked at each of them, eyes still sparkling with unshed tears.

"My girls, together at last. Thank you for coming, all of you." She clasped her hands together over her heart. "You have given me more joy than I ever expected, than I ever deserved."

She wiped her cheeks with shaking hands, and Sasha had to sit on her own hands to keep from rushing over and begging her to stop. This kind of emotional display had never happened when they were growing up. Mama was always brisk and matter-of-fact, quick with a bone-crushing hug or an unexpected swat with a kitchen towel.

"I wanted my girls home, not just because it's my birthday, though I thank you from the bottom of my heart for sharing this day with me. No, I want something more from you three oldest."

Sasha exchanged raised eyebrows with Eve, but Cat wouldn't meet her eyes.

"Of course, Mama. Whatever you want," Sasha said.

"If we can give it, we will," Eve qualified.

Mama smiled. "Always a negotiator, my Evelyn."

"I just meant—" Eve began before Mama interrupted.

"I know you do not make promises lightly, nor would I want you to." She smiled and took a deep breath, looking from one to the next. "You all know about the chemo, yes? Pop has filled you in on the details."

Everyone nodded.

"Good. He also told you they are trying an experimental therapy?"

Sasha, Cat, and Eve nodded, but Blaze sprang up and ran from the room, both dogs at her heels. Pop would have followed, but Mama laid a hand on his arm, a familiar gesture that jabbed Sasha in the heart. "Let her go. It may be best she not be here just now."

Sasha fingered the mariner's cross at her neck and exchanged another furtive glance with Eve. "What's this all about, Mama?"

Again, the gentle smile. "Sasha, my impatient one." She coughed, a deep, racking sound that raised goose bumps on Sasha's arms. Mama leaned her head back and took several deep breaths before continuing.

Sasha leaned forward, hands clasped between her knees. "Mama, please. What do you need? How can we help?"

Mama smiled once more, and Sasha swore she could see right through her skin. It made her want to bang on the cypress paneling, so she gripped her hands tighter and waited.

"You remember Tony, no? My baby who was stolen from my arms before you girls came?" She pulled a ratty-looking teddy bear from the basket beside her chair, and Sasha's heart clenched.

"Of course," Sasha said. It was a story they'd heard many times. Mama and Pop's biological son, Tony, had been three the day he disappeared. He had been playing in the yard, and Mama had gone in for another load of laundry. The phone rang while she was inside, and when she finally returned, Tony had vanished. Despite an exhaustive search by police and, later, a private investigator they'd hired, no one had ever been able to find a single trace of Tony. The prevailing opinion was that Tony had fallen in the water and drowned, his body swept out to sea.

Mama stroked the ragged bear, and apprehension flitted down Sasha's spine, mingling with her confusion. "But what does that have to do with us?"

Mama took a deep, rattling breath and focused first on Eve, then Cat, then Sasha before she said, "I want you to find him."

Sasha fell back against the sofa as though she'd been pushed. She locked eyes with Eve, whose shock no doubt mirrored her own. Cat looked equally shaken. "Find him?" Cat said. "Mama, what are you saying? What are you asking?"

Some of the familiar fierceness returned to Mama's faded brown eyes, and Sasha's shock eased a fraction. "I have not lost my mind. I am sick. I have been sick." She held up a hand. "And before you all tell me I will be fine and I will get well, we don't know that. Although I have faith that God will heal me." She patted Pop's hand. "So, in either case, I need to know what happened to my boy, my firstborn."

Eve cleared her throat. "Um, what if he's, ah . . ."

"Dead?" Mama nodded. "It is a possibility. They never found one single trace of my baby. But in here"—she patted her heart—"I believe he is alive. I want to meet him. I want to know he is healthy and happy."

"But-but that was—" Sasha scrambled to do the math, never her strong suit.

"Twenty-three years ago," Pop said.

Sasha leaped to her feet and paced. "You should hire another investigator, someone who finds people for a living, someone who knows how to do this stuff."

Eve moved to stand beside her, stopping her momentum. "I agree. While I understand why you want to do this, truly, we're not the people who can help you. You need professionals."

The whole time her daughters spoke, Mama simply shook her head. "You are family. Outsiders could not find him. I want you. My girls will find my boy for me. It is my final wish."

"Don't say things like that!" Sasha hissed, but Mama's eyes were closed, and she pretended to be asleep. Discussion over.

Oh, Mama had strong-armed them into things before, innocent requests like helping around the house or keeping little secrets from Pop, but this—this was nuts.

Eve plopped down on the couch and covered her face with her hands. Cat wore a shell-shocked look Sasha understood. She had to get outside. The walls were closing in.

Her flip-flops smacked the knotty pine floor as she marched from the room and across the porch. She stomped across the soggy grass and onto the docks at the marina. She didn't stop until she reached the farthest point. She stood, hands on hips, trying to catch her breath as Bella sidled up beside her.

By all that was holy, how on earth were they going to give Mama what she wanted?

Chapter 2

Sasha wasn't surprised when she heard footsteps on the dock behind her. But she was surprised to see Pop. She'd been expecting Eve to chew her out for running away. Again. But her emotions and all that internal churning were why she'd stayed away to begin with.

Pop came and stood beside her, slipped his arm around her waist, and tucked her against his side. "It is good you are here, my Sasha. Mama has missed having you girls around."

Sasha smiled at him, feeling warm all the way inside for the first time in years. "You were just glad to be rid of me."

He pulled off his fisherman's cap and pointed to his bald head and the wispy bit of fringe around the edges. "When you girls were young, you turned my hair gray. Then you left and it all fell out."

"Hey, I can't take all the credit. That you can blame Blaze for, I'm guessing."

He settled the cap back on his head and laughed. "She is a handful, that one." He paused, speared her with his dark eyes. "She reminds me of you."

Sasha leaned in and rested her head against the reassuring beat of his heart. Pop's easy affection had been the one constant in Sasha's young life. Mama could be laughing one minute and screaming in Italian the next, but Pop . . . he was steady. Her anchor.

"You hanging in there, Pop?" Sasha felt him stiffen at the question, but he didn't answer. She raised her head. "Pop? Is there more? Is it worse than you've said?"

He shook his head. "No, Sasha. It is bad enough, no? There is no more."

She looked directly into his dark eyes, noticing how deeply the crow's-feet had etched his skin, how worry had aged him. "I wish you had told me."

He studied her face, then looked away. "I did not want to leave the news on your answering machine. I figured you would call—and come home—when you were ready."

She started to say she would have come immediately, but didn't. She wasn't sure she would have, and the knowledge shamed her. She'd run long and hard to escape Safe Harbor. Instead she asked, "How bad is it really?"

"Your mama, she never gives up hope. Never. She is sure that this new experimental regimen will work, even though the others did not."

She heard what he didn't say. "You have doubts." It hurt to even say the words.

He nodded once and looked out at the Gulf, calm as glass now after the storm had passed through. "I will pray. And I will hope."

Sasha waited, watching his throat work as he studied the water. She could tell he had more to say but couldn't seem to force the words out. Finally he turned to her and gripped her shoulders. "This quest, it is nonsense, Sasha. Pure nonsense. Tony has been gone for twenty-three years. This is the foolish hope of a desperate woman."

Sasha agreed with him, though she wouldn't have put it in quite those terms. She reached up and patted his hands.

"Maybe foolish, maybe not." She shrugged. "But I'll do my best." She forced a smile. "And if we get Eve involved, well, then our chances go way up, immediately."

He wrenched out of her grasp. "No!"

Sasha watched, stunned, as he paced. Back and forth, back and forth, hands fisted at his sides. Beside her, Bella whimpered, and Sasha reached down to reassure her. "It's OK, girl."

When Pop turned back her way, Sasha stepped into his path. "Pop. Stop. Please. Tell me why not."

He wouldn't meet her eyes, just kept shaking his head, muttering in Italian.

She reached out and grabbed his arm, holding him still. Finally he looked up, jaw clenched.

"It is a fool's errand. A waste of time. And when nothing comes of it? Then I will be left holding her as she cries in the night again, desperate for her baby. I can't, Sasha. I can't watch her go through it again. He's gone. Our Tony was gone years ago, and she can't—" He stopped and wiped tears from his eyes. "Your mama, she can't let him go. And I can't watch her suffer anymore."

He cleared his throat and visibly calmed himself. "Tell her no, Sasha. Tell her you cannot do this. Please. For me."

Sasha swallowed the lump in her own throat, trying to find words, but nothing came out. How could she refuse him? This was Pop, the man who had found her living behind the marina in an abandoned shed when she was twelve years old, a filthy, starving runaway with nothing to call her own but the clothes on her back, a gold mariner's cross she wore around her neck, and an attitude that screeched like rusty armor. It had taken almost a week, but Pop had finally coaxed her out of the shed with Mama's homemade bread and deep-fried fish he'd caught that day.

Pop and Mama had saved her in every sense of the word. They'd loved her despite her attitude and had given her a home, no questions asked. After a while, she'd become part of their family and, later, part of their faith, too.

So how on earth could she tell one of them yes without breaking the other's heart?

And how would she ever choose?

Jesse figured he should head to Clarabelle's, start packing up and pitching the endless knickknacks and doodads his great-aunt had stacked on every available surface of her pink cottage. But he couldn't seem to leave the marina. He'd waited out the thunderstorm in his truck, and now he climbed out and wandered down the dock, stopping to study the Gulf of Mexico rolling to the west as far as the eye could see. He'd been caught off guard when his feisty aunt suddenly died in her sleep at the ripe old age of ninety-three. He'd been even more surprised that she'd left everything she owned to him.

He still expected her to appear in the kitchen, cane tapping on the heart-pine floor, pointing an arthritic finger and scolding him for some childhood misdeed. What would she say about his stint in jail? He grimaced. She would poke and prod until the whole ugly mess spilled out. Then she'd tell him that doing the wrong thing for the right reason was still wrong. She'd thump his chest and tell him to confess, repent, and move on and live as the man she knew he could be.

Jesse smiled at the mental image, watching the water. He propped a shoulder against a post and scanned the aging dock, listening to the water lapping the pilings and the birds fighting over scraps from a nearby fishing boat, inhaling the smell of salt and seawater and engine fumes. He could breathe here.

He studied the slip where *The Painted Lady* rode the tide between a flats fishing boat and a sixteen-foot camo-green johnboat that had seen better days. *The Lady* was gorgeous, but her engine needed a lot of work if he expected her to win that race. And that was exactly what he expected. He needed that prize money. He had a promise to keep.

From somewhere off to his left, in one of the small outbuildings that dotted the marina's perimeter, he heard banging, followed by muttered cursing and several more loud thwacks. He grinned and started in that direction.

He stepped into the open doorway and found Sasha hunched over a boat motor, just as he'd thought. Since they were teens, when she got nervous or worried, she paced and fidgeted with her cross necklace. But if she was furious, she took her feelings out on machinery, usually engines that wouldn't run.

If memory served, this was Pop's workshop. Sasha poked and prodded a half-assembled boat motor hanging from a lift. She checked pieces and parts, examining one after another, completely oblivious to his presence.

She wiped greasy hands on her cargo shorts and grimaced when she realized what she'd done.

He grabbed a clean shop rag from a stack and dangled it over her shoulder in front of her face. Startled, she grabbed it and spun around, looking him over with the same suspicion she would a snake that had just slithered in.

He lounged against the workbench, arms crossed, and wondered if she knew how obvious the emotions were that marched across her face. Suspicion, no question. But unless he missed his guess, he'd also seen a quick flicker of interest flash in those beautiful eyes before she looked away. His own interest came as no surprise, since he'd spent every summer of his squandered youth pining over the aloof and beautiful Sasha Petrov.

"Don't you have better things to do, Money-boy?" She wiped her hands on the rag, then took a step back in surprise when he nipped it from her grasp and dabbed at her left cheek.

Jesse found he liked keeping her a bit off balance. "You always did get dirty when you worked."

A big yellow Lab appeared and inserted herself between him and Sasha, shooting him a concerned look.

"This is Bella. She hides when I start banging, but she never goes far."

Jesse leaned over and stuck out his hand for Bella to sniff. "She looks like the dog you had when you were a kid." Color spread up Sasha's cheeks, and she looked away. Interesting. "She's yours?" he asked, though given the way the dog hugged Sasha's legs, the answer seemed obvious.

"Since she was a pup. She goes with me everywhere."

He eyed the suspended motor. "So what crime has this motor committed to make you beat it with a wrench?"

Her eyes narrowed, as if she wasn't quite sure if he was teasing or not. She pointed. "Not the motor. Idiot owners. Gummed-up injectors. Lazy." She shook her head and continued her inspection.

"You OK?" He hadn't meant to ask; the words just popped out.

Her head snapped up. "Why wouldn't I be?"

He studied her closed expression and decided not to mention Mama Rosa's cancer. Clearly a closed topic. "Must be a bit awkward, coming back after all this time."

This pulled a half smile from her. "Guess you know all about that." She raised a brow and went back to work, leaving him to wonder just how much gossip she'd picked up. And how much of it was true.

"You all moved into Miss Clarabelle's cottage?"

"Not yet. I'm going to have to shovel out a truckload of knickknacks first."

"She did love her trinkets. And you, though you kept her on her toes."

He laughed. "I still expect her to stomp into the kitchen and chew me out for something or other."

"You always gave her lots to scold you for. She was a sweet little spitfire."

"True enough." *You're stalling, Claybourne.* "So, I was going to take *The Painted Lady* for a ride. Want to come?"

She stopped, straightened, arms folded as she studied him. "She's a pretty sweet ride. You going to let me take the helm?"

"Mama Rosa said you're a boat captain. You ever pilot a vintage boat? They take a bit of finesse."

"Not one as pretty as yours. But I've handled trawlers in heavy seas and just about anything else that floats."

He indicated the door with a nod of his head. "We'll see."

She flashed him a quick triumphant grin, dropped her tools back on the workbench, and took a minute to scrub the grease from her hands at the industrial sink before she followed him out to the boat slip.

She stopped, hands on hips as she surveyed the boat. She let out a slow whistle.

"They sure don't sell these babies at the local discount lot."

All sleek wood and beautiful lines, ready to fly across the waves, *The Painted Lady* could tempt men into foolish, foolish decisions.

His gut knotted when he thought of just how much he had riding on the upcoming race. He stepped aboard and turned to offer her a hand.

She grinned. "Permission to come aboard?"

He wiggled his fingers. "Yeah, yeah, hop in." He eyed Bella. "She needs to stay here."

Sasha looked like she wanted to argue, but then she patted Bella's head and said, "Sorry, girl. I'll be back soon." She untied the bow lines, turned, and in one smooth move, grabbed his hand and stepped aboard.

Jesse turned on the blower and reached back to untie the stern lines. Once they'd cast off, he expertly maneuvered them out of the small marina and followed the channel markers into open water. Out here in the Gulf, the water deepened about a foot per mile, so a smart man stayed in the channel and knew the tides or he could end up running aground on an oyster bed.

The small cockpit barely had room for both of them, but he sat behind the wheel, studying the gauges, judging *The Lady*'s performance. When he'd used the key from Aunt Clarabelle's lawyer to unlock the air-conditioned storage unit, pulled back the cover, and gotten his first look at *The Lady*, he'd been stunned. Why had his aunt kept her hidden all these years? She looked showroom new, but her engine needed work, lots of work, after sitting idle for who-knew-how-many years. She wasn't race ready. And he didn't have a lot of time or money to get her in top form.

A few minutes later, he eased up on the throttle and moved to the side, one hand still on the wheel. "You ready?"

Her eyes widened even as a slow grin split her face, jabbing him like an unexpected fist. Did she have any idea what that smile did to him?

"I'm always ready." She eased behind the wheel, took a moment to look over the various gauges, then smoothly eased the throttle forward. Faster, faster, faster. The 630-horsepower Chevrolet marine motor pushed *The Lady* up on plane, and they skimmed over the surface of the water with ease. He'd expected jerky movements and had braced accordingly. Sasha's smooth handling made him relax.

She pushed her sunglasses down and peered at him over the top, grinning. "This is not my first rodeo, Money-boy."

"I can see that."

Neither spoke for several minutes while she inched the throttle forward in smooth increments. They were far enough out in the Gulf now that they had several feet of water. No fear of running aground this far from shore.

He sank down on the padded bench seat. "Go ahead and open her up."

She grinned, the sun glinting off her sunglasses. "You sure?"

He smiled back, enjoying the little-kid sparkle in her eyes. "Let's see what you've got."

She nodded once and took him at his word. She pushed the throttle wide open until they were flying over the water. This late in the day, most boats had already come back in, so it felt like they were alone in the world. She made big sweeping turns, learning how *The Painted Lady* handled, changing speed and direction like the pro she'd claimed to be.

Time and distance lost all meaning as he watched the pure joy in her face. She tilted her head to the wind, long hair flying behind her, and let out a whoop worthy of a Seminole warrior.

Watching her, Jesse forgot all his troubles. He simply took in the moment and admitted he'd never met anyone like her, never been so drawn to anyone. Then or now.

He mentally shook his head at his own foolishness. She'd followed the call of the sea since she left. He'd be kidding himself if he started hoping she'd stick around.

Without thinking, he reached over and brushed the back of his hand down her cheek.

Sasha looked over at him, and their eyes met. She gradually throttled back and slowed to a stop. Time seemed to stretch as the boat settled into the water, the only sound the gentle lapping of water against the hull.

Sasha looked into Jesse's eyes, and her heart skipped a beat. Behind his easy smile and confidence, she caught a quick flash of . . . something before it disappeared. She felt a blush steal over her cheeks as she broke eye contact and eased away. She'd felt that same tug every time she looked at him. She always had, and it scared her silly. Time to get things back on an even course.

"That was incredible." She patted the dash. "She handles like a dream. The engine runs a little rough, but I'm guessing you know that." When he simply smiled, she said, "This baby is going to win you some races, Money-boy, and she won't even break a sweat doing it."

"That's the plan. Provided I can get her in top shape in time." He paused. "You ever drive in a race before?"

"You want me at the helm in the upcoming race?"

"Not a chance. But you'd be good at it. You have experience on the water and some serious natural skills. The rest is just practice." He studied her face, but she didn't know what he was thinking. "I could teach you, if you want to learn."

She wanted to shout *Yes!* but she bit her lip as responsibility splashed her like a bucket of cold water. "Tempting, but no."

"You have a job you need to get back to?"

"No, but I have obligations here. People depending on me. Sorry."

They drifted into silence as Jesse guided them back to the marina and eased *The Painted Lady* into her slip. Did he have any idea how much she wanted to say yes? Then she thought of Mama, and the *no* became easier. She hopped off and secured the lines. By the time she straightened and he'd turned the engine off, Bella was prancing around like they'd been gone forever. Behind them, Eve marched down the dock, completely out of place in her heeled sandals and fancy white outfit.

Jesse stepped onto the dock to hear Eve demand, "Where have you been?"

Sasha stiffened, but before she could say anything, he held out a hand. "Hey, Eve. Good to see you again. I stole Sasha for a quick ride. Hope that's all right."

Eve stared at his hand but kept her own at her side. He lowered his arm, and Sasha stepped between them.

"Look, Eve—"

Eve poked one manicured finger into Sasha's chest. "No, you look. You're not here one day and already you're blowing off the family to run off and play."

Sasha stepped back and slapped her hands on her hips. "I went for a ride, Eve. How is that blowing off the family?"

"Mama went to the effort of cooking dinner. You didn't show up to eat it."

Sasha swallowed hard and closed her eyes for a moment. "How was I supposed to know that?"

Eve narrowed her eyes. "We waited for you for thirty minutes. By then the food was cold." She leaned close and hissed, "You made Mama cry."

Sasha spun toward the house. "I'll go apologize, right now." She looked over her shoulder. "Thanks for the ride, Jesse."

"Don't bother," Eve called after her. "Mama already went to bed." She blew out a breath. "Typical," she muttered.

"Maybe you could cut her a bit of slack." The moment the words left his mouth, he wanted to call them back. *Dumb move, Claybourne.*

Eve spun to face him, sparks fairly shooting from her eyes. "When I need advice from a spoiled rich kid, I'll be sure to let you know. Until then, butt out, Claybourne."

Jesse exhaled a slow breath as she stomped off after her sister. He straightened when that itchy feeling started between his shoulder blades again. The only time he'd ever ignored that instinct, he'd gotten knifed in the jail yard for his stupidity. He wouldn't make that mistake again. Casually he scanned the marina, the boats, the outbuildings, but he didn't see anyone.

That didn't mean he wasn't being watched.

Sasha had one foot on the porch steps when the screen door slammed open and Cat marched out and started for the steps without a word.

"Where are you going?" Sasha asked.

Cat stopped as though surprised, and Sasha noticed a fine tremor in her hands.

"Home."

Cat tried to step around her, so Sasha blocked her path while she scrambled to find the right words.

"What about Mama's request that we find Tony?"

"It's ridiculous. How is anyone supposed to find him after all these years? He's probably been dead all this time. I'm not looking for a grave."

Sasha watched her sister's face, noticing the way her eyes darted around, the strained, tight look of her mouth, the much-too-skinny body. She hadn't seen her in ten years, true, but something was very wrong.

"Are you OK, Cat?"

Cat's head snapped up. "I will be as soon as I get away from here."

"Will you stay? At least a couple days? It would mean a lot to Mama."

Her eyes narrowed. "Are you going to be here?"

"Yes. I told Mama I'd try to figure out what happened to Tony. Maybe give Pop a hand with the marina, too."

"Then there's your answer. If you're staying, I'm going."

Sasha took her arm when Cat tried to brush past.

"I'm sorry about that day, Cat. I always have been. How can I make it up to you?"

Cat shook her off, eyes blazing. "You can't. Don't you get that? You ruined my chances for the career I wanted, the career I deserved, by being your usual selfish self. I never got the chance. Never got the life I wanted—that you knew I wanted more than anything. All because of you." She shoved her sister so hard, Sasha almost lost her balance. "I never want to see you again."

Sasha bit her lip as Cat climbed in an aging Honda and took off with a spin of gravel. She let the unfair accusations slide in the face of much bigger issues. Since she'd seen her last, Cat had gotten into trouble, bad trouble, and if Sasha had to guess, she'd put her money on serious drug use. The twitchy movements, darting eyes, and loss of weight were unfortunately things she'd seen in other users. Maybe she was wrong. She hoped so.

Did Eve know? She snorted. Eve knew everything. Maybe the two of them could figure out what was really going on with Cat, how to help.

Sasha held the door as Bella bounded up the steps and went inside to flop down by the sofa, but Sasha knew her own rest wouldn't come anytime soon. Between Mama's request and now this with Cat, every cell in her body screamed to grab her backpack, hop in the Jeep, and never look back.

But she wouldn't. The time had come to stop running.

Chapter 3

After a night of tossing and turning, Sasha woke to Bella nudging her arm and whimpering. She sat up in the narrow twin bed and looked around the sloped-ceiling room, trying to get her bearings. Home. Right. Based on the angle of the sunlight spearing through the rusting metal blinds, she'd overslept. Another black mark in Eve's ledger. That sister's bed was already neatly made, of course, while Cat's hadn't been slept in. So much for hoping her estranged sister had changed her mind.

First, coffee and an impatient dog. She pulled on clean clothes, gave her hair a quick brush, then pulled it into a ponytail as she and Bella thumped down the steep stairs. She let Bella out, then turned toward the coffeepot, mumbling, "Morning," to the shapes at the table. After adding lots of sugar and a dollop of cream, she swallowed half the cup before she felt her brain cells come to life again.

She turned and kissed Mama's cheek before she slid into a chair. Eve stood at the old-fashioned gas stove, scrambling eggs. Mama and Pop sat at the table, mugs cradled in their hands. The scene was so different from her memories, it made her heart hurt. Mama had always reigned over the stove and Pop would be out greeting the fishermen before the first pink streaks painted the horizon. Eve had never wanted to cook.

Mama looked up from her tea with such a hopeful expression, Sasha couldn't tell her what she'd decided during the night. She swallowed more coffee, hoping for the courage to get the words out, but they wouldn't come. She couldn't snuff out Mama's tentative hope, couldn't tell her what she asked was impossible. Instead, she lightly patted Mama's hand. "I'm so sorry I missed dinner. I didn't know—"

"Hush, Sasha. No apologies." Mama maneuvered the tea to her mouth, and Sasha had to look away as some of it sloshed onto the table. Had the chemo worn her out that much?

Mama set the mug down. "Eve, honey, come sit. Where is Blaze?"

"Still asleep when I peeked in," Eve said as she spooned the eggs into a large bowl and set it on the table beside a plate of bacon and basket of toast. She sent a quick, disapproving glance Sasha's way, wiped her hands on a dish towel, and perched on the edge of her chair. "Eat, Mama. You need to keep your strength up."

Mama smiled again, and this time, it reached all the way to her brown eyes. Then they filled with tears, but she wouldn't let them fall. Sasha clenched her hands around her mug. It would be less painful if someone simply reached in and ripped her beating heart right out of her chest. She drank more coffee and rubbed the ache in her heart. Mama reached over and patted Eve's hand.

"You're a good girl, Eve." She reached out to her other side and took Sasha's hand, too. "And so are you. You will never know what it means to me that you two will do this for me. Maybe Cathy will also . . ." She let the thought drift off.

Desperate to change the subject, Sasha blurted out what had kept her up most of the night. "Mama, what if we can't—"

Eve gave a sharp, negative shake of her head.

"What if you can't find my Tony?" Mama asked.

"It's been a long time," Eve added gently.

Mama looked from one to the other. "Someday, if God blesses you both with children—and I hope and pray he does—you will understand why I need to know where he is. And why I know, I *know*, he's still alive." She patted her heart. "In here, a mother knows."

"We'll do whatever we can, Mama," Sasha heard herself say.

Pop hadn't said a word the whole time, and now he shoved his chair back from the table, kissed Mama on the top of her head, and left, the screen door slamming behind him.

Not sure what to say, Sasha choked down a piece of toast and noticed Eve doing the same.

"He is afraid I will get my hopes up again," Mama said. "He does not want to see me disappointed."

"Neither do we," Eve said. They ate in silence for several minutes. Then she reached over to the sideboard and grabbed her iPad. "I've made a list of places to start."

"Of course you have," Sasha murmured.

Eve drummed her long, elegantly painted nails on the scarred wooden table. "Do you have a better idea? If so, I'm all ears."

Sasha stood and started clearing the table. "I thought we'd start with the police station and ask to see the file."

Eve's eyes widened briefly, as though she was surprised her sister had an actual plan, then she gathered the rest of the dishes. "Do you want to wash or dry?"

Sasha grabbed the dish soap and metal wash pan, grinning. "What do you think?"

Eve smiled and said, "Guess I'll dry then. Imagine that."

For those few minutes, as they stood shoulder to shoulder, some of the awkwardness faded, and Sasha caught a glimpse of the sisters they'd been, the closeness they'd shared, and was glad she'd come home.

Eve insisted on driving, so they arrived downtown in the air-conditioned comfort of Mama's aging but immaculate Buick. She parked on the street and Sasha paused a moment to glance around. Nothing had changed, as far as she could see. Main Street still boasted the same tired-looking storefronts: the Blue Dolphin Restaurant, Johnson's Hardware, Annie's Attic—which was part thrift store, part antiques—Ned's Appliance Repair. She wondered if old Ned still smoked marijuana in the narrow alley out back. The library and Beatrice's Hair Affair anchored one end of the downtown block, while at the other, Barry's Quality Cars obviously still sold everything from barely running jalopies to shiny new pickups. Progress had not moved into Safe Harbor, and that suited the locals just fine, thank you very much.

The police station occupied the first floor of an 1890s boarding-house a block off Main Street, just as it had for seventy-five years. A lawyer and several other businesses rented space on the second floor. The whole building listed slightly to port and needed a fresh coat of white paint, but the black shutters all hung straight, so it didn't look too bad.

She'd been inside only once, just before high school graduation, the night Pop asked her to stay in Safe Harbor and eventually take over the marina. She'd freaked at the idea of being depended on, had gotten drunk, egged several downtown businesses—including the police station—and promptly got arrested. That was the same night she ruined Cat's life, since the whole family took off searching for Sasha, worried something horrible had happened. Cat missed her vocal audition with a big-shot talent scout and had never been able to reschedule or get another opportunity like it—for which she'd never forgiven Sasha. Two days after graduation, Sasha left Safe Harbor.

"I wonder if they've painted the shutters since you had to after the egg incident," Eve said, heading up the steps.

Sasha laughed. "Doubt it. I did a dang fine job the first time." Their eyes met and the laughter died. Sasha knew they were both thinking of Cat. And Tony. But neither said anything. They would deal in facts. Let Mama deal with the emotions.

They walked into the lobby and waited a moment for their eyes to adjust. A late-twenties officer in a green Safe Harbor police uniform stood behind what had once been the boardinghouse reception desk. He looked up from his computer with a smile, and Sasha recognized Nick Stanton from Mama's party. She figured the combination of dark hair cropped close and a tanned, toned body that came with puppy-dog brown eyes inspired the local ladies to search for reasons to call the police. She smiled back.

"Nice to see you ladies again. How can I help you?" he asked as he clicked the mouse and gave them his full attention.

Eve stepped forward, hand extended in what Sasha thought of as her diplomat persona.

After smiles and handshakes, Eve said, "We'd like to see the file on the disappearance of our brother, Tony Martinelli."

Officer Stanton frowned as he tapped keys on the computer. "We haven't had a disappearance here in Safe Harbor in a very long time. When did this happen?"

"March fifth, 1991," Eve responded.

Since no one had mentioned the actual date until now, Sasha raised a brow at Eve, who shrugged. "Research. I couldn't sleep."

Officer Stanton nodded and kept clicking, scrolling, checking. After a moment, he looked up.

"I'm sorry, but I don't see any case files with that name listed anywhere."

"What? How is that possible?" Sasha asked.

He held up a hand. "That only means it's not in the computer. We're still in the process of digitally scanning all our archives. This far back, they are probably still in the storage building, awaiting their turn."

A form spit out of the printer, and he handed it over the counter along with a pen. "If you ladies don't mind showing me some identification, you can fill out the form and I'll get the process started."

"We have a bit of time. What if we grab lunch and come back?" Sasha asked.

He shook his head. "I don't think I made myself clear. I can put the request in right now, but getting the actual file will take a few days, at least."

Eve's eyebrows shot to her hairline, and Sasha bit back a smile. Eve worked in a high-tech office with lots of clout and instant access.

"I don't have days. I have to catch a plane tomorrow."

"I'm sorry. I'm guessing it will take until the middle of the week, minimum."

Chief Monroe sauntered through the front door, and Sasha sighed inwardly. He removed his hat and extended a hand, his grin as fake as his teeth.

"Eve, Sasha, good to see you girls again. Heard you were in town for your mama's big birthday bash. I would have been honored to offer my congratulations in person, but someone had to keep the citizens of our little corner of paradise safe."

Sasha nearly rolled her eyes. He'd always been pompous and treated her like something he'd scraped off the bottom of his shoe, especially after what he termed her "crime spree" ten years ago. Still, they needed his help.

"We'll be sure to pass your good wishes on to Mama," Eve said.

The chief's grin faded. "How is she, bless her heart?"

"She's holding her own," Sasha said. "She had a wonderful time at the party."

"Good, good. Glad to hear it. So what brings you ladies downtown?"

"They want to see the file from their brother's disappearance," Officer Nick supplied.

The chief scratched his head. "Well, now, I remember my daddy talking about that case, God rest his soul. That was a long time ago. I'm sure those files are in the archives somewhere. Why would you want to see them now, after all this time?"

Eve and Sasha exchanged a quick glance.

"Call it family curiosity," Sasha said, smiling. "That happened before our time, so we want to get a sense of the whole thing."

"Well, the file won't tell you much, I know that. It was a tragedy, pure and simple. Your mama went in the house, quick-like to get more wash, got distracted by a phone call, and when she came back out, the poor boy had drowned."

"But they never found his body," Sasha said.

"No, they sure didn't. But it was the only thing that made sense. There were no strangers hanging around, never a trace of the boy found. He probably fell into the water and got washed out with the tide."

"We appreciate the insight, Chief," Eve said, "but we'd like to see the file just the same."

"Sure, sure. Just fill out the—"

"Already done, Chief," Officer Nick said.

"You told them it'll take a while to get the file?"

"I did."

The chief turned back to them. "So how long you girls staying in town?"

"Eve flies out tomorrow, but I'll be here a while, helping out with the marina."

The chief frowned. "I heard you're a boat captain these days. Seems an odd job for a pretty gal like you."

Sasha smiled through her teeth. "I enjoy it."

"Well, good luck to both of you. Now if you'll excuse me." He didn't wait for a response, just turned and headed down the hall.

"Miss Petrov, if you'll give me a phone number where I can reach you, I'll let you know when I get those files."

Sasha ignored Eve as she said, "My cell phone died, so as soon as I get a new one, I'll call you with the number. Until then, let me give you the number at my folks' house."

Then she mentally counted down as they walked out of the building and back to the car. Eve wouldn't be able to resist. *Ten, nine, eight, seven, six, five—*

"What happened to your cell phone?"

Sasha thought of Pete and his hideous treatment of Bella and tried to shrug off her fury. "It went for an unplanned swim, and turns out it doesn't like water."

"Very funny. Why can't you take care—"

"Don't, Eve. I'll get another phone, and yes, you'll have the number. Stop harping, OK?"

Eve sighed. "Sorry. I just hate that you don't think about your personal safety. What if something happens and you can't call anyone? Wait a minute. Did you drive cross-country without a phone?" Her voice rose with every syllable.

"I did and look, I'm still alive and kicking. Stop, already. You're making me crazy."

"I'm sorry. But I worry. And with Mama sick and everything—"

"You need to back off. Seriously. You are not in charge of me—or anyone else, for that matter. And worrying is nothing but borrowing trouble. It will be what it will be."

They stopped at the car, and Eve stared at her over the roof. "Aren't you scared? What if they can't stop the cancer?"

"Of course I'm scared. Terrified. I'm trying not to think about it. And to have faith. Our job is to find out what happened to Tony. That's what I'm focused on." Sasha pulled open the door and slid into the furnace-hot car.

Eve got in beside her and blasted the air-conditioning, which thankfully kicked in quickly and provided blessed relief. Sasha leaned her head back against the seat and closed her eyes as Eve pulled away from the curb, trying to pinpoint what about their meeting with the chief bugged her most.

"So when you get those files next week, what are you going to do?" Eve asked.

Sasha cracked her eyes open, wishing she'd remembered to grab her sunglasses from the Jeep.

"I'll read them and then tell Mama what they say." She shrugged.

"You need to call me—" Eve began. Sasha turned her head toward Eve and narrowed her eyes.

Eve cleared her throat, started over. "When you get the files, will you call me and let me know what they say?"

"Of course, but I'm not expecting much. It sounds like what we've always thought. That Tony drowned. Why do you think Mama is so convinced he's alive?"

Eve gnawed her lower lip. "Maybe it's like she said. It's a mother thing, a feeling. I don't know."

Suddenly Sasha sat up and stared hard at Eve. "There isn't more to the cancer than what you've told me, is there?" Pop had said there wasn't, but Pop wouldn't want anyone to worry.

"How can there be more? What are you saying?"

"Is it much worse than everyone has let on? Is that why she's pushing so hard?"

Eve swallowed hard, and Sasha wondered if she would tell her the whole truth, or try to protect her as always. "Don't sugarcoat it, Eve. Just spit it out."

"If there's more, they haven't said anything to me. All I know is what I've told you. The cancer has come back and they're trying this experimental treatment."

Sasha tried to imagine a world without Mama, but her thoughts couldn't go in that direction. She couldn't, simply couldn't. She knew they would lose their parents someday, but not yet. It was too soon. She looked around as Eve pulled into the big Stuff Mart in the next town. She hadn't even realized they'd left Safe Harbor. "What do you need to get?"

Eve opened her door and stepped out of the car. "Not me. You're getting a new phone."

Sasha thought of the few hundred dollars left in her checking account and the money due from her last job she would likely never see and sighed. Might as well cough up the cash.

When Sasha fell into step with her sister, Eve asked, "What made you decide to quit your job and come home? From your email a few months ago, I thought you really liked this job."

Sasha sighed. "I did like it." She paused, not sure why she didn't just spill the whole ugly tale. Maybe because she knew Eve would just shake her head, as though it were Sasha's fault. Which, yeah, it probably was. "It's a long, boring story. It was time to go, that's all."

Eve looked like she wanted to ask more questions, but she didn't. She just nodded as they headed toward the cell phone display.

Sasha wasn't quite sure how it happened, but half an hour later she was the reluctant owner of a shiny new smartphone that absolutely terrified her. What the heck was she supposed to do with this fancy thing?

"Once you get the hang of it, you'll love it," Eve said. "Trust me. This is so much better than that old flip phone you had."

"I liked my flip phone. I understood my flip phone. Mostly. This is . . ." Words failed her. She sat down in the car, relieved that she remembered how to unlock the screen. "We should take it back. I'll get one of the other—"

Eve reached over and tapped a finger on Sasha's lips. "Stop. It's my birthday-slash-Christmas gift to you. Besides, this way we can stay in touch better."

Sasha grinned. "Always a salesman, aren't you? What you're really saying is that I can run, but I can't hide."

Eve laughed out loud. "Guilty."

"But really, it's too much—" Sasha said for the second time.

"Sasha, please. I wanted to do this. For you, and yeah, for me, too. If you're going to be here with Mama and Pop, I want to know I can reach you. Besides, they don't have Internet at the house, so this way, you can do research, too, if you need to."

Sasha just looked at her blankly. "You forget who you're talking to here." She waved a hand. "OK, thank you. I'll do my best to learn how this beast works, just for you."

Chapter 4

It was still dark outside when Sasha stumbled down the steep stairs the next morning, Bella right on her heels, and followed the smell of coffee to the kitchen. The light was on above the stove, and Pop sat at the kitchen table reading the local paper, coffee dripping into the pot. Sasha let Bella out, kissed Pop on the top of the head, and reached for a mug. Once she had swallowed enough to wake a few brain cells, she smiled at Pop over the rim. "Bless you for getting this started."

"Can't have you running off the road in your sleep."

Sasha plopped down beside him at the table and sipped her coffee while she listened to Eve rustling around in the tiny upstairs bathroom. "Mama still asleep?"

Pop shrugged. "She's pretending to be. She doesn't sleep much, but she doesn't want me to know. Or worry."

"So you don't sleep well, either. You keep watch."

When he looked up and nodded, Sasha's heart clenched. She fingered the mariner's cross around her neck, pushing back a wave of emotion. Pop had always kept watch. Especially during her teen years. It was his job, he'd once said, as the family protector. She imagined Blaze was costing him more than a little sleep these days, too.

As if the words had conjured her, Blaze clumped into the kitchen in jeans, a tight T-shirt, clunky black boots, and attitude. She reached for the coffeepot, her blue hair shimmering in the meager light.

"You're up early," Sasha said.

"I'm going to the airport with you." She didn't turn around, just fixed a mug of coffee and joined them at the table.

"OK," Sasha said.

"Just OK? That's it?" Blaze smacked her mug on the scarred wooden table.

She wanted a fight, but Sasha wasn't giving her one. Not now, with Pop there and not enough brain cells working to keep up.

"You want to come along, come. Doesn't matter to me."

Eve thumped down the stairs with her rolling suitcase, laptop case, and a purse big enough to hold a Saint Bernard. She piled everything in the corner and said, "Good morning. I sure didn't expect a crowd this early." She helped herself to coffee, and Blaze rolled her eyes behind her back.

"Blaze's coming to the airport with us. And Pop got up to start the coffee."

"And kiss my little girl good-bye," he said.

Sasha looked away as Eve's eyes filled with tears. Her own emotions were too close to the surface this morning to deal with Eve's, too. She pushed her chair back and stepped to the coffeepot for a refill.

"Time to hit the road, gang. Traffic in Tampa will get ugly fast." Sasha grabbed Eve's suitcase and laptop and headed for the door. "I'll meet you at the car."

Outside, she stowed the bags in the trunk of Mama's Buick, spread an old beach towel on the backseat, and motioned Bella inside. When Blaze clumped down the porch steps and plopped onto the backseat like she was headed for prison, Sasha bit back a grin and shut the door after her. Eve hurried out moments later, wiping her eyes. She climbed into the passenger seat and leaned her head back.

"I hate good-byes," she mumbled.

Sasha ignored her and started the car, tuning the radio to a local jazz station. The sky was just beginning to lighten, and within five miles, she heard snoring from the backseat, in stereo. She glanced in the rearview mirror and saw Bella's head on Blaze's lap, both sound asleep.

She turned to share a smile with Eve, but her sister stared out the window, still wiping at tears, so Sasha said nothing. Eve had always cried over the dumbest little thing, and Sasha never knew what to say. Mama's cancer wasn't a little thing, but still, tears made her uncomfortable. Back in Russia, her papa had told her crying solved nothing. Action solved problems. Instead of crying, she fixed things. Or threw something.

When Sasha reached the airport access road, Eve straightened and went into what Sasha called checklist mode. "So listen, you don't have to park the car. Just drop me off at the curb. It'll be cheaper and quicker."

Sasha ignored her and headed for short-term parking.

"Did you hear what I said?" Eve demanded.

"I heard. But I don't agree. Pop asked me to see you off."

Eve huffed out a breath. "OK, fine. Do you have your—"

"New cell phone?" Sasha said. "Yes, and it's charged and it's turned on, and yes, I will text you back when you tell me you've arrived in DC. Did I miss anything?"

Eve narrowed her eyes at her. "And you'll let me know—"

"When I get the police files. Right. We've talked about this, Eve."

Eve sighed. "I know. I'm sorry. I don't want to leave."

"And you don't want to be out of the loop on what's going on," Sasha said, grinning.

Eve snorted. "Fine. Yes. That, too."

They parked, walked to the terminal, and waited while Eve checked her bag. Then they walked to security together, Blaze trailing three steps behind.

Eve set her carry-ons at her feet and turned to hug Blaze, who held herself stiffly but didn't squirm out of her grasp.

"Thanks for the way you're helping out, Blaze. I'm glad you're there."

Sasha watched Blaze's face, her usual glare softening at the words. "They're family. It's what you do."

Eve pulled back and looked her in the eyes. "It's what we do, yes, though not every family does."

Blaze scowled at Sasha. "Some of us take that seriously."

Sasha wanted to snap at her, but this wasn't the time or place. Instead she hugged Eve when it was her turn. "Be safe, Sis. I'll keep my phone on, promise."

Tears ran down Eve's cheeks. "I'll call you as soon as I land. I'll—"

Sasha turned her toward the ever-growing line for security and handed her bags to her. "I know. Go, or you'll miss your flight."

Sasha and Blaze waited and waved one last time before she disappeared from sight. Once they were back in the car, Blaze up front and Bella sprawled across the backseat, Sasha said, "So what's up, kid?"

Blaze's eyes widened before she looked away. "Who said anything is up?"

"You wouldn't be here right now—not this early—if you didn't have something to say, so out with it."

"Maybe I just wanted to say good-bye to Eve."

"And maybe I'm Lady Gaga."

Blaze folded her arms and huffed out a breath. "I know you and Eve went to the police station to ask about Tony."

Sasha tried to remember when she and Eve had talked about it and whom they'd said anything to. "So after you ran from the room, you came back for a little eavesdropping?"

"It's the only way I find out what's going on. Nobody tells me anything. I'm not a little kid!"

Sasha looked over at Blaze and was reminded, once again, of how very much she had been like Blaze at that age. "It's rough to be a teenager, no question. Adults think you're too young to understand. Or they think you don't care."

"I do care. This is Mama we're talking about. And nobody tells me anything."

Sasha gripped the steering wheel when Blaze swiped angrily at her tears. What was it with crying females this morning? She hadn't even had breakfast yet.

"Look, Blaze, nobody is trying to exclude you. Yes, Eve and I went to the police station. We asked for the report on Tony's disappearance."

"What did it say?"

Sasha shrugged. "We don't know. They said it will take a couple of days to get it out of storage."

"Don't they have it on the computer?"

"Not yet. They said they're working on scanning in all their old files, but they haven't gotten that far back yet."

"That really stinks. So now what? What's our next step?"

Sasha turned to stare at her, taking in the stubborn chin and determination in her green eyes. "What do you mean, our next step? When they call, I'll go take a look."

Blaze crossed her arms. "I'm going with you. Now that Eve isn't here, I'm your partner in this investigation."

"I, ah, that is . . ." Sasha tried and failed to come up with a good reason why she shouldn't have this surly teenager underfoot for the foreseeable future.

"Don't even try to get rid of me. I'll camp out in front of your bedroom door if I have to. I want to help with this. I need to."

Sasha glanced at her again and sighed. Oh yeah, she understood. Better than most. "Look, Blaze, you're welcome to come with me, see what we find out." She scrambled for the right words and finally said, "But none of that, and nothing we do or don't do, is going to change what's happening with Mama."

Tears rolled down Blaze's cheeks as she stared out the side window, but she didn't say anything. Sasha reached over to take her hand, but Blaze jerked it away and swiped the tears from her face.

They drove in silence for the next thirty miles, then Sasha pulled into the drive-through of a fast-food restaurant.

"OK, partner, what'll ya have?"

They ordered breakfast and got back on the highway, neither saying a word. But all the way home, Sasha tried to figure out how on earth she was going to find answers for Mama. And how they would all live with them once she did.

Jesse woke before sunrise and winced when his almost-healed knife wound protested as he sat up. He'd be glad when he didn't get reminded of his stint behind bars every time he moved without thinking.

He eased out of the sagging twin bed he'd slept in throughout his childhood summers and padded to the kitchen to start coffee. At some point he'd move into Aunt Clarabelle's bedroom, but not yet. He wasn't ready. Besides, he couldn't see sleeping under flowered sheets and waking up to flowered wallpaper. He shuddered and headed for the bathroom while the coffee did its thing.

The sun hadn't yet peeked over the horizon when he trotted down the porch steps to his truck and stopped short, coffee sloshing out of his mug. The security light from the neighbor's house illuminated the truck. Both tires on the driver's side were flat. Jesse muttered a curse and marched over for a closer look. Not just flat. Slashed.

He walked around to the other side and froze. Whoever it was had slit all four tires. He slammed a fist against the side of the truck, then cursed the pain that radiated up his arm while hot coffee sloshed over his other hand.

He shook out his aching hand and threw the coffee mug onto the straggly lawn. Not only would he lose time he didn't have, but given the size of the truck, replacing the tires wouldn't come cheap. He stood for a moment, fighting to bring his frustration under control. He'd known there'd be some who wouldn't welcome a guy who'd spent time in jail to their tidy little community. But the fact they'd done this right after he arrived showed a level of animosity that ticked him off.

He just wanted to prep his boat and win the race. And OK, yeah, start over in this little one-horse town. That didn't seem like too much to ask. Apparently, it was. He wasn't one to go looking for a fight, but someone had brought this one right to his door.

He stomped over and scooped up Clarabelle's flowered mug, annoyed the stupid thing hadn't smashed. He scrubbed a hand over his face. Whatever. He had work to do. He double-checked the size of the tires, marched back inside, traded flip-flops for tennis shoes, and tossed some water bottles and a sandwich into a backpack. The sky was gradually lightening as he started the two-mile trek to Safe Harbor Marina. That should give him plenty of time to get his temper under control.

Sasha pulled into the gravel parking area next to the house. She really wanted to crawl back into bed for another hour or so, but she'd told Pop she'd help him at the marina when they got back.

Blaze opened her door and slid out, then said, "Don't try to weasel out of this and go without me."

"I told you I'd take you with me."

"I've heard about how much your word is worth."

Sasha winced at the accusation. Before she could respond, Blaze slammed the door behind her, and Sasha wanted to yell that she shouldn't slam doors when Mama was trying to sleep.

The irony made her sigh. Oh, that girl could get under her skin. She eased the car door closed—they'd made enough racket already—and looked up, surprised to see Jesse walking down the drive from the road.

"Morning."

He raised a hand in greeting and kept walking. Well, that was rude. She turned and intercepted him just as he reached the shed Pop was letting him use as a workshop.

"What's the matter with you, Money-boy? You don't even say good morning?"

"I was trying to be considerate by not yelling at the crack of dawn."

"I wasn't yelling."

"Didn't say you were."

He nudged her out of the way, unlocked the padlock, and slid the door open. He stepped inside and pulled the chain on the overhead bulb. Weak light filled the space.

She looked around. "Where's your truck?"

He set his backpack on the workbench. "Home."

"Why would you walk all this way? It's got to be, what, a couple of miles."

He sighed and spoke without looking at her. "Go away, Sasha. I have work to do."

Something wasn't right. She stepped closer and peered at him in the gloom. "What's going on?"

"Somebody slashed the tires on my truck last night."

"What? Did you call the police?"

"No. Just let it go."

"Tires, plural. How many?"

"All of them, OK?" He stepped around her and headed for the dock and *The Painted Lady*.

Sasha dogged his heels. "Why won't you call the police?"

He stopped, turned, annoyance in every hard line of his body. "Somebody obviously doesn't want a possible felon in their little town. I expected as much."

"It isn't right. I'm going to—"

She turned to go and he grabbed her arm so fast she stumbled. He spun her around and waited until she met his eyes.

"No. You are going to do nothing. This is my business and I will handle it my way."

"But it isn't righ—"

He leaned in and silenced her with a quick kiss that was over before she'd even registered what happened. She pulled back in shock and looked at his stunned expression. She figured her own probably looked the same.

"What was that about?"

"You make me crazy," he muttered, walking away. "Leave it alone," he tossed over his shoulder.

Sasha watched him go, her mouth still tingling from his kiss.

She heard a noise and spun to see Pop struggling under a heavy box near the marina store. She rushed over to take it from him.

"Pop, that's too heavy. Why didn't you say something?"

He looked at her over the box. "Would have, if you'd been here."

Chastised, she tugged the box from his grasp and said, "Where do you want it?"

He pointed, and she spent the next two hours moving inventory, cleaning the store, and trying not to think about somebody in town slashing Jesse's tires.

Mostly she thought about that unexpected kiss. When she was with him, everything else faded away, and that's what worried her. She had responsibilities here and was determined to do right by her family. Even in high school, she'd been drawn to more than his sexy smile. The way he seemed so comfortable in his own skin attracted her like fish to bait.

More importantly, he'd always treated her like she was a competent, skilled person, not a constant disappointment.

She shook her head. Now what? She'd heard all the gossip about his time in prison for drugs, and none of it jibed with the man she knew. Which was the real Jesse? Until she knew for sure, she'd have to keep her guard up—for everyone's sake.

Jesse hated asking for help, but he didn't have a lot of options. He set down his wrench and scrubbed the grease from his hands. He needed new tires. Today. Ideally he'd have the truck towed to the tire place, but he didn't see that happening. He couldn't afford it. Plan B would be to borrow a vehicle big enough to hold his air compressor and all four tires, so he could replace them in his driveway. Then he'd drive the truck over to get the new tires balanced and aligned.

He stepped out of the shed and looked around. There was no way he'd ask Pop if he could put tires in Mama Rosa's pristine Buick. Pop's ancient pickup was gone, so he couldn't ask to borrow that. Time for plan C. He'd hoof it to the tire place and roll two tires at a time back to the cottage. It'd be a pain in the butt and take forever since the auto repair and tire place was downtown, at least another mile past his cottage.

Sighing, he loaded the compressor and a tire iron on a hand cart, locked up the shed, and started walking.

Fifteen minutes later, he heard a vehicle behind him and turned to see Sasha pull off the road in an old Jeep that looked like it was held together with rust and duct tape. Bella woofed a greeting from her perch in the passenger seat.

"Hey, Bella." Jesse walked over and scratched behind her ears, getting a doggy kiss in return.

"You heading home to call a tow truck?"

He kept his tone neutral. "Not in the budget. But I am heading to the tire place."

She muttered something about small-minded idiots. "Hop in. I'll give you a ride."

"Thanks. Appreciate it." Jesse finally looked at her, and was glad his expression was hidden behind his sunglasses. Despite his seething frustration about the tires, Sasha could stop him dead in his tracks. She'd changed since this morning. With her gorgeous hair tucked into a tidy braid, eyes hidden behind movie-star sunglasses, and athletic frame wrapped in a snug tank top and shorts, his body took one look and said, *Oh yeah,* while his mind screamed, *Run!*

He never had been very smart. He loaded the compressor in the back and opened the passenger door.

"Scoot over, Bella." The dog obediently hopped into the backseat as he climbed in and slammed the door. She put the Jeep in gear and hit the gas, and he grabbed the roll bar, just in case. "You late getting somewhere?"

"I have a lot to do this afternoon."

"If it's a problem, I can walk, Sasha."

"Did I say it was a problem?"

Jesse looked at the set of her jaw and figured something was the problem. "Mama doing OK today?"

"I guess. Maybe. I don't know, OK?"

"Okaay."

"She hasn't been out of bed today. Pop says it's because of all the excitement of the party, but I don't know. I haven't been around enough to know what's *normal*"—she made air quotes—"and what's not."

"I'm not sure there is a normal in this situation, but I get what you're saying. And it's really OK. You can let me out here."

She waved that away. "Don't be stupid, Money-boy. I'm going that way anyway."

Her irritation fueled his own, so he said nothing until they pulled into the parking lot of Safe Harbor's only car lot and auto repair.

"Thanks for the ride, Sash. I really appreciate it." He gave her a tight smile and Bella another scratch, grabbed the compressor and headed into Safe Harbor Auto.

A little bell jangled above the door. While vehicles old and new lined the lot outside, the inside was clearly divided between the tire and auto parts sections, with the garage and its work bays in the back. Captain Barry, who had inherited the business from his father but spent his weekends as a charter-boat fishing captain, came out from the small office. When he saw Jesse, the welcome-the-customer smile slid off his face.

"We're not open yet."

Jesse hitched a thumb over his shoulder. "Sign on the door says you opened two hours ago."

"Well, I don't have—"

"Look, you don't have to like me or want me in your town, but my money's green. I need four tires for my truck." He rattled off the make and model he wanted and waited.

Barry cleared his throat and rubbed a hand over the back of his neck, not meeting Jesse's eyes. Finally he said, "Four of them there model don't come cheap. You have cash? I don't take no plastic."

Jesse nodded. "I have cash."

Barry peered out the door. "Where's your truck? The tires come with alignment and balance."

"I'll put them on myself and bring the truck in for the alignment and balance."

Barry scratched his bald head. "Wouldn't it be easier just to—"

"It would, if someone hadn't slashed all four tires during the night." He hadn't planned to say anything, but now that the words were out, he watched Barry's reaction.

"Well, dang, probably a bunch of kids."

Their eyes met, and Barry finally looked away. "I'll get the paperwork started and get them tires for you."

When Jesse rolled the first two tires outside twenty minutes later, Sasha was still sitting in the Jeep with her head against the headrest, eyes closed. Bella saw him and stood on the seat, tail wagging. Sasha sat up and folded her arms over the steering wheel.

"We can get all four of them in here if Bella sits on your lap. I have bungee cords to tie them down."

She still had that mutinous look to her, so Jesse didn't say anything, just went back inside and came out with two more tires. He helped her secure everything in the back and motioned Bella up on his lap. He waited until they were almost at his cottage before he said, "Thanks for waiting. You didn't have to do that, you know."

She slid her sunglasses down the bridge of her nose and peered at him over the top. "I know you're not stupid, so quit acting like it."

"I could have—"

"I know. And rolling them two at a time would have taken all afternoon." She roared into his driveway.

Bella hopped out of the Jeep, and he followed and hauled the compressor and the tires out of the back. As soon as the last tire hit the ground, Sasha put the Jeep in gear and Bella quickly hopped back in. Jesse reached over and laid a hand on Sasha's arm.

"Let me buy you dinner."

She shook off his hand. "You don't owe me anything."

He grinned. "Didn't say I did. I just want to take a pretty lady to dinner."

He wished he could see what was going on behind those dark glasses, because her whole body stiffened.

"I'll think about it." She sped off.

He shook his head. He'd never understand women, Sasha Petrov least of all. But dang, that haughty-yet-vulnerable look got to him every time. Always had. He sighed and went to work. Probably always would, too.

He had the second tire off when that familiar tingle slid down his back. He was being watched. He stood slowly and stretched his back, studying the tidy cottages on either side, but he didn't see a curtain twitch or anyone outside. Just because he didn't see them didn't mean someone wasn't there. He hadn't known he had that early-warning system until it had saved his life in jail, more than once. He supposed he should be grateful.

After several minutes, he went back to wrestling with the tires. But he positioned himself so he had a clear view of the street, with the cottage at his back. Just in case.

Chapter 5

Sasha drove back into town, hands clenched on the steering wheel and gearshift. Why had Jesse's simple question rattled her so badly? It wasn't like she didn't get asked to dinner on a semiregular basis. This was different. This was Jesse. And Jesse mattered. He always had.

She could never risk hurting Jesse.

Her cell phone rang, and she tugged it out of the pocket of her shorts, too late to answer the call from Eve. She'd call her back when she got to the police station. Half a mile later, Eve called again.

By the time she pulled into the parking lot, it rang a third time.

"What? I'm driving, here."

"Why didn't you answer?" Eve demanded.

"And hello to you, too, Sister. I can't talk on a doggone cell phone and drive stick, OK?"

"Sorry. Why didn't you call me?"

Sasha held the phone out and stared at it for a moment. "Seriously? Weren't you supposed to call me when you got back to DC?"

"Oh, sorry. Forgot. So what did you find out? Do you have the files yet?"

"Back up. You read me the riot act when you're the one who forgot to call?"

Eve sighed. "You're right. I'm sorry. As soon as I landed, I got a call from work and I've been going nonstop ever since."

"It happens. Just remember to cut me the same kind of slack you expect."

Another sigh. "Touché. So, anything?"

"I'm heading in now. Officer Stanton called and said he had the file."

"Call me as soon as—"

"Bye, Eve. Gotta go."

Her phone rang again before she reached the reception desk, so she turned the ringer off and tucked the phone back into her pocket.

"I appreciate your calling me right away, Officer Stanton."

He smiled. "We're not that formal around here. Call me Nick. I admit your request made me curious. I haven't been here long enough to know a lot about our old cases, so I wanted to look myself." He handed her an envelope and she untied the string holding it closed.

"You're welcome to sit in the conference room if you'd like."

She nodded and followed him down the hallway, her stomach churning with a greasy mix of anticipation and dread.

"Have you lived here long?" she asked, trying to keep the past at bay. Police stations always reminded her of the awful time after her family died in the car wreck back in Russia. She still didn't know how she survived the accident. Afterward, at the police station, she was terrified and so very cold, but the policemen got in her face, demanding answers to questions she didn't understand, asking about people she'd never heard of, making it sound like everything was somehow her papa's fault. Even at nine years old, she knew better. It had been her fault, but she hadn't been able to get the words past her tears.

Sasha blinked and forced her mind back to the present.

"I came about two years ago. Chad Everson and I went to college together. He called me when a job opened up on the force and, well, here I am. I like it here."

She gave Papa's mariner's cross a quick kiss as they entered the conference room. Goose bumps that had nothing to do with the air conditioning popped up on her arms.

Nick pulled out a chair for her. "Would you like me to go over it with you? Cops sometimes use their own kind of shorthand."

Grateful suddenly not to be doing this alone, Sasha nodded. She swallowed hard as Nick pulled the contents from the envelope and spread them out on the table.

She picked up a photo of three-year-old Tony in Pop's arms and stared. She looked back and forth between father and son, and Pop's reluctance suddenly made sense.

"I hadn't realized he looked so much like Pop." They'd all been concerned about Mama, but what must it have been like for Pop to lose his son?

Nick sat beside her and leaned closer. He smelled good, like some spicy aftershave, but being around him was nothing like the electric current that hovered in the air when she and Jesse were this close.

"There isn't much, is there?" Sasha asked. The envelope held a scant handful of pages.

"From what I gathered, there was never much to go on." He picked up one of the pages. "This is the first page of the report, with the date, responding officer, reason for the call, et cetera."

Sasha scanned the page. "Wait, Chief Monroe was the one who responded?"

He shook his head. "No, this was Chief Monroe's father, right before he became chief. He was lead on the case."

Sasha started reading, the brief listing of events a stark contrast to Mama clutching Tony's teddy bear the other night and asking them to find out what happened to him.

Nick pointed to the report. "So, according to what your mother said, Tony was playing in the yard and she was hanging laundry. She went inside to get another load, and while she was in there, the phone rang. When she came outside a few minutes later, Tony was gone. They searched the area, especially the dock and waterfront, but they never found a single trace of him."

"Who was Mama on the phone with?"

"Good question." He scanned the report. "It doesn't say." He pointed to a spot halfway down. "But it does say here that half the town showed up to help search, and they kept at it for several days. They also sent divers down, but nobody ever found even one clue."

"Do you find that strange?"

He narrowed his eyes as he considered. "No, not really. I've been out to the marina—Chad and I like to go fishing—and the house isn't that far from the water. A little boy could have chased a bird or a butterfly or something and fallen into the water."

Sasha squeezed her eyes tight as an image of a lifeless Tony superimposed itself on flashbacks of the day her parents died.

He patted her hand. "I'm sorry. I'm not trying to be insensitive."

She summoned a smile. "It happened a long time ago." She read the rest of the report, but there wasn't much. Transcripts of interviews with Mama Rosa and Pop, several of the local captains, their neighbors—anyone who was anywhere near the marina that day. There was a list of the divers' names and where and when they searched, plus a list of the volunteers who helped.

Sasha pointed to the bottom of the third page. "I can't read this. What does it say?"

Nick squinted and held the page up to the light. "Near as I can tell, it says they used tracking dogs, too. The scent ended at the dock."

Sasha nodded, picking up the photo again. She turned it over. On the back, someone had printed, *Tony Martinelli, age 3, born January 31, 1988.*

She looked at Nick. "So they searched the area and the water, even using dogs, talked to everyone around that day, and concluded that he drowned."

He flipped back through the pages and pointed. "Presumed drowned."

"My mother believes he's still alive," she said. She watched his eyes widen, then fill with pity.

"I can certainly understand that—can't you? A mother's hope for her children never dies. Sorry, bad choice of words."

"I understand. But do you believe it's possible?"

"That he's still alive?"

"Yes. That maybe he got washed away and someone found him?"

"I highly doubt it." He flipped back through the pages. "The news crews came from Tampa and Orlando, and your parents showed Tony's picture and asked anyone who had seen him to please call. I'm sure the usual wackos called, but nothing here indicates there were ever any good leads, nothing that made anybody think it was anything other than a terrible tragedy."

Sasha nodded and watched him gather the pages and slide them back into the envelope.

"Can I have a copy of that?"

"It's against policy to—"

"Please."

He glanced toward the open doorway of the conference room, then back to her. "I'm going to get a soda from the machine." He stood and nodded to the copy machine at the back of the room. "I'll be back in a few minutes."

Nick winked and eased the door closed behind him. Sasha rushed over to the copy machine and tapped her foot while she waited for it to warm up. She removed the staples and stuck the pages into the feeder and pressed "Start," eyes glued to the door. The machine clunked and thumped as it worked, and Sasha was sure it could be heard across the street.

"Come on, come on," she muttered, catching the first page as the machine spit it out.

The copier squealed and ground to a stop. "No! Please don't be jammed." She leaned over the display and saw the flashing "Out of paper" message. She yanked open the cabinet under the machine. Empty. She scanned the room, frantic. There had to be more paper.

She jumped when she heard footsteps outside the door. She grabbed the pages and shoved them back into the envelope just as the door whooshed open and Chief Monroe poked his head in.

"Oh, howdy, Sasha. What brings you here? I thought I heard the copier, but no one was in this room."

Nick slipped into the room behind the chief and placed a can of soda next to her. "I hope that's OK. I wasn't sure what kind you drink."

Sasha forced a grateful smile and popped the top. "This is perfect, thanks." But she still didn't have copies of the file.

Nick glanced at the copier, then met the chief's eyes. "Sasha came to look at the report of her brother's disappearance."

The chief nodded and picked up the envelope. Sasha's heart rate went into overdrive. Would he notice the extra copy of page one? And the missing staples?

"Sad case, that one. Happened just before I joined the force. My pa always wished he could have given your parents something more concrete. Closure."

"Mama thinks he's still alive," Sasha said, watching his reaction as she had Nick's earlier.

The chief paled, then red raced up his neck. He scrubbed a hand over the back of his neck.

"While I have the utmost respect for your mama, Sasha, the facts don't support that position."

Sasha tapped the table for emphasis. "The only real fact we have, Chief, is that Tony disappeared."

"And was never seen or heard from again," he shot back. He sighed. "What are you saying, girl? This department did everything they could to try to find that boy and bring him back to his mama. Watching your parents' grief—" He paused. "It haunted my pa until the day he died. Tony Martinelli drowned. There is no other explanation that makes sense."

Sasha stood. "I'm not doubting what you've said, Chief. There are just a lot of unanswered questions." She turned to Nick. "Thank you for taking the time to go over the report with me."

By the time she slid behind the wheel of the Jeep, she was scowling. What was it about that man that bothered her so? And how much did her dislike of him affect her judgment? Just because he struck her as slimy didn't mean his father hadn't done right by Tony.

She banged a hand against the steering wheel. She still didn't have a copy of the report.

"Sasha, wait up."

Nick jogged toward her, a legal pad tucked under his arm. He leaned over and slid several pages into her hand, blocking anyone from seeing what he was doing. "I noticed the machine was out of paper."

Her shoulders slumped in relief. "Thank you, Nick. This means so much."

"I hope you find the answers you're looking for, Sasha. Wish there was more I could do."

She drove back to the marina, waiting until she could pace the dock before she called Eve.

"So, what happened?"

"Not much," Sasha admitted. "The report is only three pages. I didn't learn anything new except that half the town joined the search, for days."

"I believe it. They would have all been horrified."

"Something's not right, Eve."

"What do you mean?"

"I can't explain it, but Nick went over the report with me, and then he left the room so I could quickly make a copy of it, and then the chief suddenly showed up."

"You have a copy? Can you scan it and send it to me?"

"You're missing my point."

"Which is?"

"There was something off about the way the chief told the story. Too neat and tidy."

"You think he was lying?"

"I don't know. It's nothing I can put my finger on. Just a weird sense, like we aren't getting the whole story."

"But the report didn't show anything new, anything we can use?"

"Nope. Except the list of everyone who helped in the search."

"So, OK, you should . . ." Her voice trailed off, and she cleared her throat and started over. "What's your next step?"

Sasha smiled. "Thank you." Giving up control of anything, no matter how insignificant, was huge for Eve. "I think I'll see how many of the people they interviewed that day are still around, see what they remember."

"That sounds good. You'll send me a copy of the report? And keep me posted?"

"Absolutely."

Silence hummed over the line. Finally Eve whispered, "What if he's still alive?"

The thought had crossed Sasha's mind, too, but she thought it far more likely he wasn't. "Then we'll find him."

They said good-bye, and when Sasha hung up the phone, she turned and almost tripped over Blaze. Shoot, she'd forgotten her.

The teen had her hands clenched at her sides, fury radiating from every pore. "You promised! You promised and then you went without me."

Before Sasha realized her intent, Blaze shoved her with both hands. Sasha windmilled her arms but couldn't keep her balance. She landed backward with a mighty splash, water rushing up her nose. She came up sputtering to see Blaze standing on the dock, shock apparent right alongside the fury on her face. Beside her, Bella barked and spun in a frantic circle before she leaped into the water to get to Sasha. Footsteps pounded on the dock, and Sasha looked up to see Jesse racing toward her.

He got down on his knees and extended a hand, the other braced against the dock. She put her hand in his, and before she could blink, he hauled her up onto the dock and into his arms, barely keeping their momentum from carrying them into the water on the other side. Below, Bella paddled and barked. Sasha turned and pointed toward the boat ramp.

"That way, girl. Go on."

Bella swam until her paws touched solid ground, then marched up the ramp and onto the dock. She walked right up to a guilty-looking Blaze before she shook the water off her coat. Sasha crouched down and rubbed her behind the ears.

"Good girl, Bella. Thank you for coming to my rescue."

"I think I helped, too," Jesse said, a mischievous twinkle in his eyes.

Sasha stood. "I appreciate it. Would you like a doggy biscuit, too?"

Blaze stepped between them and demanded, "Why didn't you take me with you?"

Sasha swiped the water off her face and propped her hands on her hips. "Did you go somewhere with Pop this morning?"

Blaze's eyes widened and she shrugged. "Yeah, so? He needed me to help with some errands."

"So if you had been here when the police called, I would have taken you with me."

Jesse said, "Pushing her into the water wasn't cool, Blaze. You need to apologize."

Blaze crossed her arms and narrowed her eyes. "You don't tell me what to do."

"If you did the right thing, nobody would have to tell you what to do."

She huffed out a breath and shot Sasha a quick glance. "Fine. Sorry."

Sasha bit her lip to keep from saying things she knew she'd regret. Instead, she took a deep breath and locked eyes with Blaze.

"I'm going to go change, and then I'll tell Mama what I learned from the police report. You are welcome to join us."

Blaze nodded. "Sorry," she muttered again.

Sasha turned and sloshed back toward the house, her stomach in knots. How was she going to take Mama back in time to that awful day without breaking her heart all over again?

After a lukewarm shower in the tiny upstairs bathroom, Sasha found Mama dozing in her padded rocker on the porch. She still couldn't get used to how sick Mama looked, as though someone had taken all her features and rearranged them in a way that didn't make sense. *Oh, God, I need courage.*

She dropped the copy of the police report on the small wicker table and eased down in another rocker. While Mama slept, she rocked and tried to figure out the best way to phrase things.

Blaze clumped out to the porch and let the screen door slam shut behind her with a thwack before she saw Mama. When Mama twitched and woke up, she mumbled, "Sorry," and took the rocker next to Sasha.

Sasha gripped the arms of the chair, debated chewing her out again, but let it go.

Mama started smiling before she came fully awake.

"My girls," she whispered. Even her voice sounded wrong, and it made Sasha want to hit something. She couldn't stand to watch this disease take her mother from them in little chunks. For a moment, she wished she'd never come home. This emotional torture was why she stayed away. She could get the facts from Eve, dispensed in tidy email messages so she wouldn't have to deal with all the heart-wrenching realities.

Instead, she forced herself to smile back. "Hey, Mama. Did you get a good snooze?"

"It is so beautiful out here. The sound of the water, the smell of salt in the air, they help me rest."

"Pop says she doesn't sleep much at night," Blaze said.

Sasha experienced a moment's jealousy that this ornery teen had the relationship with Pop that she herself used to have. For years, she had been the one at Pop's side. While Cat baked and cooked with Mama and Eve and Mama tended the garden, Sasha hung out at the marina with Pop, working on boat motors, helping the other captains, learning to be a captain herself.

Suddenly Mama's gaze landed on the pages on the table, and she jerked her eyes up to Sasha. "You got the police report."

Sasha nodded and picked up the papers. "I managed to get a copy. But," she said, pausing to look directly at Mama and send a stern look Blaze's way, "we are not supposed to have these. I don't want to get anyone in trouble, so we can never say where they came from, OK?"

"How could we, since we don't know?"

Sasha smiled at Blaze. "Exactly."

Mama's eyes stayed on Sasha and made her want to squirm. "What did you find out?"

Though she wanted to, Sasha wouldn't look away. "Nothing, really, that we didn't already know. Everything that happened that day is neatly spelled out, along with the searches over the next week by volunteers and divers."

Mama reached into the magazine basket beside her and pulled out Tony's teddy bear, clutching it to her. Sasha swallowed the lump in her throat.

"Mama, do you remember who called you that day? It wasn't in the report."

"Captain Roy's wife, Mary Lee. She wanted to talk about a bake sale coming up at church. I kept telling her I had to go, and I finally just hung up on her."

"Did she call you a lot?"

"Not really. But I had the feeling she and Captain Roy were going through a difficult time. It seemed like she was lonely and just wanted someone to talk to." Mama's eyes filled. "After . . . I was angry with her for a very long time. I blamed her for what happened to my Tony. And then—then I blamed myself. If I hadn't been on the phone with her . . ."

Sasha shot from her chair, knelt down in front of Mama, and took both frail hands gently in her own. They felt so fragile, not at all like the tough hands that used to run this family. "Mama, no. Whatever happened is not your fault."

Silent tears slid down her cheeks. "What if my baby is dead because I was on the phone?"

Sasha squeezed her eyes shut and tried to think of something, anything, to say that would help.

"Mama, you said you think Tony is still alive. How do you know?"

Mama blinked back more tears. "I feel it, in here." She patted a hand over her heart. "Even from the day it happened, I could still feel him, feel the connection. I still do."

Sasha leaned forward and gently wiped the tears from her cheeks. "Then that's what you hang on to, OK?"

Mama swallowed and nodded. "What will you do next?"

"I'm going to talk to everyone who was here that day, go over everything again. Maybe there is something the police missed, some question they didn't ask."

Behind them, the screen door closed, and Sasha looked over her shoulder to see Pop marching off toward the marina. If she'd known he was in the house, she's have waited to have this conversation.

Mama looked Sasha in the eye. "I know Sal doesn't want you to do this—for my sake. But please, I need to know."

Sasha nodded and slowly stood. She bent and kissed Mama's cheek. "I will do my best."

"That is all I ask. God will provide the answers."

Sasha held the screen door open for Bella, and they slowly walked toward the marina. She had to talk to Pop, try to explain.

Sasha stepped out of the marina bait shop when she heard car doors slamming and women arguing. She shaded her eyes and spotted a shiny blue Lincoln, 1980s vintage, angled in close to the house and two women bearing casserole dishes marching up the porch steps, still in heated conversation.

She jogged off the dock and back to the house, hoping to intercept them before they got to Mama, but she didn't make it in time. She and Bella burst onto the porch to see the two women alternately bending to kiss the air near Mama's cheeks.

When the screen door slammed behind her, both women straightened in surprise.

"Sasha! How good to see you again." The tiny woman with unnaturally black hair stepped over and pulled Sasha's head down so she could kiss both her cheeks. The smell of baby powder triggered Sasha's memory.

"Mrs. Markos, how are you?" She bent down and kissed Captain Demetri's wife on both cheeks as well, then pulled back to look at her. The years had taken their toll on her lined face, but her hair gleamed its usual glossy black, no doubt from regular trips to Beatrice's beauty shop in town. "You haven't changed a bit."

The older woman patted her teased do and gave a wan smile.

"How is Christina?" Sasha asked, then wanted to kick herself as Helen's smile slid off her face.

"She is the same, always my sweet baby." She glanced at Mama, then back at Sasha. "But I am grateful for every day."

Christina Markos had been a surprise, late-in-life baby and had been born severely handicapped. She needed round-the-clock care, which Helen Markos had provided for all the years of her daughter's life.

"I have a wonderful caregiver who comes for several hours here and there, allowing me to get out for a while and visit friends." She turned back to Mama and perched in the rocker beside her, gently taking her hand.

The woman who had arrived with Helen turned and offered a hand.

"I don't know if you remember me, sugar, but I'm Patty Monroe, the chief's wife."

Sasha shook hands and gave the woman a quick once-over. She would have remembered this walking stereotype with her big hair and big chest paired with a tiny skirt and high heels. That shade of red hair only came in a bottle, but the shrewd blue eyes looked to be original equipment.

Sasha waved at another chair. "Please, have a seat. What brings you ladies out this way?" Wasn't it interesting that the chief's wife suddenly happened by, right after Sasha's visit to the police station?

Helen patted Mama's hand and looked up. "I've been wanting to come by and wish your mama a happy birthday, since I couldn't get here for the party." She motioned toward the cake carrier and casserole dishes on the coffee table and smiled at Mama. "A couple of my Greek specialties. Your favorites."

"Thank you, Helen. You're a good friend." Mama smiled, then looked at Patty, who shrugged.

"I don't bake or cook much, so I brought you a scarf I crocheted." She reached into a gift bag and pulled out the most hideous-looking scarf Sasha had ever seen. Mama's eyes widened with alarm as Patty loomed over her and wrapped the fuchsia-and-purple fuzzy caterpillar around her neck.

When Mama's hands fumbled, Sasha stepped to her side and loosened the puffy wool so she could breathe.

"Looks great on you, Rosa," Patty pronounced, and settled into a wicker chair. Then she turned her laser-sharp gaze on Sasha. "So what's all this nonsense about you nosing around in an old police case?"

Mama made a small sound of distress, and Helen snapped, "Patty, please. Not now."

Patty took in Mama's wounded look and crossed her arms before she fastened her gaze on Sasha. "You haven't been here three days and you're already causing trouble."

"How exactly am I causing trouble by asking questions?" Sasha raised her eyebrows and mirrored Patty's pose.

"The past is dead and gone—pardon the expression, Rosa—and should be left alone. Why are you digging around in something that happened so long ago?"

"Why should anyone care, then? Where's the harm?" Sasha shot back.

Patty came out of her chair, and suddenly they were nose to nose.

"The harm is that bringing up the past reminds people of a terrible tragedy." She flung out a manicured hand in Mama's direction. "I would think you'd want to protect her from that."

"I asked her to look for answers."

Helen gasped at Mama's quiet statement, and Patty's eyes widened as she turned toward Mama.

"Why on earth would you do that, sugar?"

The fierce look in Mama's eyes made Sasha smile inwardly. She might be sick, but she wasn't done fighting, not by a long shot.

"I want answers. Is that so hard to understand?"

They stared each other down. Patty looked away first. Helen, always the local peacemaker, hopped up from her chair and gently kissed Mama's cheeks again.

"It was good to see you, Rosa. I will come back when I can."

Mama smiled. "You've been a good friend, Helen. Kiss Christina for me. We'll enjoy the food you brought."

Patty stepped in behind Helen and patted Mama's hands. "Take care of yourself, Rosa. I heard chemo makes you cold. Hope the scarf helps."

As Patty passed Sasha on the way out, she hissed, "Leave the past where it belongs."

Sasha waited until they pulled away, then turned to Mama. "How long has Patty been married to the chief?"

Mama shrugged. "Twenty years, at least. But she was away a lot while her mother was ill." She paused. "She and Chief Monroe have always had a strange relationship."

"Strange, how?"

"I've heard her treat him like he wasn't worth her time, yet both of them act like they're royalty and the rest of the people in this town are beneath their notice."

Interesting. That meshed with her own feelings about Chief Monroe. Mama leaned her head back in the chair and fumbled with the scarf. Sasha reached over and tugged it free, then tossed it back into the gift bag.

"Should this conveniently disappear?"

Mama nodded. "It was a nice gesture, but it's horrible, isn't it?"

Sasha smiled. "I'll take care of it."

She took the bag to the trash can and continued to the bait shop, wondering what had brought Patty Monroe to their door. To warn Sasha off, certainly. But why?

Chapter 6

Sal stood in his workshop the next morning, desperate to get his emotions under control. Last night, Rosa had cried herself to sleep again, blaming herself for Tony's disappearance. He pounded a fist on the workbench, trying to block the memory of her sobs, but they wouldn't go away. Her tears shredded his heart into little tiny bits. Every single time.

It took every bit of his willpower, and the sure and certain knowledge that if he confessed to what he had done, things would get much worse, to keep him silent. *Oh, my Rosa, I am sorry. I couldn't fix it then, and I can't seem to fix it now, either.*

"Why is she asking for the police report, Sal?" a voice asked from behind him. Someone wrenched Sal's right arm up behind his back with enough force to nearly pop it out of the socket.

Sal sucked in a breath as pain radiated down his arm and his heart raced. He had been so focused on his own guilt, he hadn't heard either of his onetime friends come in.

"Rosa asked her to." He didn't know what else to say.

The same man shoved the arm higher, and Sal gasped.

"I hear she thinks Tony is still alive."

Sal said nothing, just gritted his teeth to keep from crying out. He wouldn't give them the satisfaction.

"Now why would Rosa be thinking a thing like that, after all these years?"

The pressure tightened and Sal had to force the words out.

"She says it is mother's intuition, a feeling, that he's still alive somewhere on this earth."

"Why haven't you dispelled that foolish notion?" the other man asked.

"I've always thought the less I said, one way or another, the better."

"So you've said nothing."

Sal nodded. "Nothing." He raised his chin. "Just held her while she cried for her Tony, you heartless monster."

From out of nowhere, a fist slammed into his gut, and Sal doubled over. He would have fallen except the first man still had his arm in a death grip behind his back.

"Tell Sasha to stop looking, stop asking questions."

"I have told her. But her mother has asked her not to stop."

"Then you'd better convince her, Sal, old friend. And fast. We don't have to remind you what happens to people who don't listen, do we?"

Sal shook his head, and finally they let him go. Once they left, he collapsed on the floor, cradling his aching arm, silent tears wracking his thin frame. It was happening all over again.

Dear God, what was he going to do? He understood Sasha's need to find answers for Rosa. But somehow, he had to convince his strong-willed daughter to give up the search. He had failed his family before. He wouldn't do it again. He would find a way to make Sasha stop.

Sasha nodded to several of the captains as she and Bella roamed the dock, her emotions too churned up to settle anywhere. Bella stopped and looked up at her every few feet. Sasha reached down and ran a hand over her head.

"I'm OK, girl. Just a lot on my mind."

Eventually, she headed to the marina office. She had to say something to Pop, although for the life of her, she didn't know what. He wasn't in the office, so she tried his workshop next.

She stepped into the dimly lit room. The bulb overhead flickered and the door stood ajar, but she didn't see him anywhere.

"Pop? You in here?"

She heard a faint rustling noise from behind the massive workbench. Bella gave one sharp bark and shot in that direction. Sasha rounded the bench and stopped short.

Pop was on his knees on the concrete slab, struggling to get to his feet. Bella licked his face and he awkwardly patted her head.

"Pop, what happened? Can you get up? Are you hurt?"

Pop waved her outstretched hand away, but he couldn't get to his feet without help. Once Sasha helped him up, he leaned heavily against the workbench, pain etched in every line of his face.

"What happened? Let me make sure you're all right." Like all boat captains, Sasha had lots of first-aid training. Actually, she had more than most since she often worked in remote locations. She reached out a hand to check Pop's ribs, but he stopped her.

"I am fine. Please. I just lost my balance." He straightened, slowly, painfully.

Possible reasons for his fall raced through her mind, from simple causes like low blood sugar to far more serious concerns. At least there was no sign of a head injury. "Let me call the paramedics, get you checked out."

"No, Sasha. Let it go. Mama has enough worries."

"But we need to—"

He held up his hand, palm out. "Enough. I am fine."

He turned and picked up a rag and began to wipe the grease off his hands.

Sasha read the pride and determination in his stance and swallowed another plea that he get medical attention. Instead, she stayed several more minutes, offering water and making small talk while she watched for signs of serious injury. Satisfied he would be OK, she leaned over and gently kissed his cheek. "I love you. Let me know if anything changes."

Sasha went back to the house and found Mama dozing again, still in the same rocking chair. Blaze sat in the living room with the shades drawn, playing a handheld video game. Sasha sat down beside her.

"I think Pop fell a little while ago," she said quietly.

When Blaze opened her mouth to ask questions, Sasha held up a hand. "Mama's outside asleep. I don't want her to know, or to worry. He seems fine, but he's moving slowly. I need you to stay here and keep an eye on both of them while I run an errand. I'll leave Bella here, too."

Blaze narrowed her eyes. "What's going on? Where are you going?"

Sasha stifled her irritation and met her gaze. "I don't know that anything is going on, but Bella will let you know if anything happens to Pop. I'm going to talk to Captain Roy's wife about the day Tony disappeared. Before you get your panties in a knot, yes, I will tell you whatever she says as soon as I get back. But I don't feel right about leaving them alone. I need you here."

Sasha breathed a sigh of relief when Blaze nodded. "I'll be here."

It didn't take long to reach the craftsman-style house Captain Roy and Mary Lee had lived in since they got married, about the same time Pop and Mama did. The yard was mowed, the hedges trimmed, but the blinds were closed in all the windows, giving the place a deserted air.

She wondered if Mary Lee had gotten a job and wasn't home. She and Captain Roy had never had any children, though everyone knew they'd wanted them desperately. Sasha walked up onto the deep porch and used the heavy brass anchor-shaped door knocker.

She thought she heard movement inside, but no one came to the door. She reached past the screen and knocked again.

Several minutes later, Mary Lee opened the door a crack and peered around it, blinking against the bright sunlight. She shaded her eyes with her hands, the nails bitten down to the quick. Her thick southern drawl oozed like honey.

"I'm sorry, whoever you are, but whatever it is you're selling, we're not buying."

"Hi, Mrs. Winchester. It's Sasha Petrov."

She opened the door wider and squinted at Sasha.

"Why, as I live and breathe, it is you, child. Well, come on in. What brings you out this way on a sweltering day?"

Sasha followed her into the house's gloomy interior and stubbed her toe on the coffee table. She finally sank down across from Mary Lee on the nubby tweed couch, circa 1975, and waited for her eyes to adjust.

"Mrs. Winchester, I know this question may seem like it's coming out of left field, but Mama has asked me to look into Tony's disappearance."

The other woman sucked in a sharp breath, but Sasha didn't stop. "I wondered if you could tell me what you remember about that day, what you and Mama talked about, that sort of thing."

Mary Lee hopped up from her chair, obviously agitated. "Is your mama dying, Sasha? Is that what this is about?"

Sasha ignored the ache the question caused and kept her tone light. "I hope not, Mrs. Winchester. She is undergoing cancer treatment, though."

The other woman waved that away. "Of course. I know all that. But why bring up the past, after all these years?"

Sasha tried to smile. "Mama just celebrated her sixtieth birthday. I think she's thinking how fast time goes by."

Mary Lee stopped pacing and plopped down on the sofa, her hands folded primly in her lap, skirt spreading across the sofa, looking every inch the debutante she'd been decades ago.

"Of course, sugar. Forgive me. It's just that it happened so very long ago."

Sasha shrugged. "For Mama, I imagine it seems like yesterday."

Mary Lee produced a lace-trimmed hankie from the pocket of her skirt and dabbed at her eyes.

"Oh, bless her heart." She sniffed, then raised her chin. "I don't know what I can tell you, but I'll try. What do you want to know?"

"That day, do you remember why you called Mama?"

"I was in charge of the bake sale and it was my first time being the chairperson of that committee, so I was going over everything with all the ladies to make sure the event ran smoothly."

"Did you talk for a while?"

Mary Lee cocked her head as she thought. "I don't think it was more than twenty minutes. Maybe half an hour at most. I remember your Mama trying to rush me through the whole process."

"Did she tell you Tony was outside by himself?"

"She may have. I don't remember." She wrapped her arms around herself. "I always wondered if I had put off calling . . . but Helen kept pressuring me to get everything done."

"Helen Markos? Captain Demetri's wife?"

"Yes, she'd been the chairwoman for years and wanted to make sure I did everything right."

Sasha stopped, considered. "Did she call you that morning, ask you to call my mother?"

Mary Lee gnawed on a fingernail but wouldn't meet Sasha's eye. "You know, I don't rightly recollect. Why?"

"Just curious. Trying to get the events of that day fixed in my mind. Is there anything else you can tell me?"

"Not a thing except that boy's death changed your mother. She was never the same after that." She hopped up. "Let me show you something."

She disappeared into what appeared to be a small library off the living room and returned carrying an old photo album. She flipped the pages until she came to a yellowing group photo that looked like it had been taken at a picnic on the lawn behind the community church.

"That's your mother, there, laughing. Wasn't she beautiful?"

Sasha grinned. Her mother looked so carefree and happy in that photo, smiling widely, holding a laughing Tony in her arms.

"When was this taken?"

Mary Lee tilted her head. "Just a week or two before Tony disappeared, I think."

"Do you know who everyone is in this picture?"

From somewhere in the other room, Sasha heard what sounded like a pinball machine. Then there were chirps and the sound of people cheering, and a phone rang.

Mary Lee's head snapped up, and she closed the album and stood in one fluid motion. "I need to get that. If you'll excuse me."

After she disappeared, Sasha took the album and flipped back to that page. She carefully slid the photo out of its protective sleeve to get a closer look. Some of the faces were easily identifiable; others she didn't know.

Mary Lee reappeared, slightly flushed.

"I'm sorry. But you need to leave." Before Sasha could say a word, she found herself standing on the porch, the door closed at her back.

She looked down at the photo still in her hand. Who were the other people in the photo? Did any of them know something that could help her?

Sasha climbed back into her Jeep and headed to the old brick building a block off Main Street that had housed the *Safe Harbor Gazette* for decades. A hand-lettered sign on the door read "Closed due to death in the family." She wondered if Mr. Ames still ran the *Gazette* or if he was the one who had died. To Sasha he'd always been old, and she couldn't remember ever seeing him without his bow tie or an unlit cigar clamped between his teeth. Even in church.

She tapped a finger on the steering wheel. If she couldn't get into the newspaper archives . . . She spun around, drove a few blocks, and pulled up in front of the aging Victorian that housed the local library, grateful for a parking spot in the shade. She headed up the wooden stairs into the two-story building. Just down the block from the police station, the library looked like a poor relation compared with the former boardinghouse. The pine floors were worn from thousands of feet, the railings dull from too many hands. But it held its own magic: the wonderful smell of musty books that took Sasha back to her teen years.

"Hello, dear. How may I help you?"

Sasha looked down at the tiny woman's name tag, pinned to a gray cardigan that hung loosely on her thin frame.

"Hello, Mrs. Robertson. It's Sasha Petrov. Do you remember me?"

Behind thick lenses, blue eyes brightened, and Mrs. Robertson hurried out from behind the counter to give Sasha a hug.

"Oh, Miss Petrov. How lovely to see you again, child."

The tiny woman didn't even reach Sasha's chin, so Sasha bent down to give her a careful hug, afraid of breaking her. Mrs. Robertson gave her a surprisingly hard squeeze before she let her go, keeping Sasha's hands in both of hers.

"How is your dear mother? Is that what brought you back?"

"She's holding her own. Yes, Eve and I came back for her sixtieth birthday."

"Rosa is a fighter. If anyone can beat this thing, she can." She patted Sasha's hand, then said, "So, young lady, what brings you here? You never did come just to browse. You always had a mission."

Sasha grinned. "Today is no exception." She looked around, but the few patrons weren't paying them any mind. "I'm looking for anything you have from the time my brother, Tony, disappeared. Newspaper articles, television clips. Anything."

Mrs. Robertson's blue eyes darkened in concern. "That was such a tragedy. Your mama was never the same after that. But why now, after all these years?" Then she gasped. "Is the cancer worse?" she whispered.

Mrs. Robertson was a dear, but she was also a devoted member of the Safe Harbor grapevine, able to spread gossip in a single bound.

"Mama wants closure. She wants to know what really happened. I told her I would do some research. The *Gazette* office is closed."

Mrs. Robertson shook her head sadly. "Yes, poor Mr. Ames passed just a week ago, right there at his desk, that old stogie still between his teeth from what I heard. But at least he died doing what he loved."

She led the way into a back room and pointed to a bulky machine and a crowded wall of labeled containers.

"This is where we keep the microfiche. I'm afraid we don't have the resources to digitize all of this. You'll want 1991." She walked to a shelf and pulled out a container, then deftly set up the machine. "There you are. Let me know if you need anything else, all right?"

Sasha nodded, sat down in front of the machine, and froze. Her fingers hovered over the controls and she tried to figure out why she was hesitating. Normally she dove in with both feet and checked the water temperature after it closed over her head. But this time it all mattered so much. *Please, God, I need answers.*

"Just get on with it already," she muttered as she started scrolling. Suddenly there it was in black and white. Tony's picture, and according to the caption, it was taken just three weeks before he disappeared. It was the same photo Mama kept on her dresser. Tony sat on the grass behind the house, all sturdy limbs and covered in dirt, grinning at the camera with Pop's brown eyes and Mama's dimples. He looked so much like them, there could be no doubt who his parents were. What would he look like now?

She scanned the article, looking for anything she hadn't already learned through the police report, but there was nothing new. It listed Tony's clothing the day of the disappearance: a pair of blue shorts, a blue-and-yellow tank top, and tennis shoes.

She kept reading, following the progress of the search, scanning pictures of dozens of townspeople who had come to help. She stopped, enlarged a picture, and studied each face, trying to match a name from memory, but she couldn't. She recognized some people, of course, but she had come to live with Pop and Mama years after Tony vanished.

She sat back and rubbed her eyes, frustrated. There had to be more. It was technically possible for him to have been washed out to sea, but it seemed unlikely. Even if Mama Rosa had been on the phone for twenty, even thirty, minutes, if he'd fallen in the water, they would have found him. From what the reports said, people waded into the marina in a line, holding hands and dragging their feet, just in case. They came up empty.

So where did he go?

Sasha wrapped her arms around herself. If Tony didn't drown that day, someone took him. But who? And why? Even more important, what did they do with him?

Either he is alive and well and living . . . somewhere. Or—Sasha swallowed hard—*there is an unmarked grave hiding his body.*

Both options made her heart hurt.

She steeled herself and looked through the rest of the articles, but as time wore on with no developments in the case, the stories simply rehashed what they'd already said. She put the microfiche away and went to find Mrs. Robertson.

"You don't, by chance, have any copies of the newscasts from that time on tape, do you?"

"Actually, I do. When it first happened, I recorded them thinking I'd give them to your folks later, after Tony was returned home safe and sound. But then . . . well, I didn't have the heart. So I brought them here and put them in the archives. His story is part of our town's story, you know."

Within minutes, Sasha sat in front of a television while Mrs. Robertson inserted a videotape into the player. She tried to shut out the emotion of the situation, to distance herself from what was happening and see it as an outsider, but it proved impossible. When Mama Rosa stood and pleaded on television for whoever had taken their son to bring him back, Sasha squeezed her eyes shut to block out the pain.

"The town of Safe Harbor has offered a reward for information leading to the safe return of Tony Martinelli."

Sasha stopped the tape. Hit "Rewind." This was the first she'd heard of a reward.

She hurried back out to Mrs. Robertson's desk and waited while she checked out another patron. "Mrs. Robertson, I just learned about the reward. Do you know anything about it?"

"Of course," she said, and came around the counter again. She leaned close. "I thought it was such a nice thing, the local captains all doing that. They set it up and let anyone in town contribute who wanted to. They ended up with over two thousand dollars in the fund."

"Who kept track of it?"

"Well, it was set up at the bank, and Mr. Hamilton, the bank president, said he would personally oversee it."

"Did anyone ever come forward with any clues or information? Who were they supposed to call?"

"Why, the police chief, of course. He said his phones rang off the hook for weeks with crazies trying to get hold of that money. None of it ever panned out."

"What happened to the money?"

Mrs. Robertson cocked her head. "Why, I don't know. I suppose it's still sitting in that account."

"Thank you, Mrs. Robertson. You've been so helpful." She put everything away and walked down the block to the police station. Luckily, the chief was in.

He didn't look especially happy to see her. "Sasha. What brings you into town today?"

"Hello, Chief. I was just in the library, doing a bit of research, and I found something I didn't know before."

"Libraries are good for that sort of thing, I hear." He laughed at his own joke, but Sasha didn't join him.

"At the time Tony went missing, the local captains posted a reward. I heard all kinds of tips came in, but nothing ever came of them." She paused until he finally met her gaze. "I never saw a single mention of any tips in the police report."

"None of them ever panned out. The poor kid died and we were never able to find his body. That's what happened."

Sasha wanted to say, *Maybe,* but instead she asked, "What kind of tips?"

"Well, now, that was a long time ago."

"Come on, Chief. This was a big deal in this town. You haven't forgotten."

"The usual nonsense. Someone saw him with Elvis. We even had somebody say they saw Marilyn Monroe carrying him down the street. Someone else saw him being swept up into a spaceship on the high school football field."

"Nothing useful at all."

"Why are you still asking about this, Sasha?"

"Mama asked me to."

"We did have a few calls that seemed promising. Somebody saw a car leaving the marina when everyone else was heading toward it. That kind of thing."

"Nothing?"

"No. The guy was late picking his kid up from ball practice. The two came back together a little while later."

"Did you keep a record of all the calls?"

"Of course. Police procedure."

She locked eyes with him. "May I see them?"

"They should have been with the file Officer Stanton showed you."

She shook her head. "They weren't."

He spread his hands. "Then they must have been misplaced over the years."

"Chief, phone for you," the dispatcher said.

"I need to go. I'm sorry, Sasha."

Sasha thanked him and walked out, unsure what he was sorry for, exactly.

She also wondered about information that conveniently went missing just as she was looking for clues.

Maybe she was tilting at windmills, looking for conspiracies that weren't there. But she didn't believe that.

Somewhere in this town, someone knew what had happened to Tony. It was up to her to find the truth.

Sasha got back into the Jeep and headed for the marina, one eye on the rearview mirror. She didn't see anyone, but she couldn't shake the feeling she was being followed.

Jesse knew Sasha was back a half second before he heard her Jeep crunching down the gravel drive. Since high school, he'd had a sixth sense about her. Not that he'd ever tell her that. He stayed bent over the propeller he'd been inspecting and waited until he heard Bella's bark and Sasha's footsteps coming down the dock.

He wiped the grease from his hands and stepped out of the shed to meet them. Bella bounded over, tail wagging, and got a scratch for her trouble. He looked up and met Sasha's troubled expression.

"Everything OK?"

She glanced around. "I think Pop took a spill earlier."

Jesse stepped closer, studied the concern in her blue eyes. "You think there's more to it."

She punched the air in frustration and started pacing. "I don't know what to think anymore."

Jesse got that twitchy feeling between his shoulder blades again and looked around, but didn't see anyone. "About what, exactly?"

"Everything. That's the problem. Something's off around here, and I can't figure out what."

Jesse chose his words carefully. "Are you sure some of it isn't the whole cancer thing? That throws everyone's world out of whack."

"I think that's part of it. But . . ." She stopped, and he could see some internal debate. "How much do you know about Tony, their biological child who disappeared years before they became foster parents?"

"Not much, except that he was just a little tyke, and after he disappeared, nobody ever found a trace of him again."

Sasha nodded, kept her eyes on his. "Mama wants me to look into it. Find out what really happened."

"Don't the police think he drowned?" When she flinched, he added, "Sorry."

"They do. But all the evidence is circumstantial. Or should I say, the lack of any evidence whatsoever made drowning the only explanation that made sense."

"Mama Rosa doesn't believe it?"

"She says she would know in her heart if he were dead."

"Why now, after all these years?" He thought for a moment. "Right. The cancer." He paused. "Is it worse than anyone is letting on?"

Sasha shrugged. "I've been asking the same question. They say no. It has come back, but this new drug has had promising results."

Jesse nodded. "You need a break. What time do you want to go to dinner tonight?"

"Who said anything about dinner?"

"I did. Yesterday. What time is good for you?"

"I'm not sure I can. Mama—"

"Has Pop. And Blaze, when she isn't acting like a scalded cat. They'll be fine for a few hours. Say yes." He gave her his best grin, then waggled his eyebrows for good measure.

She laughed and threw up her hands. "Fine. What time is it now?"

"Five twenty. You don't have a watch or cell phone?"

"Yes, I have a cell phone. It's right—" She pulled it out of her pocket and sighed. "I turned it off when I went to see Mary Lee and forgot to turn it back on." As soon as it finished its warm-up routine, it started dinging with texts and voice mails. Lots of them.

Jesse leaned over and looked at the screen. "Looks like somebody has been trying to get hold of you."

"Eve. Forever and always." She slid the phone back into the pocket of her shorts. "How about seven?"

"Great. Meet me here." He waved a hand at her shorts and tank top. "You can just wear that if you want." He figured she'd wear something flirty and floaty, just to be contrary. At least he hoped so. Sasha in a dress could take his breath away.

Blaze clumped down the dock toward them. "Hey, Jesse. Did you find the package? I left it on the seat." She pointed toward the boat.

Jesse turned to look, just now noticing a small brown paper sack. "What is it? When did you put it there?"

"I found it on the porch a little while ago with your name on it, so I put it in the boat, thinking you'd find it when you were working."

He'd been so focused on the engine, he hadn't noticed.

At that moment, Nick Stanton, in uniform, walked toward them, and something about his stance put Jesse on full alert.

"Howdy, Jesse. Sasha. How's it going, Blaze?"

"What brings you out here, Officer?" The caution he heard in Sasha's voice matched his own.

Nick looked out at the water, then back again, clearly uncomfortable. "Well, it seems the chief got a tip that you might be, ah, taking up your former profession again, Jesse."

"What are you talking about?" Blaze crossed her arms over her chest, ready to defend.

Suddenly Jesse knew, and he saw his future slipping from his grasp. "Somebody said I've got drugs."

Nick nodded. "Can I check your boat and the shed you're using?"

Jesse wanted to say no, but what good would it do? "Sure. Go ahead. I have nothing to hide."

He hadn't when he'd been arrested before, either, but that was different. He'd taken the blame on purpose. This time, the stakes were even higher. If the police took everything from him again, there was no way he could keep his promise to his friend and win that race.

Nick pulled on gloves, climbed into *The Painted Lady*, and picked up the paper bag. "What's in here?"

"I put it there. Someone left it on the porch steps with a note saying it was for Jesse." Blaze's tone dared him to contradict her.

Nick looked at Jesse. "That true?"

He ignored the frustration churning in his gut. "She told me about it just before you got here. I haven't touched it."

"So I won't find your prints on it."

"That's right."

Nick opened the bag and Jesse heard Sasha gasp, but he wouldn't look at her. His eyes were focused on the little bags of white powder. Cocaine. He'd bet his life on it. He wanted to smash something. He'd known people didn't want him here, but this went far beyond the tire incident.

Sasha stepped up to Nick, right in his face. "Isn't it just a little too convenient that the chief gets a tip after someone has Blaze plant the drugs in Jesse's boat?"

Nick pulled out an evidence bag and looked from one to the other. "I'm not a big believer in coincidence, but I do have to get all the facts. Jesse, you'll have to come to the station with me." He reached for his handcuffs, then stopped. "You'll come willingly?"

Jesse nodded. What choice did he have?

"This is crazy!" Blaze threw her hands up and she marched toward Nick. Sasha wrapped an arm around her waist from behind to stop her.

"Slow down. We'll follow them and get this worked out."

"No. Stay here. I will handle this. My way." Jesse stared Sasha down. He would never let on how much their defense meant to him and how much he hated for them to be involved in this in any way. He thought he'd left all the ugliness behind in Tampa. "When I get back, I'll fill you in." He turned to Blaze. "Both of you."

He walked up the dock with Nick. As he got in the patrol car, he heard Blaze say, "I can't believe you just let him go!"

Far worse than his frustration about being falsely accused was the fear that no matter how he tried, he couldn't make amends, couldn't set the past to rights.

But he wouldn't give up, not without a fight.

Chapter 7

"I can't believe this. Does that cop really think Jesse is doing drugs? Do you?"

Sasha tried to find the right words as she and Blaze paced the dock. She didn't believe it, no, not for a minute. She would have known. And selling them? Definitely not. She hadn't looked up Jesse's past online yet, but rumors were that it had to do with drugs. So suddenly drugs show up in his boat? Please.

"No, I don't think Nick believes that. But he has to follow the rules. If Jesse's fingerprints aren't anywhere on the drugs, but yours are, hopefully whoever left the bag left theirs on it, too."

"This sounds like people wanting to get rid of Jesse, but it's so freaking obvious. Why would anybody believe it?"

"I agree with you. It sounds like a setup to me."

Suddenly Blaze slumped against a piling. "They won't put him back in jail, will they?"

So, she knew about Jesse's past, too. "I think if there's no evidence that the drugs are Jesse's, then no, they won't. We'll have to pray Nick can get all the facts."

"Praying doesn't seem to be doing much for Mama. I'm not sure it matters."

Oh, she and Blaze were a lot alike. "I won't lie. I've thought the same thing. But here's what I know. Praying always matters. The hard part is that God's timing is usually not the same as ours."

"Well, I wish He'd get on with it, already."

Sasha couldn't help a grin. "Amen, kiddo."

"What did you find out from Captain Roy's wife?"

Sasha met Blaze's determined expression. "She didn't have much to add. Just confirmed that she'd been talking to Mama at the time. Something about a bake sale. She showed me an old photo taken just before Tony disappeared, but she got a phone call and I didn't get to ask about the people in it."

"You kept the pic, right?"

"She ushered me out before I could return it."

Blaze studied her a moment. "You're going to show it around town, aren't you?"

Sasha smiled. The girl had quills like a hedgehog, but her brain was sharp. "That's the plan. Though it may not help us much."

Blaze nodded, apparently satisfied. "The new meds are making Mama pretty sick."

Sasha's heart started pounding. "Stomach-sick?"

Blaze nodded. "She spent most of the afternoon throwing up."

"I was going to change the spark plugs on Jesse's boat, but I'll help you." She turned toward the house.

Blaze blocked her way. "No. Mama is asleep right now. Pop is with her." She crossed her arms. "We have it under control. We don't need you."

The words stung, but a split second before she retaliated, Sasha registered the pain in them. Just like her, Blaze was trying to find her place in the family and protecting those she cared about with everything she had. Sasha met the teen's eyes.

"Will you let me know if something changes or you need me? I'm not a nurse, but I have lots and lots of first-aid training. I'll help if I can."

Blaze nodded once before she headed up to the house.

Sasha went back to *The Painted Lady* and went to work. She couldn't think of any other way to help. Jesse had made it clear he didn't want her underfoot at the police station. Which was probably smart, since she was mad enough at the chief to spit nails. Still, she couldn't just sit on her hands.

She angled her gaze heavenward. "God, I don't know what you're doing here. This thing with Jesse is crazy. And no matter how many questions I ask about Tony, all I get are more questions. If you're going to provide answers, as Mama seems to think you will, it would be good if you could send a few my way."

Her phone chirped with a text from Eve, asking for an update. She filled her in, then tried to make sense of everything happening while she changed the plugs and checked the adjustment on the stuffing box in Jesse's boat. It was almost dark when her phone rang again.

"Hey, Sash. It's me. They let me go finally. You still game for dinner?"

Sasha straightened, shocked at his casual tone. "What happened? Did they figure out who set you up?"

"Yeah. I'll tell you over dinner, OK?" He sounded exhausted.

"Ah, sure. OK. As long as they're OK with me being gone for a bit. Mama is having a rough day."

"I'll be there in twenty minutes."

He hung up and Sasha flew into action, putting the tools in the shed, buttoning up *The Painted Lady*.

Twenty minutes? By the time she raced upstairs to her old bedroom, her heart was pounding and her hands were shaking. She spun around and smacked her forehead on the low-hanging beam. She plopped down on the bed and rubbed her head with both hands. She had to get a grip. Her thoughts were spinning so fast, she was making herself nuts. Between trying to find answers about Tony and worrying about what was going on with Jesse, she couldn't think straight. And then there was the man himself. A simple dinner invite had her so tangled up, she almost knocked her idiot self out cold.

With any other man, she would have said either yes or no, whatever suited her mood at the time, and not given it another thought.

But this was Jesse. When it came to him, her gut twisted into knots and she behaved like a complete nitwit. She reached into the closet and pulled a sundress over her head, one of two dresses she owned. The other was a little black dress completely wrong for Florida in the summer. She'd planned to wear the sundress for Mama's party, but she'd been late and gotten scooped up by Pop and Eve before she had the chance to change.

Should she wear it tonight? She stood and went back to the mirror, mindful of that beam. Was it too much? Did it send the wrong impression? What signal did she want to send? Or not send?

Annoyed with herself, she flopped down, undid her braid, and ran a brush through her hair. She dabbed some concealer on the growing knot on her forehead, pushed her hair out of her eyes with a beaded headband she'd bought from an Indian woman she met in Seattle years ago, and spritzed body spray here and there. It would have to do.

Sasha checked in with Mama before she walked into the living room and looked around. "Is Jesse here?"

Blaze hitched a thumb over her shoulder. "He got tired of waiting, so he's outside with Bella."

She walked out onto the porch, watching Jesse and Bella play together. Had she ever been that carefree in her life? As though they were both attached to her by an invisible chain, man and dog stopped and turned toward her. Bella woofed and bounded over, while Jesse's blinding smile took her breath away and his determined walk made her feel like prey in the hunter's sights.

He stopped much too close and took both her hands in his, lifting them away from her and giving her a thorough once-over. Sasha squirmed and tried to pull her hands away, but he wouldn't let go. Finally he met her eyes. "You look absolutely beautiful tonight. Thank you."

She narrowed her eyes. "For what?"

"For dressing up for me."

Heat raced up her cheeks and made her response sharper than she intended.

"I didn't do it for you." She turned and motioned Bella to go inside. "Stay with Blaze," she told the dog.

When she walked toward Jesse's truck, he fell into step beside her. "So are you meeting some other guy tonight?"

"What are you talking about, Money-boy?"

"If you didn't get all spiffed up for me, then who?"

"For me. I felt like wearing something pretty." Why did the man forever get her all mixed up inside and babbling like an idiot? She never babbled. And she didn't like feeling out of step all the time. "Stop it, OK? Just stop it."

If anything, his grin got wider, and those gorgeous eyes sparkled with mischief. She wanted to slap him. Or kiss him. She wasn't sure which, and that more than anything flustered her. She reached for the door handle on his truck, but he blocked her with his arm.

"Please, let me." He opened the door and offered her a hand up into the big vehicle. She caught him sneaking a peek at her legs as her dress rode up her thighs. He reached over to tuck her skirt in so it wouldn't get caught in the door, and despite her resolve not to let him get to her, a little shiver shimmied up her insides.

Once he had the diesel engine rumbling, he turned that grin her way again.

"Choices are the Pizza Palace and the Blue Dolphin for all-you-can-eat shrimp night. Or we can drive toward Tampa for something more upscale."

"I didn't think you could afford upscale. But let's go to the Blue Dolphin. I don't want to be gone too long."

"How's Mama doing with the new treatments?"

"Blaze said she spent most of the afternoon throwing up."

He glanced her way, genuine concern in his eyes. "I'm sorry. It's hard to watch a family member struggle."

"Are you going to tell me what happened at the police station, or will I have to beat it out of you?"

He grinned, but she could see the exhaustion he'd been trying so hard to hide. "The chief was ready to throw me in jail—no surprise there—but Nick did some more digging. Sure enough, Blaze's prints were on the outside of the bag. Mine were nowhere, not on the bag or the drugs. But they did find the prints of some low-life drug dealer from a couple towns over. The dealer said somebody ordered the drugs over the phone and asked him to drop them off on the porch with a note."

"Were they able to trace the caller?"

"Burner phone. So, the dealer is in jail and they let me go."

"But not without the chief telling you he'd be keeping an eye on you, I'll bet."

"Of course. I don't want to talk about this anymore tonight, OK?"

Sasha totally understood. Besides, she needed time to collect her thoughts—and stop acting like her sarcastic, insecure, high school self. She couldn't figure out how to stop. Maybe if she ignored the way just looking at him made her insides shiver, and the way his grin made her want to kiss him, and the way his hair made her want to slide her fingers through it . . . She sighed and shook her head.

Jesse parked in the crushed-shell lot. Since the Blue Dolphin was one of the few restaurants in Safe Harbor, it was crowded, as always. The smell of fried fish and french fries wafted out onto the street and spilled over the outdoor seating area. She and Jesse wound their way inside to the hostess station, surprised to find an old high school friend manning the booth.

"Hey, Sasha. Heard you were back. How many tonight?" LuAn asked.

Sasha tried not to stare at how much weight the former cheerleader had gained.

"Just two. Thanks, LuAn. How have you been?"

LuAn laughed and patted her belly. "Me and Joey got hitched right after graduation and I'm still trying to lose the weight after baby number four. But I wouldn't trade any of them. Except maybe Joey, sometimes."

She laughed, and then her eyes landed on Jesse and her entire demeanor changed. "Jesse Claybourne. Didn't expect you to show your face in town again. This here is a nice, God-fearing, family community."

"Hello, LuAn. It is that. Congrats on your family. I'm sure you're a wonderful mother."

She narrowed her eyes at him. "Are you making fun of me?"

Jesse sent her a lopsided grin. "No, ma'am. I have the utmost respect for mothers. Hardest job in the world."

"We don't want your kind in this town," she hissed. She left them cooling their heels for several minutes while she seated other customers who came in after them.

When another table opened up, Sasha leaned in and slipped the menus from LuAn's hands.

"Don't let us bother you, LuAn. We'll just take that table right over there." She pointed and started walking in that direction.

LuAn sputtered and rushed after them, and Sasha wondered if she'd make a scene. She looked over her shoulder as LuAn stared daggers after them and whispered to Betty, the rail-thin sixty-something chain smoker who had been keeping her pencil tucked in her bright-red beehive since 1972. Betty walked right up to their table.

"Well, hey there, Sasha. How you been, sugar?" Then she leaned closer. "You all are pulling the tiger's tail getting LuAn all riled up. Her daddy owns the Blue Dolphin, don't forget." She looked Jesse in the eye. "Your aunt Clarabelle was a devoted Christian and a good friend of mine. You going to cause trouble in our little town, young Jesse?"

Jesse shook his head. “No, ma’am. I don’t plan to. I have good memories of Safe Harbor. I thought it might be just the place for a fresh start.”

“It’s a good place, I’ll grant you that. But folks in these parts have long memories. They thought very highly of your aunt. Folks might think you were taking advantage of her good name.”

“She left her cottage to me.”

Betty raised one penciled eyebrow. “Well, now, that ought to give the gossips something to talk about. I’ll be sure they hear about that.”

“Much obliged,” Jesse responded. He turned to Sasha. “You know what you’d like?”

Betty grinned. “All-you-can-eat shrimp?” When Sasha nodded, Betty laughed. “You always could pack them away. How about you, Jesse?”

“I’ll have the same, thanks.”

Betty smiled. “I’ll get this right out. Don’t let those old biddies get to you, ya hear?”

“Was she talking about LuAn?” Jesse asked, and they shared a laugh.

“She shouldn’t have treated you that way.”

Jesse shrugged. “I expected it. Hopefully, they’ll get over it. Eventually.”

“You ever going to tell me how you ended up in jail in Tampa?”

He met her eyes, gaze serious. “I figure if you want to know, you’ll read about it online.”

Sasha nodded and looked around the crowded room, surprised at the downright hostile looks aimed in their direction.

“When people act like this, I remember why I left this place.”

Jesse grinned. “You wanted to do your own thing and not have to answer to anyone.”

Sasha grinned back. “That, too. I was eighteen and stupid.”

“I’m glad you’re back. Are you going to stay?”

She should have expected the question, but it caught her off guard. “I’ll be here for a little while at least, helping Pop. I, ah, haven’t made any long-term decisions yet.”

"You never make long-term decisions if you can avoid them. You ever going to tell me why?"

Sasha looked away and tried not to squirm. How could he still know her so well after all these years? She looked around the room again and stopped. Wait. She knew those men at the back table. They helped search for Tony.

She slid from the booth with a murmured "I'll be right back" and headed in their direction. She walked up to their booth and slid in beside the youngest of the three men. "Hi, guys. How's it going?"

The younger man slid closer, a cocky grin on his face. "Well hello, beautiful. What brings you to our table?"

"Knock it off, Romeo. That's Sal's daughter," the older man across the table said. "Sasha, right?"

"Hello, Captain Harvey. I thought that was you. I haven't seen you out at the marina. You still taking dive trips out to the wreck?"

He shrugged. "Not as often as I used to, what with the economy and all."

The heavyset man beside him added, "These days the tourists want snorkeling, not dive trips. It's cheaper. But on that wreck . . ." He shrugged.

Sasha nodded. "Too deep to see much from the surface."

"Right. And then they complain about the trip," the young man they'd called Romeo added.

"I'm sorry to hear that, guys. That's tough."

"Thanks, Sasha. How's your mother?" Harvey asked. "We heard she's fighting the Big C."

"She is and holding her own. Thanks for asking."

Romeo leaned closer. "So what brings you to our table? Especially since the guy at yours does not look happy."

Sasha looked over her shoulder to see Jesse frowning at them. She turned back to the men and smiled.

"He'll get over it. I have a question for you, Harvey. You remember when Sal and Rosa's boy, Tony, disappeared years ago?"

Harvey's eyes widened and he exchanged a nervous glance with the heavyset man sitting next to him. "Sure. Terrible, terrible thing. Your folks were inconsolable. Why are you asking about that now after all these years?"

"Wait. What happened?" Romeo wanted to know.

"My parents' biological son disappeared from their house when he was three." She turned her attention back to Harvey. "The police report says you were one of the divers who tried to help find him. Can you tell me anything about that day?"

Harvey scrubbed a hand over his chin. "It was a long time ago, and there wasn't much to tell, then or now." He hitched his thumb at the man beside him. "Frank helped search the water, too."

Frank shot Harvey a scowl before he turned to Sasha. "I brought my airboat. We were out there at first light for days, checking around docks, marshy areas, little lagoons, checking the tides." He stopped and shook his head.

Harvey picked up the tale. "There were three divers, and we did the same thing, thinking maybe he got trapped underwater somehow. We never found anything. Not one piece of clothing, a shoe, nothing. We all figured he fell in and got swept out to sea."

Frank nodded. "They had teams of volunteers from town, too. I think everyone in Safe Harbor joined the search. They never found anything, either. It was a very sad time."

Harvey studied her under beetle brows. "Why now, Sasha, after all this time?"

Sasha met their eyes and shrugged. "Mama asked me to look into it again, see if we could find answers."

The two oldest men exchanged another look. "I don't think there are any answers, but I hope your Mama beats this thing," Harvey added.

"She's doing her very best." Sasha started to leave, then changed her mind. She slipped the photo out of the pocket of her dress and set it on the table. "This was taken not long before Tony disappeared. Can you all help me identify these folks?"

Harvey's eyes widened, but he picked up the picture. "Well, now. Looks like the usual church crowd. Most of the captains, the preacher, your folks, Chief Monroe, Clarabelle. All locals." He passed it to Frank.

"You looking for strangers, Sasha? None here." He tapped the photo and handed it back. "Sorry."

She waited, but nobody said anything else. She slid out of the booth. "Thanks for telling me what you know."

"You ever want to go out for a ride—" Romeo started. "Ow. What?"

Frank answered him with a look. "You give our best to your mama and Sal, you hear? Let her know we'll say a prayer for her."

"Thanks." Sasha pushed back unwanted images of a little boy tangled underwater in sea grass as she headed back to their table.

"Why, Sasha Petrov, as I live and breathe. Is that you?"

Sasha's head snapped up just in time to keep her from crashing headlong into Mayor Dunbar. He steadied her and grinned, his dentures as blinding white as his hair.

"Hello, Mayor. Good to see you again."

"Mary Lee told me you were back in town." His grin faded as he leaned closer, and the scent of mothballs assaulted her nose. "My daughter also said you're stirring up the past. Leave it be, Sasha. Let young Tony rest in peace."

Sasha reared back, eyes narrowed. "We don't know if he's dead."

The mayor's bushy eyebrows climbed to his hairline. "Nothing else makes sense but that the poor child was snatched from this world far too soon. All this turmoil must be devastating to your poor mother after all this time."

"She's the one who asked me to find answers."

He looked stunned for a moment, then his face hardened. "Let the past go, Sasha. For everyone's sake." He let go of her and pasted another smile on his face. "Have a lovely evening."

Sasha shook her head as she slid back into the booth. Seemed like everyone in town said the same thing. Why were they all determined to sweep it under the rug?

She indicated the other table with a nod of her head. "The two older captains helped search for Tony."

Jesse watched her, eyes intent. "They give you any more insight into what happened?"

"Not really. Harvey dove and Frank manned the airboat. They both said they never found one single trace, nothing. It was like he vanished."

The silence lengthened, and finally Sasha asked, "Are you thinking what I'm thinking?"

"That maybe someone took him? Yeah, it crossed my mind. But who would do that?"

Sasha shook her head. "If someone here in Safe Harbor took Tony, where would they hide him? Everyone knows everyone's children. Someone would have recognized him immediately. If it was a stranger, people would remember seeing someone around who didn't belong." She showed him the photo. "This was taken just before Tony disappeared. Do you recognize the people in it?"

Jesse turned it so they could both see it and started naming various captains. He came to one face and stopped. "I remember seeing him, but I can't place him."

Betty delivered heaping baskets of fried shrimp and french fries and looked over Jesse's shoulder. "That sure takes me back." She pointed to a woman in the second row.

"You haven't changed a bit," Jesse teased, and she laughed, her raspy voice like an old saw. "You know this guy?" He pointed to a face in the back.

Betty's smile died. "Poor Captain Alby. After his wife died, his mind went, and he lives in the assisted living place just outside town."

"He was around when Tony disappeared?"

"Oh, sure. He and Sal were good friends. He helped with the search, just like everyone else. But these days, he just shuffles around and mumbles to himself. It's very sad."

"Thanks, Betty." After they finished eating, Jesse took care of the bill, then nodded to Sasha. "You ready to go?"

Sasha climbed into the truck, thoughts still on kidnapping. She didn't realize they'd arrived back at the marina until Jesse hurried around to open her door and help her down. "Thanks for dinner. I enjoyed every bite. Sorry I was distracted."

"No problem. I thought LuAn was going to have the kitchen cut you off if you ordered a third shrimp basket." He grinned and took her hand as they walked down the dock.

Sasha tried to ignore how right her hand felt in his callused one. "*All you can eat* should mean what it says."

"I don't think they were counting on you."

"I like food. Sue me."

He pulled her into his arms in a lightning-fast move that made her squeak in surprise. He leaned in and said, "You smell good. Citrusy. With just a hint of fried shrimp." His hands ran up her arms to her bare shoulders, and a lovely shiver raced over her skin. "You look beautiful tonight. Have I mentioned that?"

He leaned in and nuzzled her neck, and Sasha sank into the moment, feeling his arms pull her closer, his lips on her cheek. She turned her head and met his gaze. She couldn't see the color of his eyes, but his expression was unmistakable, even in the waning light. He was going to kiss her. It would feel wonderful, she knew. But what about after? She thought of Pete and his assumptions and stepped away before she gave in.

"You want this," Jesse said.

Sasha couldn't lie. "I do, but it's not a good idea. You said it yourself. I don't do long term."

He laughed at her. "Who said anything about long term? It's a kiss, not a lifetime commitment."

"You're an idiot, Money-boy." She turned and was halfway up the dock when he took her arm and spun her right back into his arms. This kiss wasn't tentative or questioning. This was a full-on assault on her senses. He gripped the back of her neck to hold her steady and kissed her like he would never get enough.

Sasha put her hands on his shoulders, thinking she'd push him away, but then she stopped fighting and gave as good as she got. Oh, the man could kiss. But it wasn't just technique; it was Jesse. He poured his whole heart into what his mouth was doing. Every nerve ending in her body came to life and begged for more. She growled low in her throat and he pulled her closer, his hands roaming over her back and down over her hips. He trailed kisses along her throat, kissed her mariner's cross. His callused fingers skimmed the straps of her sundress, and he planted featherlight kisses as he went.

"Ah, Sasha," he murmured. The tender, urgent way he said her name smacked her like a rogue wave and brought her back to reality. She couldn't get involved. Not with Jesse. Never Jesse. He deserved so much more than she could ever give him—or any man.

She deliberately stepped away before her selfishness trapped them both. They faced each other in the fading light, both breathing hard. "I'm sorry. I have to check on Mama."

Jesse reached out and brushed his thumb over her mouth. "Sweet dreams, hummingbird."

The longing in his eyes almost made her leap back into his arms, but she turned and walked back to the house without a backward glance. She felt his eyes on her with every step.

The house was quiet, but night-lights glowed from outlets here and there. She tiptoed down the hall, but the door to Mama and Pop's room was closed. She hoped they were sleeping. No light glowed under the door to Blaze's small room, but she could hear music, muffled, probably headphones. She went back to the living room, and Bella stood and licked her hand before heading for the door. Sasha let her out and leaned against the porch railing while she waited. She could see the light on in Jesse's shed and wondered if that kiss had shaken him as much as it had her.

She never bothered much with if onlys. Therein lay madness. But she had learned not to make the same mistakes twice. Reckless, restless, selfish people like her should not get involved. Inevitably, she let people down. The other person wanted you to stay, build a life, settle down. That she couldn't do. She wasn't wired for picket fences and PTA meetings and sharing her life. She was wired for the sea, and adventure, and the view from the next horizon. No responsibilities. No obligations.

Hadn't what happened to her biological parents proven she should be alone? If only she had done what she was supposed to that day—

From somewhere in the darkness, Bella barked and it jolted Sasha back to the present. She stepped off the porch and followed the sound.

"Bella," she hissed. "Come here, girl. Time to go in."

She waited, listening, but she couldn't hear her. "Bella. Come, girl."

After a few minutes, Bella appeared beside her, soaking wet. Sasha laughed and leaped away just before the dog shook.

"You crazy mutt." She went to the laundry room and grabbed a rag to wipe her down before they went inside. When they got to the door, Bella looked over her shoulder and barked again. Sasha scanned the area, but didn't see anything. She opened the door. "Go on in, girl."

Bella ignored the command, something she almost never did. Instead, she lay down in front of Mama's rocking chair, head on her paws, watching the darkness beyond the porch.

"Bella?" Sasha crouched down and scratched behind her ears. "What's wrong, girl? This isn't like you." She stood, went to the inside door, and called her again, but Bella simply lifted her head and whined before she settled back down. "OK. Have it your way." Sasha locked the door and headed upstairs, unsettled. From her bedroom under the eaves, she studied the marina. Light spilled out from under the doorway of Jesse's workshop, but that wouldn't upset her dog.

She checked her phone and found several texts from Eve. She responded, *Too tired to call tonight. Will update in a.m. What's up with Cat? Do you know?*

She put the phone on the nightstand and started down the steps to go talk to Jesse. Halfway down she stopped, closed her eyes, and sighed. *Don't be an idiot.*

She turned and went back upstairs. The house didn't have internet, so she picked up her fancy new phone and finally figured out how to do an online search. She read all the articles she could find about how Jesse ended up in jail, but none of them really answered her questions. According to the articles, he and his friend Ethan started fixing boat motors after high school. Following a short stint in Afghanistan, they started their own boat repair shop and built it into a high-end boat dealership in Tampa. By all accounts they were doing quite well.

But then, drugs were found on one of their boats, and they were both arrested. Jesse claimed the drugs were his. Before the trial, Ethan committed suicide in jail and left a note saying Jesse had no knowledge of the drug operation. Jesse was ultimately released for lack of evidence, but the government never returned any of his assets. He really had nothing but what his great-aunt Clarabelle left him.

Had he known about the drugs? Was he involved? The Jesse she knew years ago would never have gotten near them, but . . . somehow there was a piece missing. Why had he said the drugs were his?

She finally climbed into bed, but sleep was a long time coming.

Chapter 8

Jesse tightened the last bolt and straightened, putting both hands on his lower back. He felt the grease on his hands and grimaced, glad he'd taken off his only decent shirt before he started working. He reached for a clean shop rag and grinned as he put his tools away.

Just a few more tweaks and the motor would be ready. He planned to test it again tomorrow. Once he was sure the engine ran like a top, he could get serious about practicing for the upcoming race.

He had just stepped out of the shed, ready to lock it behind him, when his phone rang. He glanced at the caller ID. Adelaide's mother wouldn't call at 1:00 a.m. unless it was important. "Hey, Tracy, what's wrong?"

"Oh, Jesse. I'm sorry to call so late, but I needed someone to talk to." She stopped and blew her nose. "Adelaide is back in the hospital. Her blood oxygen levels were horrible and her heart keeps getting weaker. I just can't-can't watch my baby fight anymore. I'm afraid she won't-won't . . . that she won't live long enough to have the surgery."

Jesse tried to block the images of little nine-month-old Adelaide stuck full of tubes, the way she'd been last week. "She's a fighter, Tracy, just like her mama. Her daddy was one tough son of a gun, too. I was glad to know he had my back over there with bombs exploding in the desert. Adelaide is going to get through this. She will have that surgery and be running around like a little terror before you know it."

"Do you really believe that, Jesse?"

"I do. You have to keep the faith, and keep being strong. For Adelaide's sake."

"I don't know how I'm going to keep paying the bills." Her voice trailed off and Jesse heard her sobs. With any other woman, he might have been suspicious of the tears, but Ethan had told him how much some of these treatments cost, even with insurance.

"You know I'll do what I can, and I'll keep doing it. I just need a little time to get some funds together. But I will. Trust me."

"I do trust you, Jesse. I know Ethan did, too. Thanks for listening."

As he talked, he walked to the gravel lot and climbed into his truck. "You can call me anytime, day or night. Get some sleep. Your girl will need you to be strong and smiling tomorrow."

She let out a laugh, a bit shaky, but still a laugh. "Thanks, Jesse. You're the best. Night."

Jesse disconnected and heaved out a sigh, then slammed a fist against the steering wheel. He'd promised Ethan he'd take care of his girls, and he'd meant it.

He had to win that race.

Sasha gave up trying to sleep and padded downstairs, avoiding the creaky steps. Bella silently fell in behind her. The screen door squeaked and Sasha grimaced, hoping she didn't wake anyone. Head down, she wandered toward the marina office, mind jumping from worry to worry, but she always came back to Jesse. How did everything she'd learned about him affect her opinion of him? Or did it? Should it? She had no idea what to do with all the crazy feelings he churned up inside her, especially the ones that made her want to stay right here in Safe Harbor with him. Maybe forever. She snorted as she opened the door to the office and flipped on the light. She held the door for Bella, surprised she wasn't right behind her.

Sasha started a pot of coffee and settled into Pop's ancient desk chair. The house had always been Mama's domain, but the marina office, that was hers and Pop's. She'd always had free run of the place and had begun helping him keep the books when she was fifteen. In many ways, this felt more like home than her bedroom under the eaves.

She started opening drawers, searching for . . . something. When it came to Tony's disappearance, Pop's reactions—then and now—didn't make sense. The odds were minuscule, but maybe his office would yield answers. Or at the very least, insight.

The top desk drawers held the usual assortment of office supplies, the other drawers neat stacks of receipts going back ten years, some still with her handwriting on them. Sasha pushed back and headed to the four-drawer metal file cabinet against the wall. It was locked, but the key had always hung from a nail beside it. She started flipping through folders, not surprised to find more of the same. Hadn't she helped create the filing system?

Still, she felt compelled to search all of it. When she came to the bottom drawer, she knelt down on the floor and moved the hanging files. Something slipped down into the bottom of the drawer.

She picked it up and found a postcard. The front said *Happy Birthday* in large block letters. She flipped it over, and her heart stuttered. It was addressed to Mama and simply said, *I'm so sorry.*

Sasha sank down onto the floor, heart racing. No signature or return address, but the postmark was dated five years after Tony disappeared, stamped in Tampa.

What kind of birthday card was this? Who did that? Her first thought: it had to do with Tony. A chill raced up her arms. Had someone accidentally killed him and felt guilty? What was the postcard doing in here? Did Mama even know about it?

Sasha hopped up, ready to confront her parents, when logic kicked in. She stopped. Took a breath. She was letting her imagination run away with her. There could be any number of completely logical, innocent reasons someone sent that card. A spat with a friend. Even something as simple as a missed birthday and feeling bad.

She looked at the time. She had to get some sleep before she ran off half-cocked. Tomorrow she'd ask about it, like a normal, rational person.

She turned off the light and closed the door.

"Bella?" she called quietly.

No answer. A prickle of unease slid up her spine. Bella never ran off. When she climbed up the porch steps, Sasha studied the marina, but nothing seemed out of place. Nerves humming, she went back upstairs.

Something wasn't right.

Sasha must have fallen asleep, because her phone's alarm clock scared her awake before dawn. She lay still for a moment, struggling to get her brain in gear. Right, she had told Pop she'd open the bait shop this morning so he could spend time with Mama.

Where was Bella? She pushed up on her elbows and scanned the floor by the bed. Slowly, events clicked into place. Bella wouldn't come inside last night. Which she'd never done, ever. Between Jesse's kiss, the news articles, and the postcard, Sasha had been distracted. She should have looked for her.

In the kitchen, she started the coffee and hurried out to the porch, not surprised at the number of fishermen milling around the docks and ramp, launching boats.

"Bella? Here, girl." Nothing. Her anxiety grew with every passing second. If not for her promise to Pop, she'd start a search right now. Maybe she was overreacting. Wouldn't be the first time.

Instead, she'd act like a calm, responsible adult and hope Bella showed up in a little while, muddy from a romp in the woods. Cup in hand, she walked out on the dock and unlocked the marina office.

"Morning, all. Come on in."

"You're not usually here this early," Harvey said.

Sasha went straight to the industrial coffeepot and got that going. "Not usually, but I thought Pop could use a little extra shut-eye. You taking a group out today?"

Harvey grinned. "Yeah, they found me through that website my twelve-year-old grandson set up for me. Go figure."

Sasha laughed and handed him his coffee and change. "Times are changing, aren't they?"

"I can't keep up." He held the door for a family staggering in, trying to wake up. "Take good care of my customers for me, Sasha, will you?"

"Sure, Harvey. Good morning and welcome to Safe Harbor Marina. What can I get for you?"

Several minutes later, Chad Everson and Nick Stanton stepped up to the register, sodas, snacks, and a bait bucket in hand.

"Don't you have school today?" she asked.

Chad grinned from under his ball cap. "The main air conditioner quit, so I get an unexpected day off."

Beside him, Nick flashed white teeth. "And I was off today, so we're taking advantage." He sobered. "Sorry about yesterday."

Sasha ignored the last. "Didn't realize y'all were fishermen."

"I grew up near Crystal River." Chad nodded to Nick. "He grew up near Miami."

"I spent every minute I could out on the water with my father." He looked around the bait shop. "Somehow, this place reminds of me home."

She wished them good luck and spent the next two hours ringing up coffee, bait, and candy bars for the fishermen and soda, sunscreen, and Safe Harbor Marina ball caps for the tourists.

By the time Pop came in a little after nine, Sasha couldn't wait any longer. "Pop, have you seen Bella? Was she up at the house?"

Pop leaned over and gave her a quick kiss on the cheek. "Nope, haven't seen her. Figured she'd be here with you."

"She wouldn't come inside last night and I haven't seen her this morning. This isn't like her. You mind if I take a look around, make sure she's all right?"

"Sure. Just watch for snakes if you go in the woods."

This time, she leaned over and kissed his cheek. "Grew up here, remember? Haven't forgotten."

"Well, get on with you then, miss know-it-all."

Sasha started by checking inside the house again, then the area around the house. She called Bella's name as she walked in an ever-widening circle around the marina.

"Sasha! Over here." She spun and saw Jesse striding toward her, a limp Bella in his arms.

She started running and met him in the middle of the parking lot. "What's wrong with her? Where did you find her?"

"I heard her moan when I went out to check on my boat trailer." He kept walking toward his shed. Sasha jumped in front of him and fumbled to open the door.

She grabbed a tarp and threw an old towel on top of it, and Jesse gently laid Bella down. Sasha dropped on her knees and stroked Bella's silky head. "Hey, girl. What's wrong? Did you eat something you shouldn't have?"

Bella fluttered her eyes and finally got them open, but they were glassy. She whimpered and Sasha made soothing noises, stroking her head. Suddenly Bella staggered to her feet and retched. Sasha leaped out of the way just in time. It took a few minutes to empty her stomach, but when she was done, Bella swayed on her feet and staggered outside to crop grass.

Sasha watched her for a few minutes, then turned back to see Jesse studying the mess on the floor.

He met her eyes and said, "Call me crazy, but I think she may have been poisoned."

Chapter 9

Sasha's heart stuttered. "Poisoned?" She crouched down by the tarp where Jesse poked the mess with a screwdriver. "What makes you think that?"

"Did you feed Bella hunks of salami or anything like that last night?"

"No. Never. She loves it, but it doesn't digest well."

Jesse poked again. "Looks like someone gave her quite a bit."

Sasha leaned closer and wrinkled her nose. "Maybe someone gave it to her while you and I were out last night."

Jesse shrugged. "I know my friend Ethan always buried his dog's meds in sausage or salami so the smell would disguise the taste and distract the dog."

Bella wandered back in and plopped down beside Sasha. Her eyes looked less glassy and her tail thumped when Sasha scratched behind her ears.

"She seems to be OK, thank God. But I'm taking her to the vet anyway, just to be sure." Everything inside her felt shaky as she leaned over to kiss the top of Bella's head. She kept her voice calm. "So, without jumping to conclusions or becoming a conspiracy theorist, why would someone poison my dog?"

Jesse looked around the shed, jaw clenched, and Sasha followed his gaze. She registered the destruction around her for the first time and hopped to her feet. "What happened? This place is a mess."

Jesse nodded and their eyes met. "I worked some last night after we got back. I got a phone call and forgot to lock the door when I left."

Sasha scanned the room. "Did someone just trash it, or did they destroy things?" She nodded to the carburetor on the workbench. "Did they sabotage it?"

"I'm still checking, but I don't think so." He picked several tools off the floor. "It looks like someone just wanted to be annoying."

Sasha could feel the anger Jesse kept under control, so she matched his calm tone. "Is this because they don't want you in town, or because of the race, do you think?"

He shrugged and thumped the tools on the workbench with more force than necessary. "This seems more like not wanting a guy with my quote 'unsavory past' in their pristine little town."

She furrowed her brow, thinking. "I buy that. Safe Harbor has never been known for its open-mindedness. But why drug Bella? It seems like whoever did this wasn't trying to kill her, thank God, just knock her out, keep her quiet and out of the way. So if they planned far enough ahead to do that, to bring the drugs, why just toss the place? They bought themselves time. Why not use it?"

Jesse stopped picking things off the floor and met her gaze. "I don't know. Maybe they got interrupted."

"What if this isn't about you?" Sasha scanned the room again, thinking aloud.

Jesse tossed something into the trash, where it landed with a clatter. "My shed. My mess. They already attacked my truck. How can it not be about me?"

He had a point. Still, it wouldn't quite jell in her mind. "What if it's about Tony?"

He stopped, stared at her, considered.

"What if, as we said, Tony didn't drown? What if something else happened and somebody doesn't want the truth to come out?" Even as she said the words, a chill raced over her skin, and Sasha rubbed her arms. "Of course, the idea that someone here, someone I've known forever, could have been a part of something like that terrifies me."

Jesse leaned against the workbench and crossed his arms. "I think you should tell Mama Rosa that there's nothing to find and leave it at that."

Sasha thought she must have misunderstood. "Someone may or may not be trying to get me to back off and you think I should? Is that what you're saying?"

He nodded. "They drugged your dog, Sasha. You willing to have something worse happen because you're determined to poke around in the past?"

"Just the fact someone wants me to stop is the main reason to keep digging."

Suddenly he stood before her, hands on her arms. "It's dangerous. Doesn't your family have enough to worry about right now?"

She tried to shrug him off, but he wouldn't release her. "When did you become a coward, Money-boy? When did the truth stop mattering to you?"

Her words hit harder than she'd intended, and she saw his eyes darken with pain. His grip tightened and he leaned closer. "The truth has always mattered to me. But it becomes cold comfort when you're staring down at a grave."

His words made her heart beat faster, but she couldn't agree. "You're overreacting, Jesse. Besides, we have absolutely no proof of any of this. We have a sick dog and a trashed shed and planted drugs—"

"And slashed tires," Jesse added.

She nodded. "And slashed tires. Which, frankly, could all be about you coming back to town and be somebody's misguided idea of how to get you to leave." She paused and leaned back to poke his chest for emphasis. "Or it could have nothing to do with you—and everything to do with Tony."

She thrust the postcard at him. Watched as he turned it over, studied the postmark. She waited but he didn't say a word, merely clenched his jaw and handed it back to her.

"Go away and let me get this place cleaned up." He turned his back on her, so she walked to the door, not quite sure what had just happened.

She had one foot over the threshold when he said, "Be careful, Sasha. It's obvious things in this little town are not what they seem."

Sasha stepped back out into the sunshine, Bella at her side, and scanned the fishermen milling about the docks, most of whom she'd known forever. She tried to mesh this scene with everything that had happened recently and worried that maybe Money-boy had it right.

All she had to do was figure out what to do about it.

Sasha went back up to the house to check on Mama. She met Blaze in the hallway. "How's Mama today?"

Blaze just shrugged and kept walking.

"Blaze, wait." She stopped, but wouldn't turn around. "Are you OK?"

Sasha heard a sniff and a mumbled, "Fine."

Sasha sighed and walked up behind her, unsure what to say. "It's tough stuff to watch the people you care about hurt."

Blaze turned at that, accusation in every line of her body. "How would you know? You never sit with Mama, never see the hurt."

Sasha barely kept from flinching at the punch of truth. "I've been doing what Mama asked me to do and helping Pop with the marina. Which Mama also asked."

"You're scared. So you avoid her."

Sasha forced herself to meet her eyes. "That, too. You're doing the tough stuff, sitting with Mama."

Blaze wiped tears from her eyes and streaked black mascara all over her face. "The new meds are worse than the last ones. She's puking all the time."

"Do you want me to go sit with her for a while?"

Blaze shook her head. "She's asleep right now. I'll be in my room so I can hear her when she wakes up." She looked over at where Bella had fallen asleep in the middle of the hallway. "She seems weird today. Is she OK?"

Sasha debated how much to say. "I think she'll be fine. My guess is she got into something last night she shouldn't have." Which was true, to a point. "You didn't see or hear anything strange late last night, did you?"

Her eyes behind the dark mascara smears sharpened. "What happened?"

"Someone trashed the shed Jesse is using."

"What, because he was in jail?"

Sasha shrugged. "We don't know. Just that folks haven't exactly rolled out the welcome mat."

"I hate this stupid town," Blaze muttered, and stormed off.

Jesse had the shed and all his tools almost put back the way they were when Sal walked in. He eyed the pile of trash near the door and stepped over to the workbench where Jesse was wiping down his tools.

"Sasha said someone made a mess in here last night."

Jesse glanced over his shoulder. "Appears so."

"Did they take anything?"

"Nope. Not as far as I can tell. Just tore the place up."

"Did you want me to, ah, call the cops, see if they can figure out who did it?"

Jesse turned and leaned against the workbench, arms propped behind him. "Cops aren't high on my list of favorite people right now. Besides, there isn't much they can do. I got a phone call and forgot to lock up."

Sal nodded, removed his fisherman's cap, and scrubbed a hand over his head.

"You're probably right. Not much they can do." He put his cap back on and paced the room once, twice, and Jesse wondered how long it would take before he worked up the courage to say whatever he'd come to say.

Sal stopped, cleared his throat, and looked at a point beyond Jesse's shoulder as he spoke. "Look, Jesse, I know you own part of the marina, but in light of the circumstances, it would be better if you took your boat and set up shop somewhere else. It will take me a while, but I'll come up with the money to buy you out. "

Jesse didn't move, but his heart jumped into overdrive. He couldn't go anywhere else, not and have a prayer of winning that race. Not only would he have to find dockage at another marina—at a price he could afford, which meant free—but he'd probably have to find a place to live, too, or spend a fortune commuting. Which he couldn't afford, either. And not many places would have a shed like this to work in. He couldn't leave. Not yet.

"Sal, I understand what you're saying, I really do. But—"

"I don't want any trouble, Jesse. You understand that, right? With Rosa's treatments and all, I can't risk things happening here."

Something about the way he phrased it tripped Jesse's radar. "You afraid local folks won't leave it alone? Won't leave me alone?"

Sal started pacing again. "I can't say for sure. That's what worries me. Safe Harbor Marina is a safe place, a family place. Tourist business is just starting to pick up again after a long dry spell. I can't risk our reputation."

"Looks like we have a problem then, Sal, because I'm not leaving. Every penny I have is tied into this boat and my truck. I'm staying until after the big race. I need to win that race. The prize money will help me repay a debt to a good friend. If you still want me gone after that, I'll consider it. But not before."

Sal rubbed the back of his neck. "I'd rather you not go at all, but I don't see as how I have a choice. I have to protect my family and my business."

"Unfortunately for you, it's partly my business, too. I know most folks don't realize that. I'll do my best to keep a low profile, but that's the best I can do."

Sal huffed out an almost-laugh. "You are many things, boy. Invisible isn't one of them."

He walked to the door, paused, and looked back over his shoulder. "You sure I can't convince you to go?"

"Nope, sorry."

"That's what I was afraid of." Sal sighed and left. Jesse watched him go, eyes narrowed. That had to be the oddest conversation he'd had in a good long while.

Sasha worked with Pop in the marina store for several more hours, helping charter captains restock supplies, admiring their customers' catches, processing fuel payments, wishing everyone a good evening. By the time suppertime approached, most of their business was done for the day. The last of the pleasure boaters were heading back in, sunburned and laughing, ready to head home or to the Blue Dolphin for a cold beer and a greasy meal.

Sasha finished processing the receipts and poked her head into Pop's workshop, where he carefully sanded a piece of wood for one of the model boats he loved to build.

"It's looking good, Pop. I've got the day's receipts tallied. Do you need anything else before I call it a day?"

Pop looked up, and Sasha stifled a gasp at how old he looked. Drawn and thin, without the zest for life that had always surrounded him. He looked beaten down. Hopeless. She walked over and wrapped her arms around him.

"I love you, Pop."

"I love you, too, Sasha. I—"

The marina's ancient wall phone shrilled, and Pop walked over and answered. "Safe Harbor Marina. I'm good, love. Yes, she's right here." He handed her the receiver and turned back to his workbench. "It's Eve."

"Hi, Eve. Hey, why didn't you call my cell phone?"

"I would if you kept it turned on!"

Sasha pulled the phone from the pocket of her shorts. *Oops.* She pushed the power switch and stabbed at the volume button to turn it down when it started chirping and whistling with all the notifications.

"Sorry," she muttered. "What's up? Aren't you still at work?"

"You were supposed to keep me updated on what's going on, Sasha."

The condescending tone grated. "I was going to call you later, thinking I'd wait until you were done working, and give you what little news there is."

"I don't want to be kept in the dark."

"Stop trying to control everything."

They both spoke at once, then Eve sighed. "So, anything new?"

Sasha told her about Jesse's shed and Bella, and when she hung up, she found Pop listening nearby, looking sadder than he had before.

"You girls aren't going to give up this nonsense, are you?"

For a minute Sasha just stared with no idea what to say. "Pop, we're trying to give Mama the closure she's wanted for so many years. Can't you understand her need for that? Just to know, finally, what really happened?"

Pop's eyes flashed and he thumped a fist on the workbench, making several wood chips jump.

"We know what happened. We've always known. He disappeared. He's gone. Our baby is gone, and he's never coming back. Why won't you let him rest in peace?"

Tension vibrated in the air. Sasha considered for a split second before she pulled out the postcard and held it toward him. He eyed it like a coiled snake before reaching out with a hand that trembled. He studied it a moment, and his shoulders slumped even farther.

"Where did you get this?"

"In the office, in the bottom of a file drawer. What's it mean, Pop? Who sent it?"

His head snapped up, and some of the old fire lit his eyes. "You had no business searching the files, Sasha. If you want information, you ask me."

"Since when? I used to do all the filing." She paused. "Had I asked about this, would you have told me?"

He sighed and looked away, scrubbing the back of his neck. "Rosa had a little spat with one of the local women, and things were tense when the other woman moved away. She sent this as an apology later."

"Why is it in the office? Did you show it to Mama?"

"No. She was fighting another bout of depression, and I thought this would make things worse, bring up another painful time in her life." He propped his fists on his hips, speared her with a fierce look. "I have been trying to protect my Rosa every day of our marriage. You may not like what I've done, but I did what I had to, to keep her safe. It is time to stop digging, stop making her suffer. I have had enough."

He turned and marched out, the door slamming behind him. Sasha wrapped her arms around herself as she grieved for Pop and Mama and the pain that never went away. She thought of Tony, the brother she had never known, who haunted her family to this day.

Somehow, she had to find answers without destroying the people she loved.

Jesse felt like he finally had the engine of *The Painted Lady* in racing shape. He wiped his hands on a rag before he straightened and stretched his arms over his head. Then he reached into the little cooler by his side and downed most of a water bottle in one gulp. He'd checked everything he knew to check, but until he fired her up and took her out for another sea trial, he had no way to tell if he had a prayer of winning this race.

Excitement buzzed under his skin as he turned the key and the engine rumbled to life.

"She sounds good, Money-boy. Purring like a kitten."

Sasha stood on the dock in shorts and a Safe Harbor Marina tank top. She looked about sixteen with her ponytail pulled through the back of her Safe Harbor ball cap, and Jesse fought an irrational urge to pull her into his arms and never let go.

She shot him a cheeky grin. "But can she go the distance?"

Dang if he didn't get stupid when she tossed out a challenge.

"Hop aboard and we'll go find out. Unless you're afraid." He let the words hang in the air.

"Of you? Puh-leez." She leaped aboard in one smooth move, and Jesse clenched his hands on the wheel to keep from throwing a fist in the air in triumph.

She stopped as though she'd hit a brick wall, spun around, and hopped off the boat, eyes full of apology.

"I'm sorry. I can't go. I want to, but I need to do something else first."

"Something like what?"

"It's a long shot and it might be nothing, but remember the guy Betty mentioned, Captain Alby? I need to go see him, find out if there's anything he can remember. He and Pop, they were friends."

"From what Betty said, he doesn't remember much of anything these days."

"I know, but in dementia, the long-term memory is the last to go."

When he raised a questioning brow, she added, "Got to know a café owner once whose husband had it. Learned a lot. It's very sad."

Jesse turned the motor off and tucked the key in his pocket before he stepped out onto the dock beside her. "Let's go see Captain Alby, and then we'll take *The Lady* out."

"You don't have to do this."

He kept walking. "I know I don't."

She grabbed his arm. "Jesse."

He waited, but she couldn't seem to find whatever words she wanted to say. "I'm helping you with this, Sasha. Deal with it." He took her arm and led her to his truck.

On the way to the assisted living facility just outside town, she sat with arms folded, pouting, as far as he could tell. "I don't like people telling me what to do."

"Me, either. But for the record, I simply told you what I planned to do. You can do whatever you want."

"Stop crowding me."

"I'll do my best. But I don't mind keeping you a little unbalanced, hummingbird."

Sasha didn't say anything else until they pulled up in front of a fairly small, U-shaped building. The middle section boasted a pretty courtyard, with residents sitting on benches or in wheelchairs shaded by live oaks, listening to the fountain splashing in the center.

They walked in the entrance and asked the heavyset woman manning the desk for directions to Captain Alby's room. She peered at Sasha over the top of her half readers. "Who wants to know?"

"Sasha Petrov, ma'am."

The woman's eyes narrowed. "I heard you was back in town. Heard you was stirring up trouble, too, same as always."

Sasha shook her head and kept her smile in place. "No, ma'am. Just wanted to pay my respects to a friend of Pop's."

The woman studied her a moment before her fierce expression softened slightly. "Poor Alby don't remember too many folks these days. Don't get many visitors, neither."

"I understand. If you'd just point us to his room?"

Jesse took Sasha's elbow as they walked. "Nobody seems to be rolling out the welcome mat for either one of us, are they?"

Sasha shrugged. "Story of my life."

He heard the pain behind it. "Maybe we could both change our stories a bit."

She glanced his way but didn't respond.

Farther down the hall, she stopped in front of a partly open door and took a deep breath before she stepped inside.

The old man sat slumped in an armchair by the window. He must have been a big man once, but now his clothes hung off his frame. Sasha went over to him and sat in the chair angled next to his. Jesse stood by the door, wanting to offer support, but not sure how.

"Hi, Captain Alby. I'm Sasha, Sal Martinelli's daughter. He said to tell you hello."

Faded blue eyes glanced her way, then darted around the room. "Sal. Gotta find fridge."

"Pardon?"

"Sal and Rosa."

"Right. I'm their daughter. Do you remember their son, Tony?"

Something flickered in his eyes before he looked away again and plucked at the buttons of his sweater.

"Gotta find fridge." He lurched to his feet. "Gotta find fridge."

Jesse looked over at Sasha, his own sadness for the man's plight reflected in her eyes. She shrugged helplessly as the old man started pacing the room, voice rising. "Gotta find fridge. Gotta find fridge."

Sasha tried again. "Do you remember Tony, Captain? He was only three when he disappeared. Pop said you helped look for him."

"Gotta find the fridge. Gotta find the fridge. Too many secrets. Gotta find the fridge." His voice rose with every sentence.

Movement outside the door caught Sasha's eye, and moments later a twentysomething aide slipped into the room.

"Hey, Captain Alby. You doing OK?"

"Gotta find the fridge!" he shouted.

The aide took his arm, led him back to his chair. "I know. It's OK. It's almost snack time. I'll find the fridge, OK?"

She smiled at Sasha and Jesse. "He gets like this sometimes."

"Is he hungry?" Sasha asked.

The aide shook her head. "I don't know. He hardly eats anything. But when he gets agitated, he starts muttering about a fridge."

Sasha stood. "We've upset him, and we didn't mean to."

"You might come back another day. Some days are like this. Others are . . . not as bad."

"Thank you," Jesse added as they left the room.

Back in his truck, Sasha stared out the window. "Sorry to have wasted your time."

"Time with you is never wasted."

That earned him a weak smile. "It's sadder than I thought it would be. Hard to see."

"I'm sorry he's alone. Do you remember him from when you lived here?"

"Not really. His wife was sick and he'd been taking care of her, so I didn't see him much. But when he brought her to church sometimes, he seemed like a genuinely nice man. Dry sense of humor."

Jesse couldn't stand to see more shadows in her eyes. He couldn't make this all go away, but he could give her a little reprieve. "You ready for that ride now?"

She smiled again, and this time, it almost reached her eyes.

Within minutes of arriving at the marina, she'd untied the lines and they eased into a truly spectacular Florida sunset. He kept the speed slow out of the marina and, with the tide low, made sure they stayed in the channel. Once they hit open water, he pushed the throttle and let *The Painted Lady* fly.

Sasha sat beside him at the helm, grinning. She tightened her ball cap and he flipped his around backward so it wouldn't blow off, then laughed when he realized they'd done the same thing.

Jesse wasn't given to sentimentality, but as he watched the joy on Sasha's face, he wanted to freeze this moment in time, capture it somehow so he could pull it out later and remember. She leaned forward on the seat, perfectly balanced against the Gulf's light chop, grinning as they sped over the water. She looked behind them and laughed, pointing.

He glanced over his shoulder. Three dolphins jumped their wake, playing in the waves behind *The Lady*. Life didn't get much better than this. When he looked back at Sasha and their eyes met, he thought she might be thinking the same thing.

Suddenly the engine coughed, sputtered, and died. After the third try, Jesse got it started, but it still struggled.

Sasha automatically took the helm when he moved to open the engine compartment. He used his flashlight to check connections and belts, looking for obvious signs of trouble, but didn't see anything. He poked around a bit more, then called, "Start heading back, slowly."

She expertly turned the boat toward home, the engine bucking like it would die at any moment. She flipped on the running lights as the sky darkened, holding a steady course back to the marina.

"I don't have GPS on her yet. Can you find your way back in the dark?" he called.

Her teeth flashed white in the last remnants of daylight. "With my eyes closed. Some things you don't forget. Besides, we're not far from the channel." Once inside, they would be able to see the markers.

He clenched his fist around the flashlight, his suspicion of sabotage growing by the minute. Still, when he looked back over at Sasha, he couldn't help grinning. She handled *The Lady* like the captain she had been trained to be. As a teen, he'd been incredibly jealous when she stood at the helm of one of Sal's boats, taking a fishing charter out for the day. Now, as then, she looked utterly calm, the mariner's cross around her neck glinting in the last bits of light from the setting sun.

He'd always thought of her as a hummingbird, the way she flitted from task to task and place to place, but when she was at the helm, a stillness slid over her that was absent anywhere else. She was on alert, eyes scanning, always watching the sea around them. But a calm filled her on the water like no place else.

It was full dark when they secured *The Painted Lady* in her slip. Jesse went to his shed and returned with a work light and an eighty-foot extension cord, anger bubbling under his skin.

Sasha looked over his shoulder as he unscrewed the gas cap. "Are you thinking what I'm thinking?" she asked.

He nodded and shined a flashlight into the tank, then used a siphon to suck up some of the fuel and check it.

He cursed and leaned back on his heels. He wanted to throw things, so he concentrated on taking several deep breaths instead.

"Water or sugar?" Sasha asked.

"Sugar," he bit out, too angry to say anything else at the moment.

"You think whoever trashed your shed did this?"

"It's the only thing that makes sense."

"Somebody really doesn't want you in that race, I think."

"Too bad. Because I'm going to win it." He saw something flicker across her features. "You don't think I can?"

"I have no doubt you can win. But this worries me. How far will this person go to stop you? I don't want you hurt, Jesse."

"I can take care of myself." He stood and moved in front of her. "My biggest concern is that whoever it is will mess with your family."

"What are you talking about?"

He studied her face for a long moment, debating how much to say. "Sal came to see me today."

Something about his tone alerted her, because she crossed her arms and waited. "OK. And?"

"He tried to get me to take my boat and go somewhere else."

"What? Why would he do that?"

"He's getting pressure from the dear citizens of Safe Harbor about my being here. It could hurt business."

"What did you tell him?"

"That I'm not leaving, at least not until after the race."

"How did he respond?"

"He didn't like it, but he didn't push too hard, either."

"It'll blow over after a while. People will get to know you."

"Do you know of anyone else in town with a connection to this race?"

"You mean, someone with a vested interest in you being out of it?"

"Something like that."

Sasha thought a moment. "No, I don't think so, but I could ask around."

He held up a hand. "No, don't do that. Just keep your ear to the ground in case you hear anything."

Footsteps pounded down the dock toward them. Blaze stomped in their direction, her usual scowl in place. "You took off. Again. And made Mama cry. Again."

"What? How did I make her cry?"

"Even though she's been sick as a dog all day, she got up and made homemade macaroni and cheese for you, because she said it used to be your favorite. And then you didn't show up to eat it."

"How could I have known that? Nobody told me she was planning to cook."

"If you had bothered to tell somebody you were going out for a cruise, we would have told you."

"Why didn't you call my cell phone?"

"I did. You didn't answer."

Sasha pulled her phone out and sighed. Sure enough, there was the missed call from Blaze. Along with another two from Eve.

Sasha looked up at Jesse, stricken. "I have to go."

Jesse watched them leave, then went back to work. It was going to be a long night.

Chapter 10

Sasha gave up trying to sleep just before the sun peeked over the horizon. Nothing kept a girl awake like knowing she'd made her mother cry. Her sick mother. Again. *Oh, God. Help me do right by Mama. Help me find answers.*

She got semipresentable for the day, then padded downstairs, Bella thumping along behind her. Once the coffee finished brewing, she took her cup and went over to open the bait shop.

It amazed her how quickly she fell into the familiar banter, how much she remembered about the shop's routines, about each captain and their preferences and the members of their family.

Two of her favorite captains, Demetri and Roy, came in together, bickering like an old married couple, Roy's two nephews behind them, egging them on.

"Good morning, gentlemen. What can I do for you this fine morning?"

"Turn on the air conditioning outside, will you, sugar?" Roy teased. "I hear tell it's going to top ninety-six today."

"Then you boys best get going so you can be back before it gets too hot out there."

Demetri elbowed Roy. "She's trying to get rid of you, you big lout."

"Didn't see her inviting you to stay, either," Roy tossed back.

Sasha handed Demetri his coffee and Roy a cold soda and nodded to his nephews, Al and Scooter. "How do you stand them all day?"

"As long as they're each on a separate boat, they're tolerable," Al, said, and everyone laughed.

Pop stepped in and slipped behind the counter to join her. She kissed his cheek as she reached past him for more coffee.

"Morning, Pop. You and Mama get some sleep?"

He nodded yes, but the dark circles under his eyes said no. "Morning, Roy, Demetri, boys. Need anything before you head out this morning?"

Roy leaned over toward Demetri and stage-whispered, "See, they're both trying to get rid of us."

"Only because having you in here is bad for business. You scare the customers away," Sasha said with a grin.

Demetri and Roy exchanged shocked expressions, then Roy turned to Sasha. "There is one more thing. We just got a request for a night-fishing charter tonight, and we have tickets to take the wives to some play or something in Tampa." He nodded over his shoulder and rolled his eyes. "The boys all have hot dates. Think you can take the charter out for us, Sasha?"

A little thrill of excitement passed over her skin, but she ignored it and plopped her elbows on the counter, ready to deal. "Depends. What are you offering?"

Beside her, Sal grinned. "That's my girl."

"What? No favors between old friends?"

"I'm only seeing this favor flow one way." She made a *give-me* motion with her hands. "You're going to have to do better than that, boys."

"Tough cookie, that one," Demetri said, shaking his head.

Roy leaned closer on the counter, and Sasha settled in for some serious negotiation. "How about half the fare and we pay the gas for your boat?"

She shook her head. "I get seventy-five percent of the fare, and I use your boat. Take it or leave it."

Demetri and Roy exchanged glances. "The wives would kill us if we missed the play, and neither of us is willing to take them alone, so I guess we have a deal." Roy reached over and they shook hands. He pulled a scrap of paper from a white bakery bag out of his pocket and handed it to her. "Here's everything you need to know. Family of four, tourists from Germany, never been fishing. Should be interesting."

Sasha nodded her thanks as she tucked the piece of paper in her pocket. Night charters were always fun, and the extra money wouldn't hurt, either.

Suddenly she realized the temperature in the shop had dropped and all talking had stopped. She looked up to see Jesse had walked through the door.

"Morning," he said, nodding to those he passed by.

He headed straight to the counter, and the grin that spread over his face made her want to drool, so she sent him a controlled little smile instead. "Morning, Money-boy. You're up early."

His grin faded. "Got a lot of work to do today."

Sasha poured him a cup of coffee and turned back to see several more captains standing behind him. Captain Doug, short, balding and skinny, eyed him from beneath his fisherman's cap. "We don't need no racing team here, Claybourne. Best you take that fancy boat of yours elsewhere."

Jesse turned and looked down at the other man, his face carefully blank. "I'm not starting a team, not yet anyway. Just racing one boat in one race."

Wiry Captain Tobias, who could be any age between sixty and eighty, spit into the spittoon by the door. "Seems to me that's one boat too many. We don't need your kind here."

Sasha glanced behind her, looking for Pop, and saw him fiddling with the coffee machine, head down as if he didn't hear what was going on. If he wouldn't say anything, she would.

She planted her hands on her hips and ran her gaze over all of them. "I'm surprised at you, all of you. Thanks to the gossips in our little town, we all know every single one of you has a thing or two in your past you're not proud of. Why shouldn't Jesse get a second chance, too?"

Captain Tobias crossed his arms over his skinny chest. "We don't need no jailbirds here."

"Who gave you the right to decide who's worthy to live here? If I heard right, you mortgaged your house *and* boat to pay your gambling debts. Does that mean you shouldn't live here, either?" Her voice rose with every word.

Across the counter, Jesse said quietly, "Let it go, Sasha."

She was on a roll, so she ignored him as she eyed the group. "You all ought to be ashamed of yourselves, treating folks this way. I'm disgusted with the lot of you. Now get on out of here." She made a shooing motion. "Go. And if you need something before you go, you'd best keep a civil tongue in your head while you ask for it."

A few captains slammed out the door, and a couple of others shuffled to the counter and made their purchases, heads down.

Jesse winked but didn't say a word as he set down three bottles of water and a bag of peanuts.

"Have a nice day," she said, same as she had to every single other customer. She waited until the last one left before she let out a huge sigh. "Stupid, pig-headed, small-minded—"

"You should have left well enough alone, Sasha," Pop said, coming up behind her.

She whipped around to confront him. "Seriously? Since when do we let people talk to our customers that way?"

Then she remembered that he'd asked Jesse to leave to avoid exactly this kind of situation.

"Jesse is a good man, Sasha, don't misunderstand. But our business depends on the local captains and their support." He heaved a sigh.

"And those drugs Mama is getting don't come cheap, even with the little bit of insurance we have."

There it was, Sasha thought with disgust. Principles shoved aside to deal with the practical. She could understand his reasoning, but she couldn't accept it. There had to be another way.

She spent several hours stomping around the shop, but eventually, the bigger question reared its ugly head.

Someone, probably one of the captains there this morning, had trashed Jesse's shed and put sugar in his gas tank. How much further would they go to get him to leave? She had to find out. But first, she had an overdue apology to deliver.

"Hey, Pop, you good here for a while? I need to go check in with Mama." She ducked her head when he sent her a reproving look. "I know I missed supper, and I'm so very sorry. I didn't know she was cooking, and—"

Pop held up a hand. "I'm not the one who needs the apology, Sasha. Go on up to the house. She should be up by now."

Sasha trudged up the path, Bella at her side. Why couldn't she get her act together and stop hurting the people she cared about? She never meant to. She just got . . . sidetracked. Distracted. Didn't pay attention. They got hurt, and she didn't know how to fix it.

Mama sat in her padded rocker on the porch, and she smiled when Sasha approached. Sasha crouched down at her knees, taking Mama's hands gently in her own. "Mama, I'm so, so sorry about last night. I didn't know you were cooking or I would have been here, would have eaten every bite."

"Not every," Mama teased. "I made enough for the entire week."

"Then I'll look forward to having some later. Thank you so much for going to the trouble on my behalf."

Mama waved that away. "What trouble? It is cheese and noodles." She leaned forward and cradled Sasha's cheeks in her hands. Sasha's heart contracted anew at how frail she'd become, how thin her skin was. "Besides, how can I not do a little something special for the daughter working so hard on my behalf?" She leaned back. "Come. Sit down and tell me what you've discovered. Is there any news about my baby?"

Sasha tried to smile. She told her about her conversation with Mary Lee and about talking with the divers at the Blue Dolphin. Mama listened attentively, but then her face fell. "There isn't anything new, is there?"

"Not that I can see, no. Mary Lee's story is the same as yours. She called you that morning at Helen's urging, and, well"—Sasha spread her hands—"you know the rest."

"What will you do next?" Mama asked. She leaned her head back against the chair, and Sasha knew her strength was fading.

"This afternoon I'm going to talk to those who were here at the marina that day. See what they remember. And then, before I take a night-fishing charter out, I'm going to gorge on your macaroni and cheese."

Sasha smiled as Mama's eyes slid closed. Sasha stood and kissed her cheek, then she and Bella slipped away. Too bad she'd ticked off all the captains this morning. Meant her chances of them talking to her were not good.

She walked down the dock and leaned against a piling next to *The Painted Lady*, watching Jesse work. As though he'd sensed her presence, Jesse's head snapped up, and Sasha snorted at her own foolishness. More like he'd heard her and Bella clumping down the dock.

"Hey, hummingbird, what's up?" He straightened, and as he chugged down water, Sasha fought the urge to sigh. Was there anything better looking than a shirtless, incredibly hot guy on a sweltering day? *Oh my.* He caught her staring and lifted a brow. "See anything you like?"

Sasha felt the flush spread up from her neck and scowled. "Just admiring the general scenery," she said, scanning the area.

He laughed and hopped onto the dock beside her. "What brings you down here?"

"I was killing time until the captains come in so I can talk to the ones who were here the day Tony disappeared."

He had the gall to laugh. "Good luck with that. Probably should have done that before you chewed them all out this morning. Not that they didn't deserve it."

She cocked her head at him, surprised to see a healing scar on his side. Without thinking, she reached out to touch, but he stepped out of reach. She drew her hand back and met his gaze.

"What happened?" Though she had a pretty good guess.

"Difference of opinion with some of the folks at the county jail."

Understanding slammed into her. "This is why you wanted me to keep quiet this morning. You don't want to draw unwanted attention to yourself."

His expression darkened, and he gripped her arm and pulled her close, his voice rough. "You think I'm afraid of a couple of local boys? Somebody tampered with the engine on my boat, fed your dog drugs. I don't want you or your family in the line of fire because of me."

She tried to lighten the mood. "Too late, I think." She smiled, but if anything, his expression turned even darker.

"Be careful, Sasha. Somebody is pretty serious about all this." He let her go. "Have you had lunch yet? I'll buy you a sandwich."

She shrugged. The commercial captains wouldn't be back for at least an hour, with the charter captains after that. "Sure, why not? I don't have anything else to do."

He put his tools away, then grabbed his shirt and swatted her with it. "You sure know how to stroke a guy's ego."

"Guys with an ego as big as yours don't need stroking."

He grinned, one side of his mouth kicking up. "Don't we?" He grabbed her hand and swung her around so she crashed against his chest. His mouth came down on hers all playful and inviting, and before she knew it, Sasha had opened her mouth and invited him in. Their tongues touched and teased, while his hands roamed over her back, easing her ever closer to his rock-solid frame. The kiss went on and on until Sasha leaned her head back to give him better access to her neck and locked eyes with a disapproving Pop behind them.

"Pop," she whispered, and Jesse stiffened and eased away.

They pulled apart, and Sasha felt like she had ten years ago when Jesse had given her her very first kiss. Then, as now, Pop had seen. And scowled.

"Don't start fires neither of you are prepared to put out," he said, then turned and headed up the dock to the house.

"He said the same thing the last time he caught us," Jesse commented.

"I know. But I'm still not sure what he means by it."

Jesse laughed. "Can't you guess?"

She socked him in the arm. "You know what I mean."

He nodded. "I do. Let's eat. I'm starving."

They climbed into Jesse's truck and headed for town, unaware of the eyes watching them.

When they stepped into the Blue Dolphin, all conversation stopped. Most of the captains from this morning hadn't returned to shore, yet the grapevine had apparently hummed along at top speed. They were getting the silent treatment.

"Funny how cold it can feel inside on a hot summer day," she commented, glancing around as they slid into a booth.

"We're stirring things up around here, and that can make some folks very, very nervous."

Sasha stood suddenly. "I'm about to make things worse. I'll be right back." She crossed the restaurant and sat down beside an older couple in a back booth.

"Hi, Mr. Hess. Mrs. Hess. How are you folks?"

For a moment, the tiny birdlike woman just blinked at her. Across the table, her husband, balder than when he taught her high school biology, pushed his horn-rimmed glasses farther up his nose.

"Miss Petrov. I heard that you'd returned to our fair little town. How lovely to see you. Rumor has it you're a boat captain these days."

Sasha smiled. "Yes, sir, I am, and I love it."

"Will you be staying in Safe Harbor permanently?"

Sasha shook her head. "I'm just here for a little while to help out around the marina."

"I heard your poor mother is dying," Mrs. Hess whispered.

Sasha shook her head. "Oh no, Mrs. Hess. She's fighting cancer, but she's a long way from death's door."

"Well, that's not the way I heard it," she sniffed, chin in the air.

Sasha didn't think shouting would help, but she wanted to be very clear. "You were misinformed, ma'am. My family would be grateful if you set the record straight if you hear such things again." She stared at the old woman until she gave a reluctant nod.

"So what can I do for you, Miss Petrov?" Mr. Hess asked, leaning forward on his elbows. "I've never known you to chitchat without a good reason."

Sasha would have protested, except he was right. "I've been going over the events of the day my brother, Tony, disappeared—"

"He wasn't technically your brother, was he, since the Martinellis never legally adopted you girls, did they?" Mrs. Hess interrupted.

Sasha didn't remember Doc Hadley's old nurse being quite this obnoxious in the past. "That's true, Mrs. Hess, but my point is that I'm talking to folks who were at the marina the day Tony disappeared, trying to see what they remember, piece together the events of that day, if I can."

Behind his glasses, Mr. Hess's eyes widened. "You mean there've been new developments after all this time? That seems highly unusual."

"No, nothing new, just trying to retrace that day."

Mrs. Hess thumped her bony fist on the table. "She's dying, I'm sure of it."

"She's not dying!" Sasha's voice carried farther than she expected in the restaurant's silence. She leaned closer and lowered her voice. "She's not dying, OK?" She turned back to Mr. Hess. "Could you tell me what you remember about that day?"

"Of course. It was hot, I remember that. I'd been helping Captain Barry with fishing charters, acting as first mate. We weren't there at the time Tony, ah, disappeared. We were out with a family on a half-day charter. They were from England, I believe. They came back looking like boiled lobsters, but they had a wonderful time."

"What time did you get back?" Sasha knew how long the half-day charters went, but she wanted to see how much detail he recalled.

"We arrived just before noon, about eleven fifty, to be precise. One of the children had started feeling queasy, so we headed back a few minutes early."

"What was it like at the marina when you got there?"

"Chaos, utter chaos. The town's two police cars, the fire truck, and the EMT vehicle blocked all access, and people were running all over, peering into the water, under the docks, calling Tony's name." He swallowed and met her eyes, pain visible in his. "And above it all, your mother, running back and forth shouting Tony's name with a kind of desperation that still gives me chills."

Sasha looked away for a moment, tried to close out the scene, but it didn't work. "What were the police doing?"

"They were doing the same thing as everyone else when we got there. Searching. Everyone figured he'd somehow wandered out of the yard and fallen in the water. Otis Monroe, who hadn't been elected police chief yet, arrived about the time we did, and got the other officers started interviewing those who were there at the time. By this time, word had gotten out, and folks from town were showing up on the run, trying to help." He looked off into the distance for a moment. "Even given the gravity of the situation, seeing how the community came together—it was moving." He shrugged. "It was one of the reasons we stayed in Safe Harbor. This community cares about each other." He paused again. "Although, now that I think back . . ."

His voice trailed off, and Sasha leaned forward, waiting. "What was different, Mr. Hess?" She said it quietly, not wanting to startle him from whatever he was seeing in his mind's eye.

He shook his head as if to clear it, then met her eyes. "It was strange, really. While half the town seemed to be rushing to the marina, one vehicle was headed away from the marina."

Sasha tried to curb her impatience. "Do you remember when that was, what kind of car?"

"It was shortly after we arrived, in the midst of the chaos, as it were. Let's see, it was a Chevrolet, I think. A large vehicle. Gray."

The chief had also mentioned a car leaving. Was this the same one?

"It wasn't a police car, was it?"

"Oh no. All of those were clearly marked. But it might have been the same type. Perhaps a Crown Victoria. I don't know that it means anything. I just found it odd that it was headed away, when everyone else was headed to the marina."

"Did you get a glimpse of the driver? Any impression if they were male or female?" Sasha knew it was a long shot, but she had to ask.

"No, nothing like that. I was too far away." He spread his hands. "I wish there was something else I can tell you, but it all happened so long ago."

"Was anyone acting, I don't know, odd in any way? Strange, given the circumstances?"

Mr. Hess cocked his head, sunlight glinting off his thick glasses. "Not really, except . . ." He trailed off again, and his expression turned sheepish, uncertain. "I know people handle grief and anxiety differently, but to me, the strangest thing that day was Sal's behavior."

Sasha reared back, unsure what to say. "Please tell me what you mean, sir."

"Well, as I said, your mother was in a total panic, running hither and yon, screaming Tony's name. Sal was, too. For a while. After the first hour or so, while the police started talking to everyone there, he just sort of . . . stopped. I saw him slumped on the bench outside the bait shop, face in his hands, hunched over, just sobbing. It was like he'd given up. But to me"—he sent her a quick glance, shrugged—"it seemed like it was much too soon for that. The search was just getting started."

Thoughts swirled in Sasha's mind, tangling with all sorts of questions. But they would have to wait. "You weren't there that day, Mrs. Hess?"

She snorted, a very unladylike sound from someone who always dressed so primly. She reached up with a bony hand and fluffed her white hair. "I don't get out in the sun. Does terrible things to your skin. You should watch yourself. Keep spending time out there and you'll be covered in that awful melanoma before you hit forty, mark my words. Why, a friend of mine—"

Sasha cut her off by sliding out of the booth. "Thank you both so much. I appreciate your time."

As she walked back to their table, she heard Mrs. Hess whisper, "I'll bet my last dollar her mother is lying at death's door."

Sasha ignored the old lady's words, more concerned about what Mr. Hess had said—and hadn't said. She'd have to see if anyone else had noticed the same thing.

She looked up and saw Jesse watching her, his smile getting wider the closer she got. She couldn't help smiling back. Nobody had ever looked at her quite the way he did, as though he saw past all the masks and defensive shields and liked her anyway. It was freeing.

And terrifying enough to make her hands shake.

She slid into the booth opposite him and glanced at the food on her plate and his half-eaten lunch.

"I was starved and Betty was getting impatient, so I ordered for both of us. You used to love their burgers."

Sasha inhaled deeply and popped a french fry into her mouth. Nothing like grease to help her regain her equilibrium. "Nobody does burgers like the Blue Dolphin." She had to use two hands to hold it. "This is so good," she mumbled, taking another bite.

She looked up to find Jesse watching her, heat in his eyes. An answering spark ignited deep in her belly, and she took another bite, smiling as she did so. His nostrils flared, and she felt his bare foot rub hers under the table. Just like he'd done in high school. The spark burst into flame, and she felt his eyes drawing her closer as though he were reeling in a snapper—slow and steady.

"Are you flirting with me, Jesse Claybourne?"

His foot traveled farther up her calf, and she almost jumped in surprise, especially when his grin grew positively wicked. "Me? Since when has that ever worked on you, Sash?"

He slid his other foot up her calf, slowly, then back down, and Sasha set the burger aside, determined not to squirm. How could something so innocuous be so intense?

"Aren't you going to eat that?" The gleam in his eyes said he knew exactly what he was doing—and that he was enjoying every minute of it.

She held it up. "Want to share?"

He leaned closer and they both took a bite at the same time. Someone snickered at a nearby booth, and just like that, the sensual spell snapped. Good grief, they were acting like a couple of teenagers at the busiest gossip hub in three counties. What were they thinking?

Sasha tucked her head down and polished off the burger, avoiding those knowing eyes.

"Ready?" he asked as he slid out of the booth.

She nodded and they headed out to his truck, the afternoon heat a slap in the face. He walked her around to the passenger side, but when he reached for her, she held out a hand to stop him, afraid suddenly of the wanting in his eyes. Especially since he would see the same in hers. This wasn't a simple lunch flirtation. This was Jesse, and she couldn't play games with him. Couldn't ever take him lightly. He mattered too much.

"What are you afraid of, Sasha?"

They stared at each other, tension crackling like palm fronds in a storm, but she couldn't move or speak. She clenched her fists to keep from reaching for him as fear and regret raced around and around in her head and made her dizzy. She thought of her father and that long-ago night in Russia, when he told her to stay home with her brother. Of his face when she happily skipped up to his meeting anyway, surprised at his anger, his fear. Of seeing her parents, dead in the car, just hours later.

What if she'd listened to Papa? What if she hadn't ignored the rules and done what she was supposed to do? Would it have made a difference?

Terror held her still. If she ignored the warnings and followed her heart, would her selfishness destroy Jesse, too?

"Sasha Petrov? Is that you necking like a teenager in broad daylight in front of God and everybody?"

The shrill voice broke the spell, and Sasha couldn't help a rueful smile. Imagine if they had been necking!

"Have to love small towns." She turned and saw Captain Roy's wife standing two rows over, hands on her hips, shaking her head. "Hi, Miss Mary Lee. You just heading inside? Hot out here today."

Mary Lee stepped closer. "Who is that you're . . . ooh. That Claybourne boy." She marched over and poked a finger into Jesse's chest. "You leave that girl alone, Jesse. And while you're at it, you can take yourself off back to Tampa or wherever it is you hail from and leave us alone."

Sasha glanced at Jesse. In high school, words like that would have had him swinging. "I reckon Sasha can choose her own companions, ma'am. Enjoy your lunch." He leaned closer to Mary Lee and said quietly, "Just for the record, I'm not going anywhere."

Mary Lee stood openmouthed in the parking lot. Then she spun on her high-heel sandals and marched off to the restaurant like a general heading into battle.

Sasha leaned against the truck and turned to Jesse with a little smile. "You've gone and done it now, Money-boy. Got the old biddies all riled up about my virtue."

"I like your virtue. I want to get all kinds of familiar with your virtue, just so you know."

Sasha laughed out loud. When Jesse opened the truck door, she changed her mind. "Are you in a big hurry?"

He shrugged. "Nothing that can't wait an hour or two. Why?"

"I thought since we're here, I might ask some of the shopkeepers what they remember about the day Tony disappeared."

He nodded. "I'd go with you, but I don't think you'll get anywhere if I do." He opened the driver's side door and climbed in, rolled down the windows. "I'll wait here. Take your time."

Sasha recognized the truth in what he said, but she still felt naked and exposed as she walked down Main Street. She approached Beatrice's Hair Affair and locked eyes with the owner through the window. As Sasha stepped through the doorway, Beatrice, a big lady whose tight gray curls hadn't moved since Reagan was president, blocked her path.

"I'm just closing up. Sorry."

Sasha looked around the shop. Four of the six chairs were occupied by women pretending they didn't see her and weren't listening to every word. The pink-smocked staff doing their hair were equally determined to ignore her. Sasha sighed.

"Look, Miss Beatrice, I don't need my hair done. I just wanted to know what you could tell me about the day my brother, Tony, disappeared."

Someone in the back stifled a gasp, and the silence grew louder. Beatrice opened the door and held it, waiting for Sasha to leave.

"That was a terrible tragedy that happened a long time ago. There is nothing more to be said."

Sasha studied the woman's closed expression and knew more questions were futile. "Thank you for your time, Miss Beatrice."

As Sasha stepped out, Beatrice added, "Leave the past alone, Sasha. For everyone's sake."

Sasha walked down the street, frustrated. Why did people keep saying that?

Down the block at Annie's Attic & Antiques, she had just reached for the doorknob when the blinds rattled down and the "Closed" sign appeared, followed by the lock snapping into place. Through the slats she could see Miss Annie, who'd seemed ancient for as long as Sasha could remember, staring her down through the gap in the blinds.

She sighed and continued down the street. She walked into Ned's Appliance Repair, but it was empty. "Hello? Ned, are you here?"

The smell of marijuana led her out the back into the alley, but he wasn't there. Everyone in town knew Ned smoked a joint occasionally to combat pain from injuries he'd gotten back in Vietnam. She went back inside. "Ned? I need to ask you a few questions." She waited a few minutes, but the empty feeling in the air persisted. He'd left.

She trudged the length of Main Street and up the other side, all with the same results. No one would talk to her. When she reached Safe Harbor Auto, she made it through the office before Barry stepped around a car he was working on to tell her they were closed.

"Come on, Captain Barry. I just have a few questions about—"

He held up a hand. "I know all about your poking around the past. I can't help you. It was twenty-three years ago, for heaven's sake. Let the boy rest in peace, and stop harassing people. Don't your folks have enough to worry about these days?"

She found herself on the sidewalk once more with a locked door at her back. She walked back toward the Blue Dolphin.

At the mouth of the alley that led to the restaurant's employee parking lot, someone called her name in a whisper. Sasha looked up to see Betty motioning to her. She looked over her shoulder, but no one seemed to be paying attention. Course, that didn't mean a thing.

Betty stubbed out her cigarette when Sasha reached her. "I know y'all were asking about Captain Alby the other day. Did you hear he died in his sleep last night?"

"What?" Sasha gasped, but kept her voice down. "We just saw him yesterday. His mind was pretty much gone, but physically, he seemed fine."

Betty clucked her tongue. "I wondered if you'd made it over to see him. I'm sure he's happy to be reunited with his wife, but it's still very sad. Thought you'd want to know."

"I can't believe it. He was fine yesterday."

Betty lit another cigarette, eyed Sasha through the smoke. "Strange, the timing of things sometimes."

Sasha rubbed her arms, chilled despite the temps. She met the other woman's eyes. "Do you know something you're not telling me?"

Betty looked away. "Just making conversation, sugar." She glanced over at the parking lot, where Jesse leaned against his truck. "Best not leave that one waiting too long."

Sasha studied the other woman's face, but she kept her eyes on her cigarette. "Thanks, Betty. If you hear anything else, let me know, would you?"

"Be careful, that's all I'm saying."

Sasha walked over to the guest parking lot, and Jesse offered a hand up into his truck. She climbed in without a word, mind spinning.

"No luck, huh?" he asked once they'd left town.

"None of the shopkeepers would talk to me, except to tell me to leave it alone." She rubbed her hands up and down her arms. "Makes me wonder what they're all so eager to forget."

"Maybe nothing more complicated than the knowledge that bad things can happen to good people."

She considered. *Maybe.* "Betty just told me Captain Alby died in his sleep last night." She felt him stiffen beside her. "The timing seems off, doesn't it?"

He raised a brow. "Maybe. And maybe it was just his time."

"Seems like a tidy coincidence, though, doesn't it?"

His jaw tightened but he didn't answer.

She decided to let it go for now. "Mr. Hess was at the marina the day Tony disappeared."

"He have anything to add?"

"Two things, both of them probably nothing. He said he remembered a car leaving the marina right in the middle of the chaos, which he thought was odd, since folks from town were showing up by the carload as the word spread." She clasped her mariner's cross, seeing the scene as it must have unfolded. Her mother's grief. Pop.

"Did he give you any details?"

"Not many. The chief mentioned the same thing. I wonder if there's a way to find out who had what kind of car back then."

"It's a long shot. Captain Barry would be the guy to talk to."

"Right, and he just locked the door in my face, too. But it's the second thing Mr. Hess said that's weird. He remembers seeing Pop sitting on the bench outside the marina, head in his hands, sobbing. As though while the search was heating up, he gave up."

Jesse looked over at her. "I don't think I'd read too much into that. People react differently. Maybe he just got overwhelmed for a minute and had to take a break."

Sasha heard his words, and they made sense from a logical, rational standpoint, but she'd always listened to her gut, and her gut was telling her that wasn't the right reaction for Pop. He would have been right beside Mama, searching, checking, frantic.

Unless he knew something.

Jesse glanced at her face and said, "Don't go jumping to conclusions, Sash. You weren't there. You can't possibly know what they were thinking."

"If your kid turned up missing, what would you do?"

"Move heaven and earth to find him. Or her."

Sasha folded her arms across her chest. "That's my point. So would Pop."

Her cell phone rang, and she fished it out of her shorts pocket before it went to voice mail. It was Blaze.

"Mama's having a rough day. Pop needs to take her to the doctor, so you need to man the bait shop. I said I'd do it, I know how, but he won't let me—"

"We'll be right there. Thanks, Blaze."

"Whatever."

Jesse already had his foot on the accelerator, weaving around slow-moving traffic.

"Thanks, Jesse," was all Sasha could manage. Too many emotions rushed through her system. Worry for Mama. Anxiety about Pop and what happened that day. Jesse himself. When he reached over and took her hand, that simple connection centered her more than she ever thought possible.

But she couldn't start relying on him. Or let him rely on her. She wasn't reliable.

She hopped out the minute he pulled up in front of his shed. "Thanks for lunch. I appreciate it."

"My pleasure."

She took that grin with her as she raced up the dock and to the house, worry keeping pace with every step.

Chapter 11

Sasha sat on the bench in front of the marina's bait shop as evening settled in. The captains had brought their catches and tourists in, unloaded, washed down their boats and gear, and headed home. The afternoon showers had bypassed them today, so the air remained still and hot. She leaned her head back against the rough wall of the shop, trying to understand what Pop had felt that long-ago day. Panic? Certainly. Worry for Tony's safety and Mama's sanity? No question. Why the defeated pose as he sat here? Was he simply overwhelmed at the possible loss?

Or did he know something about what happened that he wasn't saying?

The minute the thought formed, Sasha pushed it away. Her mind couldn't fathom such a possibility. If Pop had known something, anything, that could help find Tony . . .

Her brain chased round and round the many questions, no closer to answers than before. When her phone rang and she saw it was Eve, she jumped on the distraction.

"Hi, Eve. How're things in the world of environmental wackos?"

"Saying that never gets old for you, does it?"

Sasha shook her head with a little chuckle. "Nope. Never."

"Your message said Mama was having a hard day. I just got out of a very long meeting. How is she?"

"She and Pop just got back from the clinic. They got fluids and antinausea meds into her through the chemo port, since she couldn't keep anything down. Her color is a lot better. Pop's, too, now that she's feeling a little more solid." She paused. "It's hard to watch, Eve."

"I know, Sasha. If I haven't said it, thanks for being there when I can't. I'll never forget it. We have to keep believing God's going to heal her." Eve swallowed hard. Then her voice brightened and Sasha heard the effort behind the smile. "So, anything new in the search?"

Sasha filled her in on what she'd learned from Mr. Hess about the unknown car, the reactions of the shopkeepers, the odd timing of Captain Alby's death. "I'll get back to it tomorrow, but tonight I'm taking a night charter."

"I didn't think Pop was doing them anymore since Mama got sick."

"He's not. Demetri and Roy hired me. Said they had tickets to a play and their wives wouldn't forgive them if they bailed. I haven't been out in the Gulf at night for a long time, so I'm looking forward to it."

She paused, debated. Eve would tell her if she was being stupid. "So, um, Mr. Hess said something weird." She told her all about Pop's odd reaction.

"Can you blame him?" Eve shot back. Then she added, "Though it doesn't seem like the right reaction, does it? Seems like he'd have been in the thick of it, frantic like everyone else." Another pause, longer this time. "Unless . . ."

"Right. Unless . . . he knew or suspected or . . . I don't know. It feels wrong to even have this conversation."

"You need to ask him."

"What? No. I can't ask him that." Sasha stood and paced, but even as she said the words, she knew Eve was right. She sighed. "Oh, God, Eve, what if—"

"Don't borrow trouble, as Mama always says. Just toss the question out there, see if he'll talk to you about that day. He never would before, remember?"

"Maybe he fell apart and is embarrassed at how he acted, or didn't act."

"You need to ask him."

"I will. But you can't push me on this, Eve. I need to do this my way, when the time is right."

"But I—" Eve cut herself off. "Right. OK. So, have fun on that charter. Catch me a nice big fish, would you? Fresh seafood without an insane price tag is hard to come by here."

"I'll give it my best shot."

Sasha hung up and saw a family of four headed her way. European, definitely, based on the too-short shorts on the father. When you added the varying shades of blond hair and Dad's sandals worn with black socks, she decided these were her charter. She walked down the dock to greet them and held out a hand.

"Good evening and welcome to the Safe Harbor Marina. You must be the Habershams. I'm Captain Sasha and I'll be your guide this evening."

The dad's eyes narrowed a bit, but his wife's twinkled. "You are *der Kapitän*?"

"I am," Sasha said with a wink at the woman. She shook the hands of a boy and girl of about sixteen and fourteen, respectively, who were wearing the long-suffering looks of teenagers everywhere.

"I don't like fish," the girl said.

"To eat or to catch?" Sasha asked. The girl crossed her arms, and Sasha thought she looked a lot like Blaze. "Fishing can be very relaxing, and if you don't want to eat your catch, I'm sure your brother would be happy to help you out."

"I'm going to catch a big von," he said. His accent and confidence made her smile.

"Then let's get this party started," Sasha said as she held the shop door open. "Feel free to get whatever snacks you'd like to take along. I have sandwiches from the restaurant in town, as well as water and sodas." While the family wandered the shop, she loaded the rolling cooler Roy had dropped off earlier.

She secured the cooler behind the helm and went back inside to collect her guests. As she reached for her captain's bag, she noticed an envelope poking out the top, her name scrawled across it in big black letters. Inside, she found a single sheet of paper printed with what looked like a black felt-tip marker.

> Stop looking for Tony. For your families sake.

For a moment Sasha just stared. Then a chill settled in her belly and spread through her entire body. Someone had threatened her family.

"Sasha? Hey, Sasha." Jesse touched her arm and she jumped.

She folded the paper as she turned to him. "What brings you out here?"

He studied her, eyes narrowed. "What's going on? You're pale and your hands are shaking."

She tried to tuck the paper back into the envelope, but Jesse took it from her when she couldn't quite manage it. She watched his eyes widen, then darken with fury. "When did you get this?"

"Just now, hence the shaking and everything."

"They spelled *family's* wrong," he said, pointing.

"So I've ticked off an ignorant meanie?" Sasha tried to joke, but it fell flat.

"I'm trying to get a sense of who wrote this."

Sasha wrapped her arms around her middle, trying to ward off the chill. "I know. And I'm trying to stay calm. " She had to think, plan, figure out her next steps. Make sure her family stayed safe.

Mr. Habersham appeared at her elbow. "We are ready, madam, whenever you are."

Sasha nodded and reached for her bag. Right now, she had a job to do. She held out her hand for the envelope.

"What are you going to do with that?"

She glanced at her guest, then back to Jesse. "I haven't decided yet, but whatever it is, it will have to wait until morning."

Jesse nodded. "Do you have all the gear?"

"Already aboard." She turned to Mr. Habersham. "Let's be on our way."

She helped everyone aboard Captain Demetri's *Fair Isle*, started the engines, and went over the safety features and equipment. Jesse waited on the dock, and at her signal untied the lines.

He hopped aboard just as she pulled away from the dock.

"What are you doing?"

He grinned, but Sasha caught the worry in his eyes. "I'm your first mate tonight."

She glanced over at the elder Habershams, who watched the two of them with interest, to their son, who looked out to sea with his hand shading his eyes, to their daughter, who already had her phone out, texting busily.

"Thank you. I appreciate it."

The couple whispered in German, and for a moment, Sasha wondered if they had been hired to do something to her while they were out tonight. She shook her head at her own foolishness. Still, someone had threatened her family. Maybe suspecting everyone, given the timing of the note, wasn't as crazy as it sounded.

"Did you leave Bella at the house tonight?" Jesse stood beside her at the helm, and for one second, Sasha wanted to ask him to wrap her in his arms and hold tight. She pushed the thought away. She couldn't, wouldn't lean on him, physically or emotionally. When she left—and she would; she always did—she didn't want to hurt him. She'd never considered how her actions would affect others before, since she normally didn't think that far ahead. But this was Jesse, and he mattered. Maybe too much.

She glanced up and realized he was still waiting for an answer. Bella. Right. "I left her planted at Mama's feet. Bella could tell something was up, so she wouldn't leave."

"Intuitive dog, your Bella."

Sasha shrugged, not sure how to explain. "Bella had been abused, was almost dead, actually, when I found her. She's seen me through some hard days, too. She has a keen instinct to protect and comfort. I was glad to see it directed at Mama tonight."

He stepped up behind her and massaged the tension from her shoulders. "Now you have me as your watchdog," he whispered.

The words touched her in ways fancy poetry never could. She stared as he walked over to Hans, the Habershams' son, and showed him how to choose the right hook and get a live pinfish on it as bait. Sasha finally found her tongue and started her tour-guide patter, surprised at how easily she fell into the spiel she'd learned as a teen. She talked about the different fish they might catch, spun tales of memorable catches of yesteryear that had Hans wide eyed, and explained the Gulf's moods and temperatures and the many varieties of sea life that called it home. All the while she kept her eyes out for dolphins, always a hit with guests.

The tip of Hans's pole bent down sharply, and he shouted, "I got von. I got a big von." The elder Habershams crowded around as Jesse helped him reel it in. Sasha stayed at the helm and kept the boat steady while Jesse coached the teen on the best technique to use. Since they'd left the marina, the wind had picked up slightly, and the boat rocked gently in the water, which made landing the fish more of a challenge.

Once they got the snook into the boat, Jesse held the measuring stick next to the fish while Mrs. Habersham took photos of the triumphant fisherman displaying his catch. Jesse deftly removed the hook and tucked the fish into the cooler.

A while later, Hans asked, "Where did you say the sandwiches were, *Kapitän* Sasha?" They'd been out about two hours, and by now he and his parents had all caught several good-sized gray snappers. Katie, his sister, wouldn't even look at the fishing poles, determined to sulk over her cell phone. Sasha handed out the food and snacks.

Katie unwrapped her sandwich and wrinkled her nose. "Tuna fish?" She handed it back. *"Nein danke."*

"Katie," Mrs. Habersham scolded and followed it with a spate of German.

"I'm sorry," Katie mumbled, clearly not sorry. Sasha dug in the cooler and took out the turkey sandwich with her name on it. She handed it to Katie. "This is the only other option. Sorry."

Katie nodded and took a tentative bite, then almost smiled. Sasha called that a triumph.

All eyes were focused on a pod of dolphins playing nearby when Katie said, "I don't feel so good," and promptly threw up. Sasha stepped over, grateful the teen had leaned over the side of the boat. She offered paper towels and a bottle of water to rinse her mouth. "Better?"

The teen nodded. "I want to go back." She turned even paler and leaned over the side of the boat again.

Once the dolphins swam away, Mr. Habersham looked between his daughter and his son. "I think we need to go back, *Kapitän* Sasha."

"I agree." She looked at Hans's disappointed expression. "I don't think you're going to do much better than that snook. The Florida Fish and Wildlife Conservation Commission is very particular about size with them. They have to be caught in season, and be between twenty-eight and thirty-three inches long. Yours fits right in that slot."

Hans grinned and lounged back on the seat, quite proud of himself. Mrs. Habersham hovered over her daughter. "Are you all right, Katie? Do you need something?"

Katie lay back on the bench seat, a towel over her face. "Leave me in peace, please."

Jesse moved to stand beside Sasha, and they exchanged a knowing glance. German teens didn't seem a whole lot different from their American counterparts. But right now, they had a more serious issue.

"Mr. Habersham, I'd like to call the local paramedics and have them meet us at the dock to check on Katie, just in case it's a bit more serious than seasickness."

The parents whispered in German, then nodded. Sasha used her cell phone to call it in and guided them back to the marina.

The paramedics wheeled a stretcher down the dock while Jesse hopped out to secure the lines.

Mrs. Habersham kept close as the two men examined Katie.

After a few minutes, the older paramedic snapped off his gloves and reached for his clipboard. "We'd like to take her in overnight, get some fluids into her, make sure everything is OK."

Katie immediately protested, and Mrs. Habersham asked, "Is that really necessary?"

The paramedic smiled. "Always better to be safe than sorry, ma'am."

As they packed their gear and prepared to transport Katie to the county hospital, Sasha stepped beside the gurney and asked quietly, "Is there any sign this might be, ah, poison of some kind?"

The older paramedic's bushy gray brows rose almost to his hairline. "Do you have some reason to suspect poison?"

"Maybe, but I hope not."

He eyed her sternly. "You need to call the police, ma'am." He scribbled on his chart. "But I'll have the doctor check for that, too."

"Thank you. I will."

Mrs. Habersham climbed into the back of the ambulance with her daughter. Once they were gone, Mr. Habersham eyed the cooler. "Would you know where I can find someone to clean the fish?"

Sasha set the cooler by the fish-cleaning station. "I'll be happy to do that for you right now."

She and Jesse expertly cleaned the fish, then loaded the Habershams' catch into a Styrofoam cooler filled with ice to take along.

Before they left, Mr. Habersham tried to hand her a hefty tip, but she politely declined. What if it really was poison? She hosed off the fish-cleaning station, then turned to clean and secure Demetri's boat, surprised to find that Jesse had already done it.

He leaned against a piling, arms crossed. "The girl got sick eating the sandwich you brought."

"I know. I brought it down from the house earlier and put it in the little fridge in the marina office."

"Anyone could have gone back there and tampered with it."

"Or maybe the mayo went bad. Or maybe she just got seasick."

"I'd buy that if you hadn't just gotten a threatening letter."

Sasha tucked her hands into the pockets of her cargo shorts.

"Yeah, me, too." She huffed out a breath and paced the length of the dock. When she came back, she stopped in front of Jesse. "Why would someone be that adamant that I stop looking? I get that the town wants to forget it happened. But this is taking things too far. The only reason that makes any sense is that Tony didn't drown. Or maybe he did, but somebody knows how, or why, or . . . something."

"You going to call the chief?" He kept his tone casual, but Sasha heard the concern in it.

"I need to let him know, at least. Though I'm sure he'll pass it off as someone not wanting me to bring up the past."

Jesse studied her face long enough to make her squirm. "It's more than that."

She nodded. "This search has folks running scared, and that makes me wonder why."

Jesse nodded and gave her a quick hug. "Go get some sleep. Lock all the doors. I'll see you in the morning."

Sasha went up to the house and peeked in on Mama, who slept in her recliner in the living room. Bella raised her head when Sasha entered the room. Her tail thumped once, then she settled down and went back to sleep.

Sasha checked all the doors and windows and went to bed, but she knew she wouldn't sleep. An hour later she gave up and went outside to sit on the porch, wrapped in an afghan Mama had crocheted years ago.

Had Katie simply gotten seasick? Or had someone tampered with her sandwich?

Sasha wanted to howl in frustration. How had this simple—though nigh impossible—search for answers turned dangerous? She wasn't worried about her own safety—she was more than capable of taking care of herself. Whoever was behind this had threatened her family, which meant they knew what mattered to her. Memories of the car crash that killed her biological family made goose bumps pop out on her skin. She pulled the afghan tighter.

She couldn't let something like that happen again. Not if she was alive to prevent it.

All the questions boiled down to one: What happened to Tony? Everything hinged on that.

She rocked for a while, head back, watching the moon play across the slight waves, listening to water lap against the pilings. She must have dozed for a while, because when she looked up again, the moon floated higher and slid in and out of view behind some clouds.

She heard a low hum and realized that was what woke her. A pickup approached the boat ramp, pulling an empty trailer. His lights were off, but maybe he didn't want to wake her parents. Still, not even running lights glowed in the darkness.

The moon shifted behind a cloud, and Sasha strained to see who was loading a boat in the middle of the night. It wasn't that uncommon, but the way this person behaved seemed stealthy. Like they had something to hide.

She stayed where she was, eyes trained on the water, but the angle of the dock kept her from seeing the approaching boat. She heard the boat motor shut off, then splashes as the truck slowly pulled the boat from the water and stopped in the shadows. Long minutes passed as she watched.

When the truck finally drove past, she strained to see, but all she could make out of the boat was a dark, formless shape, which meant someone had covered it before they left. She tried to determine the type of truck or catch a glimpse of the driver, but couldn't.

As the engine noise faded, she sat up straight. Wait a minute. Had someone stolen a boat? Maybe Jesse's *Painted Lady*? Not on her watch. She tossed off the afghan, tiptoed off the porch, and ran full out to the marina. But when she got to Jesse's slip, *The Painted Lady* rocked gently right where she was supposed to.

Just in case, she walked up and down the dock, checking every slip. Every boat was accounted for.

She stopped, tried to slow her racing heart. She had to get a grip or her imagination would make her nuts. Nobody had stolen a boat. It was probably just a local fisherman with an expensive boat he wanted protected on the ride home.

Except, you had to rinse salt water off a boat and especially out of the motor, or it would corrode in a hurry. Nobody covered a boat that hadn't been washed down.

Unless they had something to hide.

"Could be someone just doesn't want anyone digging around in the past," the chief said when he arrived at the marina the next morning. "Folks don't like to remember tragedy."

Sasha shot Jesse a triumphant look. He simply raised his eyebrows.

"What if that's not it, Chief?" Sasha asked.

Chief Monroe looked up from studying the threatening message and frowned. "What do you mean? That someone in this town actually had something to do with that little boy's disappearance? And then they poisoned your sandwich?" He threw his head back and laughed, long and loud. "Sasha, honey, if you believe that, then you've been gone longer than I thought. People round here don't do things like that. Leastways they sure didn't back then. Don't forget, my daddy was nearly chief then, and I'd just joined the force straight from the police academy. Got high marks in all my classes, too." He rocked back on his heels and dared them to contradict him.

"Good to know, Chief. I mainly just wanted to make you aware. The hospital says Katie Habersham is fine."

"I stopped by there on my way over. The little girl is being released. Doc says the culprit was most likely bad mayo."

He pushed his Stetson lower on his head, signaling the meeting was over. "I'll keep a closer eye than usual on all the comings and goings out here, and you all do the same. To my way of thinking, if you stop this search, Sasha, this will all blow over."

Sasha almost said she had no intention of stopping the search, but some little voice inside stopped her just in time. They bid the chief good-bye, and she glanced at Jesse.

"Told you that's what he'd say."

Jess muttered a curse and rubbed the back of his neck. "Yeah, you did. That is one arrogant son of a gun. If I remember right, he's just like his daddy."

"Do you think I should quit?" She searched his eyes, watched emotions chase each other. She'd always relied on her own instincts, but in this case, she didn't want to miss something obvious.

He spun away from her to pace. "I want to send you to Tahiti, because I don't want you—or your family—to get hurt by someone who's lost a few screws along the way."

She smiled. "Probably not a realistic option."

He shot her a scowl. "You're in tough spot. Mama Rosa wants answers. Sal wants peace. They're mutually exclusive. And now we have a local who's gotten really nervous."

"That's the part that tells me to keep looking. If there was nothing to find, someone wouldn't be trying so hard to get me to quit. If I get to the bottom of this, if I find answers, then both Mama and Pop will get what they want. Eventually."

He studied her face, then nodded. "Promise me you'll be careful."

His casual acceptance of her ability to handle this situation bolstered her strength in ways she'd never experienced. She had no idea how to put that in words, so all she said was, "I will."

Her fancy phone chirped, and she saw the email icon. Eve must have set that up, too. She opened it, read the message, and felt temptation whisper in her ear.

> Dear Captain Petrov,
> We'd like to have you join our racing team. We're in need of a backup captain, and your experience and recommendations indicate you may be a good fit for our team. If you are interested, please call us at the above number so we can discuss this further. You would need to start work at our racing facility in Ft. Lauderdale, FL, within sixty days.

She read the info several times while she let the possibilities sift through her head. The job wouldn't start for another couple of months. She could finish up here, get Mama the answers she needed, and then . . . go. New adventures. No responsibilities but the boat under her feet. No chance of disappointing her loved ones.

"Good news? You're grinning like a kid on Christmas morning."

Sasha looked up, and her smile faded. Jesse. Her other temptation. "Ah, possible job offer. Wouldn't start for a while yet, though."

"You're planning to leave." He tried to hide it, but she caught the flash of hurt.

She couldn't stay, not even for him. "This was never supposed to be permanent. You know that."

"I hoped . . . never mind." He leaned over and kissed her forehead. "I need to get busy on *The Painted Lady*. Taking her out later. You in?"

"Definitely," she said. Nothing cleared her head like flying across the water. And maybe, she could find a way to explain.

As she greeted customers at the shop the rest of the morning, several questions played in her mind: What did someone know about Tony's disappearance? How could she find them?

What had she seen last night? Was it possible it had anything to do with her search? The idea seemed ludicrous, but two days ago she would have said that about a possible poisoning, too.

None of it made sense. But someone in Safe Harbor had secrets they would go to great lengths to hide.

Her stomach churned. The bigger question was, how far would they go?

Chapter 12

Blaze stepped in front of Sasha as she went into the house. "I could do it without you, but it would be easier if you helped me with my psychology project."

Sasha hid a smile. "OK, what is this project I could help make easier?"

"I have to watch this stupid television show and then ask someone to answer questions about it."

"I think I could manage that. When is it?"

"Tonight at seven."

Sasha saw how much asking for help grated on the teen, so she smiled and acted like it was no big deal.

"Sure thing, kiddo. I'll be here. You're not going to make me run on a hamster wheel and then watch me puke or anything, are you?"

This got an eye roll. "Just the stupid show."

"Sounds fascinating. See you later."

"Don't forget."

"I won't forget. You taking care of Mama today?"

Blaze nodded. "Pop said he'd be back from the marina in a little while, but he hasn't shown up yet. I have homework to do."

"I'll go down and see if I can relieve him and send him up here."

"You haven't found anything new about Tony, have you?"

Sasha sighed. "No, not really. I've told you everything I know about that." She decided not to mention the threat. For now.

Blaze nodded and left the room. Sasha walked off the porch and down to the marina, Bella running off to sniff and pee before returning to her side. When she reached the marina store, she was surprised to find it empty.

"Pop? You in here?"

A trickle of unease skittered over her skin. It wasn't unusual for him to leave the shop, but these weren't regular days. Anything could happen.

"Pop?" She poked her head into his office, but he wasn't there. A check of the storage room behind the office yielded the same. She scanned the floor, making sure he hadn't collapsed again, but there was no sign of him.

She walked around the building and finally spotted him walking along the water's edge, rubbing a hand over his heart. She automatically sped up, cataloging details as she got closer. His color didn't look good and he seemed to be panting.

She took off running, Bella loping alongside, thinking this was a new game. She skidded to a stop, Bella prancing at her feet.

"Hey, Pop. How's it going?" She kept the worry out of her voice.

Was that panic in his eyes? "Pop? How can I help? What's wrong?" Sasha started a mental checklist of symptoms.

He waved her away. "I'm . . . fine." But he didn't sound remotely fine.

"Why don't you come inside where it's cooler?" She led him by the arm, easing him inside and into the chair at his desk. Bella sensed something because she started to whine and nudge him. "Bella doesn't think you're fine. Is your arm stiff?"

"Not . . . heart . . . attack," he huffed. "Just need . . . a minute."

Sasha brought him a glass of water and watched, relieved when his color improved and he stopped panting. After a few more minutes, his breathing returned to normal and so did his color. Bella relaxed, dropping her muzzle on her paws and falling asleep on his feet.

Sasha laughed. "Well, Bella thinks you're out of danger."

She expected Pop to laugh, but he didn't. His dark eyes pierced hers. "I may be. But you're not."

"What are you talking about?"

"You have to stop this search, Sasha. For all our sakes."

She leaped to her feet and paced to the door of the shop and back. She held his eyes as she asked the question. "Is someone threatening you, Pop?"

He looked away. "Why would you say something like that?"

"Because you just said we're in danger."

He waved that away. "That isn't what I meant." He locked his gaze on her. "But you have to stop this, Sasha. For me. Please."

"I don't understand, Pop. Help me see. Don't you want to know what happened to Tony? How can you not?"

He sighed and seemed to collapse in on himself. He leaned forward, hands clasped between his knees, his posture one of defeat.

"How many times do I have to say it before you understand that it won't change anything? There are no answers to find. Not after all this time. Digging only gets Mama's hopes up. And when you find nothing?" He met her eyes, his bleak. "Mama cried for months, Sasha. Months. This cancer treatment is hard enough on her. On us. The stress of this might kill her. All because you're too stubborn to stop?"

Sasha reared back as though he'd slapped her square in the face. "I'm not trying to hurt her. Or you. I'm trying to bring healing, closure. Why is that wrong?"

He stood so quickly, Sasha stepped back in surprise. "The cost is too high. That is what your young foolishness can't understand. This can't be fixed, and you can't fix it." He stopped, grabbed her arms. "If you love your mother and if you love me at all, you will stop this. Today. Right now." He shook her slightly. "Promise me."

Sasha's heart shattered into little pieces, though she kept her gaze on his face. How could she promise such a thing, when Mama had asked her to promise the opposite, to keep looking and never give up until she had answers?

"How can I promise that, Pop? You know what Mama asked me."

"And I'm asking you to stop. For her sake, above all else."

"You're putting me in an impossible situation. How can I make you both happy?"

"Do what I tell you, Sasha. In the end, Mama will understand you did it to protect her."

Sasha swallowed hard. "I can't," she whispered.

Pop shook his head and slumped back into the chair. He wouldn't look at her. "Then God help us all."

Sasha shook her head and slowly backed out of the shop. When she looked up, she stood on the dock beside *The Painted Lady*. Her heart had automatically led her to Jesse, her anchor. He looked up from the engine and studied her face. "What's up, Sash?"

She shook her head, not sure how to put what just happened into words.

"I'm about ready to take her out for a test run. Finally got the motor running again. Are you coming?"

"Absolutely." She needed to get away, clear her head.

As they headed out of the marina, she and Jesse exchanged nothing but small talk while the wind whipped her hair and the waves soothed the ache in her heart. She let her mind wander, figuring it would offer up a solution in its own good time. When Jesse put his arm around her and pulled her close, she let herself sink into the warmth of his embrace. For this brief period, she wouldn't think, wouldn't choose—she would just be.

Sal had known deep in his bones that Sasha would never back down. He would have to stop her another way. He stepped up beside her ancient Jeep and casually scanned the interior. Where would she have put that file?

He found her tote bag on the floor on the passenger side and pulled it up onto the seat. He fished around inside, and sure enough, there it was. He pulled out the file and flipped through it, just to be sure. Seeing the details of that day, spelled out in blunt copspeak, cut deeper than he'd expected. He tried to stay detached, to read all of it as though it had happened to someone else, but he couldn't.

The thing he remembered most was the agonized sound of Rosa's screams. Hair rose on the back of his neck just thinking about it. It was a sound he hoped never to hear again. He didn't know if he'd survive it.

He couldn't think about this now. Maybe never. He closed the folder, turned, and smacked right into Blaze.

He reached out to steady her. "Blaze, honey, I didn't hear you come outside. Did you need something?"

She scanned the folder he held. "What did you take out of Sasha's bag?"

"She asked me to get something for her." He hated lying, especially to this teen who generally saw far more than most people gave her credit for. He steered them back toward the house. "How is Mama? Is she resting?"

"No. That's why I came to find you. She says she's hurting." Those kohl-rimmed eyes filled with pain. "I couldn't stand it, so I left. I'm sorry."

He pulled her into a one-armed hug, the most she would ever allow, and said, "I understand. It's OK. It really is hard to watch." They climbed the steps to the porch. "Why don't you take a break while I take care of Mama?"

She stopped, studied him with those wide eyes that made him want to squirm. "Are you OK, Pop? You don't look so good."

He smiled. "I'm fine. Just worried is all. Go on, relax. I'll see you later."

Once inside, he went to their room. He perched on the side of the bed, noting the extra strain around Rosa's eyes. Her skin looked so pale, he could see the veins under her eyelids and the bruises below them. It tore at his insides to see her hurt and not be able to change it, not be able to fix it or make it easier. His job was to protect his family. To keep evil and heartache from his door. He had failed miserably once before. He couldn't do it again.

He plastered a smile on his face, leaned down, and kissed her cheek. Her eyelids fluttered open, and she clasped his hand. He brushed a gentle hand down her cheek. "How are you, *mi amore*? Blaze says today is not a good day."

"Hurts, Sal. Everything hurts."

He reached for the pills on the bedside table and helped her wash them down with water. He sat, stroking her hand until she fell asleep again.

Then he went outside to the burn pile, tossed the folder on top, and lit a match. He stood, watching to be sure there was nothing left, before he went to find Blaze.

He would let nothing and no one hurt his Rosa.

Not even his own daughter.

The sea helped Sasha breathe again, finally. Just as it always did. When life closed in and didn't make sense, being out on the water made everything right again. Here, things followed a pattern. Tides, waves, fishing seasons. There was rhyme and reason, order. True, the sea could be a dangerous mistress, and a gorgeous day could turn deadly in a heartbeat, but there was beauty in that, too. A power and majesty all its own.

Jesse had been content to leave her to her thoughts for most of the afternoon, something else she hadn't expected. Most people wanted to talk all day long, fill the air with words. He seemed as satisfied as she was to simply enjoy their time on the water.

She studied his profile as he handled the wheel: the strength of his jaw, the way the wind molded his T-shirt to his admittedly impressive chest. Just looking at him made her heart give a funny little twist.

As though sensing her gaze, he turned, eyes hidden behind his sunglasses but his grin unmistakable. "You ready to take the helm? It's too pretty out here for such deep thoughts. Time to feel, Sash."

It startled her, the way he read her mind. She smiled back and nudged him out of the way. He let her slip in next to him, but he didn't back away. Instead he wrapped his arm around her, nuzzling her neck. "This is much nicer, don't you think?"

She shot him a saucy grin. "Trying to navigate here, Money-boy."

"So navigate. Don't let me distract you."

His lips did something amazing to the sensitive spot behind her ear, and a shiver raced over her skin. She instinctively leaned closer and loosened her grip on the throttle. He chuckled against her neck.

"Why don't we idle for a while?"

Without consciously agreeing, she lowered their speed until *The Painted Lady* bobbed gently in the late evening twilight. Together they watched the sun sinking lower and lower on the horizon. Jesse continued his tender assault on her neck while his arms pulled her closer. Sasha could barely breathe. She felt surrounded by his nearness, completely enveloped and unsure where he ended and she began. It should have been terrifying. Instead, she felt . . . safe. Cherished.

Jesse turned her in his arms so they faced each other, and she wrapped her hands around his neck and pulled him close for the kiss they'd both been waiting for. As the boat rocked gently, their mouths met and clung, their bodies swaying with the boat's motion. Sensation pooled low in her belly, every nerve in her body came alive, and every thought in her head narrowed to one: *more.*

The kiss went on and on, Jesse's hands on her back, pulling her ever closer. Sasha heard a low moan and couldn't tell if it came from her throat or his. She only knew she wanted more. More of this delicious sensation of being loved.

Wait. What? Loved? Who said anything about love?

She must have stiffened, because Jesse muttered, "Stop thinking."

But the thought had lodged in her brain and wouldn't leave. She couldn't do this. Couldn't get her heart tangled up and then walk away without a backward glance. Not without breaking her heart. Worse, not without breaking his.

Slowly she pulled away.

"We should head back," she whispered.

He stroked a hand along her cheek as he studied her face in the deepening shadows. "What are you afraid of, Sash?" His voice was quiet.

It was the second time he'd asked the question. She still didn't have an answer, not really, but maybe if she told him, he'd understand.

"It's a long story."

Jesse smiled. "I've got lots of time. Tell me."

Sasha wondered where to begin. She'd never told anyone what happened. Ever.

"Just start at the beginning."

She took a deep breath and started talking. "You know I was born in Russia. One December night when I was nine, Papa said he had to go out, but told me to stay and help my seven-year-old brother, Alexi, with his homework since Mama hadn't come home from work yet. I begged him to take me along, but he told me not to argue. He said he had a meeting. That was all I needed to know.

"The minute the door closed, I grabbed my coat. Alexi told me not to go, but I ignored him. 'Papa won't mind once he sees me.'

"Alexi snorted. 'You just want to be near the water.'

"I remember grinning and saying, 'That, too,' as I pulled the door shut behind me. It was a game to me."

Jesse stroked a hand up and down her arm, and his touch gave her courage.

"I ran down three flights of stairs and out into the street. Papa was a block and a half ahead of me, so I hurried to catch up, but got caught by a traffic light. When the light changed, I raced across the intersection, eager to reach him. I knew he would scold me, but then he would smile and take my hand and take me aboard the big ships he helped load at the docks. I loved being near the ships, filled with grain and bound for ports around the world. Papa would tell me stories of places and people far, far away from our little world.

"I chased him across the next intersection, trying to catch up. He was almost to the port, so I raised my mittened hand to wave and call to him, when a man came out of a dark alley and stepped up beside him. Something about the way Papa shifted away made me drop my hand. I'd never seen the man before, and Papa seemed afraid, which made no sense to me. My Papa tossed bags of grain like they were feathers. He was never afraid.

"Once they reached the docks, I hid behind the corner of a building and watched. I couldn't tell what they were saying, but the man sounded angry. Papa kept patting the air like he was telling the other man to stop shouting.

"Suddenly the other man pulled out a knife. I gasped and clapped a hand over my mouth.

"When both men turned toward me, I ran, desperate to get home before they realized I'd been there.

"The man caught me, and I almost peed my pants. I kept my head down, panting from my run. 'Who are you?'

"I could barely get my name out.

"He grabbed my chin. 'What did you hear? Where are your parents?'

"My eyes automatically went to Papa, but I knew right away that was the wrong thing to do.

"'You know her?' the man demanded.

"Papa pleaded with the man. 'Please, she's just a little girl. She knows nothing. She'll say nothing.'

"The man shook me like a rag doll, then shoved me toward the street. 'Go. Get on home. And if you ever breathe a word of anything you saw or heard here, I'll kill you.'

"I only made it a block before I had to stop running because I couldn't catch my breath. I kept looking over my shoulder, but no one was behind me. I ducked into a storefront, huddled in a dark corner, trying to stop crying, to get enough air.

"Suddenly Papa was there, hauling me into his strong arms. 'Hush, little one. It's all going to be all right.'

"He carried me home while I sobbed on his shoulder. 'I'm sorry, Papa. I just wanted to go with you.'

"When we got back to the apartment, Mama's eyes were wide with panic. 'Oh, thank you, gracious Father, you are both unharmed.'

"Papa told me everything would be OK in the morning, but as I huddled in the narrow bed I shared with Alexi, I couldn't sleep. Mama and Papa were arguing in hushed voices, and the fear in Mama's voice kept me wide awake.

"I must have fallen asleep, because suddenly Papa crouched beside the bed, shaking my shoulder. 'Wake up, children. We are going on a trip.'

"We hurried into warm clothes and coats. Alexi whispered, 'Where are we going, Papa? How long will we be gone? Will we miss lots of school?'

"Papa laughed quietly, but I could tell it was forced. 'So many questions, my Alexi. All will be answered in good time. Come. We must go.'

"I glanced at Mama, who wrung her hands even as she tried to smile, and I knew something was very wrong. We tiptoed down the stairs and out to our ancient Citroën and climbed in.

"Alexi chattered nonstop, but Mama and Papa said nothing, just kept checking the side mirrors. Suddenly Mama gasped. Papa gripped her hand and kissed her clenched fist. 'It will be all right. God will protect us.'

"Something slammed into us from the side, and Alexi and I were thrown against the doors. The Citroën didn't have seatbelts. 'Children, are you all right? Sit back up, quickly,' Mama whispered.

"I glanced at Papa, his hands tight around the steering wheel, jaw clenched as he checked the rearview and side mirrors, and fear gripped me like a living thing. Papa was never afraid.

"The car hit us two more times and Alexi and I braced our legs against the front seats. Mama prayed quietly.

"'Sasha, my pet, this is—'

"Papa never finished the sentence. There was another loud crash behind us, and then the car started to bounce and roll. I heard screams, but had no idea where they were coming from. The car thumped and bounced, over and over. Glass shattered. I heard Papa moan."

Jesse pulled her close and kissed the top of her head. She blinked and came back to the present, surprised when she realized her cheeks were wet with tears. She turned to look at him.

"I think I was knocked out. When I woke up, there was an eerie silence. I called their names, but no one answered. The car was upside down, and Alexi was on top of me. Somehow I got out of the car and checked on them. They were dead. All three of them, gone."

Sasha swallowed hard and wiped the tears from her cheeks. She fingered the mariner's cross around her neck. "This was Papa's. It's all I have left."

Jesse gently stroked her cheek. "It wasn't your fault, Sasha."

Sasha studied his face. "If I hadn't followed Papa that night, if I had done what he asked, been responsible . . . my family would still be alive."

He made a dismissive sound. "You don't know that. You don't know what your father had gotten mixed up in. Besides that, you were nine, Sasha. A child. This was not your fault. My guess is that if someone showed up with a knife that night, the trouble started way before you got there."

Sasha's mouth dropped open. She'd never thought of that before. But it still didn't excuse her. "I do that, Jesse. You've seen it happen. I act on impulse and don't think, and people get hurt." She eased out of his arms and took the helm, turned them toward home. "I'm better off on my own. That way, my irresponsibility doesn't hurt people I care about."

"What about the search for Tony?"

She stared at him. "What about it?"

"Are you being reckless and irresponsible?"

Her head jerked up. "No. Although Pop might think so. I'm doing what Mama asked me to. I'm trying to do right by my family. To make amends."

"Then what? You'll leave with a clear conscience? Alone?"

"I told you I got a job offer today. Fort Lauderdale. To help pilot a racing boat. Be part of a two-man team."

He gripped her chin and forced her to look at him. "You want to drive fast boats, I'll give you a job with me when I'm set up. But that's not the issue, and you know it."

She wanted to look away, but he wouldn't let her. "You didn't kill your family, Sasha. And when you find out what happened to Tony—and I have no doubt you will—it won't undo what happened in Russia. And it won't make Mama Rosa or Sal love you any more than they already do."

"You don't understand," she mumbled.

"Oh, I understand perfectly. You're trying to earn your family's love, but you don't realize you already have it. You believe you're not worthy of love and should spend your life alone. Which is a total crock."

His words pierced deep and made the picture of her past she'd carried in her heart seem distorted, like a kaleidoscope that had been turned upside down.

He reached over and fingered the cross she wore. "The cross for faith, the anchor symbolizing hope. Your family were people of faith, Sasha. They loved God and they loved you. Don't reject that gift."

Sasha couldn't think, couldn't talk. Instead, she turned back to the helm and flipped on the running lights. As they headed back to the marina, Jesse stayed beside her, his words echoing in her mind.

It was after eight when they docked. "Want to grab dinner?" he asked.

Sasha shook her head. "I need to go check on Mama, see how things are going." She pulled her cell phone out of her pocket. Three texts from Eve. "And I need to check in with Eve."

Jesse nodded and pulled her close for a quick kiss on the tip of her nose. "It wasn't your fault."

She managed a weak little smile and headed toward the house, their conversation heavy on her mind. She needed to think, process.

The living room was dark when she got inside. She turned on a lamp and walked down the hall, surprised to see the doors to both Mama's and Blaze's rooms closed. She heard low voices in Mama's, so she knew Pop was with her. Some sort of screaming metallic sounds came from Blaze's, so she figured she was busy, too.

She went into the kitchen and peered in the fridge, wondering what everyone had for dinner and who cooked it. Pop and Blaze both tried hard, but neither were very good at it. She saw a dried-out piece of chicken, a shriveled baked potato, and a nice-looking salad. No sign of Mama's macaroni and cheese. She sighed, nuked the chicken and potato, and carried her plate out to the porch.

She rocked slowly while she picked at the food. She was almost done when Blaze appeared on the porch. She looked over at Sasha, shook her head, and kept going, slamming the screen door behind her.

"Hey, what's that all about? Where are you going?"

Blaze ignored her and headed toward the dock. It wasn't until she disappeared from sight that Sasha remembered. She'd told her she would watch some program with her tonight for a homework assignment. What time was it now? She checked her cell phone. It was after nine. Guilt slapped her hard. She'd done it again.

She dropped her plate on a side table and hurried after her. She finally found her on the bench outside the marina office and plopped down beside her.

"I screwed up, Blaze. I'm sorry."

"Yeah, well, I waited for you. You were too busy with Jesse to bother."

Sasha heaved out a sigh. "It was lousy of me. I'm sorry. I don't know what else to say."

Blaze hopped up. "Don't say anything. Just go back to where you came from. And don't tell people you're going to do something and then blow them off. That just sucks."

She ran back to the house, and Sasha leaned her head against the rough boards of the building. Oh, dear God. Would she never get it right? She meant to help, to show up and be responsible. But she didn't always remember to do what she'd promised. She let people down.

Disgusted with herself, she walked back to the house but detoured past her Jeep to grab her bag. She washed her dishes and took the bag upstairs to go over the file and call Eve. She'd get that much right tonight, at least. Her sister would no doubt have an itemized list of next steps for her to take.

She set the tote and her phone on the bed and reached in the bag. The file wasn't there. She leaned closer and went through everything inside, then upended it on the bed. Nothing.

Her phone rang. "Hi, Eve." She propped the phone between her ear and shoulder and tried to remember when she had the folder last.

"You're ignoring me again." As greetings went, it could use some work.

"Not on purpose. Just busy here."

"Bring me up to date on what's going on."

Sasha filled her in on the note and the sandwich incident.

"A threat? You actually got a threat? Is everyone in that town crazy?"

"Maybe just one," Sasha said, rifling the drawers of the dresser, though she was pretty sure she hadn't tucked it in with her underwear.

"What are you doing?"

"Right now? Trying to find the file Nick gave me."

"You lost the police file?" Sasha pulled the phone from her ear as Eve's volume went to screech level.

"No, I didn't lose it. I put it in my bag. I haven't taken it out."

Silence lengthened while they both considered the implications. "You think someone took it."

"Someone obviously doesn't want us looking into this, so yes, I think someone took it."

Even huffed out a breath. "Now what?"

Chapter 13

Jesse went back to his shed, Sasha's story on his mind. He knew all about regret, about trying to undo the past. Maybe he should have told her about Ethan's death, but it wasn't the right time.

He wiped his hands on a rag and shook his head as his thoughts slipped back in time. He hadn't realized what Ethan was doing. Not until the moment they were arrested. If he had, he would have done . . . something. Even tried to borrow money from his father. He'd been so wrapped up in their business, in proving to his father he didn't need him or his money, he'd let his friend down. It wasn't a mistake he would make again.

But right now, he had to stay focused. He couldn't get so tangled up in his feelings for Sasha that he missed some clue that would keep her safe.

Tied up in his thoughts, he didn't hear the whisper of movement behind him until it was too late.

He turned his head toward the sound and saw a wrench headed for his head. He reached out to block the blow, but it wasn't enough.

Pain exploded in his head, and he slumped to the floor. He heard men arguing, but he couldn't place their voices, couldn't distinguish anything but the throbbing in his skull.

Someone flipped him over, and he thumped his head on the concrete floor. Nausea threatened, but he tried to hold it back as he struggled to open his eyes. He wanted to fight back. Or, at least, see who was doing this. But he couldn't get his eyes to open.

He took shallow breaths, trying to gather his strength to fight, when something pounded him in the middle of his chest. Once. Twice. Three times.

A low moan escaped. Through the haze of pain, he heard more whispered arguing. So at least two men, based on the voices.

He put his palms down beside him, prepared to stand up.

Another sharp pain in his ribs. He turned his head and threw up.

The beating stopped.

The voices stopped.

Blackness descended. This time, he didn't fight it.

Jesse woke to someone moaning beside him. He tried to move, to see what was wrong. But then the sound came again, and he realized he was the one moaning. Everything hurt. He opened his eyes and slammed them shut again as sunlight poured through the dusty window and hit his face. His head throbbed, and when he opened his eyes and tried to focus, he realized there were three of everything. *Dang. Concussion.*

He tried to sit up and clenched his teeth against the pain. Since it had happened before, he knew he had some bruised ribs at the very least, if they weren't fractured. What worried him was how hard it was to draw breath. He had to get up.

He rolled to his knees and waited for the room to stop spinning before he crawled over to the shelves along the wall and used them to pull himself to his feet. One agonizing inch at a time.

By the time he got all the way up, sweat ran down his back and his breath came in pants.

He turned, slowly, and shuffled his way toward the door, using the wall for support. The room wouldn't stop spinning, but he couldn't stop. He had to get these ribs looked at. Make sure he didn't have a punctured lung. He couldn't race with a punctured lung.

He wasn't sure he could race with broken ribs, either, but he wouldn't think about that right now. For the moment, he just needed air. *Please, just enough air.*

He stumbled out into the daylight and turned to look for Sasha. She would help him. He just had to find her. But the dizziness grabbed him again and spun him around, and somehow he was on the wooden dock. He felt something lick his face, and then everything went black.

Sasha handed the man his change. "There you go. Enjoy the charter. Captain Doug will make sure you have a good time."

"Thanks. The family is looking forward to it."

They both turned as Bella barked and bounded into the store, still barking. She raced over to Sasha and barked and nudged her knee. "What's up, girl?"

Bella barked and raced back out, Sasha hot on her heels. She'd learned to pay attention when her dog acted like that. As she ran up the dock she wondered if the problem was with Mama, or Pop, or—

She skidded to a stop. Jesse lay facedown on the dock, halfway out the door of his shed. The back of his head was matted with dried blood. She immediately reached down and checked for a pulse. Thready, but there. She pulled out her cell phone and dialed 911, giving the particulars in short order.

Several people gathered around, and Pop pushed his way through. "Back up, folks. Give him some room."

Sasha crouched beside him. "Jesse! Jesse, can you hear me?" He didn't respond. She ran her hands over his body, looking for other obvious signs of trauma, but found nothing but the wound on his head. She didn't want to turn him over and put that wound on the dock, maybe causing further damage.

Pop crouched down beside her. "Any other injuries?"

"Not that I can tell. He's panting, so I know he's breathing. I don't want to cause more harm."

Pop nodded, and they looked up as the county EMS vehicle pulled into the marina parking lot. Two muscled men in their twenties hurried down the dock, rolling a stretcher.

They cleared the crowd and crouched beside Jesse. Sasha gave them Jesse's name and age and told them what she knew of his injuries. They conducted their own tests and quickly rolled him to his side, then loaded him onto the stretcher. The blond EMT looked at her. "Looks like a couple broken ribs, too. Do you know if he fell? Or if someone beat him up?"

Sasha stilled. "I really don't know."

Until that moment, she hadn't thought about how Jesse got hurt. She stood and hurried back into the shed, but saw no signs that he'd fallen somewhere and hit his head. And how would he break ribs if he fell backward?

She shivered despite the heat and went back outside as the EMTs started rolling the stretcher toward the ambulance. Jesse hadn't stirred.

"You taking him to County General?" she asked. When they nodded, she said, "I'll be right behind you."

She told Pop where she was going, instructed Bella to stay with Pop, and followed the ambulance to the hospital. She slammed a hand on the steering wheel, hard. This whole thing had gotten completely out of hand. Could this really boil down to locals who didn't want Jesse in their little town? In sleepy little Safe Harbor, this kind of violence seemed completely over the top.

It seemed far more likely someone didn't want Jesse in the race. Why should anyone care? She shook her head, searching for answers and coming up empty.

Part of her knew keeping her mind busy also kept her feelings at bay. If she let herself think about how close she'd come to losing Jesse . . . she rubbed a hand over the ache in her heart. No, she couldn't, wouldn't think about that. He would be fine. They would figure this out.

She would accept nothing less.

The pain came first, poking through the fog in his brain like a burning stick. His head pounded, and every breath made his ribs feel like someone kept jabbing that same stick into his midsection.

He couldn't draw a full breath, and panic edged in alongside the pain. He gasped, then made himself stop. He had to clear his thoughts, focus, figure out where he was and what was going on.

"Dear God, let him rest. Let him breathe. Don't take him. Please don't take him."

It took a minute to recognize Sasha's murmured voice. He'd never heard her sound so worried. He cracked open his eyes and couldn't hold back a moan at the harsh sunlight. He slammed his lids closed and within moments, felt the room dimming.

"I closed the blinds. See if that helps." Sasha's low voice came from somewhere near his ear.

He slowly opened his eyes again and found her crouched over him, fear in her eyes. "Sorry to make you worry." His voice came out scratchy, not like his at all.

She straightened and pasted a grin on her face, her phony smile trying to hide her discomfort. "You must have hit your head harder than we thought, Money-boy."

"You care about me," he insisted.

She nodded. "Like I do a lost puppy." Her expression eased into a real smile. Then she turned serious again. "Do you remember anything about what happened?"

He took a moment and looked around the hospital room. He raised an arm, surprised to see an IV running from it to a stand by the bed. He felt the back of his head and touched a heavy bandage. But even that small contact made him wince. He lowered his hand and stifled another moan as his ribs screamed.

"I was in the shed. Working."

He stopped, tried to think, to remember what happened after that. Nothing came to mind. Just darkness. And pain.

"Did anyone come by to talk to you?" Sasha prodded.

He tried to see past the darkness, but nothing penetrated.

The door to his room swung open, and Chief Monroe strolled in, his Stetson in one hand. "How you feeling, Claybourne? You up to a few questions?"

"Can't remember."

The chief pulled up a chair and leaned over the bed so he filled Jesse's line of sight. "The doctor says severe concussion and some broken ribs. And you did some damage to the knife wound that hadn't healed completely yet."

He'd figured that much out already, given the pain levels.

"I wandered around in that shed of Sal's you've been using. No sign that you fell. Doesn't make sense anyway, given the ribs. You remember what happened? You tick anybody off lately?"

"Big race. Lots of money for winner."

The chief stroked his chin. "I've thought about that." He looked over at Sasha. "You or Sal seen any strangers around lately? Anyone seem a little too interested in Claybourne's boat?"

Sasha shook her head. "Couple of charters in the past couple of days. *The Painted Lady* is eye-catching, but nobody seemed to take more than a passing interest."

The chief stood and picked up his Stetson. "You take care, son. If either of you think of anything, you holler, ya hear?"

Sasha waited until he left to lean closer. "Did you see more than what you told the chief?"

He started to shake his head, then stopped. "No. There's a gap between when I went into the shed and when I woke up here."

"Do you have any idea who would do this? And why?"

"The race. Who? No idea."

"What will you do now, Jesse? You can't race with those broken ribs."

He sighed. "I know." He paused, wondered what she'd say. "Will you do it, Sasha? Drive *The Painted Lady* for me?"

He saw the excitement that flashed in her eyes. Then it disappeared behind the caution he'd come to hate.

"I'll, ah, have to think about it."

"Why? You love flying over the water."

"You know why. I'm here to help my family. It would take lots of practice, and I can't be running off to do that when they need me."

"You can do both. Being here to help doesn't mean you can't do anything else."

"I can't be irresponsible." Before he could protest, she stood and placed a gentle kiss on his forehead. "I need to go. I'll be back later."

Before he could formulate more arguments, the darkness claimed him again. When he woke, a white-coated man stood at the foot of his bed, scribbling on a clipboard.

"I'm Dr. Gamble. How are you feeling, Mr. Claybourne?"

"Like I got run over by a truck," he mumbled.

The fifty-something doctor smiled, eyes kind. "Maybe not a truck, but you took quite a hit to the back of the head. Any idea who did that? Or why?"

"It's all a big blank in my mind."

The doctor scribbled some more. "You've got several broken ribs, too. And we had to repair the knife wound you got a while back. You also have some really ugly bruises, making me think someone kicked you. Hard. For your own protection, you may want to tell the chief who's angry enough to do that to you." With that he patted Jesse's foot and left the room.

Jesse let the words roll around in his head for a while. Every thought still felt like it had a fur coat over it. Finally something the doctor said clicked, and he lunged up in bed. Pain ripped through his midsection, and he moaned and fell back against the pillows. If someone beat him up this badly to keep him out of the race, Sasha couldn't drive for him. He couldn't risk putting her in more danger. There were enough people angry with her about Tony.

Reality set in, and despair washed over him. He would have to withdraw from the race.

He pictured little Adelaide's face and felt his throat thicken. He'd have to find another way to pay for her heart surgery. He had no idea how, but he couldn't risk anything happening to Sasha. He'd have to find another way.

Chapter 14

Sasha drove back to the marina, and as the fear wore off, her fury grew. She sent Pop up to the house to be with Mama, then paced in front of the bait shop, more furious than the day Pete had the nerve to throw Bella overboard. *How dare somebody show up here, in tiny Safe Harbor of all places, and beat Jesse to a pulp?*

She knew whoever it was had to have caught him off guard, or Jesse would have given as good as he got. There was no way he would have stood still for a beating. No, some cowardly slimeball hit him from behind and then, when he was down, kicked him, too.

As for the chief's handy theory about outsiders? Sasha snorted. Please. You couldn't bandage a hangnail in this town without someone commenting on it.

Bella paced with her, whining every so often. Sasha stopped and bent down to pet her. "Sorry, girl. I'm just angry."

When Eve called, Sasha picked up right away. She could use a little objective advice. "Hey, Eve. How're the crazies?"

"Still crazy. Sometimes right. So, what's new there?"

"Jesse is in the hospital." She had to work to keep the worst of the fury at bay. "He was working late last night, and someone knocked him on the head from behind. Then they kicked him enough times to break several ribs. Bella found him. He needed stitches and has a bad concussion."

"Dear God. Who would do that?" She paused. "Somebody doesn't want him in that race."

"That's my take on it."

"What does the chief say?"

Sasha snorted. "I don't know if he's naive or covering something up, but he asked about strangers around the marina. As though someone just breezed in here under everyone's noses, did the deed, and walked off. And no. One. Noticed."

"Oh, please. He can't be serious."

"I think he'd rather think that, and rather we think that, than point fingers at local folks."

"Then *we* have to point fingers at local folks. Who could have done this, Sasha? Who was around yesterday, late in the day? Who has made comments about Jesse's boat?"

"Who hasn't made comments? *The Painted Lady* draws attention. But I know what you mean. Nobody has been directly nasty, at least not to that degree. The local captains don't want any more racing boats here, only because it would mean competition for them if this place became well known. And we know people have made comments about Jesse's past. Other than that, I can't think of anyone who has come right out and made threats."

"What about the stranger theory? Anybody come through the marina in the past week who seemed, I don't know, off? Too interested, maybe?"

Sasha thought back and came up blank. "None of it seems connected or makes any sense, Eve. Somebody clearly doesn't want us looking for Tony, given the sandwich incident and threatening note and the fact my files were stolen. And Jesse had his tires slashed, some idiot put sugar in *The Painted Lady*'s fuel tank, and now this. Why would someone go to so much trouble to get him out of town? Is the race reason enough?"

"The purse it pretty big, isn't it?"

"Yeah, fifty thousand dollars. I guess that's motivation enough to get him out of the race. But . . ." Her voice drifted off as she tried to figure out what was nagging at her. What little thing didn't fit, didn't make sense?

"Sasha? What are you thinking?"

"I'm not sure. I think we're missing something, but I don't know what." She paused. "Jesse asked me to drive *The Painted Lady* in the race."

The silence lengthened. "I can't say I'm surprised. There's nobody else in town who could pull that off. Are you going to do it?"

"I don't know."

"If you do, I wouldn't let anyone know about it, given what happened to him."

"I thought of that." She paused. How to put it into words? "I don't want to disappoint anyone in the family."

"How would doing what you love disappoint anyone? Everyone is proud you're a captain, Sash."

"But I get distracted. Forget things." Though it was true, the admission didn't come easily.

"True. But one has nothing to do with the other. Families get frustrated with each other. We get over it. But supporting each other? That's something different." She paused. "You care about Jesse."

Sasha felt her throat tighten as she thought of how battered he looked. "I always have."

"I know, but be careful. Maybe whatever happened has nothing to do with this race and everything to do with his past."

Sasha had considered that, too, but she'd never admit it to Eve. "And maybe it doesn't."

"Has he ever told you what happened?"

"I looked it up online." How could she not?

"Either way, be careful, Sash. Pop and Mama have enough to worry about without this, you know?"

"I know. Hey, Eve, what's up with Cat?"

Silence hummed over the airways. "I have some guesses, none of them good."

"Drugs?"

"Maybe. I'll see what I can find out. Talk to you soon."

After she hung up, Sasha resumed her pacing. She felt like a jigsaw puzzle without all the pieces. She could see some of the edges: the search for Tony, the upcoming race, Jesse's mysterious past. But the center? How they all fit together? She couldn't make sense of any of it.

By the next day, Jesse couldn't stay cooped up another minute. When Dr. Gamble made his rounds, Jesse grabbed his wrist. "You have to spring me, Doc. I'm going crazy."

The doctor grinned and scribbled on the chart. Then he looked up, still smiling. "I think we can let you go, but only if you have someone to stay with you overnight."

"I'll be fine, Doc. I don't need a babysitter."

Sasha walked into the hospital room and smiled. "Hi, Doc. Hey, Money-boy, are you ready to go?"

"He needs someone to stay with him tonight. Just in case."

"In case what? You did a CAT scan and checked everything last night and today, and I'm fine, right?"

"It was a serious concussion, young man. Nothing to fool with."

"I'll stay with him," Sasha said.

Jesse looked over and saw her wide-eyed expression, as though the offer had surprised her, too. "You don't have to—"

"Hush, or I'll have the doc change his mind."

Within an hour they were in Sasha's Jeep, heading back to Aunt Clarabelle's cottage in Safe Harbor.

"How are you really?" she asked.

"I feel like I've been trampled by a herd of wildebeests."

"Really? Does that happen often?"

He started to laugh, then coughed and grabbed his ribs. "Do not make me laugh, I beg you."

"Sorry," she said, but she didn't look the least bit sorry.

Sasha kept a white-knuckled grip on the steering wheel the whole drive to Jesse's cottage. What had she been thinking? She wasn't ready to deal with this . . . this whatever it was between her and Jesse. Especially after she'd told him about her past. And the way he kept looking at her lately threw her off balance. These looks were different, deeper or something. Whatever this was, it scared her.

She pulled into his driveway, and he reached over and unwrapped one of her hands from around the steering wheel. Her eyes flew to his face, caught the laughter in his expression.

"A drive from the hospital should not be the scary part."

Her chin came up. "Who says I'm scared, Money-boy?" The response sounded like she was ten years old, but it was the best she could do. He could see through her way too easily. That annoyed her almost as much as her anxiety about her feelings.

"I promise to restrain myself from attacking you if you come inside and help me get settled."

He eased the door open and gingerly climbed out, inch by inch. She wanted to smack her own forehead at her stupidity. Here she was worried about attraction while he was doubled over in pain. The idea of Jesse hurting made her furious all over again. When she left here, she planned on having a little chat with Chief Monroe. *Stranger, my eye. Somebody has to pay for this.*

She reached his side of the Jeep just in time to see him sway on his feet. He didn't protest when she carefully wrapped an arm around his waist and helped him up the overgrown walk, up two steps onto the porch, and finally into the living room, where he eased into Aunt Clarabelle's old pink recliner. He moaned and the recliner creaked, and Sasha wondered if they'd both end up on the floor.

His eyes slid closed, and she stood in the living room, trying to decide what to do. Go or stay? She really wanted to talk to the chief. But she didn't want to leave him alone. He cracked one eye open.

"Go, already. I'm fine."

She looked closely and saw fresh pain etched in his face. The meds they'd picked up at the pharmacy on the way here were still clutched in her hand.

"It's time for your pills, right?"

She took his nod for assent, went back to Clarabelle's fussy kitchen, and fetched a glass of water. She set it and the pills beside him, but he didn't stir. She gently touched his shoulder.

"Money-boy. Pop a pill and then you can sleep, OK? You need to stay ahead of the pain if you can."

He shook his head, but took the pill and swallowed it. His eyes were closed again before his head hit the headrest. She grabbed an afghan crocheted in red, white, and blue from the back of the flowered sofa and tucked it around him. Then she leaned over and kissed his forehead. "I'll be back in a little while."

"Thanks," he mumbled. "My hummingbird."

Sasha smiled, then quietly let herself out the door without locking it so she could get back in.

All the way back to town, she worried she should have locked it, because what if whatever crazy person beat him up followed him home to finish the job? When she realized she was panting as she drove, she took a deep breath.

"Calm down, you idiot. Who is going to attack him in his house on a sunny afternoon in Safe Harbor?"

Minutes later, she marched into the police station, demanding to see the chief.

"I'm sorry, Ms. Petrov," the officer manning the desk said. "He left a little bit ago."

"So maybe you can help me. Where are you with the investigation into Jesse Claybourne's attack?"

He looked blank for a moment. "Oh, you mean your friend that got hit in the head at your marina?"

"Right. Bad concussion, stitches, broken ribs. What's being done to find whoever did this?"

"We're doing everything we can, Sasha," the chief said from behind her. She hadn't heard him come in.

"Really? What kind of everything are you doing?"

He folded his arms over his barrel chest, obviously not liking her tone of voice. "We do not divulge the details of an ongoing investigation."

Sasha made her pose mirror his. "So there is an actual investigation?"

"Of course. We take care of our own in this town." He paused, cleared his throat. "Though I don't hold out much hope of finding whoever did this."

"Why is that?"

"Nobody reported seeing any strangers in the vicinity at the time of the attack—or any locals, either," he added.

"It happened at night. How many people did you think were at the marina at that time? Did you interview my family?"

"Now, Sasha, your family has enough to worry about right now. I spoke to Sal, but he didn't see anything. The young girl was asleep, as was your Mama, from what he said."

She eyed him. "You're not even going to try to solve this, are you?"

"Listen, young lady, this is a small department, but we know our jobs and we do our best. Now if you'll excuse me, I need to get back to work."

Sasha huffed out a breath as he walked away. She looked over at the other officer, but he was on the phone.

She stopped at the marina office to see Pop.

"Sasha, my girl, how's Jesse?" He wrapped her in a big hug, and just like that, some of her anxiety fell away.

"He's home resting. The chief says he talked to you. You didn't see anyone out here, did you?"

He raised bushy eyebrows. "Why wouldn't I have told him, if I had?"

She shrugged and paced the small office. "The whole thing just doesn't sit right is all. The chief all but said it had to be a stranger, and since nobody saw anything, well, what are you going to do?" She pushed back a strand of hair that had come loose from her ponytail. "It's making me crazy that he doesn't seem to be taking this seriously."

"Taking it seriously and finding answers may be two different things, Sasha."

She turned and looked at him. "You may be right." She leaned over and kissed his cheek. "I'm going to go make supper, then take some over to Jesse. How's Mama today?"

He shrugged and wouldn't meet her eyes. Which meant she was having one of her bad days. They usually happened after a treatment. "I love you, Pop."

"I love you, too, Sasha, *tesora mia*."

She walked up to the house and found Blaze and Mama in the living room, the ceiling fan circling slowly, a talk show on the television. Mama's eyes were closed as she dozed in her recliner. Sasha slid onto the sofa next to Blaze. "How's she doing?"

Blaze shrugged and looked away. "How's Jesse?"

"He just got out of the hospital. I figured I'd cook supper, then take some to him, make sure he's OK. I saw some chicken in the freezer."

Blaze made a face.

"What's wrong with chicken? I can cook chicken."

"Is that all you can cook?"

Sasha stood. "That and chili, maybe soup. So, sue me. Besides, I figure it's better than takeout. Or another one of the frozen casseroles the church ladies keep bringing."

"The church ladies are nice. And we don't have takeout in this stupid town."

Sasha grinned over her shoulder. "My point exactly. Chicken it is."

Blaze cleaned her plate, but Mama barely took a few bites of dinner. Every single day she seemed to be shrinking a little bit more, drifting a tiny bit farther away, and it made Sasha want to scream. Or run and hide. Sasha packed up dinner for Jesse and left Bella with Blaze. Or rather, Bella had sensed Blaze's pain and wouldn't leave her side, so Sasha left her home. Which was just as well, or she would've had to keep her from eating the overcooked chicken on the way to Jesse's.

The lights were on inside Jesse's place when she arrived, giving the pink cottage a fairy-tale look. She knocked once on the screen and poked her head around the door. "OK to come in?"

Jesse sat up in the recliner, looking much better than he had earlier. She stepped inside, plate in hand. "Please tell me that's food and that it's for me," he said.

"Yes, and yes, though Blaze did not give it rave reviews."

"I'm hungry enough to gnaw a leg off the table, so I'll take it."

She took hunger as a good sign. She went to the kitchen for a napkin, water, and silverware, then sat down opposite him on the couch. He turned down the volume on the small television set on a frilly table across the room.

"I'm surprised that old thing even has a remote."

"I got it for Aunt Clarabelle a couple Christmases ago. It came with a larger TV, but she didn't want it. Told me to leave the remote and take the TV back."

Sasha laughed. "That sounds like your aunt Clarabelle." She eyed him as he dug into the baked chicken and rice. "You look a whole lot better than you did earlier."

"I slept most of the day." He chewed, then chewed some more, and finally took a gulp of water and swallowed. "It's a little—"

"Dry? Overcooked?" Sasha shrugged. "Martha Stewart I am not. Like I told Blaze, this is a take-it-or-leave-it proposition."

He took another mouthful, chewed, swallowed, and smiled. "I'll take it. Thanks for going to the trouble to make it." He looked around. "Is Bella in the Jeep? You can bring her in."

"She decided to stay with Blaze." Sasha looked down. "Mama's having a rough day, and it was hard on Blaze."

"Hard on all of you, I expect," he said.

Sasha nodded, the fear wanting to wrap itself around her. She couldn't lose Mama. Not now. Certainly not before they found out what happened to Tony.

After he finished eating, Jesse moved to the flowered sofa beside her and slowly pulled her into his arms. He eased her head onto his shoulder, and his hands slid slowly up and down her arm. It felt so incredibly good to be held, to feel like someone else was shouldering the burden, that she wasn't alone. Emotions threatened to overwhelm her, but she pushed them away. She had to be strong. She tried to ease away, but he tightened his hold.

He tucked her head under his chin. "Let me be the strong one for a little while, OK? For right now, you don't have to be."

How did he always know what she was thinking? What she needed? She nestled closer, ever mindful of his ribs. Right here, in Jesse's arms, she always felt a sense of home she'd never experienced elsewhere. It was wonderful. And as always, it scared her to death.

She was ready to pull away when he cupped her chin in his hand and rubbed his thumb over her cheek.

"My beautiful hummingbird," he whispered, just before his lips closed over hers. The kiss started out as a light brush of lips against lips, but quickly moved to a deeper hunger. Before long, their mouths were saying all the words neither one could say. *I care about you. I want you. I need you.*

A cell phone rang, startling them both. Sasha realized it wasn't hers, so she reached for Jesse's and handed it to him. He frowned at the caller ID before he answered.

"Hi, Tracy. What's up?"

Sasha went into the kitchen and washed up the dishes, giving him some privacy. She shouldn't be jealous of some woman named Tracy, but she couldn't seem to help it. Who was she?

Once the dishes were done, she went back into the living room. Jesse was back in the recliner, feet up, clearly exhausted. His eyes opened as soon as he heard her. "Did you ever look up my past online? Check out the story of my arrest?"

She nodded and sat on the couch. "The other night. Article said the cops found drugs on a boat that belonged to you and your business partner, Ethan. You said the drugs were yours, you were both arrested, and the boat and your boat dealership were confiscated. You both went to jail, but before the trial, Ethan . . . ah, killed himself, but he also left a note saying you knew nothing about the drugs."

She looked up. Jesse sent her a half smile. "The short and sweet version."

"Doesn't sound sweet. Sounds very sad. He was dealing drugs?"

Jesse nodded. "Yeah, but he had a good reason. His little daughter, Adelaide, needs heart surgery."

"He was trying to pay for it."

"Right." He gripped the armrest. "He couldn't live with the guilt."

"Were you friends a long time?"

Jesse finally smiled a real smile. "Since we finished high school and I refused to join my father's bank. We started fixing boat motors in his parents' garage, then did a short stint for Uncle Sam overseas, during which Ethan saved my life, by the way. Afterward, we started our own shop and eventually built up a nice boat dealership and hired other people to do the hard labor."

Sasha studied his deliberately casual expression and decided she'd ask about the lifesaving part later. "Even after you were released from jail, the cops didn't give back what they'd confiscated, did they? Like your business? Other assets?"

He grimaced. "Nope. Said since we were partners and they couldn't prove or disprove whether I had any knowledge of his activities, I was free to start over with a clean slate."

Sasha leaped from her seat. "That isn't right! They should have—"

He grabbed her hand as she stormed past. "It's OK, Sasha. I've made my peace with it. I like the idea of a fresh start. And I plan on paying my debts."

Understanding dawned, and she sat back down. "That's why you came back." She realized something else, too. "I'll drive *The Painted Lady* in the race. Help you get that fresh start."

He came up out of the chair fast enough to make him clutch his ribs and suck in a breath. But his voice was firm. He towered over her. "I don't want you anywhere near that race. Not after what's happened."

"You're in no shape to do it, Jesse. Let me help."

"Either I'll do it, or I'll withdraw. But that's it. I don't want you hurt."

Her chin came up. "I can handle *The Painted Lady*."

He pulled her to her feet. "Of course you can. You know that's not what I mean. You matter to me, Sasha. I need to know you're safe."

He yanked her into his arms and winced, then his mouth came down on hers in a possessive kiss unlike any she'd ever experienced. Sensation swamped her, and she wrapped her arms around his neck to steady herself. Slowly, he gentled the kiss, letting her know without words how much she mattered to him. She could feel it and taste it, and it seared her heart like a physical pain.

"I can't," she whispered, and kissed his cheek as she pulled back. "I'm not sure I can ever give you what you want, Jesse. I'm not staying; you know that. I can't. Even if I did, I'm not a . . ." She waved a hand around the cottage. "I'm not a pink-house, dependable, picket-fence kind of girl."

He tried to say more, but she covered his mouth with her hand before she stepped away. The silence lengthened as they stared at each other.

"You're beautiful, you know," he said.

"I think the meds are making you loopy," she shot back.

She expected a grin, but he frowned instead.

"Don't cut yourself down, Sash. You are beautiful. If you don't believe it for yourself, believe I believe it, OK?"

Something in her heart flipped over at his words, but she couldn't think about them right now. She swallowed hard and grabbed her car keys. "You'll be OK by yourself?"

"Absolutely. Besides, we don't need to give the gossips any more ammunition."

"You'll call my cell if you need me during the night?"

He winked at her, his grin wicked. "Oh, I'll need you all right, but I won't call."

She rolled her eyes as he locked the door behind her. Back outside, the humidity wrapped around her like a blanket. Overhead, stars winked down, and she took a steadying breath as she climbed into the Jeep. She had to walk away from Jesse before she broke his heart. And her own. But how could she, when he'd somehow become everything she'd never known she wanted?

Back at the house, everything was quiet. She could hear Mama and Pop talking quietly. She tapped on the door before she poked her head in.

"I'm back. Do you all need anything?"

They were sitting up in the adjustable bed, Pop with his arm around Mama's bony shoulders.

"We're fine, honey. Sleep well," Pop said with a smile.

She blew them a kiss, then listened at Blaze's door. Bella lifted her head from her spot in front of it, tail wagging. Sasha could hear the music from Blaze's headphones through the door. She tapped lightly, but Blaze didn't answer, so she went back down the hall and out to the porch, Bella padding along beside her.

They walked out toward the marina, pausing for Bella to do her thing. Then Sasha sat down on the bench outside the marina store, hoping the waves and the scent of the sea would calm her as they usually did. What was she going to do? About any of it?

She felt like she was spinning her wheels in the search for Tony. She hadn't found a single clue or bit of information that could help her figure out what really happened that day. Maybe because she hadn't looked in the right place yet, hadn't asked the right questions. Or maybe because the original answer was the right one: Tony fell into the water and drowned, his body washed out to sea. For some reason, that answer just didn't sit right. It never had.

She wrapped her arms around her middle and Bella sidled closer, pressing her head against Sasha's knee. Sasha leaned down and tangled her fingers in Bella's thick fur.

"We can't lose her, Bella. We can't lose Mama. She's the glue that holds this family together. But when I look at her . . ." Her voice drifted away, and she swallowed hard. She had to keep trusting, keep praying, keep looking for answers.

Then there was Jesse. She could still taste his kiss, and just thinking about it made her tingle all over. More than that, she knew beyond the shadow of a doubt that he would protect her with his life if need be.

Jesse would stand by those he loved no matter what, just like he'd stood by his friend. He'd never let anything keep him from protecting those who mattered to him.

She knew she mattered. And she knew she would break his heart, and her own, when the inevitable wanderlust hit and she moved on. As much as she loved this place, these people, she'd never imagined staying forever. Could she? For Jesse? Could she make promises and keep them?

The thought brought the panic back, and she stood to pace. Bella clambered to her feet, and they walked out past the fuel tanks where the shop blocked their view of the boat slips. Out here, with the gentle waves slapping the pilings, she beat the anxiety back. She didn't have to decide today. Maybe Jesse wouldn't stay, either.

Her phone chirped again, and she saw another email about the job offer. Did she have an answer yet? When could she come down for an interview?

She closed the app and plopped down on the dock to watch the light from the moon play across the water while she petted her dog. She wouldn't think about anything else tonight. Despite all her agonizing, peace lived here by the water.

The moon had ridden higher in the sky when something caught Sasha's eye. She froze and squinted into the darkness, trying to figure out what she was seeing. It looked like a light, but it wasn't the usual red and green running lights of a boat, or the white of the stern light. This looked orange.

What out here would have orange lights? She watched as the object disappeared from view below the surface, the orange glow fading and eventually vanishing altogether. *What in the world?*

She waited, wishing she'd brought her binoculars, trying to find it again. Was someone out diving in the middle of the night? If so, where was their boat?

That familiar tingle that said something wasn't right raised the hair on the back of her neck, and she stayed put, watching. Waiting.

She checked the time on her cell phone. A little after midnight. She waited and watched for another hour, scanning, always scanning the area, before her efforts were rewarded. The orange glow appeared below the surface again, then the whole thing popped above the water.

Sasha froze. At first it looked like a bubble, but she realized it was a small submarine. The cockpit was the bubble, and the orange glow now mixed with green on the console. Someone sat in the pilot's chair, but it was too dark for her to make out any features.

Who would be out here in the middle of the night in a minisub? Why?

The sub, now completely on the surface, moved steadily toward the marina and its boat ramps. From somewhere behind her, a truck started. They were going to take it out of the water.

Beside her, Bella gave a low growl, deep in her throat. Sasha crouched down. "Shh, Bella. No. Hush."

In response, Bella growled again.

Sasha eased them back around the side of the building, where they could watch the progress without being seen. The sounds of the truck grew louder as the driver backed the trailer into the water. The truck door opened, but the dome light had been turned off, so she couldn't see the person's face. But judging by the size and the way they moved, it was a man.

Beside her, Bella grew restless, and Sasha crouched down again, trying to see without Bella giving their location away.

Bella let out one sharp bark before Sasha could stop her. The man's head snapped up, and he leaned back into the cab. When he slid back out, Sasha's blood ran cold at what he held in his hand.

Chapter 15

Dear Jesus, was that what she thought it was? Sasha poked her head around the side of the building, one arm tucked around Bella to keep her close and her other hand over Bella's muzzle so the big Lab couldn't bark again. "Shh, girl. It's OK. Shh."

She squinted in the darkness, trying to get a better look at the man slowly peering around the hood of the truck.

The clouds shifted, letting several shafts of moonlight through.

He had a bow in his hand, and as Sasha watched in growing horror, he reached back and fitted an arrow into the slot, pulling the string tight.

Beside her, Bella whimpered, prancing in place, trying to get Sasha to let her go. "Shh, we need to stay here."

Bella ignored her, tugging harder, and Sasha knew if she didn't do something, Bella would knock her over and go charging off after the man. That couldn't happen.

The man suddenly lowered the bow and lifted a cell phone to his ear. A glow appeared in the bubble of the sub as whoever was in there answered. Moments later, the sub backed away from the dock and vanished.

Sasha looked back at the truck, but the man had disappeared too. Where had he gone? She shifted position to get a better look, and as she did, Bella used her movement to break free and race toward the dock, barking and growling. Sasha had never heard her bark like this, and it raised goose bumps on her arms.

Behind the corner of the building, Sasha froze, terrified for Bella. If she ran after her, she'd make herself a target, too, and Bella an even bigger one. She couldn't do that.

She heard a splash, then more barking.

A whistling sound sliced through the quiet, followed by a yelp. She couldn't tell if it was from Bella or the man, but it didn't matter. She couldn't stay here. She had to get to Bella.

She broke free of her cover and raced toward the dock in a crouch, hoping the moon would stay behind the clouds long enough for her to take cover. Just as she crossed the open area, she heard that whistling sound again. Acting on instinct, she dropped to the dock just as an arrow zipped past her and embedded itself into the corner of the building where she'd been hiding.

Merciful heavens, he was shooting at her. She pushed up on her hands and knees, trying to catch her breath and figure out where her assailant was hiding. She crawled over to a supply box fastened to the dock and hid behind it.

Another arrow shot past her and lodged in a dock piling. Sasha tried to keep her breathing quiet, settle the shaking in her hands, but her heart pounded so loud she figured they'd hear it. Why were they shooting at her? And where was Bella?

She scrambled up on her knees to look around, and another arrow whizzed past her head. She ducked back down and tried to think. Forcing a calm she didn't feel, she took several deep breaths, studying the arrow closest to her. Based on direction, the arrow came from over by the boat ramp. Which she already knew.

Another bark, this one muffled and frantic, propelled Sasha to her feet. When the bark was followed by splashing, she ducked down a row of boats, peering between them, trying to find Bella.

She didn't have to go far before she heard another bark, more splashing, and then enraged cursing. *Atta girl, Bella.* Still in a crouch, she kept inching along, trying to pinpoint their location. Ripples below the dock let her know she was getting closer.

Suddenly she spotted movement in the water. A flash of yellow, together with the larger shape of a man. When Bella yelped, Sasha didn't stop to think. She simply stepped off the dock, surfaced, and plowed through the water in that direction, using the dock as cover.

It took a minute for her eyes to adjust to even less light under the dock, but when she got closer, she realized the man was in the water with Bella, holding her head under the water.

Oh no, that wasn't going to happen. Sasha surged out of the water and grabbed the man around the neck.

"What the—" He cursed and tried to shake her off, but Sasha hung on. He let go of Bella so he could reach for her, and Bella's head popped out of the water. The man turned around and managed to get Sasha off his back, and now he had his hand around her throat and was trying to wrestle her head down.

"Go, Bella." Sasha tried to say more, but the man cut off her air. Instead of swimming to safety, Bella lunged up and clamped her jaw on the man's arm. He tried to shake her off, but she wouldn't let go. And he wouldn't let go of Sasha's throat.

Who was this crazy person? Sasha tried to see, but he had something over his face that hid his features.

Her vision blurred as she tried to pry his hands from around her throat. He plunged her head down, and she instinctively took a breath and closed her mouth, just in time. He held her head underwater while her heart beat faster and faster as panic grew. *Dear God, help me.* She needed air. Right. Now.

She could feel her struggles getting weaker, the darkness closing in. She kept struggling, but she knew it wasn't doing any good. She was going to die.

Everything inside her rebelled at the thought. No, she wasn't. Not without fighting with everything she had.

She tried to grip his hands again, tried to pry them off, even as the darkness closed in and her lungs felt like they were going to burst from the pressure.

Suddenly she heard the man shout in pain, and the hands around her throat loosened. She felt Bella nudge her, then her head burst up into the night air.

Air. *Thank you, Jesus.* She gulped in air as Bella tugged on her arm. It took a moment to realize Bella was urging her under the dock. The man had disappeared. Where had he gone?

An arrow struck the water right where they'd been, and Sasha knew. She and Bella quickly moved farther away from the ramp, Sasha trying not to wheeze like a racehorse after the Kentucky Derby. They swam quietly, trying not to create any sound, but they still made ripples in the water.

Another arrow hit the water.

Sasha grabbed Bella's collar and took a deep breath, and they swam underwater to the cover of the next dock. They popped up to take a breath, then headed for the next one. Then the next. All around them, arrows hit the water, but Sasha and Bella were getting farther away.

Sasha held on to Bella's collar with one hand and treaded water. How were they going to get out of the water without being found? Or impaled by an arrow?

Beside her, Bella was tiring, starting to whimper. Sasha grabbed her around the middle to keep her afloat.

Maybe they could get to Pop's old johnboat, they one he kept at the end of the marina, just in case. Except that was the opposite end of the marina from where they were hiding.

Footsteps sounded one dock over, and Sasha heard quiet talking.

"I lost them. They can't be far, but we have to get out of here. We don't need anyone showing up asking questions."

Sasha moved slowly toward shallower water, Bella clutched in her arms, until finally her feet touched bottom. She stayed hidden under the dock, holding Bella, listening as the footsteps drifted away. Then came the sound of the truck engine and more ripples when the truck and trailer went into the water.

Sasha heard the low hum of an engine and peered around the pilings. Sure enough, they were loading the minisub onto the trailer. As soon as it was loaded, the truck pulled it out of the water.

Bella whimpered again. "I know, girl. Hang on. Just a little while longer." If they did the same thing as last time, they would move to the darkest corner of the parking area and cover the sub before they left.

Sasha wanted to wait to get out of the water until she was sure they were gone, but Bella couldn't wait that long. She was flailing and her whimpers had gotten louder. Sasha eased them quickly from the cover of one dock to the next until they were under the main dock, right by the bait shop. Keeping a tight grip on Bella's collar, she walked out of the water in a crouch and ducked behind the marina building and out of sight.

Bella tried to shake the water off, so Sasha let go just long enough for that, then grabbed her collar again. Together they watched the far corner, but Sasha couldn't see anything clearly in the dark. Finally the truck pulled down the drive and disappeared. They had no lights on inside or outside the truck or trailer, so Sasha wouldn't have seen them if she hadn't been watching the whole time.

When she was sure they were gone, Sasha led Bella into the marina store and grabbed an old towel to dry her off. She stopped when she saw blood on her snout. "What happened, girl?"

Bella just looked at her, big brown eyes full of pain. Sasha held her snout in her palm, but couldn't find an injury there. She carefully ran the towel over Bella's flanks and stopped when the Lab flinched. She parted her fur and found a two-inch gash in her flesh, but thankfully it didn't look deep.

She went into Pop's office to retrieve the first-aid kit and had Bella bandaged in no time, though it wasn't easy, given her thick fur. She checked the old-fashioned clock above the counter. Two thirty in the morning. They both needed sleep. If she thought it would do a bit of good to call the police, she would. But given the chief's attitude . . . she didn't have the energy to deal with him tonight. She'd call Nick in the morning. Maybe he could help.

Quietly they walked up to the house and eased in through the porch. Bella tried to follow Sasha up the stairs, but her strength gave out. Sasha's heart clenched, and she squatted beside her.

"You did good tonight, girl. I'm thinking that crazy person has a nice-sized gash in his arm, thanks to you. Get some sleep."

Bella curled up beside the couch, so Sasha grabbed an afghan Mama Rosa had crocheted years ago and bedded down on the couch beside her. She didn't have any reason to think the men would be back tonight, but if they did show up, she wanted to be ready.

It didn't take five minutes before Bella snored quietly, but Sasha couldn't settle down. Somebody was out on the water at night with a minisub. Strange, but OK. Maybe it was a prototype and they didn't want anyone to see it yet. She could understand that. Maybe.

But they'd tried to kill her and Bella both. With a doggone bow and arrow, for Pete's sake. That made no sense.

So now what? Whom to trust? The question replayed over and over in her mind with no answers until she finally drifted into a light sleep.

She woke to Bella nudging her hand. She cracked one eye open, surprised at the streaks of dawn lightening the sky. She rubbed her eyes and forced her brain to wake up. It felt like she fell asleep ten minutes ago. She tossed the afghan aside, then remembered to fold it neatly on the back of the sofa. She let Bella out before she stumbled to the kitchen and started a pot of coffee.

She had just let Bella back in and poured the first cup when Pop walked into the kitchen. She rose to kiss his cheek. "Morning, Pop. Coffee?"

He nodded, and she studied him over her shoulder while she grabbed a mug and poured him a cup. He looked exhausted, like he hadn't slept any more than she had. She opened her mouth to ask him if he'd heard anything around town about a minisub, but closed it again. Pop had enough to worry about. She wouldn't add any more to his load.

He sipped his coffee in silence, head down. Sasha went over and wrapped an arm around his shoulders.

"You OK, Pop? Another rough night?"

His glance flashed up to hers for just a moment, and in it she saw such anguish, such grief, she sucked in a breath.

"It is always a rough night these days, my Sasha."

Her eyes widened. "Did something happen? Is Mama worse?"

He shook his head sadly. "It isn't so much that she's worse. It is that she is not getting better."

Sasha plopped down in one of the old wooden chairs surrounding the table where they'd shared so much laughter over the years. Meals, game nights, homework.

"The treatment isn't working?" She said the words quietly, afraid speaking them too loudly would give them more power.

"I do not think so, no. Your mama, though." He shrugged and raised his mug in salute. "She is a fighter. And she decided that she will dance at the wedding of each of her daughters, so this must work. No matter what the doctors say."

"She may be right," Sasha said, trying to summon a smile. "Mama has always bent the world to suit her needs."

Pop's shoulders slumped, and she wanted to call the words back. "Not always, Sasha."

She swallowed. She had no idea what to say.

"Can I make you some breakfast?"

He stood, wrapped an arm around her shoulders, and gave her a kiss on the cheek. Then he reached past her and took a frozen breakfast sandwich from the freezer. He filled a travel mug and took his fisherman's cap from the hook by the door. One hand on the screen, he looked over his shoulder.

"I love you, my girl, but cooking is not your gift." He raised the sandwich. "I'll nuke this at the store. It's safer." He said the last with a chuckle and left.

Sasha laughed, as he'd wanted her to, and went to pour another cup of coffee.

She spun to see Blaze glaring at her from the doorway, arms crossed over her middle. Did the teen have no other expression?

"Good morning, Blaze. Can I get you anything?"

"Yeah, you can pack your bags and leave already."

"That seems a bit harsh at"—she glanced at the black-cat clock with the swishing rhinestone tail—"six forty-five in the morning. Did you want coffee?"

"You don't get it, do you?" Blaze snapped, opening the refrigerator and taking out a gallon of milk. She reached into a cupboard for a cereal box and a bowl, then added milk to the sugary mess before she faced Sasha across the table.

"I guess I don't. Will you tell me?" She kept her tone even, calm, trying to figure out what bee the prickly teen had lodged in her ball cap this morning.

"You've changed everything. This whole stupid quest. It's making Mama Rosa cry more, and she and Pop are fighting more. I don't want to hear them fight. You need to stop this stupid search and go away."

Sasha sipped her coffee, choosing her words with care.

"But Mama asked me to do this, Blaze. Should I have told her no? Would you?"

Blaze jumped up from her chair. "You could have. She would have listened to you. But now you're talking to the cops and getting old files and upsetting everybody. Mama has to get better. Don't you get that?"

"I want her to get better, too. Of course." She stopped. "Finding out what happened to Tony won't change her health, Blaze. One way or the other."

"I know that. I'm not an idiot. But it can't be good for her to be so worried about it."

"That's true. I didn't know she was worried, though. I thought she was OK with me trying to find answers, no matter what they turned out to be."

Blaze dumped her cereal in the sink. "Shows what you know."

Something Blaze said earlier caught Sasha's attention. "Speaking of those old police files, they seem to have disappeared. You wouldn't happen to know where they are, would you?"

"I didn't take them."

Sasha held her hands up, palms out. "I didn't say you did. But do you know who might have taken them?"

"Maybe you just lost them in that mess you made upstairs."

Interesting. So Blaze had been snooping in her room. She stifled a grin. Which is exactly what she would have done at Blaze's age. Anyone who got shuffled around foster care learned to get information wherever and however they could. That way you weren't blindsided.

"Help me out here, Blaze? Do you know anything?"

"Even if I did, why should I tell you?"

"Because ultimately, we're on the same side, you and me. We both love Mama Rosa and Pop, and we both want them to be healthy and happy."

"Yeah, so?"

"So who wants me to stop the search, besides you?"

"And besides Pop and every single person in this stupid town?" She tugged her ball cap farther down on her head. "He even—" She stopped herself and slammed out the door.

Sasha hurried outside and caught up with her halfway across the yard. "He what?"

Blaze ignored her and kept walking. Sasha reached out and grabbed her arm to stop her. Blaze shook her off, but wouldn't look at her.

"Talk to me, Blaze. Please."

"Pop asked you to stop and you won't."

Sasha waited as the silence lengthened. Finally she said, "Because Mama asked me to keep going."

Blaze glanced her way, eyes full of the same pain and confusion Sasha saw in her own eyes when she peered in a mirror.

"Check the fire pit." The words seemed like they were torn from somewhere deep inside. Then the teen spun on her heel and hurried away, earbuds already in her ears.

Sasha watched her, her own frustration boiling. Did Pop and Mama have any idea the impossible situation they'd put their daughters in?

She turned and marched over to the fire pit. In what passed for winter in Florida, when temps dropped enough to merit a sweatshirt, Sasha and her sisters used to light the fire pit and roast marshmallows and hot dogs and tell ghost stories in the dark. The rest of the year, the fire pit was a handy place to burn branches and other yard debris.

She leaned over the rock-encircled pit and saw several charred tree branches and a big pile of ashes. She looked closer. After a quick glance over her shoulder, she crouched down and fished a yellowish object from the ashes, her heart knowing what it was before her brain completely registered it. She plopped down on her backside and brushed soot from the tiny remnant of the police file Nick had copied for her.

Goose bumps popped out on her skin. If what Blaze had hinted at were true, Pop had taken the file from her Jeep and burned it.

She knew he wanted her to stop the search.

But the familiar question wouldn't go away. Was there more to it than simply not wanting to upset Mama?

How much more?

Chapter 16

When Jesse arrived at the marina the next morning, still hunched over like an old man, he stopped in the bait shop and was disappointed to see Sasha wasn't behind the counter. "Morning, Sal. How're things?"

Sal looked up from an order form and offered a weak smile. "Can't complain. Nobody wants to hear it anyway, right?"

Jesse laughed as he was meant to, but he could see that worry and sleepless nights were taking a toll.

Sal eyed him and said, "You look like you've been keelhauled. Do you feel as bad as you look?"

Jesse nodded. Even that small movement proved painful. "It hurts no matter what I do, so I might as well get some work done."

"You're not still planning to race, are you?" Sal's raised eyebrows left no doubt as to his opinion of that.

"We'll see," he said. "Mama Rosa holding her own?" He wasn't sure how else to word the question.

Pop's eyes darkened as he nodded. "She's a tough one, my Rosa. If anyone can beat this thing, she can."

"I have no doubt of that, Sal. None. Give her my love, would you?"

Sal nodded and rang up Jesse's purchases. Jesse scooped up his bag and nodded to several captains in line behind him as he went out the door.

Jesse had his head bent over *The Painted Lady*'s engine compartment, ribs screaming while he tried to see if his attackers had wreaked any havoc on the boat, when he heard footsteps on the dock. He knew who it was before he looked up. Her stride, her scent. And Bella's nails clicking on the boards.

He looked up with a smile. "Hey there, beautiful. How are you?"

"Didn't expect to see you here this early. And that's Captain Beautiful to you." Her own lips curved in a smile, but something seemed off. "Permission to come aboard, sir?"

"Aye, aye." He studied her as she boarded nimbly, but she wouldn't meet his eyes. He stood slowly as his ribs protested, and turned to her. "What's wrong?"

Her head snapped in his direction. "Who said anything is wrong?"

"Every bit of your body language."

"What, you're a psychologist now?"

"Don't evade, Sasha. What's up?"

Her sharp gaze swept the marina, stopping for a moment at each of the boats moored in the slips, as though looking for something. Then she turned around and scanned the parking lot, crowded with pickup trucks pulling boat trailers of every size, description, and vintage.

He wanted to pull her close and wrap his arms around her, kiss a smile back on her face. But he didn't think she'd appreciate the gesture. Certainly not in full view of everyone in the marina.

When she looked up at him, her eyes were troubled. "I saw something last night and I'm not sure what it means—if it's something we should be worried about."

The more she talked about the minisub, the wider his eyes got.

"I've heard of those. Seen pictures online. Even had one of our customers in Tampa ask about them once, but I've never seen one."

"It was really cool looking. But why were they sneaking around in the middle of the night with it?"

"That's an easier answer than you might think. My guess is someone is testing a prototype and doesn't want anyone to see it before they've run it through its paces, so to speak."

"That was my first thought, too. But in the dark? How much can you reasonably see? Why not launch it from some remote place and test it there?"

"Could be they were trying to see how it behaves at night." He looked over at Bella, who had curled up on the deck. "What happened to Bella? Why the bandage?"

"She's fine. Just a little scrape."

Jesse's radar twitched. "Right, but how did she get that little scrape?"

Again, Sasha looked around the marina before she answered. "When they went to load the minisub onto the trailer, Bella made a racket, which they took exception to."

He carefully folded his arms over his chest. And waited.

Sasha glanced at him, fidgeted, checked the marina. Finally she said, "They tried to shoot her, with an arrow."

For a moment he didn't think he'd heard right. But one look at Sasha's face and he knew he had. He bit back several choice words and stepped even closer. "Is she OK?"

"It just grazed her. She's fine."

He took her chin in his hand. "And did they hit you anywhere you're not telling me?"

This time, she met his gaze squarely. "No. Bella and I hid under the docks until they left."

Just thinking about someone stalking them in the dark with a bow and arrow made him want to smack something. Perhaps it was due to the pain meds, but it took him a minute to realize what she hadn't said.

"They know you were out here."

She tried for a careless shrug. "Yeah. Wouldn't be hard to identify Bella or me."

Now he scanned the marina, too, but no one seemed to be paying them the slightest bit of attention. "Did you get a license plate or anything on the truck? Description of the driver? Anything?"

She shook her head. "Believe me, I tried. They had all the lights off on the truck, trailer, and the little sub." She took a deep breath. "And the guy with the bow had a stocking or something over his face."

"So they were making sure no one could identify them." That changed everything. Somebody just testing a prototype wouldn't hide their faces. Someone was up to no good out here. "You need to be—"

Sasha hopped off the boat. "I know. I have to go."

Before he could stop her, she and Bella were gone.

Either she wasn't taking this seriously or, and this was more likely, she didn't want to worry him, so she'd downplayed the whole thing. Well, his ribs might've felt like someone had taken a saw to them, but he wouldn't let anything happen to her. Like it or not, he'd protect her. Whether she wanted protection or not.

Sasha waited over an hour before she could say what she'd come to say. Every time she opened her mouth, someone else popped into the shop or the phone rang. Finally the last of the customers walked out, and she followed Pop into his office and closed the door. He looked up in surprise, then settled in his sagging desk chair.

"What's wrong, Sasha?"

She'd never thought of herself as all that easy to read, but twice in the space of an hour she'd given her emotions away. She sat in the seat opposite the desk and tried to ask the question the right way, instead of just blurting it out.

"Look, Pop, I know you want me to stop looking for Tony."

When he opened his mouth, she held up a hand to stop him. "I know all the reasons. I don't agree with you, but I get it." She paused, watched his face. "I found the burned ashes of the police report." Pop's eyes widened, but other than that, he didn't react. "Did you burn them?"

He nodded once. Looked away. "Sometimes, the past needs to stay in the past. For everyone's sake."

Sasha studied him. "What are you afraid of, Pop?"

He started as though she'd slapped him, then he narrowed his eyes and leaned back in his chair.

"I'm afraid of exactly what I told you before, Sasha. Mama has been through enough. You weren't here then, to see her waste away, hiding in her room crying day and night. I almost lost her, too. I won't risk that again. Why is that so hard to understand?"

"It's not hard to understand." She paused. "If it were true."

His palm came down on the desk and made her jump. "Now I'm a liar?"

Sasha's frustration slipped its leash, and she hopped from her chair and leaned over the desk. "I've never thought you were a liar. But I think there is a whole lot of this story that you know—or that you suspect—that you won't say." She stopped as another thought struck. "You know who took Tony?" she whispered.

She watched all the color drain from Pop's face, and then his whole body seemed to fold in on itself as he let out a huge sigh. "I don't think he was kidnapped. I think he's dead. There is no other explanation that makes sense."

"A whole lot of this doesn't make any sense at all." She studied his face, tried to see beyond the fatigue to what he was really thinking, but he'd put up a wall she couldn't penetrate. "Pop, what if he's not dead? What if someone took him?"

"If that's true, then what? We show up now that he's a man and turn his world upside down?"

"Don't you want to know for sure?" Sasha didn't understand his thinking at all.

"I am satisfied with the police report that says *suspected drowning*." He pierced her with a look that could always get her to spill her secrets years ago. "Tell Mama you've tried and come up with nothing—which is true."

"I can't. There are too many holes in the whole scenario, too many other possible answers. The police quit looking much too soon."

"Because I told them to."

Sasha's mouth dropped open, and it took a stunned moment before she found words. "He was your son. Weren't you at least curious, never mind completely desperate, to find out exactly what happened?"

"He was gone. There was nothing left to know. Besides, curiosity killed the cat." He stood. "Go, Sasha. It's done. Don't bring it up again."

Sasha stood frozen, unable to move. She studied his shuttered expression and wondered if she'd ever known him at all. The Pop she grew up with would have moved heaven and earth if something had happened to her or one of her sisters.

She walked to the door and glanced over her shoulder to see him sitting with his head in his hands, just like people said he did the day Tony disappeared.

As she walked out, the pieces of the puzzle suddenly clicked into place. Fear and frustration propelled her to the end of the dock where she paced, heart pounding, as she tried to settle her racing thoughts. Time lost all meaning as one thought repeated over and over in her mind, settled deep in her heart. *He knows. He knows who killed Tony. Or who took him.* It was the only explanation that made any sense.

Why wasn't he telling? Why wasn't he screaming from the rooftops for justice? What—or who—had kept him silent all these years?

She didn't know. But she was going to find out.

Chapter 17

Sasha hurried into the screened porch and saw Blaze in a rocker, petting Bella.

"There you are. Will you keep an eye on Mama and Bella while I take a quick ride?"

Before Blaze could question her, Sasha heard shuffling down the hallway, and a minute later Pop appeared, Mama leaning heavily on his arm.

"Is everything OK? Where are you going?" Sasha asked. Mama's pale face sent alarm skittering down her spine.

Pop held the screen door open. "The doctor wants to see her. Do some blood work, check on the dosage for her meds." Sasha went to Mama's other side and helped her down the steps and into the car. "We won't be long," he continued.

Sasha leaned in, kissed Mama's cheek, and buckled her seat belt. "Love you."

Once they were gone, she climbed back up to the porch.

"Where are you going?" Blaze demanded. "And don't give me some lame half answer."

Sasha leaned against the doorjamb and studied Blaze's determined expression.

"I'm going to go check out a hunch. Want to come along?"

"What kind of hunch?"

"I'll tell you on the way." She crouched down and scratched Bella behind the ears. "I need you to stay here, girl. Keep an eye on the place for me."

Bella whined in protest but collapsed on the floor, head on her paws, a pitiful expression on her face.

"You little stinker," Sasha said, giving her an extra pat on the head. "But you're still staying here."

Once they left the marina, Blaze didn't waste any time. "So where are we going?"

"Do you know who Captain Alby is?"

Blaze scrunched her face, thinking. "No idea."

"He used to be a boat captain, and he and Pop were friends way back when. After his wife died, his mind went and he lived in the local assisted-living place."

"Wait. I heard Pop talking about him. He just died, like, the other day."

Sasha nodded as she turned off the paved road and onto a dirt path.

"Right. In his sleep. Jesse and I had gone to see him the day before. He didn't make much sense, unfortunately, but he kept shouting about finding the fridge."

Blaze scanned the trees all around, the way the path kept narrowing the deeper into the woods they went. "What does that have to do with wherever we are?"

Sasha stopped at a fork in the path, studied the area in each direction, and finally turned toward the left. The tracks that way looked more recent. "Old Ned—you know, the appliance guy—used to dump the things he couldn't fix out here somewhere."

"Was Captain Alby friends with Pop when Tony disappeared?"

When Sasha nodded, Blaze said slowly, "So you're thinking maybe Captain Alby knew something about Tony and it has to do with old appliances?"

"Maybe. Or maybe not. It's a total long shot. I figured it couldn't hurt to look."

A branch swept over the Jeep's open top, and Blaze ducked just in time.

"When's the last time you were out here?"

Sasha grinned. "High school. We'd go four-wheeling and mudding out here."

Blaze merely snorted as Sasha hit one pothole after another, the Jeep bouncing over the rough terrain. Suddenly they burst into a clearing, and Sasha grinned in triumph.

"Found it."

Piles of rusted appliances littered the small area, victims of time and weather. Sasha and Blaze climbed out and walked closer to investigate.

"Watch for snakes," Sasha warned, and Blaze rubbed her arms, eyes darting all around. "You can wait in the Jeep if you want."

Blaze stepped closer until she practically stood on Sasha's heels. "I'll just stay with you."

Sasha eyed the piles, shading her eyes with her hand. "Captain Alby kept talking about a fridge, so let's focus on those. There aren't that many."

Blaze rolled her eyes, but kept pace as they climbed over and under the rusting hulks to peer inside every fridge. Most were missing their doors; others had them propped open. But several were closed. Sasha took a deep breath before she grabbed the handle of the first one. Would she find evidence of her brother? Maybe even his body?

Her heart pounded and her hands shook as she slowly pried the door open. Her breath whooshed out when the inside revealed nothing more than a nasty mildew growth. Behind her, Blaze let out her own relieved sigh.

By the time they'd worked their way to the last fridge on the back side of the last pile, they were both sweaty and swatting at mosquitos.

"Last one." Sasha climbed on top of an old stove to reach the latch. She yanked, but it wouldn't budge. One try. Two. Finally the seal let go, and Sasha tugged it open and used her shoulder to keep it from slamming shut while she looked inside.

She froze. What was that? Her hand shook as she reached down into the bottom and pulled out a large freezer bag. As she gazed at the contents, the words from the newspaper article ran through her mind. Blue shorts, blue-and-yellow tank top, tennis shoes. *Sweet Jesus, these were the clothes Tony was wearing the day he disappeared.*

From below, Blaze said, "What did you find?"

Before Sasha could answer, a loud *crack* sounded, right before something slammed into a rusting dishwasher not twenty feet away. It took Sasha a moment to catalog the sound. The second it registered, she shouted, "Duck!" and leaped down, taking Blaze with her.

The sound of metal hitting metal exploded all around them.

"What's happening?" Blaze whispered, shaking.

Sasha tried to keep her voice steady. "Someone's shooting at us. Stay down."

They waited several minutes, then Sasha slowly eased up and peeked around the pile. Another shot rang out, too close for comfort.

She had to get them out of here. She looked back over her shoulder, picturing her Jeep and where the shooter had to be standing, based on where the shots hit.

"This way," she whispered, and took Blaze's hand as they melted back into the cover of the trees behind them. Sasha put a finger to her lips, and together they inched their way around to where they'd parked the Jeep. Heart pounding, Sasha peered around the side of a pine tree, scanning the area, looking for the shooter. She held herself perfectly still, watching, waiting. Finally she saw a flash of yellow heading back around behind the appliance pile. This was the best chance they were going to get.

She whispered in Blaze's ear. "We're going to make a run for the Jeep. Hop in and get down on the floorboard, OK?"

The moment Blaze nodded, Sasha gripped her hand again and they took off running. They opened their doors, and the Jeep roared to life almost before Blaze got all the way in. She was still pulling the door shut as Sasha raced back the way they'd come.

Several shots rang out, but they came from too far away to hit their mark. Sasha kept one eye on the rearview mirror as they raced back to the main road, clouds of dust in their wake.

"We're easy to follow," Blaze commented, coughing against the dust.

"I know. But I'm heading for town, thinking nobody is dumb enough to start shooting there."

Sasha didn't slow until the shops of downtown Safe Harbor came into view. Then she looked over at Blaze. She'd stopped panting but still gripped her seat belt like a lifeline.

"You OK, kid?"

Blaze smiled, but it wobbled a bit at the edges. "Guess your hunch was right on."

Sasha grinned, glad Blaze could smile. "I guess it was."

"What did you find?" She nodded toward the floorboard, where Sasha had stashed the bag under the front seat.

"I'm pretty sure they're Tony's clothes."

Blaze slumped back against the seat. "Was there any, like, blood or anything on them?"

"Not that I saw. It looks like someone took them off him. Let's get home, then we can take a closer look." She sped up again as they left town and turned toward the marina. "You did good today, kid. Nerves of steel."

Blaze wrapped her arms around her middle. "I almost peed my pants, I was so scared. Somebody really shot at us."

"They really did. Maybe, let's not mention this to Pop and Mama."

Blaze snorted. "Duh. I'm not stupid."

"I've never once thought you were. You are incredibly smart."

As they drove the rest of the way, Sasha tried to gather her jumbled thoughts. Could Tony still be alive?

Jesse breathed a sigh of relief when Sasha pulled her Jeep into the gravel lot next to her folks' house. She had poked the hornet's nest but good. Every instinct screamed that danger was closing in. Around Sasha.

He didn't know how Tony's disappearance, the upcoming race, and a minisub fit together, but he knew they did. Somehow. Which put Sasha right in the line of fire.

He walked over, surprised to see Blaze riding shotgun. Everything still creaked and groaned when he moved, but he felt better than he had this morning. Which wasn't saying much.

They had almost reached the porch when he caught up with them. "Hey, ladies, what's up?"

Sasha turned, and her expression had him up on the porch beside her in two painful strides. "What happened?"

"Somebody shot at us," Blaze blurted.

The words hit like a fist.

"Tell me what happened," he barked. "All of it. From the beginning."

Sasha patted the air in a "calm down" gesture as she dropped into a wicker chair, clutching something in her lap. There was a fine trembling in her hands. "We're fine. We had quite a scare, though."

Blaze took Mama's rocker, and he sat beside Sasha where he could keep an eye on both of them.

"I kept thinking about what Captain Alby said about finding the fridge—and his sudden demise—and decided to check out Ned's old appliance graveyard."

"The one out in the woods all the kids used to hang out by when we were in high school?"

"Right. It was just a crazy hunch. But then someone started shooting."

"Do you know what kind of weapon the shooter had? Shotgun, rifle or pistol?"

"My guess is rifle, based on the sound. I didn't really stop to analyze."

He'd get back to that. "Did you find anything?"

She slowly pulled out the sealed plastic bag, brittle after all this time. "Based on the newspaper articles I saw, these are the clothes Tony was wearing the day he disappeared."

He froze, stunned. She carefully handed him the bag, and he studied the clothes through the plastic. No sign of blood. He blew out a relieved breath.

"Speaking of analyze." He nodded to the clothes. "What now?"

She reached in her pocket and pulled out her cell phone.

"I'm going to call Nick. Hand them over to him. See what he can find out."

As she spoke to him on the phone, the Martinellis pulled up to the house. "Meet us at the end of the drive, would you, Nick? I don't want anyone, including my folks, to know about this yet."

Twenty minutes later, the three of them climbed out of the Jeep to meet Nick when he pulled up. "What's with all the cloak-and-dagger stuff, Sasha?"

She handed him the bag, hands almost steady. "I think I found Tony's clothes this morning."

Nick's eyes widened, and he said almost the same thing Jesse had. "Start at the beginning and don't leave anything out."

Sasha told him the whole story, just as she had Jesse. He didn't interrupt, but his face gave nothing away, either.

Nick finally looked up from his little notebook. "We have all your fingerprints on file, so we can easily eliminate your prints."

Sasha glanced at Blaze, who sighed. "Yeah, mine are in the system, too. Shoplifting. Long time ago."

Blaze turned to Sasha and held out her hand. "Let me have your phone." When Sasha raised a brow and handed it over, Blaze took pictures of the bag of clothes from all angles. "Just in case," she mumbled as she handed them back.

"Given everything that's been happening lately, is there some way you can check on all this . . . quietly?" Sasha met Nick's eyes, and Jesse watched the two study each other for a long moment.

Nick seemed to come to some decision. "I'll get them to a friend of mine at the law enforcement lab in Jacksonville. Have her check out the clothes on the down low. See if she can find prints, DNA, anything that will help. I'll also head out to the woods and try to get hold of those spent cartridges, see if I can get a lead on the shooter. I'll be in touch. In the meantime, you guys be careful." He paused. "I wouldn't mention this to anyone just yet."

Nick headed back to town, and they went back to the marina. The minute Sasha stopped the Jeep, Blaze headed inside.

Jesse leaned against the vehicle.

"She's OK?" he asked.

"Shaken up, but she's tough."

"Kind of like someone else I know." He studied her eyes, but whatever feelings she had were carefully hidden. Her emotional distance suddenly made him furious.

His control snapped and he yanked her into his arms. "I could have lost you today. Don't ever scare me like that again." His mouth met hers in a frantic kiss, every worry pouring out of him. She met his emotional storm with her own, and the kiss went on and on, pulling them both under. He couldn't lose her. He wouldn't.

When he finally eased back, her eyes looked a little dazed.

"Have dinner with me." He took her hand and started leading her toward his truck.

"Wait. Stop. I need to check in with the family."

He stopped. "Right. Sorry. Go and I'll wait here."

She grinned and quipped, "You've got it bad."

He laughed. "Yes, ma'am, I do."

She disappeared inside the house and he paced, trying to get his fear under control. Frankly he didn't want her out of his sight. This had gotten way out of control. Every primal instinct shouted for him to hide her away—along with her whole family—and hunt down this shooter, make sure they were safe. But he knew if he tried that, she'd eject him from her life forever.

He shoved a hand through his hair. This need to protect unsettled him with its depth. He'd never felt this way about anyone, and he wasn't quite sure what to do with it.

When she reappeared twenty minutes later, she'd changed into a pair of jeans that hugged every curve, wedge-heel sandals, and a little black tank that played well with the jeans. She'd left her hair down, and it swung around her shoulders.

"You look amazing," he said, and gave her a quick kiss on the cheek. "Everyone OK?"

"Mama is tired after the doctor appointment, but her color is better." She wouldn't meet his eyes, so he cupped her chin and turned her to face him.

"What else?"

She shrugged, looked at the house, saw Blaze sitting on the porch. "Let's talk about it later."

He nodded and helped her into the truck, then headed toward town. "The Blue Dolphin? Or the new barbecue place out by the highway?"

"Let's go with the Dolphin. I need comfort food."

"Which for people like you and me is seafood."

She smiled, but it was frayed around the edges.

"What are you thinking?"

"There was no blood anywhere. I checked every fridge out there. What if he's alive? That changes everything."

Jesse nodded. It did. Then they were looking at kidnapping, not drowning or murder. "It's one heck of a tangled mess and means there are more secrets in this town than we thought."

"But wouldn't someone, somewhere, have seen or known something?"

"People have all kinds of reasons for keeping secrets, Sasha. Sometimes good ones."

"How can this be one of those times?"

"I don't know. But we'll find out."

He pulled into the parking lot of the Blue Dolphin and walked around to help Sasha out of the truck, unsurprised to find her already striding toward the door. He hurried to catch up so he could at least hold the door open.

Once they had ordered drinks and were mindlessly glancing at the menu, Sasha suddenly peered at him over the top of hers. "So are you going to tell me what's on your mind?"

"Besides you, you mean? Have I mentioned you're gorgeous?"

She just raised a brow.

He debated, again, where to start, and decided just to go with his gut. "I'm going to stay in this crazy little town after the race, settle down. Maybe paint over the pink of Aunt Clarabelle's cottage."

If he hadn't been watching closely, he would have missed the way the shutters came down over her eyes and hid all her emotions.

"Really? After the warm welcome you've received, I thought you'd be eager to leave this place."

"There is a lot to love about Safe Harbor. Namely—"

"What will you do for an income, exactly? It's not like there are races all the time."

He let her shift the conversation. For now.

"I'm going to start a racing team. That wasn't just talk, Sasha. I'm also going to see if Sal will let me take on some of the mechanic's and boat-repair work at the marina. That will free him up to take care of Mama Rosa, do other things."

Her eyes widened. "You've been thinking about this. You think Pop will go along with you doing his job?"

He shrugged. "We haven't talked about that part yet. But I'm hoping he'll like the idea." He reached across the table and took both her hands in his. When she glanced around at the other diners and tried to pull away, he simply held tighter.

"Look, Sasha. I'm staying. Safe Harbor is a good place. With good people."

"Except the ones who've been trying to kill us."

"We're going to figure all that out."

"You're seriously not worried?"

"Of course I'm worried. Somebody shot at you and Blaze today. Whatever this is, it's escalating."

"Then we need to come up with a plan and—"

"Not tonight. Let's talk about something else. Like you and me, for instance."

She snatched her hands away and folded them across her chest. "There is no you and me."

"Isn't there? Come on, Sash. You know that's not true."

She huffed out a breath, sent him one quick glance, then went back to studying the other diners. "I told you from day one that I'm not staying. I don't want to hurt you. Why do you keep talking like this?"

Her panic and desperation hit him hard, but he couldn't back down. He knew she had feelings for him, but her past wouldn't let her admit it. He reached over and laid his hands on the table, palms up, and waited until she finally put hers in his again. He breathed a small sigh of relief.

"I'm saying this all wrong. Here's the truth. I want you to stay here in Safe Harbor. With me." He let go of one of her hands and reached into his pocket with the other. He held up the ring, a square-cut ruby surrounded by gold shaped like rope. "Marry me, Sasha."

All the color drained from her face, replaced by pure panic. She started to get out of the booth, so he set the ring down and reached for her hands again. "Easy. It's OK. You don't have to give me an answer right now. Just think about it, OK?"

"Why?" she whispered.

"Why what?"

"Why do you want to marry me?"

Now it was his turn to panic. Could he tell her everything he felt for her? Bare his soul? Memories of his mother telling him at twelve years old that she needed more than his love to stay cut off his voice. He opened his mouth, but no words came out. "Because I . . . I . . ." He cleared his throat and tried again. "Because we're good together. We enjoy the same things—"

Her eyes were great pools of misery when she looked at him. "It's not enough. I can't stay. I'm sorry," she whispered, and raced out of the restaurant.

Her words froze him in his seat. *It's not enough.* The words were hers, but in his mind, it was his mother speaking. By the time he dug out his wallet, threw some bills on the table, and slammed out the door, she was gone. He searched by the truck, looked up and down the street, but it was as if she'd vanished.

"Sasha!" He circled the parking lot again, looked in the alley leading away from the restaurant, then ran back out to the street. Which way would she go? Right or left? He knew she was tough and could take care of herself, but there was a crazy person with a rifle running around Safe Harbor. He ran several blocks along one side of the street, checked every cross street, then raced back down the other side. This time of night, most of the shops were closed and very few pedestrians roamed the streets. Where had she gone?

Heart pounding and ribs screaming in protest, he ran back to the Blue Dolphin and hopped into his truck. The tires squealed as he raced out of the parking lot.

Chapter 18

Sasha woke to pain. Everywhere. She opened her eyes but couldn't see a thing. For a moment she thought she'd gone blind, but then she realized she was blindfolded. Not good, but better than blind.

Why did everything hurt? Where was she? She closed her eyes again and tried to determine if anything was broken. She'd only felt like this once before, when she'd tumbled halfway down a mountain while skiing.

Her brain felt like it had been wrapped in cotton. Putting two thoughts together took a lot more effort than it should have.

Slowly, bits and pieces of memory surfaced. The Blue Dolphin. Jesse's crazy proposal. Didn't he know she was a bad risk? Everyone she loved, she disappointed. Or worse. Look at the mess she'd made here with her family. And before that, in Russia. Her birth family died because of her.

Jesse thought that was crazy, but what did he know? The memories tried to push in, but she shoved them away. She had to focus on now. Today. *Think, Sash. What happened?*

OK, he'd proposed, the crazy man, and she'd run out of the restaurant like a coward. Not her finest hour. But she hadn't been able to stay.

If she had, she might have said yes. Probably would have. Jesse made her want things she'd never considered wanting, like a home, maybe even a family. Could she stay? For Jesse?

Her heartbeat sped up, so she forced out a slow breath. *Focus. Don't think about that now.*

So, she'd run outside, and then—

She searched her fuzzy brain and came up empty. What happened next? She couldn't remember.

Maybe she'd been drugged. But why?

Tony.

It was the only answer that made sense. This had to do with her search for Tony. She tried to sit up and couldn't. Her hands were tied behind her back. She shifted her legs again and realized why she couldn't move them. They were bound, too.

Panic washed over her, but she forced her mind to calm down. In her years as a captain, she'd learned the best way to survive an emergency was to take a few precious seconds and think before you acted. Assess the situation.

She rubbed her fingers back and forth and decided she was lying on a dirt floor. She sniffed the air. Musty, with a layer of hay and the underlying smell of dung. So chances were someone had stashed her in a barn.

What were they going to do with her?

The smart thing would be to get out of here before they came back.

She wiggled herself to a sitting position and tried to figure out how to get her hands free. Whoever had tied her up knew what they were doing and wanted to ensure she wasn't going anywhere. Instead of rope, they'd used duct tape, and it wouldn't budge. Her feet were bound the same way, and no amount of twisting and tugging loosened the tape. At all.

The blindfold had to go, but she didn't want it completely off, lest they notice if they came back. She rubbed her face against the ground, back and forth, back and forth, getting dirt in her mouth and spitting it out. Finally whatever smelly bit of cloth they'd tied around her head moved the slightest bit, and she could see splinters of light between the cracks in the building. She scooted her body around to see better.

Yes, she was in a barn. A big old one. There were several holes in the roof that let in shafts of light. Streaks of pink colored the sky. It must be morning.

How was she going to get out of here? *Think, Sasha. What day is it?* She tried to shake her head, but pain shot through her temples. *Come on, fog, clear.* Today was . . . Friday. Which meant the big race was tomorrow. Jesse needed her to captain *The Painted Lady* and win that race.

He said he didn't need her, but he did. He couldn't take the helm with those ribs.

But first, she had to get out of here before whoever took her came back. Just thinking about the shooter in the woods sent a chill down her spine and propelled her into action. Tied up like this, she was at their mercy.

After a lot of groaning and panting, she managed to get up on her knees. From there, she tried to hop to her feet, but she lost her balance and crashed face-first onto the ground.

She spit out dirt and wondered briefly if anyone had missed her yet or if they just figured she'd run off again, as usual. Either way, it didn't matter. She had to get out of here.

She rolled until she was next to the wall, then maneuvered to her knees again. This time, when she hopped up, she crashed into the rough barn wall, but at least she was upright. *OK, now to get out of here.*

She stood, leaning against the wall, trying to catch her breath and figure out her next move. As her eyes scanned the gloom, searching for a way out, a shadow separated itself. She caught one quick glimpse of a dark figure before something jabbed her in the arm.

Everything went black.

Jesse pulled in to the marina just as the sky began to lighten. He'd spent several hours last night trying to find Sasha before he called the police, not sure what else to do. He'd asked for Nick, but the dispatcher said he was off duty and patched him through to Chief Monroe instead. Not surprisingly, the chief speculated she'd just run off for a few hours to clear her head.

Had she? She used to do it when they were in high school. When she was overwhelmed, she took off for a while. Last night he'd called her cell every fifteen minutes, but it went right to voice mail. Meaning she didn't want to talk to him. He'd said he'd give her time to get used to the idea. Which was fine, but he had to know that's all her disappearance was. A little voice had been hounding him all night, telling him she wouldn't vanish without a word. Not now, not with things with Mama Rosa the way they were and a crazy with a rifle on the loose.

When he'd run off the road because he'd nodded off behind the wheel, he went home set the alarm, and forced himself to sleep for exactly one hour. He wouldn't do her any good if he crashed into a tree.

He now headed down the dock to the marina store, worry building even as he hoped to find her behind the counter so he could give her what for.

"Morning, Jesse." Sal looked up from an account ledger as he walked in.

"Morning, Sal. Is Sasha working this morning?"

"Not today. She has the morning off." He raised a brow. "I heard you caused quite a stir at the Blue Dolphin last night, something about candlelight and a ring."

Jesse grinned. "Yeah, there was a ring involved, but she didn't take it." He held up a hand. "I really didn't expect her to."

Sal's eyes narrowed. "Are you toying with my daughter's affections?"

"Not at all. I'm completely serious." Jesse met Sal's gaze. "You OK with me marrying your daughter, Sal?"

"You've always been a good boy, Jesse. Even as a scrawny teenager. I think you're man enough to love my Sasha without trying to control her."

"Thanks, Sal. Now all I have to do is get her to say yes." He scanned the bait shop, but no one seemed to be within earshot. "Have you seen our girl yet this morning?"

"No, and I missed her. She's been getting up first and getting the coffee going. Had to make my own today." His smile faded. "Is something wrong?"

"She left the Blue Dolphin in a hurry last night and I haven't seen her since."

"Ran off, did she?" He waved a dismissive hand. "Don't let that worry you. She's been doing that since we first met her. Sometimes, she just needs a little bit of time and room to clear her head." He stopped suddenly, and the color drained from his face. "But with the strange goings-on around here lately . . ."

Jesse waited for him to say more. When he didn't, he thanked him and left, but his worry kicked up another notch. Too much had been happening to ignore it.

He sent a text this time, asking her to let him know she was OK. Then he walked up to the house and found Blaze on the porch, Bella prancing and whining at her feet.

"Morning, Blaze. How ya doing?"

Blaze reached over and stroked Bella's fur, trying to calm her. "Shh, Bella. It's OK." She glared at Jesse. "Somebody who isn't going to take care of a dog shouldn't have one."

He stilled. "What do you mean?"

Blaze narrowed her eyes. "Did Sasha spend the night with you? Because her bed hasn't been slept in. I woke up to Bella nudging me awake."

"No. She didn't. And she never has, by the way." He walked up the steps and onto the porch, Bella still whining and running to the screen and back to Blaze. "You checked her bed?"

"Of course. How else would I know that?"

He thought a moment, a chill running down his back. He didn't want to scare Blaze, though.

"Can I take Bella with me? We'll take a spin, see if Sasha's around somewhere. Maybe she went for a run?"

Blaze snorted. "Sasha doesn't run unless someone's chasing her."

That wasn't reassuring in the least. He managed a confident smile and motioned to Bella. "Come on, girl. Want to go for a ride?"

Bella barked once and raced to his truck, where he had to help her scramble up into the passenger side. She perched on her haunches, scanning the area, and Jesse could have sworn he heard her telling him to hurry up already.

"Take it easy. We're going."

He put both windows down, and Bella hung her head outside as they left the marina, sniffing the air as they drove.

Jesse drove slowly to be sure he didn't miss her if she'd been injured at the side of the road or something, but every instinct urged him to hurry, too. Sasha was in danger. He could feel it.

They led a line of cars from the marina to the Blue Dolphin. Jesse wouldn't go above thirty-five so he could scan both sides of the road. Vegetation grew so thick on the edges, he could drive right past and not see her if she were lying in the bushes. A driver behind him laid on the horn, then crossed the double yellow line on the two-lane highway to get around him. Any other day, that would have ticked him off. Today, he couldn't care less. He had to find her.

Beside him, Bella sniffed the air. He wondered if there was any way she could find Sasha, or if that was just wishful thinking on his part. Bella was a Lab, not a bloodhound. Still, when she started barking frantically out the window, he pulled over. Before the truck stopped, Bella had leaped out and tumbled to the ground. He ran around to check on her, but she was already racing into the underbrush at the side of the road, barking as she went. Jesse ran after her, wishing he had worn boots instead of flip-flops. Snakes loved this kind of terrain.

Bella stopped suddenly and Jesse almost fell over her. He caught his balance and saw what had gotten her attention. A scrap of cloth hung on the spines of a scrub pine, as though it had been snagged as someone went by. He pulled it off, and Bella started jumping in a circle.

When Jesse recognized it, he took a deep breath. It was part of the tank top Sasha had been wearing last night. So where was she?

"Sasha? Are you here?" He waited, listening, eyeing the crisscross tire tracks in the soft sand. Even Bella seemed to understand, for she stood motionless beside him.

They heard nothing but the cry of a hawk and the rumbling whir of the cicadas. He looked up, thankful he didn't spot any vultures overhead.

Which way had she gone? He wanted to hurry, but he was afraid he'd miss something, so he walked in an ever-widening circle with Bella before he realized there was nothing more to find here. The tire tracks went in several directions. This wouldn't help him find her.

He slammed a hand against the truck as he and Bella climbed back in. Someone had to have some idea where she might have gone. Or been taken.

His phone signaled an incoming text from Sasha. *Stop searching. I'm fine.*

Instead of easing his mind, the text cranked his worry even higher. Would she think he was searching for her? Knowing Sasha, if she was trying to clear her head, she wouldn't give him a thought right then.

He had ignored the nagging feeling that something wasn't right the last time he talked to Ethan. He wouldn't make that mistake again. His gut said someone had taken Sasha. The trick was to find out where, and then he could deal with who later.

He stopped at the Blue Dolphin, determined to act nonchalant and praying he would get answers along with his breakfast. He walked in and several conversations ground to a halt.

Marge, the daytime waitress with the gray braid and smoker's voice, handed him a menu and said, "Sit anywhere you like, handsome."

Outside, Bella stared in through the window and finally settled her muzzle on her paws to wait. Marge came over and filled his coffee cup without being asked. "So I hear you popped the question to our Sasha last night and she ran out on you."

"Heard that, did you?" He sipped his coffee and tried not to wince.

Marge grinned. "Honey, everyone in town has heard it by now."

"What else have you heard?" He smiled widely.

She looked both ways and suddenly lost her carefree expression. She leaned closer and said, "I hear there are those not too happy with your coming to town with that fancy boat of yours, and your past, and living in dear Clarabelle's cottage."

"Anybody say why that was such a crime?"

Again, she glanced around the busy dining room before she spoke. "This town has its own routines and schedules and things that happen on a regular basis, and folks don't like that messed with."

Jesse wanted to shake her until she stopped talking in riddles and told him exactly what she meant. Every single detail. Instead, he kept his voice equally low. "Any examples you might be willing to share?"

"Well, now, if someone in town had a new toy to try out, for example, something they might could use to transport certain things . . . they might not take kindly to other people knowing about it, see?"

He met her eyes, thinking of the minisub. "What are you saying, Marge?"

"I'm saying this town has secrets, and Sasha has been trying to dig them out. That can be a dangerous game."

"It's not a game."

"No, it surely isn't. Somebody could get hurt bad." She paused. "It's time to back off, Jesse, and tell Sasha to back off, too. Before it's too late."

Jesse clenched his hands around his coffee mug. "It might already be too late."

She reached down and gripped his forearm so hard he thought she might draw blood. "Then grab that lady of yours and leave town. Today."

Now it was Jesse's turn to scan the room. "If someone in this town were hiding . . . something, where would you start looking?"

Someone called out, "Hey, Marge, refill?"

"Coming, Ed," she answered, and walked away.

She didn't say a word as she brought Jesse his breakfast, but when she came by later and handed him his check, he realized she'd slipped another piece of paper under it. He slid it in front of the check and read, *Old Donovan place. Cedar Road.* Their eyes met, and she nodded.

When she rang him up at the old-fashioned cash register, he said, "Thank you, Marge."

"I wouldn't dawdle. I think time is running out."

The hair on the back of Jesse's neck stood up. He'd been thinking the same thing.

Where was the danger? Who had Sasha? Why?

He held the door for Chief Monroe and debated asking him for help for about five seconds. He discarded the idea and headed for the truck. He didn't trust the chief. With Sasha's life on the line, he was going with his gut.

When he reached the truck, Bella started barking like crazy. He stopped, looked at the frantic dog. "What is it, girl?" She tugged his shorts and tried to pull him away from the truck. Jesse looked up and down the quiet side street, every sense on alert.

He tuned out Bella's barking for a moment as he studied his truck. He crouched down, and for a split second, he thought he saw a flame under the cab. He didn't have time to do anything but grab Bella—all ninety pounds of her—and dive around the corner of the building just as his truck exploded.

Chapter 19

Jesse ended up on his back with Bella on top of him, both of them shaking. He slowly sat up and wrapped his arms around the dog, rubbing her fur.

"Good girl, Bella. Good girl. Are you hurt?" He ran his hands all over her, but she seemed fine.

He heard pounding footsteps and shouts in the distance, then the telltale wail of a siren. He and Bella stayed where they were, trying to catch their breath. Clouds of smoke billowed around them, coating everything in acrid fumes.

But in that moment, clarity speared him like a sword.

They thought he was dead.

He eased to his feet, feeling worse by the minute, and motioned for Bella to follow. It might be good to let them go on thinking that for a little while.

The two walked down the side street to the alley, then off into the woods. Before long, he found himself on a narrow path he hadn't walked since he and Sasha used to ditch class back in high school. Old memories flooded through him, and it felt like he'd never left.

They followed the trail all the way back to the woods behind the marina, searching for any sign of her.

He found nothing.

He spun in a circle, heart pounding as the seconds ticked away. *Where are you, Sash?*

When Sasha woke again, it took a few minutes to clear the fog in her brain enough to figure out where she was. She took several deep breaths through her nose, trying to control the nausea. If she didn't know better, she'd think she had the world's worst hangover. Once her stomach settled a bit, she lay quietly for a while, as she worked to get her fuzzy brain to cooperate.

They had drugged her. She tried to sit up, but she'd forgotten about being tied, and she immediately flopped back down.

"Ow, dang it."

She swallowed hard and rubbed her face against her shoulder, trying to slide the blindfold up a bit again from where it had slipped down. The room spun, her stomach churned, and she held herself perfectly still until everything settled. She had to get out of here before they came back and drugged her again. Or worse.

Once she could see under the blindfold, she scanned the darkening space and realized another day had gone by. She was running out of time. Fast.

Something glinted, metal of some kind, and she realized they'd left her a dog's water bowl. She wriggled over, incredibly grateful to find it full of water. She was so thirsty, her tongue felt swollen. She knelt in front of the bowl and tried to lap up water without pitching forward and dumping the bowl. Without her hands for balance, she got several mouthfuls before she fell, knocking the bowl out of reach and sloshing precious water over the side.

She lay there panting, trying to figure out what to do. Her thoughts seemed to float away before she could grab them, and she found her eyes drifting shut.

"No, stay awake, dummy." Her voice seemed to ricochet around inside her head, and she squeezed her eyes shut. OK, focus. She had to focus.

She rolled to her side and squinted at the walls, trying to find a glimmer of light, something that would offer a chance to escape.

Suddenly her stomach heaved, and she emptied all the water she'd swallowed. The room spun, pain making her ears ring.

Before she could formulate a plan, the blackness overtook her again.

Jesse and Bella combed the woods behind the marina but came up empty. He needed a vehicle to search the place Marge suggested. He eased up beside the shed, Bella tucked at his side. He kept a grip on her collar lest she run up to the house.

"They all think you're dead, you know."

He pulled back his clenched fist just in time, heart pounding.

"Holy cow, Blaze, I almost took you out."

She stepped out of the shadows and shrugged. Then she threw herself into his arms, and he sucked in a breath as his ribs screamed in protest.

She immediately pulled back. "Sorry, I forgot about your ribs. I'm glad you're not dead."

He grinned. "Yeah, me, too."

She cocked her head, studying his face. "Why are you letting them think you died in the explosion?"

How much to tell this too-smart teen? He decided she could handle the truth. "Because I don't think my truck randomly exploded."

At his words, Blaze wrapped her arms around her chest. "You think it was deliberate."

"I do."

"Did you find Sasha?"

"No. Not yet," he added, refusing to think about any other outcome.

"Pop and Mama Rosa were asking about Sasha. I told them she was with you so they wouldn't worry."

"That was probably smart. But that left you to worry all by yourself."

Her chin came up, and he was reminded—again—of how much she resembled Sasha at that age. "I can handle it."

He stepped closer and wrapped her in a gentle hug. "I know you can, Blaze. But that doesn't mean you should, not alone."

She leaned back and met his eyes. "Where is she? Do you think someone took her?"

Right now, that was his working theory. "I'm trying to check all the angles."

She pulled out of his arms. "Please. That's the kind of grown-up doublespeak I hate."

He huffed out a breath. Debated. "OK, truth. Yes, I think someone took her. I don't know who and I don't know why. Maybe the search for Tony. Maybe because they don't want me to race tomorrow."

"What are you going to do?"

"I'm going to keep looking. Will you look after Bella? I don't want anything to happen to her."

"You don't have a car."

"Right. I was hoping you could bring me Sasha's keys."

She shook her head. "I already looked for them. They're not here. She must have had them with her when she . . . when . . . I couldn't find a spare," she finished.

Jesse grinned. "Then it's a good thing I remember how to hot-wire a car from my misspent youth."

"When they ask about Sasha, what should I say? I don't want to lie."

"Nope. Don't. Just say you haven't heard from her."

"You'll find her?" In that moment, Blaze looked every bit the scared teen she was. He walked over and gave her another quick hug. "I won't stop until I do. Take care of Bella and your folks for me in the meantime." In moments, he had the Jeep hot-wired and was roaring out of the marina.

He headed out toward the place Marge at the Blue Dolphin had recommended. He pulled out his phone and plugged what little he knew of the location into his GPS, which he'd named Linda.

"Come on, come on, Linda. Tell me where it is," he muttered as Linda tried to figure out where he wanted to go. Finally she spit out a location about twenty-five miles north of Safe Harbor.

He felt the minutes tick by the farther he drove. His only consolation was that this location seemed remote enough to effectively hide someone. He refused to dwell on the possibility that whoever took Sasha might have done more than hide her.

The two-lane highway narrowed to one. Then the pavement gave way to dirt and gravel. He bounced over ruts in the road, ducking whenever palm fronds slapped the Jeep as he went by. This road obviously wasn't well traveled, which upped his conviction he was headed in the right direction. Linda continued to give instructions, and he dutifully turned left, then right, then left again before he skidded to a stop before a huge, gaping hole. It stretched the width of the dirt track, and had he not been paying attention, the Jeep would have disappeared into the opening. He stopped inches from the hole and climbed out, peering into the darkness below. This sinkhole must have opened up recently.

Behind him, Linda announced he had reached his destination. He stopped and turned in a circle, looking for the place Marge had described, but he saw nothing but pine trees and scrub palms. There was nothing here.

Frustrated and feeling he'd just wasted precious time, he plugged the name in again. Linda directed him to another dead end. And another. And one more. When his GPS finally spit out an area about fifteen miles southeast of town, in what looked like the back end of a nature preserve, he decided to give it one more try.

He glanced up at the sun, appalled at how much time had gone by. Wincing as the Jeep bounced over the ruts in the dirt track, he retraced his route to Safe Harbor, then headed southeast. Not sure what else to do, he followed Linda's instructions off the pavement and onto yet another dirt road, which wasn't unusual out here, but proved tricky with darkness closing in. He'd forgotten just how fast it got dark away from the ambient light of town.

Even with the high beams on, visibility steadily decreased. Heavy underbrush scraped both sides of the Jeep as he went by, and mosquitos the size of small birds swarmed around his head. He tried to see into the woods and find whatever Marge told him was out here, anything that resembled a homestead, but he couldn't make out a thing.

Clouds of dust billowed behind him as he bounced over potholes and tracks left by other vehicles.

Wait. He stopped the Jeep and climbed out to get a better look. Yes, these were fresh tire tracks. It hadn't rained in what, three days? Otherwise, they would have been washed away. Someone had driven this way recently, in a vehicle with big tires and deep treads.

Hope filled him. Finally. He followed the tire tracks, aware that if someone were watching him, his headlights would make him an easy target. He couldn't worry about that now. He had to find Sasha.

He wished he had his gun, but he hadn't gone to the trouble of getting it back from the Tampa police yet. He hadn't thought he'd need it.

He shook his head. He wouldn't think about that. If he had it to do over, he'd have done the same thing to protect Ethan, so it was a moot point.

Ahead, water ran across the road, which wasn't unusual in this low, marshy area. He kept his foot steady on the accelerator and drove into the water. Suddenly the ground fell away, and the Jeep sank down farther than he'd expected. *No, no, no. Don't quit on me now.*

He struggled to keep the Jeep moving forward, but the steep drop had stopped his momentum.

He kept giving it steady pressure, hoping that would get him moving again, but mud spewed out from under the tires and made him sink even farther. He slammed a hand on the steering wheel. He reached over to the glove box and rooted around. He spotted a small flashlight.

"Atta girl, Sash," he mumbled as he flicked it on and climbed out of the Jeep.

He stepped out into calf-deep water, mud sucking down his flip-flops. He aimed the light around and up onto the banks, looking for something he could put under the tires to provide some traction.

Just then the Jeep sputtered, coughed, and died.

"No, dang it." He sloshed back to the driver's side and looked at the gauges. He'd run out of gas. He wanted to throw something or howl in frustration. He'd like to blame Sasha, but he hadn't even looked at the gauge when he climbed in. *Stupid, stupid, stupid.*

Now what? How was he going to find her? He thought for a moment, then turned off the headlights. He climbed up into the Jeep and stood on the driver's seat and waited for his eyes to adjust. Then he took his time, scanning in every direction, searching for a building or something that would give him a target.

He was ready to give up when he saw something in the distance, between a stand of trees. Was that a roof? He waited, eyes steady on the location. Yes, he'd swear that was the roof of what was probably a barn. Since there wasn't anything else out here for miles, that had to be what he was looking for. Now all he had to do was get there.

If that wasn't the place . . . he wouldn't let his mind go there. He just had to keep moving.

He rummaged around under Sasha's seat, hoping she kept some type of weapon stashed. He grinned when his hand closed over the handle of a knife. He pulled it out and strapped it to his belt, then took the flashlight and started running.

His best bet was to keep following the tire tracks. With any luck, Marge hadn't sent him on a wild goose chase and he'd find Sasha there.

Just the thought of what she might be facing had him racing down the road, ignoring his aching ribs. He kept moving, flashlight pointing the way. He had to find her.

Quick.

Chapter 20

Sasha woke to the sound of voices. Daylight filled the barn. She forced herself to stay perfectly still so they would think she was still out cold. Her muscles wanted to clench, but she deliberately relaxed her limbs.

The voices were male, and while she mostly heard nothing but a faint rumble, one word suddenly became clear. Her breath caught. Jesse. They were talking about Jesse.

She strained to hear, trying to quiet the hammering of her heart. When she realized what they were saying, she bit her lip to keep from crying out.

"The explosion took out his truck . . . couldn't have survived . . . haven't heard . . . has to be dead."

The words hit Sasha like hurricane-force winds—relentless, unforgiving, unmistakable.

Jesse was dead? *No, oh please, God, no.*

She forced herself to take slow breaths. She couldn't draw attention to herself now. What did they mean by an explosion? What happened? Her muscles wanted to shake from the effort of holding herself motionless, but she wouldn't make a sound. She had to know more.

". . . still take the sub . . . in case we need it . . . boss doesn't want any screw-ups . . ."

Silent tears tracked down her cheeks as the truth sank in. Jesse was dead. Gone from her life forever. And she'd never told him how she felt about him, never had the guts to confess she loved him. Always had.

Even with his ridiculous proposal, she'd let fear keep her silent. And for what? Her foolish pride? *Oh, God. Please don't let this be true.*

Maybe she'd misunderstood. Not that unlikely, given her foggy brain. But in her heart, she knew she'd have to face the truth that he was gone. She blocked the pain, mentally packing it in a trunk for later, because she knew if she let her emotions run free right now, they'd swamp her and take her under.

If something horrible really had happened to Jesse—and she'd deal with that later—then she had to race *The Lady* today and show whoever was behind this that they hadn't won. She'd get there on time and she'd win Jesse that money. Her mind skimmed back to their conversation about Ethan and she suddenly realized what she'd missed until now. Ethan saving Jesse's life, Ethan's sick little girl, Jesse talking about repaying a debt. This wasn't about a fresh start. Jesse had needed that money for Adelaide's surgery. Well, Sasha would make sure Adelaide's mom got it. It might very well be the last thing she could ever do for him. She wouldn't let him down. Not this time.

She tuned in again to what the men were saying, but they'd moved out of earshot. Thankfully they weren't paying any attention to her. They were focused on something on the other side of the barn. She heard rustling, metal clanking, and then what sounded like a pickup truck's engine, but she couldn't be sure.

Within a few minutes they were gone, the barn door closed behind them.

She waited a few more minutes, listening to the silence, to be sure they were really gone.

It was now or never. *Oh, Jesse.*

She rolled over until she faced the room and made out several pieces of old farm equipment and square hay bales, piled in towering heaps. One bit of equipment had disc-looking things you pulled behind a tractor. That had to have sharp edges, right? Even if they were rusty.

She rolled over and over, then maneuvered herself around until her bound hands were up against the edges of one of the discs. She pulled the duct tape tight over the edge and sawed her hands back and forth. She was breathing hard by the time the tape started to give. Finally it split, and she fell forward, landing face-first in the dirt. Again.

She lay there a minute to catch her breath, then used her hands to push herself up and pull the blindfold off. She shook out her arms and flexed her hands to get the circulation going again.

She gripped the sides of the machine and pulled herself to a sitting position, then raised her bound feet over the edge of one of the discs and started the process all over again. Her stomach muscles protested the longer she worked. "Should have kept up with the sit-ups," she panted.

Finally her legs popped free.

She tried to stand and almost fell off her wedge sandals, so she slipped them off and took them with her in case she needed them later. Her legs tingled and wanted to collapse under her, and the room had an annoying tendency to spin, but she figured that was from hunger. First things first.

She walked around the barn, searching for a way out. She tried the big door, but it wouldn't budge. She peered through a crack and saw the large padlock on the outside.

Frustration swamped her, but she wouldn't give up. She had to do this for Jesse.

Finally she spotted a small shuttered opening about twelve feet off the ground. Maybe they used to pour corn or something through it. But it looked like the shutter opened from the inside. If she could get up there, she should be able to climb out.

She scanned the pile of hay bales below the window and headed up, her sandals hanging over her left wrist. She'd almost reached the window when her foot slipped, and she almost tumbled to the ground. She hung on, panting, until her heart rate settled enough to keep going.

Hurry, hurry, hurry.

She scrambled the rest of the way to the top and smacked her fist against the shutter clasp until it gave way. She swung it open, and the sunlight almost blinded her. Without giving herself time to think, she tossed her sandals out the window and then wiggled through the opening, head first.

Her hips got stuck. Of course. She wiggled and tugged until she pitched forward through the opening, rolling into a ball just before she landed on the grassy sand below.

Ouch.

She lay there for several minutes until the world stopped spinning. All her moving parts still worked, so she slowly sat up and groaned. Even her hair hurt.

A gash on her leg oozed blood, so she wiped it with a handful of grass and slowly got to her feet.

She looked up at the sky. Based on the position of the sun, it was already nearing nine o'clock. She turned in a slow circle, getting her bearings, then hurried away from the barn and headed west, toward the Gulf and Safe Harbor.

She would win that race for Jesse and Adelaide. No matter what.

The sun was barely above the horizon when Jesse heard a vehicle on the road. He'd headed toward what he thought was a barn hours ago, only to find nothing but dead trees and tricks of his mind when he got there. Frustrated, he'd spent most of the night going in circles, desperate to find her.

He ducked into the thick underbrush beside the road, crouched down, and waited to see if they passed by.

It didn't take long before an aging pickup came into view, pulling what he thought was a boat behind it under a tarp. But the shape wasn't right. Was this the minisub Sasha had seen?

He tried to see into the cab of the truck, but whoever was in it—and it looked like there were two people—had dark glasses on and ball caps pulled low over their heads.

The truck looked vaguely familiar, but he couldn't remember where he'd seen it before. He could follow them back to town, but he had to make sure Sasha wasn't being held hostage wherever they'd come from.

In the morning light, he finally saw the building. That had to be it! He ignored his screaming ribs as he ran. *Don't let me be too late, God, please.*

It looked deserted. He walked around, tugged on the padlocked door. "Sasha! Are you in there?" He wasn't surprised when no one answered. The place had an empty feel to it.

Still, he had to be sure. He kept walking until he found a smaller door, wedged closed. He braced himself, then rammed it with his shoulder. He gasped at the pain, but grinned when it opened just far enough for him to squeeze through.

Once his eyes adjusted, he looked around, then headed toward the far side, where rusted farm equipment leaned against the wall. She'd been held here. He'd bet his life on it. His fury grew as he spotted a dog's upended water bowl. Something glinted a dull silver. He picked up a jagged piece of duct tape from the floor and noticed another piece stuck to the teeth of the tiller. They'd tied her up, but she'd gotten loose.

Atta girl, Sash.

He turned and almost tripped over a wooden crate half buried under a pile of hay. He stepped closer and realized it wasn't hay; it was the straw used in packing crates. Whatever had been shipped in the crate was gone. His heart pounded, and memories of his military days came rushing back. Unless he'd completely lost his mind, weapons were transported in crates like these. He froze when he found a label.

His heart slammed his bruised ribs as he tried to process what he was seeing. There had been two torpedoes in this box. Now it was empty. What would someone do with two torpedoes? In Safe Harbor, of all places? Sasha said she'd seen a minisub, possibly the same vehicle he saw this morning. Were they connected? How?

Both had to do with water. Given the lengths someone had gone to in order to keep him and his boat out of the race, the only thing that made sense was that someone wanted him out of the way today. Sasha, too, if they thought she might race in his place.

Sweet Jesus. He had to find her, make sure she was safe. Then he had to prevent whatever evil someone had planned for today's race.

He thought of Adelaide, and his heart clenched. He'd get the money for her surgery another way somehow—even if it meant going to work for his father's company to get it.

He saw the opening far up on the wall. That had to be how she'd escaped.

He hurried outside, and despite his growing panic, a slow smile spread over his face. Sasha was flat-out amazing. She had jumped out that crazy-high window to the ground. His blood froze when he saw a clump of bloodied grass on the ground. His heart rate slowed to slightly less than full gallop when he found footprints leading away from the barn.

She was heading for the marina.

One hand around his bruised ribs, he raced after her, eyes on her tracks as he went.

Sasha hadn't gone far before palm fronds sliced her arms and tree roots attacked her toes, but she didn't stop, didn't slow down. She could do this, for Jesse.

Suddenly she stopped, listened. She'd heard a car. She veered off in that direction and was rewarded a few minutes later when a single-lane road appeared.

She heard another car behind her and stopped. Hide? Or ask for a ride?

She moved off to the side and huffed out a breath when a police SUV came into view. What if Chief Monroe sat behind the wheel? She decided to take the risk. She was exhausted, physically and mentally. When she stepped out into the road, the driver slowed.

"What are you doing way out here, Sasha?" Nick asked.

"I could ask you the same thing." Could she trust him?

"I got a call out this way to do a wellness check on old Mrs. Donnelly. Her daughter hadn't heard from her since yesterday and she was worried."

She searched his eyes but saw no sign of lying, no nervousness, nothing that made her instincts twitch. She'd trusted him with Tony's clothes. Why doubt him now?

"Is she OK?"

He grinned. "Oh yeah. Drunk as a skunk and singing at the top of her lungs while swinging in her hammock."

He looked her over. "You OK? Do you need a ride? What happened to your leg?"

She climbed in the passenger side. "It's a long story, but the short version is that someone drugged me and stashed me in an old barn back that way." She hitched a thumb over her shoulder.

His eyes narrowed, and the good old boy instantly morphed into a cop on duty. "Start at the beginning. When did this happen? Did you get a look at who did this? I'll take you to the hospital, get you checked out. Then we'll figure out what's going on."

Sasha held up a hand. "I'm fine, physically. I don't need to get checked out. And I'll do whatever I can to help you figure everything out, but right now, I'm kind of in a hurry. Can you get me to the marina, quick? My family must be worried." She wanted to tell him she was scrambling to make the race in Clearwater, but she worried that he might try to stop her. For her own safety or some such nonsense. Better to skip that part for now.

He nodded grimly and flipped on the flashing red and blue lights. "I'd rather take you to the hospital, but I know you won't go."

Sasha didn't say anything else until Nick reached down to a small cooler on the floor and handed her a cold bottle of water. She wanted to gulp it down, but forced herself to sip it slowly. "Any news yet from your friend at the lab?"

"Still waiting. But it's early days yet."

Several minutes later, he flipped off the lights and pulled into the marina's gravel lot. Before she could escape, he stopped her with a hand on her arm. "Reassure your family and get some rest while I start trying to figure this out. I'll be back in a little while to hear your story in detail."

She nodded her thanks as he left the marina.

She turned and almost got knocked down by Bella, who stood on her hind legs and licked her face. Sasha laughed and pushed her down.

"Yes, girl. I love you, too. Now, down." She rubbed her back and scratched behind her ears.

Welcome greeting completed, Sasha came face-to-face with a scowling Blaze. "Did Jesse find you?"

Sasha's heart stopped, and fresh pain threatened to buckle her knees. How would she tell Blaze about Jesse's death? "No. I, ah, haven't seen him in a while."

"Someone blew up his truck. He let them think he was dead so he could go looking for you."

"He let them think he was dead? But he's OK?" Joy wanted to burst free, but she had to know, had to be sure.

Blaze eyed her. "He's fine. He said Bella warned him."

Sasha grabbed Blaze in a bone-crushing hug before she could pull away. "Oh, thank you, Jesus! He's OK." Blaze squirmed out of her grasp, and Sasha wiped unexpected tears from her face.

"Stop, you're getting me all wet."

Sasha grinned. "Sorry, kid."

Blaze crossed her arms, met her gaze. "You thought he was dead."

Sasha nodded and looked around. "I did. Wow. So glad that's not true. Where is he?"

"He went looking for you."

Sasha glanced up at the house, thinking, trying to make sure she didn't miss something important. "How much have you told Mama and Pop?"

"As little as possible. I let them think you were with Jesse. He took your Jeep."

Sasha tried to take a step, and the world spun. "I think I need to eat."

Blaze stepped over and wrapped an arm around her waist, keeping her upright. "A shower wouldn't hurt, either."

"I need to get to Clearwater for the race."

Blaze's eyes widened. "I don't think that's a good idea. Jesse was really worried about you." She looked Sasha up and down. "You're bleeding, too."

"I'm fine. I just need to eat, I think. Will you grab me something with protein, while I shower? I need to get there on time. Jesse needs to win this race." She stopped and looked deep into Blaze's eyes. "It's important."

Blaze started walking. "Yeah, yeah. Whatever. Just don't pass out and crash, OK?"

Sasha smiled. "Wasn't planning on it."

Sasha hurried upstairs and took a quick shower, wincing when she saw the bruise on her cheek and the scratches all over her arms. She reached for her mariner's cross and stopped. It was gone. Unexpected panic filled her. It was her last link to her biological family; it was her anchor. She wanted to rush out and find it, but Jesse needed her more. She tried to remember when she'd touched it last and decided she must have lost it in the barn or on the way home.

She doctored the gash on her leg with a couple of butterfly bandages, since it still wanted to bleed. She braided her hair before she took a few minutes to cover the bruises on her face to limit explanations.

When she returned to the kitchen, Blaze handed her a plate of scrambled eggs, several slices of bacon and cheese, and two pieces of buttered toast. Sasha gave her a quick hug before she could pull away, then piled all the food onto the bread for a sandwich. She washed it down with a big glass of milk and glanced at the clock.

Pop came in. "Sasha. There you are." He leaned over and kissed her cheek.

She rinsed her glass and grabbed a ball cap. "I've got to go."

"Go where?"

"Clearwater. The race starts soon."

Their eyes met, and he studied her face for a long moment, his look troubled. "I don't think this is a good idea, Sasha, given . . . everything that's happened lately."

Sasha raised her chin. "Which is exactly why I'm going. Somebody thinks they got Jesse out of the race. So I'll go on his behalf." Now was not the time to express her worry that maybe her own kidnapping could have something to do with the race. Though she still wasn't sure how.

"I worry for you, Sasha."

His words pierced her heart, but she pushed them away. She gave him a quick kiss on the cheek. "I know, Pop. But I need to do this."

"Where's Jesse?"

Sasha grabbed the small cooler filled with water Blaze handed her, and sent her a grateful smile. "I don't know. He must be running late. You coming to the race?" As soon as the words slipped out, she wanted to call them back. "I wasn't thinking. Take care of Mama. Wish me luck."

"You go, Pop. I'll take care of Mama," Blaze said.

Sasha turned and grabbed her in a quick hug before she could protest. "Thanks, Blaze," she whispered.

"It's Bethany," Blaze hissed.

Sasha stopped, halfway out the door. "What?"

"My name is Bethany." Her chin came up, challenge in her eyes.

"It's a beautiful name. Thanks for telling me. See you later." She rushed down the dock, smiling. Blaze, aka Bethany, would be all right.

Sasha let herself into Jesse's shed and fished the boat key out from where he kept it hidden. She hopped aboard *The Painted Lady* and turned the blower on, checked the fuel levels—bless Pop for filling the tanks!—and ran through her pretrip checklist.

Within minutes she was heading south, the clock ticking in her head. She had to get there in time. She had to. Luckily, *The Painted Lady* could get her there with no trouble. Jesse had her purring like a kitten. There wasn't much wind today, so the water was pretty calm, too, which helped.

The farther she went, the better she felt. She flung her head back and laughed at the feel of the wind in her face and the sun on her back. There was no other feeling like it in the entire world.

She could do this. She'd win this race. For Jesse.

Sasha's footprints ended at the side of the road. Jesse figured either she'd kept walking on the pavement, or someone had given her a ride, since there was no sign of her on the arrow-straight road.

He heard a vehicle behind him, but instead of flagging it down, he ducked into the bushes. Something about the engine sounded familiar.

The hair on the back of his neck stood up when he saw the same pickup he'd seen that morning.

He waited, searching his memory.

He thought back to his breakfast at the Blue Dolphin with Bella, and the pieces clicked. He'd glanced out the window and seen that same truck turning into the street from the alley where he'd parked his truck.

Was he spinning conspiracy theories like a lunatic? Maybe, except that ten minutes later his truck exploded.

When the truck made a U-turn and headed back in his direction, Jesse eased farther back into the underbrush. They were looking for him.

Or for Sasha. She'd said she'd seen what looked like an ancient pickup the night she saw the minisub. He'd bet money he saw the same one this morning. Which meant these were the people after him—and Sasha.

He had to get to the marina. Make sure she was safe. And then, get hold of Nick. If these guys had a minisub in the water, armed with torpedoes no less, he knew they wouldn't hesitate to kill either of them.

As soon as the truck disappeared from view, he started running toward Safe Harbor.

His ribs hurt so badly he could barely draw breath. He had slowed to a walk, trying to take shallow breaths so he could pick up the pace again, when a big boat of a Buick pulled in behind him and Mrs. Robertson hopped out. Hard to imagine the tiny woman could maneuver that barge, but she did. She rushed over to him.

"Jesse Claybourne, are you all right? You look terrible, young man."

"Hello, Mrs. Robertson. Any chance you could give me a ride to Safe Harbor?"

"Of course. But aren't you supposed to be in that big highfalutin race today in Clearwater?"

Jesse climbed in the passenger seat and sighed as his aching body sank into the soft leather. "Yes, ma'am. But my ribs won't let me."

She started the car with a roar, and Jesse studied her for a moment as she eased onto the highway at thirty-five miles per hour.

"Mrs. Robertson, I really need to get to the marina. Sasha may be in danger."

Her eyes widened behind her spectacles, and she gripped the steering wheel. "Well, why didn't you say so?" She clenched her jaw and stomped down on the accelerator, and the car rocketed down the highway like it had been shot from a cannon.

When they arrived at the marina in a spray of gravel, he leaned over and kissed her cheek. "Thanks, Mrs. Robertson."

"You look out for our Sasha, young man."

"Yes, ma'am. I intend to."

When she barreled out of the parking lot, Bella raced up to him, Blaze hot on her heels. "Where have you been?"

He looked over at *The Painted Lady*'s empty slip, and his heart kicked into overdrive. *Please, God, don't let her have gone to Clearwater.* But in his heart, he knew. He looked back at Blaze. "Sasha's on *The Lady*?"

Blaze nodded. "Headed for Clearwater like her pants are on fire."

"Where's Sal? I need a boat."

"He just went down to the marina store to get something. Then he's going to Clearwater to watch the race. Mama had a rough morning, but she's sleeping now."

He leaned over and kissed her forehead. "Thanks for holding down the fort, Blaze." Then he ran to the marina store as fast as his ribs would let him.

Jesse burst into the store and headed straight for the office in the back. "Sal, I need a boat."

Sal's head snapped up. "Thank God you're OK. What's wrong?"

"I need to intercept Sasha. You have a boat I can borrow?"

To his credit, Sal didn't waste time asking questions. He simply reached into a drawer and tossed him a key.

"She's in the last slip on the south side. Tank's full. You need me to ride with you?"

"No thanks. But I appreciate it." He turned to go. "You going to Clearwater?"

Sal nodded. "Absolutely. How can I help?"

Jesse thought for a moment. "Knowing you'll be there means a lot. If I need anything else, I'll let you know."

"I don't know what's going on, Jesse, but you keep my girl safe, you hear?"

"That's the plan, Sal." He held up the keys. "Thanks."

He hopped into the boat, started her up, and raced out of the marina.

If only he could get there in time.

Chapter 21

Sasha made it to the small marina just north of Clearwater with scant minutes to spare. She tied up at one of the slips and raced into the marina office just in time to check in with the race official and refuel the boat.

"Captain Sasha Petrov of *The Painted Lady* of Safe Harbor Marina, on behalf of owner Jesse Claybourne," she announced, hand outstretched.

The man looked her up and down as he shook her hand. "Do you have credentials?"

Sasha merely raised a brow as she reached into her hip pocket. "Of course." She handed him her captain's license and other official paperwork, hoping he wouldn't question Jesse's absence.

"You just made it. Starting gun is in thirty minutes." He handed her a T-shirt with a number pinned to the back of it. "Good luck."

"Thank you, sir." Relieved, she shook his hand again, then ducked into the ladies' room to don the shirt before heading back outside. It didn't take long at all before she was out in deeper water, idling at the starting line with the other vintage power boats.

A quick glance showed she was the only lady captain, but she wasn't worried. Let them send her their smug looks and nod like they were so superior. She'd show them soon enough.

She was going to get Jesse that prize. She could feel it.

The announcer started jabbering and the boats moved into position. Another boat, two feet longer than *The Painted Lady*, tried to edge her out of position, but Sasha held *The Lady* steady, forcing the other boat to back off or risk bumping into her. The man glared, and Sasha smiled serenely.

She wouldn't show her hand too early. Let them think she didn't have a clue.

As soon as the starting gun fired, she hit the throttle. *The Lady* leaped under her commands and soon she was in fourth place, gaining on the number three boat.

Out of the corner of her eye she saw something in the water ahead at about one o'clock, and her heart skipped a beat. What was that? She eased *The Lady* farther west to avoid whatever it was that bobbed just below the surface.

Sasha kept her eyes on the boats ahead of her, with quick glimpses behind to see who was gaining on her. So far so good. The other boats were maintaining speed behind her.

She glanced over at what she'd seen, and suddenly her brain registered what it was.

The minisub! What was it doing out here in open water—and barely submerged? If someone wasn't paying attention, they'd run right into it.

She gave it wide berth as the boats raced down the straightaway, everyone holding their position.

They made the first turn without a problem and were heading back toward the marina when Sasha spotted some idiot racing right toward them—from the wrong direction. Was the guy crazy? What was he doing?

Sasha lost sight of him as the boats made the next turn, passing in front of the grandstands on shore and the cheering crowds. She dutifully waved, but never took her eyes from the boats around her. While the other captains were busy smiling and waving, Sasha inched the throttle forward and *The Lady* eased into the number-three spot. The crowd went wild, but Sasha ignored them. Only two more laps to go and she could win that money for Jesse.

She made the next turn, and suddenly the *Griffon*, which had tried to get her spot at the starting line, pushed ahead of her, forcing her to slow or risk a collision. Sasha eased back on the throttle, then picked up speed again.

She could so win this.

Jesse thought his heart would hammer right out of his chest when he saw that idiot try to maneuver right under *The Lady*'s bow. Was the guy nuts?

Sasha didn't panic, though; she just eased around him and, in a burst of speed, got *The Lady* back into the number-three slot.

Win or lose, he'd be forever grateful. But right now, he had to find that sub, see what they were up to. He throttled back, looking over the area he thought he had seen it in. He waited, scanning, always scanning, and was rewarded when sunlight glinted off the bubble dome.

It had moved and now bobbed right in line with the boats currently at the other end of the racecourse. What were they planning?

He maneuvered Sal's little johnboat back around and idled behind the minisub. He watched as the boats came screaming toward them again, but he kept his eyes glued to the little submarine. He rummaged around under the seat and could have kissed Sal when he found a pair of binoculars. The glass was a bit cloudy, but he wiped the lenses on his T-shirt and trained his eyes on the minisub.

As the boats raced past his location, Jesse finally caught a glimpse of the operator, a man, fiddling with the console, aiming the minisub directly at Sasha. The man's eyes never left *The Painted Lady*.

A wave brought the sub partway up out of the water, and Jesse caught a glimpse of what was underneath. His blood ran cold as his suspicions were confirmed.

Dear Jesus, they'd mounted the two torpedoes on the minisub. He couldn't let him hurt Sasha. He reached over and pulled on a life jacket, tightening the straps. Then, as the boats rocketed toward him again, he set his little boat on a course straight for the minisub. He whipped off his belt and used it to secure the throttle in position, hoping it was enough to keep the boat moving in a straight line.

He got as close as dared, keeping out of the sub's line of sight until the last possible moment, which wasn't hard, since the operator was completely focused on Sasha and *The Lady*.

Just before his johnboat crashed into the minisub, Jesse leaped off the boat.

He surfaced just in time to see the two vessels collide.

And explode.

"Sorry, Sal," he muttered, treading water.

He watched the racers take note of the commotion and steer clear of the burning wreckage and floating debris.

Once they passed him again, he started swimming toward shore. Sasha had been in the number-two spot when she went by. He had no doubt she would win.

He tried not to think about whoever had been in that sub.

When what looked like a fireworks barge exploded just outside the racecourse, Sasha gripped the steering wheel and tried not to let it distract her or throw her off course. Had someone detonated them too early?

Was there a fireworks display planned for later? She had no idea, but she couldn't worry about it right this second.

She had one more lap to get *The Lady* into first place. She pushed the throttle farther forward, and *The Lady* increased speed. The *Grey Goose* in the lead wasn't going to make it easy. As Sasha tried to pass on the starboard side, the *Goose* moved in front of her, keeping her just behind him the whole way.

As they entered the last turn, Sasha decided to let him get a little bit ahead so he'd relax, maybe get a little cocky. The minute he did, she gunned the throttle, and *The Lady* blew right past him and across the finish line.

Sasha eased back on the throttle and headed back to the marina, a satisfied smile on her face. She'd done it. She'd won the race for Jesse.

As she approached the marina, she scanned the crowds lining the dock, hoping to spot him, but if he was there, she couldn't find him. Anxiety slid down her spine. Surely by now he knew she'd taken *The Lady*. Where was he?

Not far from the grandstand, she spotted Pop. He tipped his hat, and the gesture made her heart clench. "Love you," she mouthed, and he blew her a kiss and gave her a thumbs-up.

Where was Jesse?

She secured *The Painted Lady* and let a race official congratulate her and lead her to the podium, where they handed her an enormous trophy and a big fat check. She smiled as the cameras flashed, but all she wanted was to get away, to find Jesse.

Something wasn't right. Blaze said someone blew up his truck.

She thought of the explosion on the water and spun in a circle, scanning the crowd, looking for him.

"Sasha!" Pop called, elbowing his way through the throng. She wrapped her arms around him, surprised at how weak her knees felt all of a sudden.

"You did good, Sasha, *mia bella*."

She pulled back to look at him. "Where's Jesse?"

He wouldn't meet her eyes. "I don't know." He took her hand. "We should go. Leave *The Lady* here. We'll come back for her."

Sasha nodded. Now that the adrenaline was wearing off, bone-deep exhaustion was setting in. All around them, people were talking about the explosion. Official boats milled around the site, lights flashing.

"Do you know what happened?" Sasha asked as Pop led her through the crowd.

"I'm not really sure."

Reporters swarmed around her, thrusting microphones in her face. Sasha stopped, held up a hand to get their attention. "I am honored to have won the race today and am grateful for the skill and great driving exhibited by all the captains in the race today. Thank you."

"What did you think when you saw the boat explode?" a balding reporter asked.

Sasha's smile vanished, and her anxiety reached new levels. "I was unaware it was a boat. I thought some fireworks detonated early. Is the captain OK?"

"No word yet. What are your thoughts?"

In that moment, Sasha had no thoughts but to find Jesse. "Thank you all for being here."

The reporters chased her all the way back to Sal's truck, shouting questions, but she ignored them. There was only one person she wanted to see. Once they were headed home, Sasha said, "Tell me what's going on, Pop."

Pop glanced her way. "I wish I knew, Sasha. I know Jesse was worried about you, and he borrowed a boat in a hurry . . ."

Sasha's stomach clenched as she turned to Sal. "Your johnboat? That's what he borrowed?"

Sal kept his eyes on the road.

Sasha studied his expression and tried to voice the fear that suddenly gripped her heart. Her voice came out a whisper. "Was he in that explosion?"

"I pray not."

"Pop!"

He sighed. "He didn't say much, Sasha. Only that he thought you were in danger and he needed to borrow my boat."

"Then we need to get out there and see if he's OK. Turn around! Go back!"

But Sal didn't change course, just kept driving.

"Pop, what are you doing? Go back!"

"No, *mia bella*. Jesse also asked me to keep you safe." He patted her hand. "If he's hurt, the official boats will take care of him. I think you should lie low."

Sasha had to figure out what was going on. "My name will be all over the news."

Pop sent her a half grin. "All over Tampa and Clearwater, sure. But it wasn't that big a race."

Sasha tried to think, to make sense of it all. "I don't understand any of this." Jesse couldn't be dead. Not after everything they'd been through. He had to be OK. He had to be. She had to get back to the marina and make sure he was alive.

Pop reached over and gripped her hand. "Let's just get you home and hope Jesse is OK."

She turned on him, disbelieving. "Are you crazy? We have to make sure he's OK." She lunged for the steering wheel, but Pop fought her off. Jesse needed her. She had to get to him. A dull roar filled her ears as she fought Pop for control of the vehicle, arms flailing, desperation making her crazy. Pop tried to bat her hands away, to keep the truck on the road, but she wouldn't stop, couldn't stop.

Jesse.

Suddenly, in all the flailing, Pop's elbow connected with her cheek, and her head snapped back and hit the door frame, hard. She heard him murmur, "I'm sorry," as the last few days caught up with her and she slid into oblivion.

Jesse hadn't thought his ribs could hurt more than they already did, but he was wrong. It was getting harder and harder to draw breath, and he wondered if the jump from the boat had punctured a lung. Thank God for the life jacket. It was a fisherman's vest, not one of those orange horse collars, so he turned on his back and floated. His brain still seemed fuzzy, so he had to work to focus. Was the tide going in or out?

In. *Thank you, Jesus.* It would push him to shore, as long as there weren't any odd currents that caught him. Or rocks.

Worry for Sasha gnawed at him and he fought the urge to close his eyes and sleep. No. He had to stay awake, get to shore, find Sasha.

Jesse opened his eyes and glanced around at the dark water, the dark sky; he was disoriented. Something slammed his head, and he realized he'd drifted into some rocks. Sasha, he had to find Sasha. He forced himself to turn over, and his feet touched bottom. He scrambled for a handhold on the nearest rock and pulled himself up out of the water.

He sat there a few minutes, still unable to draw a deep breath, and tried to climb over the rocks to shore. It wasn't that far, but he couldn't seem to make himself move.

"Hey, you there, on the rocks. Are you OK?"

A flashlight shone in his face, and he put up a hand to block it. The voice came closer. "Well, dang, son, you're a bloody mess." A hand appeared, as rough as the male voice that went with it. "Let me help you."

Jesse wondered briefly if this was a trick of some sort, but then decided it didn't matter. He couldn't fight back right now no matter what. He let the man pull him to his feet and half drag, half carry him to the sandy shore.

They walked a couple dozen feet across the sand, and the man said, "Hang on and let me get my truck. You need a doctor."

Jesse collapsed the moment the man let go and sank onto the sand. The man helped him into the truck, and that was the last thing he remembered.

Sasha woke on the couch with Pop shaking her awake. "Sasha. Wake up. The hospital called. They have Jesse."

Thank you, Jesus. He was alive. Her breath whooshed out in a big sigh. She sat up and winced at the pain in her cheek. "You knocked me out with your elbow."

Pop raised his chin. "Not on purpose. But I had to keep you safe."

Sasha wanted to argue, but now wasn't the time.

"Is Jesse OK? How did he get to the hospital?"

"Shirley's an ER nurse, and she said some old guy brought him in, saying Jesse washed up behind his house and just kept telling him to take him to Safe Harbor."

Sasha forced her aching body up to a standing position. "I need to get there, to see him, find out what's going on."

Pop put a hand under her elbow and led her out to his truck. "That's where we're headed."

Sasha never cried; she wouldn't let herself. Her Russian papa had always told her tears solved nothing; only action helped. But unbidden tears rolled down her cheeks when she walked into the ER cubicle and saw Jesse's battered face. Both eyes were black and blue, and he had bruises everywhere. She leaned over and gave him a gentle kiss on the cheek.

When his eyes opened, they were red and bloodshot, but Sasha had never seen a more welcome sight.

"You're OK," he whispered, and pulled her close. "I thought I'd lost you."

"That's my line." Sasha swallowed hard and pulled back to look at him. *Thank you, Lord.*

He studied her face, then brought his thumbs up and wiped her tears away. "You're crying. You never cry."

"I thought I lost you, too." She tucked her cheek into his palm, then raised her head and met his gaze. "What happened, Jesse?"

"You first," he said. "Do you know who kidnapped you? I found the barn."

"No, I never saw their faces. But I think it was the same guys who tried to put an arrow through me. I think I saw the sub in the barn."

"I think you're right. I also think whatever they were trying to do isn't over yet." He pushed back the covers, winced, and started climbing out of bed. "We need to get to the marina."

She put a hand on his arm. "Jesse, no, this is crazy. You need to stay here and get your strength back."

He reached for his shirt, realized they must have cut it off him, and leaned down right in her face. "They tried to blow up my boat today, with you in it. But I don't think they were gunning for you. I think they were after me."

"But we still don't know why."

"I have a theory. Let's go."

Sal shot up from his chair in the waiting room. "Jesse, are you sure you should be up and around?"

"Just get us home, Sal. OK?"

Sal said nothing, just nodded and led the way to the truck. Sasha tried to figure out what was going on, but the last couple days were catching up to her.

Once they were back at the marina, Jesse said, "Walk down to the dock with me?"

Sal gave a knowing smile. "Good night. I'm heading for bed."

Sasha kissed his cheek. "Kiss Mama for me."

Sal turned and looked at Jesse, his expression pained. "Be careful. You put things in motion that may try to take you down with them."

Sasha waited until they were alone before she said, "What gives, Jesse? What did Pop mean?"

"Do you trust Nick?" he asked instead.

"I do. He gave me a ride today so I would make the race."

He held out his phone. "Then call him and ask him to take a drive down here, quietly, without telling anyone."

Sasha did as he asked, then turned to him. "Are you planning to tell me what you're thinking?"

"Let's just watch for a while."

Barely ten minutes later, Nick pulled up, Chief Monroe right behind him. Jesse muttered a curse and stepped back into the shadows of the bait shop. "I thought you asked Stanton to come alone." His voice came out a harsh whisper.

"I did. You going to tell me what's going on?"

He didn't answer, simply shifted farther into the shadows. Chief Monroe sauntered up, Nick behind him. "Evening, Sasha. What's wrong? Why did you ask my officer to come out here this time of night?"

Sasha glanced at Nick, who shrugged. "The chief and I were going over a case file when you called."

She met the chief's gaze. "Jesse suggested I call."

"He's in the hospital. That was quite a close call he had today."

Jesse stepped out of the shadows, and even in the gloom, Sasha saw the chief's ruddy face pale. "I don't think whatever happened today is over yet." He held pairs of binoculars out to each of them. "Humor me, and let's watch awhile."

Monroe propped meaty fists on his hips. "I don't have time for games, Jesse. Just tell me what you're trying to prove."

Jesse cocked his head and listened. In the distance, Sasha heard a vehicle approaching. Jesse hitched his thumb over his shoulder, and the four of them stepped out of sight behind the marina building. They didn't have to wait long.

An ancient pickup pulled into the marina, towing a sport-fishing boat. The driver launched it easily, parked the truck, and hopped aboard the boat, vanishing into the night.

The chief lowered the binoculars and thrust them at Jesse. "Since when is it a crime to launch a boat late at night?"

"Give me half an hour, Chief. If nothing else happens by then, I won't argue. But I don't think it'll take that long."

They waited. For a while they heard nothing but the lapping of water against the pilings, but then they heard the sounds of a propeller. They looked up and saw a small plane in the distance. It flew closer to shore, then turned in a circle and disappeared the way it had come.

"They dropped something," Sasha said quietly.

"That's my guess," Jesse answered.

Nick and the chief said nothing, just kept scanning with their binoculars.

Ten minutes later, they heard an approaching boat motor, and the same sport fisherman returned. The driver tied up the boat and went to get the trailer. They didn't move until he had the boat loaded onto the trailer.

Chief Monroe stepped from the shadows and turned on his flashlight, the beam hitting the driver square in the face. "Evening."

The driver threw his arm up over his eyes, and Sasha sucked in a surprised gasp. "Captain Demetri?"

He lowered his arm and met her eyes, then hopped in the pickup. Nick stepped in front of the truck, gun drawn. "Get out of the vehicle. Now. Hands where we can see them."

Sasha watched in stunned silence as the chief waved his service revolver at Captain Demetri, telling him to get out of the truck. He slid out slowly, hands in the air, a puzzled grin on his face. "What in the world is going on here, Chief? Since when does a man get arrested for night fishing?"

"Stanton, search the vessel," the chief barked, and the other man scrambled aboard and started opening cubbies and coolers, searching every square inch.

Tension grew as the minutes ticked by. Captain Demetri's smile slowly vanished, and he sent pleading glances toward the chief, who ignored him.

Nick held up a nice-sized snook. "This one's not legal size."

Captain Demetri barked out a laugh. "All this for a fish? Throw him back then."

"This one's not legal size, either," Nick said, pulling out a package sealed in plastic. He used his knife to slit the bag, and Sasha's eyes widened as white powder spilled out. Stanton took his pinky and dabbed a bit on his tongue. He nodded to the chief. "Tastes like high-grade cocaine, boss."

The chief grabbed Demetri by the hand, spun him around, and slapped handcuffs on him amid the other man's protests. "Demetri Markos, you are under arrest for—"

"What are you doing? You can't arrest me. This was all Roy's fault. He planned—"

The chief calmly recited the Miranda warning, ignoring the words pouring out of Demetri's mouth.

Sasha sank down on the bench, her mind whirling. All of this had been about drugs? Captain Roy? And Captain Demetri? She couldn't wrap her mind around it.

She hadn't seen him move, but Jesse materialized at Demetri's side. Sasha's head snapped up when she heard the chief say, "Let him be, Jesse, or I'll arrest you, too."

Jesse landed a hard jab in the man's midsection, and she flinched.

"You almost killed Sasha, you selfish son of a—" He punched Demetri in the nose, and blood spurted.

Demetri howled in pain, and Nick pulled Jesse away even as Sasha raced over to the men. She grabbed Jesse's arm.

"Jesse, no. He's not worth it."

Jesse spun to face her, rage in every line of his face. "He could have killed you."

She held his battered face in her palms. "But thanks to you, he didn't. Thank you."

Jesse wrenched from her grasp, breathing hard, hands clenching and unclenching at his sides.

"I'm sorry, Sasha," Captain Demetri said. "Truly."

"Get him out of here," Chief Monroe barked.

Nick had just stepped over to take charge of Demetri when his phone rang. He looked at the caller ID, then stepped away to answer it. If Sasha hadn't been watching, she would have missed the way he stiffened. "I'll have to call you back in a little while." Without a word, he loaded Captain Demetri into the backseat of his vehicle and headed back to town.

Chief Monroe marched over to Jesse. "I have half a mind to haul you in, too." He eyed the younger man. "But I figure you all have enough to deal with."

He turned his gaze on Sasha, anger in every line of his face. "Captain Roy died in that explosion in the water today. Preliminary reports say he was in a minisub that was equipped with torpedoes."

"But why?"

The chief shook his head. "We'll know more soon. Y'all get some rest."

He climbed back in his SUV and left.

Sasha tried to make sense of it all. She looked over at Jesse. "You knew the sub was there today to take out *The Painted Lady*."

"I found the crates from the torpedoes in the barn. It was the only thing that made sense. I think the minisub was supposed to be part of the drug smuggling, but my entering the race changed things somehow, and they decided we had to go."

"I still can't put Captains Roy and Demetri in the same sentence as drugs." She wrapped her arms around her middle and shuddered. "What about their families? Captain Demetri's handicapped daughter?"

"That may be how he got tangled up in all this to begin with. Money."

She sighed and leaned her head on his shoulder when he pulled her close. "It's so sad."

He tightened his hold on her. "I thought I lost you today, Sash."

"I thought I lost you, too. Let's not do that again. Ever."

He kissed her tenderly. "Agreed. How about you go ahead and marry me so I can keep an eye on you?"

She pulled back and eyed him in disbelief. "Seriously? That's your proposal?"

"Hey, I already did the classy one over dinner, and you said no."

"Actually I didn't say anything, because you didn't tell me why you wanted to marry me."

"Right, you ran out and got kidnapped."

Sasha shuddered. "Right. Let's not think about that tonight, either." They started walking toward the house. "You still haven't answered my question."

Jesse raised a brow, grinning. "You mean, why do I want to marry you? Because I love you, Sasha. Exactly the way you are. Just being near you makes me feel like I'm home, wherever we are. The fact that you care for a guy with a sketchy past blows my mind. Do life with me, Sasha. Be my partner, my wife." He paused. "But you still haven't answered my question."

Instead of the usual panic, peace flooded her, and she smiled back. She was done running. This was Jesse. "Yes, Money-boy. I'll marry you."

He stopped and cradled her face in his hands, a lopsided grin melting her heart. "Have I thanked you for winning the race for me today?"

She raised an eyebrow. "Not yet."

He pulled her closer. "Well, let me remedy that immediately."

When they came up for air she asked, "You needed that money for Adelaide's surgery, right?"

"Figured that out, did you? Smart girl. Since I'm no dummy, either, I think we should go to city hall tomorrow and get married before you change your mind."

"What?" She poked him in the arm. "No way, Money-boy. We're going to do this right, with the froufrou dress and the tux and the preacher and everything."

Jesse just grinned. "Froufrou dress, huh? Whatever you want, Sash, as long as I get you." He pulled her close again. "I love you, Sasha. Always have. Always will."

After a long, satisfying kiss that wasn't nearly long or satisfying enough, Sasha went upstairs to sleep while Jesse bedded down on the lumpy sofa in the living room.

Her mind was so numb, she couldn't begin to make sense of it all. There would be time enough, tomorrow.

Only one thought played over and over in her mind. She fell asleep with a trembly little smile on her lips. Holy cow. She was getting married.

Chapter 22

Instead of going to the Blue Dolphin for breakfast the next morning, Sasha and Jesse called everyone into the kitchen. Jesse stood at the stove, scrambling eggs, while Sasha set the table and poured coffee.

Mama shuffled into the room on Pop's arm, robe secured up to her chin, head wrapped in a turban, eyes worried.

"Is everything all right?" She reared back when she saw Sasha's face. "What happened to you?"

Sasha rushed over and held a chair for her. She'd forgotten about how she looked. "Everything is fine now, Mama. I didn't mean to make you worry."

"But your face?" Mama couldn't seem to take her eyes from it.

Sasha let out a sigh. "I will explain, OK?"

Blaze plopped down in a chair and crossed her arms. "Let me guess. You guys are getting hitched."

Sasha looked over at Jesse and grinned before she turned to Blaze. "As a matter of fact, yes."

Blaze stood with a yawn. "Old news, so I'm going back to bed."

Sasha gently pushed her back down and whispered. "Thanks for stealing my thunder, sis, but that's not why I called everyone together."

Sasha looked around the table as they all joined hands. "I'll say the blessing." She ignored the surprised faces and said, "Father, thank you for our family and their love for each other. Thank you for your protection from danger and for your love for us. We pray for healing for Mama and wisdom for the future. Oh, and thanks for the food. Amen."

Once the last bite was eaten, Sasha took a deep breath and clasped Mama's hand. "Mama, a few days ago, Blaze and I found Tony's clothes, the ones he was wearing when he disappeared."

Mama's choked cry had Sal at her side between one heartbeat and the next. "Show me," she demanded. "Show me my baby's clothes."

Sasha stood and reached into the pocket of her shorts. She pulled up the photos Blaze had taken and held the phone out for her parents to see.

Tears poured down Mama's cheeks as she studied the images. Beside her, silent tears flowed down Sal's face as he tried to comfort her.

Sasha sat down again, and Jesse reached over and gripped her hand. "We gave the clothes to Officer Nick, and he's having a lab analyze them, see if they can help us. Fingerprints. DNA. Fibers. Something." She paused, chose her words carefully. "There was no sign anywhere of, ah, foul play."

"You're sure?" Mama's tone broke Sasha's heart.

"Absolutely. None."

Mama swallowed hard and rocked back and forth in her chair. "My Tony is alive. He's alive." She looked at Sal. "Our baby is still alive."

Sal stood abruptly. "I have to get back to the bait shop." He left without another word.

Mama watched him go. "It breaks his heart, every day." Then she turned to Sasha and stroked her cheek. "Sasha, my precious one. I knew I could count on you."

The words washed over Sasha like a gentle shower, wiping away years of failure, mountains of guilt and regret. "But I've let you down, so many times."

Mama smiled. "We all disappoint the ones we love. But you have a warrior's heart, my Sasha. You fight for those you love. And you don't give up. Thank you for this." She hugged the phone close. "I can never thank you enough."

"We still haven't found him."

"You will."

"I love you, Mama."

"And I you, my precious one."

The knock on the door startled everyone. Blaze went to see who it was and came back a moment later. "Officer Stanton is outside. Said he wants to talk to Sasha and Jesse." She huffed out an annoyed breath. "Alone."

Sasha stepped out onto the porch where Nick paced frantically, like a man with demons chasing him. He looked up, his bloodshot eyes a testament to a sleepless night. His hair stood in clumps, as though he'd been running his hands through it. "Good morning, Nick. Can we get you some coffee?"

He shook his head, kept pacing. "No, I've had too much already."

Sasha and Jesse exchanged a look. "What brings you here so early in the morning?"

He stopped pacing, turned to face them. "Captain Demetri was pretty chatty last night before his lawyer showed up. He had a lot to say about your past, Jesse. My guess is they didn't know if you'd try to cut into their drug business or rat them out, so they wanted you gone."

"What about the race?" Sasha asked. "Was that part of it, too?"

"We were just getting to that when his lawyer walked in. I'll keep you posted. But that's not why I'm here." He stopped, looked away, then turned back to face them. "So, I, ah, got a call last night, as we were arresting Captain Demetri. From my friend at the lab."

Everything in Sasha stilled, and she felt Jesse step up behind her, settle his hands on her shoulders. She forced a calm she didn't feel. "Did he find anything from the clothes?"

"She, actually. But, um, yeah. She did."

"What did she find?" Her voice came out a whisper.

Nick looked toward the door of the house, then stepped closer. "She found fingerprints, on the tennis shoes. One really good one, actually. "

"And?"

"Come with me." He turned and strode to his official SUV, reached in for a laptop. "This is my personal computer. I didn't want to go through official channels. Not yet." He opened a folder and turned the laptop so they could all see the screen. "This is the fingerprint from Tony's shoes." He scrolled down. "And this is the match the computer found."

Sasha gasped and would have fallen backward if not for Jesse steadying her from behind. Her eyes went from the screen to Nick's face and back again. "Can this be right?"

"Fingerprints don't lie. And they don't change over time."

Sasha swallowed hard, felt Jesse grip her arms in a show of support. "We have to tell Mama."

He nodded. "Yes. But I wanted to show you first. Give you a minute to absorb it."

She grabbed him and hugged him, hard. Then she stepped back. Tears filled her eyes, but she blinked them away so she could see his face again. Her emotions could come later. First, they had to get Mama—and Pop—through the shock. She turned to Jesse.

He nodded as though he'd read her mind. "I'll get Sal." He headed off to the bait shop.

Nick followed Sasha up onto the porch. "I'll bring her out here," she said. "She likes her rocker."

A few minutes later they had Mama settled, Sal beside her. Blaze hovered near Mama's feet, Bella wedged between them, as though both sensed something important was about to happen.

Nick seemed calmer now, though his eyes were still filled with anxiety and a mixture of dread and fear. He walked to Mama and crouched down so they were eye level. "Mrs. Martinelli, Sasha told you she found Tony's clothes from the day he disappeared?"

Mama nodded, the mix of hope and dread in her eyes making Sasha want to weep. "It's OK, Mama."

"I took them to a friend of mine who works at the state law enforcement lab, and she planned to run a bunch of tests. But she hit pay dirt with the first one. There was a fingerprint on Tony's shoes, and it was good enough, clear enough, to run through all the law enforcement databases." He took a deep breath, and Mama gripped Pop's hand, where it rested on her shoulder.

"She got a match, one she says is positive. I had her check and recheck, just to be sure."

"You found my Tony?" Mama whispered.

"I did." He paused, cleared his throat. "I don't know how and there's a lot we have to figure out, but . . . the fingerprint is mine. I'm Tony."

For a second, there was absolute silence. Then everyone spoke at once. Mama lunged up from her chair and wrapped Nick in her arms, Sal with his around both of them, tears flowing like water.

Blaze stood slowly, walked over to Sasha and Jesse. "Seriously?"

Sasha swiped at an errant tear. "Seriously. He showed us the fingerprint match." She remembered something and slipped back inside. A moment later she reappeared, handed the teddy bear to Nick.

His eyes widened, and he took the bear with hands that trembled. "This was mine. I remember looking for it as a child, thinking I should have it, but never being able to find it."

Mama cupped his cheeks in her hands. "Who are your parents? Do they love you? Did they treat you right? How did you come to be with them?"

"They were wonderful to me. Sally and James Stanton, but they're both gone now. Car accident. I came to Safe Harbor because my friend Chad loved it here and invited me to join him. But I've been having these weird dreams, with this bear in them." He smiled. "I guess now I know why."

"Do you have a picture of them?" Sasha asked.

"Of course." He pulled out his wallet, flipped it open so Sasha could see.

Her breath caught, and she slipped inside again, this time charging up the stairs to her bedroom. She ducked under the low-hanging beam just in time and ran back downstairs. She held the photo she'd taken from Mary Lee's album and showed it to him. "Are your folks in this picture?"

He looked from Sasha to the photo and back again. "Sure, that's them in the back row."

Mama gasped and snatched the photo from his hand. "Where? Where are the people who took my baby from me?"

"Rosa, easy," Pop soothed, but she shooed his hands away.

"I need to see." She studied the photo and gasped when the faces registered. "That's Roy's cousin and his wife. They stole my baby?" Sal turned her into his arms, and she sobbed against his chest.

Nick looked sick. "I never knew I wasn't their biological child. Never. I had no idea until last night. They never said a word."

"But I think it weighed on them. Your mother especially." Sasha pulled out the postcard she'd found in Sal's file cabinet.

Nick took it and studied the signature, the postmark. "That's my mother's handwriting." He swallowed hard. "I can't believe they were involved in this."

Mama pulled him close again and hugged him hard. "My Tony. I can't believe I've found you." She swayed and Pop steadied her from behind, much like Jesse had done for Sasha.

Nick's face was filled with pain, confusion. "I have to go. We'll talk more."

Mama made an anguished sound, but he kept walking, got in his SUV, and drove away.

"You should rest, Rosa. Come." Sal gently guided her inside and down the hall.

Once they were out of earshot, Blaze let out a low whistle. "Holy Toledo. Somebody stole him? Somebody they knew?" She shook her head. "People are crazy." She pulled earbuds out of her pocket, held the door for Bella, and headed out.

Sasha collapsed into the nearest chair, her legs suddenly wobbly. "Wow. My head is still spinning."

"Mine, too."

They sat in silence a while, then Sal walked past them and out to the bait shop. Sasha gave him a few minutes before she followed.

"Don't push him, Sasha. He's had a shock, too."

"I know. But we need to talk this out. Now. Before he retreats into himself again. It might be my only chance to find out the truth."

He leaned over and kissed her forehead. "I'll be right here."

She found Pop standing on the dock, out of view of the house. She came up beside him and slid an arm around his middle, surprised again at how thin he seemed, how fragile. "You doing OK, Pop?"

He patted her hand where it wrapped around him, anguish etched in every line of his face. They stood in silence for several long minutes before he said, "They threatened me, years ago. Roy and Demetri. They said if I didn't let them use the marina to smuggle their drugs, bad things would happen."

Sasha's heart stuttered as she tried to make sense of what he was saying.

"I didn't believe them until the day Tony disappeared." He swayed on his feet, so Sasha led him to the bench, rubbing his back while he sobbed into his hands. "In the end, it didn't matter. They kept smuggling their drugs anyway. And my Tony was gone."

Sasha pushed the questions aside for now. He needed comfort, not an interrogation. "It's not your fault, Pop. It's not your fault. The blame lies with them."

"I wanted to go to the police, but I was afraid, for Mama. What if they had hurt her, too?"

Sobs shook his frame, and Sasha kept rubbing small circles on his back. "Will you tell the police now?"

He turned his head to look at her, tears tracking down his cheeks. "How will that help, my Sasha? Roy is dead. It was all so long ago."

"But Demetri is alive. And in jail. Maybe he'll barter the information."

Finally he nodded. "It is the least I can do for my Tony."

Sasha's throat was thick when she said, "You were in an impossible spot, Pop. But you tried to do the right thing, stick by your convictions." When he started to protest, she interrupted. "You were trying to protect your family. I can't ever fault you for that." She paused, tried to decide how to phrase it. "You know I had to do this, right?"

He leaned over and kissed the top of her head. "I know. You are our warrior, our champion. I love you, my girl."

"I love you, too, Pop."

Later, Sasha and Jesse met Nick at the police station, where they went over every single moment of the last few days until Sasha's head ached and her hands shook from all the caffeine.

When they were finally released, Jesse drove them south toward Tampa.

"Thanks for being here, Jesse."

He winked. "I'm not going anywhere."

"So, where are we going again?"

He laughed, a bit too loud. "Nice try. You'll see."

When he pulled up in front of a big medical center, Sasha figured she knew. After several miles of corridors and an elevator ride, they arrived in the small waiting area outside the pediatric intensive-care unit. A young woman in her midtwenties wearing sweats and the worried, sleep-deprived look of a parent with a sick child leaped up when they walked in.

"Jesse!" She ran over and jumped into his outstretched arms. If he hadn't braced himself, he would have fallen. "She made it through the surgery! Thank you, thank you."

Sasha's momentary jealousy at seeing this woman throw herself at Jesse dissipated as her words sunk in. The woman wiped her tears away and pushed hunks of brown hair behind her ears.

"I can't ever thank—"

Jesse stepped over and grabbed Sasha's hand. "Tracy, this is Sasha. Sasha, Tracy was my friend Ethan's girlfriend, and their sweet baby, Adelaide, just had heart surgery this morning."

Seeing Tracy's relieved expression, Sasha's love for Jesse burrowed deeper yet. This was why winning the race mattered so much.

Jesse turned to Tracy and pulled her close for another quick hug. "I'm so glad everything went well. And you can thank Sasha. She piloted *The Painted Lady* and won that prize money."

Tracy looked from one to the other, still wiping tears away. "I'll pay you back, both of you, I promise. No matter how long it takes."

Jesse just shook his head. "Stop, Tracy, OK? I promised Ethan, and I meant it. You don't owe us a thing. Just take care of that sweet girl."

Sasha stepped closer and gave Jesse's hand a squeeze. "Can we take a peek at her through the window?"

Tracy's smile could have lit up a city. "Come see."

They huddled by the glass, and Sasha's heart clenched at the sight of the tiny girl with the big bandage over her chest, tubes and wires and monitors all but burying her in the big crib.

As she and Jesse headed back to Safe Harbor, Sasha reached over and took his hand. "You're a good guy, Jesse Claybourne."

"You OK with that prize money going to Adelaide?"

She furrowed her brow. "Give me a little more credit, Money-boy."

"I'm not Money-boy anymore. Not by a long shot."

She sniffed. "That was never your most attractive feature anyway."

He laughed, and they grinned at each other like idiots.

"Eyes on the road, Money-boy."

Epilogue

"Jesse! Where are you going? It's bad luck to see the bride before the wedding." Blaze appeared at the foot of the porch stairs, arms crossed, blocking his path.

Jesse stopped and let out a wolf whistle. Blaze had dyed her hair from blue to green so it would match her bridesmaid dress. "Wow, don't you look beautiful, kiddo."

Blaze rolled her eyes. "You still can't go in. It'll ruin everything."

Jesse stepped closer. "I really need to see her, OK? And I promise, I won't ruin a thing."

When she sighed and shrugged, he leaned in and kissed her cheek before she could pull away. "You are going to break hearts, kiddo."

Then he slipped past her and took the stairs two at a time. He rapped lightly on the door. When Sasha opened it, he sucked in a breath. *Wow.* "Hey, beautiful lady."

Eve appeared next to Sasha and tried to shut the door in his face. "Go away, Jesse. You shouldn't be here."

Before she could protest, Sasha drew him into the room. "It's OK, Eve. Give us a minute." To Jesse she said, "Watch your head."

He ducked just in time, and Eve closed the door none too gently behind her. He took Sasha's hands, not surprised to feel them trembling. "Just ride the wave. Nothing to worry about."

She sucked in a panicked breath, and he held her arms out at her sides and studied her. The simple white sleeveless dress suited her perfectly. It had no frills or lace but hugged every curve. Her hair was done in some kind of fancy knot and showed off those beautiful cheekbones. "Have I mentioned how much I love you?"

Her smile was still a little shaky around the edges. "Not lately, no."

He leaned in for a gentle kiss. "I love you."

She searched his gaze. "Why are you here? Did something else happen?"

"Only good things." He reached into the pocket of his gray suit and pulled out her mariner's cross. Her breath hitched as she reached for it, but he held it just out of reach. "Nick found it. He figured you'd want to wear it today. They found it in a hay bale in that old barn."

He held it up, and her eyes widened as she saw the addition.

"I know the mariner's cross symbolizes faith and the anchor, hope. So as a wedding gift, I added a small heart, for love. I hope that's OK with you."

When he leaned in to fasten it around her neck, she blinked rapidly. "Don't you make me cry and ruin my makeup. Eve will never forgive you."

As if on cue, Eve stuck her head in the door. "Time to go, Romeo. The natives are getting restless."

Jesse placed a kiss on her forehead and winked. "Steady as she goes, Captain."

When the familiar strains of Pachelbel's Canon in D emerged from a hidden speaker, Sasha stepped out onto the porch with her arms linked through Pop's on one side and Nick's on the other. She blinked, surprised by the number of people gathered in the yard. It looked like the whole town had shown up.

She smiled at Eve and stopped to whisper, "You look beautiful, Bethany," in Blaze's ear as she went by. In deference to Mama's health, the ceremony would take place right there on the porch, with Mama presiding over the proceedings from her rocker, Bella at her feet.

As Jesse slipped a gold band designed to look like rope on Sasha's finger, he said, "You've made me the happiest guy in the world, Sasha."

She looked up, and everything faded but the love in his eyes. Even so, the familiar wings of panic started beating against her heart. She whispered, "But what if—"

He put a gentle finger over her lips.

"If you need to run, go. But know I'll catch you. Every time."

Just like that, the panic eased, and she smiled. "I love you, Money-boy."

He winked. "I know."

She threw her head back and laughed.

ACKNOWLEDGMENTS

Manuscripts may be written in solitude, but it takes a whole team to turn a story into a book. For their invaluable help in bringing Sasha and Jesse's story to life, my heartfelt thanks go to:

My agent, Susan Brower, for all her hard work and encouragement.

Leslie Santamaria, whose friendship, calm, last-minute plotting help, and invaluable feedback keep me writing—and relatively sane.

My editor, Erin Calligan Mooney, and the whole Amazon Waterfall team for their hard work in making this story a reality.

My fabulous family—who handle my creative distraction with incredible grace. Harry, Ben and Maria, Michele and Matt—you all make the journey worthwhile.

Thanks to God, the Great Creator, who gives the gift of stories and who always, always offers second chances.

Last, but not least, to all of you who've encouraged me and welcomed my stories into your lives. Thank you from the bottom of my heart.

ABOUT THE AUTHOR

Photo © 2015 Michele Klopfenstein

Connie Mann is a licensed boat captain and the author of the romantic suspense novels *Angel Falls* and *Trapped!* as well as various works of shorter fiction. She has lived in seven different states but has happily called warm, sunny Florida home for more than twenty years. When she's not dreaming up plotlines, you'll find "Captain Connie" on Central Florida's waterways, introducing boats full of schoolchildren to their first alligator. She is also passionate about helping women and children in developing countries follow their dreams and break the poverty cycle. In addition to boating, she and her husband enjoy spending time with their grown children and extended family and planning their next travel adventures. You can visit Connie online at www.conniemann.com.